FOR THE PLOT

All for Love: Book 1

KATIE VAN BRUNT

Copyright © 2024 by Katie Van Brunt

All rights reserved.

No part of this book may be reproduced in any form or by any electronic or mechanical means, including information storage and retrieval systems, without written permission from the author, except for the use of brief quotations in a book review.

This is a work of fiction. Any names, characters, organizations, events, or incidents are products of the author's imagination and used in a fictitious manner. Any resemblance to actual people or events is purely coincidental or fictional.

Cover Design & Illustrations by Lauren Gnapi at Elemental Opal LLC

Editing by Beth at VB Edits

Proofreading by Kristen Hamilton at Kristen's Red Pen

ASIN: B0CQL19H1K

ISBN: 979-8-89298-551-2

katievanbrunt.com

*To the little girl with big dreams and lots of anxiety.
We did it.*

Author's Note

I had a blast writing Cam and Joey, and I hope you have just as much fun reading.

For the Plot is an open-door romance intended for mature audiences. The characters are consenting adults, and there is explicit, on-page sexual content, explicit language, and adult situations. Not eighteen? Please come back later!

If you're someone who never reads the epilogue or bonus scenes, trust me—you don't want to miss out.

For a full list of trigger and content warnings, please visit: www.katievanbrunt.com

For the Plot is the first book in the All for Love series, but can be read on its own.

FOR THE Plot

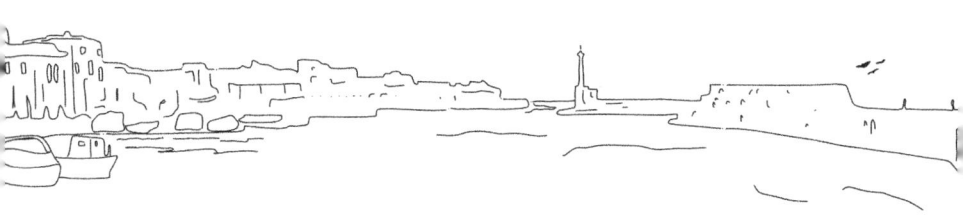

an
All For Love
novel

KATIE VAN BRUNT

Playlist

- **CHRONICALLY CAUTIOUS** by Braden Bales
- **Fictional** by Khloe Rose
- **QUARTER LIFE CRISIS** by Taylor Bickett
- **Alright** by Sam Fischer, Meghan Trainor
- **Electric Touch** by Taylor Swift, Fall Out Boy
- **How a Heart Unbreaks** by Evermoist (Pitch Perfect 3)
- **Welcome to New York** by Taylor Swift
- **Be Okay** by Oh Honey
- **Dancing Queen** from 'Mamma Mia!'
- **Under Pressure** by Queen, David Bowie
- **Put Your Records On** by Corinne Bailey Rae
- **Sun Goes Down** by Bruno Martini, ADORA
- **Trash My Heart** by Walker Hayes
- **Glad You Came** by The Wanted
- **Joey, Joey, Joey** by Leslie Odom Jr.
- **Till We Both Say** by Nicotine Dolls
- **Lose Somebody** by Kygo, OneRepublic
- **Lipstick** by Charlie Puth

- **Late Night Talking** by Harry Styles
- **Miss Independent** by Kelly Clarkson
- **Little Bit Louder** by Mimi Webb
- **Don't Lose Sigh**t by Lawrence
- **imagine** by Ben Platt
- **Perfect** by Ed Sheeran
- **Butterflies** by MAX, FLETCHER
- **Be Me** - Acoustic by VINCINT
- **I Love You Will Still Sound the Same** by Oh Honey
- **I'll Never Not Love You** by Michael Buble
- **BONUS TRACK: Gumption** by Hans Zimmer

There is no passion to be found in settling for a life that is less than the one you are capable of living.

-Nelson Mandela

I'll let you be in my dreams if I can be in yours.

-Bob Dylan

Chapter 1
Josefine

"Fuck!" All the good words are taken. I toss my notepad and pen at my open laptop with such force it flips onto its back.

On the other side of the desk we share in our quaint Santa Monica apartment, Tyler removes his headphones. "You okay?" He sets my MacBook upright.

I drop my head to my arms and let out an incoherent grumble.

He rattles my wrist. "Look at me, Beck," he says, using my childhood nickname. It's short for Beckham—my last name. (And yes, when we started dating, he exhausted all the *Bend It Like Beckham* jokes.)

I lift my head but keep my chin propped on my arms. "Yes?" I sigh.

"You're going to write this book." He grins, his gray eyes shining. "You're the most talented person I know. And I know talent."

That he does. Tyler is a music producer who works mostly with electronic dance music artists.

"You really think so?" I ask, blowing out a long breath.

I've been writing a book for the past six months, but recently, my work has come to a standstill. I wouldn't call it writer's block, per se, but I can't find coherent words to fill in the gaps in my plot. Like a dog chasing its tail, I go around and around in circles, but everything I write lately is utter shit. Maybe I should buy some of those disposable plastic poop bags, stuff my laptop inside, tie the baggie in a knot, and toss it over the Santa Monica Pier.

I'm working on a novel loosely based on my life. I considered writing a memoir, but I'm worried that if I do, my mom will sue me. It's probably better this way anyway. It allows me to be more creative. Although I feel about as creative as a sponge right now.

"Yes. Now come here," he commands.

I round the desk and climb onto his lap, relishing the way his tattooed arms engulf me. He's toned, but not a big dude, and I love how my petite frame fits against him. His blond hair tickles my nose when I bury my face in the crook of his neck and inhale his signature honey and rosewood scent, courtesy of Tom Ford.

"You need a haircut." I nip at his neck.

"Oh, do I now?" he murmurs into the messy brown knot planted on top of my head, giving my hip a playful pinch.

"No, not really." I brush a hand across his chest. "I like it this way. More to pull on." With a giggle, I bite his neck again.

"Josefine Beckham," he quips. "Am I going to have to bend you over this desk?"

"Don't threaten me with a good time."

After an adequate night's sleep, I'm feeling refreshed and motivated. I work from home most days, but staring at the same walls starts to feel like a prison after a while.

Even though Tyler could afford a nicer place in LA, I begged him to keep the Santa Monica apartment he's owned since before

I moved in. It's just the two of us, and while we're minimalistic, it does sometimes feel like we're living in a hermit crab shell. But its location can't be beat.

We're steps away from the shore, and when I need a change of scenery, I pack my laptop bag and wander to my favorite coffee shop. I swear it's the only one in all of Southern California without ridiculously overpriced lattes. Over time, it's become a sort of unofficial communal workspace. I'm one of many patrons who set up shop there regularly.

Each of us is part of the writing world in some way, shape, or form—a discovery I made because of my growing curiosity. Writing a book has helped me see the world from other angles and encouraged me to open up and learn more about the people I encounter.

As a child, I was shy. I'd tiptoe around others, observing from afar—a wallflower of sorts. It's taken years (and lots of therapy), but I no longer collect boob sweat like it's going out of style when I talk to strangers.

These days, I approach social encounters as potential material for my book. My accountability partner, Brooks, and I have a saying: *It's for the plot.* Car breaks down on the side of the road? It's for the plot. Dealing with a total asshole in the middle of Whole Foods? Potential material for the plot. Babysitting Tyler's goofy-ass clients who throw temper tantrums in the middle of nightclubs? You guessed it—it's for the plot.

Any life event—whether it's happening to me or around me—is up for grabs. The juicier, the better.

Most people working at the coffee shop prefer to be left alone with their nonprescription blue-light glasses, near-permanent hunched shoulders, AirPods, and double espressos. But picking their brains and chatting them up is what I live for.

Brooks is already waiting for me, and he's got a smirk glued to his smug face. He's wearing a baseball cap, which makes him look even more like his doppelgänger, Penn Badgley, from *You*. Like he's ready to lock someone in a glass cage at any moment.

Fantastic. We'll never get anything done; people will be gawking and asking for "Penn's" autograph all day.

"What?" I ask as I approach our usual table. Brooks & Beck may as well be carved into the wood. Technically, we can't reserve tables, but we regulars have an unspoken agreement about not taking the seats others prefer—sort of like in middle school.

"Nothing." Brooks does his best to sound bored, but his gnarly smile deceives him.

"Whatever," I huff, collapsing into my seat. "Thanks for my lat—*hey!* What the hell is this?" Instead of the usual heart or leaf latte art, a foam penis floats on top of my honey lavender latte.

Brooks bursts out laughing, along with Raj, who's standing behind the counter arranging croissants on a platter.

"You are no longer my favorite barista, Raj!" I shout over my shoulder, but when I turn back to Brooks, I'm snickering too.

"You said you had a shitty writing day yesterday. I figured you could use the laugh."

"You're evil." I blow him a kiss.

Brooks and I have a good thing going. We met back when he was in songwriting. While he still occasionally writes songs, his focus is screenwriting—the script he's been working on gives major Shondaland vibes. We meet at least once a week and spend our first few minutes together asking one another if what we wrote is worthy or utter shit. On days I don't see Brooks, I send him screenshots of pages, usually accompanied by texts like: *IS THIS STUPID? YES OR NO?* He always gives it to me straight. He pushes me in ways I would never do myself. In return, I support him through his impostor syndrome.

"What are you working on today?" I ask as I snap a pic of the penis art (quite impressive, Raj). I text the image to Tyler, then silence my phone to avoid distractions.

"I'm going to comb through the text for grammar issues. I know, super boring, but I don't want to look like an illiterate idiot when I send it out," Brooks replies. "What about you? Is it a *you* day or a *them* day?"

There is a distinction between the two. While I am writing a book, I also freelance as a copy editor.

"It's a *them* day." I sigh. "Gotta pay the bills." I once heard that to be a good writer, a person should also be a good reader. So while copy editing has polished my craft, I still find myself being sucked into an unhealthy 'why is everyone getting published but me?' vortex.

Also, it's often said that a book that hasn't been written can't be published. Dammit.

It's a constant battle, a tug-of-war, editing work for others versus writing my own. I'm forever indebted to people like Brooks who know exactly what to say to keep me both motivated and humble.

I place my laptop on the table just as Raj sets down a cranberry-orange scone, my favorite.

"A maple leaf for my favorite brown-eyed girl." His smile lights up his whole face.

"A what?" I tilt my head up and blink at him.

"You know, to say I'm sorry for my offensive art." He winks.

"Oh!" I slap a hand to my mouth to stifle a laugh, but I'm not quick enough. "I think you mean an olive branch."

"Oh, fuck off," Raj says, turning and heading to his spot behind the counter. "You try learning English as a second language."

Loud enough for all to hear, I shout, "Thanks for my morning cock!"

Chapter 2
Josefine

"Do you want to talk about it?" Brooks asks from behind his coffee mug.

It's a question I've heard hundreds of times throughout the years—spoken to me twelve years ago, after my father died. First by my Aunt Rachel, then many times by a handful of therapists. But, oddly, never by my mother. For so long, I despised that question.

The first two therapists I saw were lovely people, but during every session, they asked me some variation of "Do you want to talk about it?" While my insides were screaming *Yes!* my responses included a plethora of shrugs, awkward silences, and grunts. Even at ten, I worried about saying the "wrong thing" in therapy. I'd seen more than a few movies that included patients lying on leather sofas to know that therapists cataloged every word spoken. Too afraid that I wouldn't do therapy "the right way," I said nothing at all. After barely any progress, I was pawned off on yet another therapist—a woman named Sora.

When Aunt Rachel drove me to my first session with Sora, I was surprised to see that her office was a bungalow near the beach rather than a drab room in a stale office building. A small collection of wind chimes framed the entrance, and cloud-patterned drapes covered her windows. A calico cat sunbathed on a rainbow doormat that read *All Are Welcome*. The cat woke with a start and quickly disappeared inside when Sora opened the door.

She bent to my eye level when she introduced herself. Her smiling lips were coated in a clear gloss and her short nails were painted a summery yellow. A zillion gold bracelets covered a floral tattoo on her forearm—their clinking harmonized with the wind chimes outside. She offered me a beverage from the mini fridge by the door, and I accepted a fruit punch Capri Sun.

Sora recommended a café around the corner to my aunt and politely said we would see her in an hour. After Aunt Rachel hugged me, Sora directed me into her office. While a modest desk was pushed up against the window-lined back wall, a white leather sofa took up the main space. Colorful tapestries layered across the back gave it a warm, inviting feel. Two yellow beanbag chairs, along with a sea of pillows, sat on top of a plush white rug.

Sora, to my surprise, plopped herself onto one of the beanbag chairs, no yellow legal pad in sight.

One wall was covered in a collage of children's art that she had arranged into the shape of a rainbow. The bag of beans I settled into crinkled like Rice Krispies beneath me.

"Joey," Sora began.

I braced myself for the inevitable question.

"What was your dad's favorite food?"

For a moment, my brain short-circuited. No therapist had asked me a question like that before.

The inky-black wings at the corners of Sora's eyes tipped up when she smiled. "Was it something delicious or awful?"

When I first opened my mouth to speak, nothing came out. I closed my lips around the narrow yellow straw of my Capri Sun and sucked in the sweet nectar of childhood. Maybe that's when my affinity for emotional support drinks started.

After a long moment, I found my voice. "Tuna fish with rice and salt-and-vinegar chips."

Her almond eyes lit up with warmth and kindness when she burst out laughing. "No way!"

I found myself infected by her pure delight and couldn't help but join in with her laughter.

My new therapist, whom I stayed with until I turned eighteen and she could no longer see me, never once asked me if I wanted to talk about it. *It* meaning *my dad*. Every week for years, she dove into talking about him with ease, like it was the most natural thing in the world to discuss someone who was no longer living. It wasn't until I was an adult that I realized she was intentionally building trust, knowing that we would eventually get to the hard parts—managing my grief and understanding and navigating my mom's addiction.

I'd been seeing her for months before she asked why I go by Joey and not Josefine.

By then, she'd firmly earned a spot high on my list of trusted individuals, so I didn't hesitate to share the story.

When my mom, Elin, was pregnant, she and my father chose not to find out my gender before birth. My dad, Noah, had a dream that I was a boy, and nothing my mom said could convince him otherwise. He was so damn certain his dream was a premonition that he painted the nursery pale blue early one Sunday morning while my mom was sleeping. While I was still in her belly, he started calling me Joey. I laughed out loud to Sora that day, reminiscing about how my mom would interject during this part of the story, saying, "I felt like a kangaroo!" But my dad was so persuasive that even my mom got in the habit of using the name.

When she went into labor three weeks early, my dad—decked

out in all blue in the delivery room—got the surprise of his life. After hours of intense labor, the doctor lifted me into the air à la *The Lion King* and declared, "It's a girl!"

My parents had called me Joey for months and agreed that they couldn't come up with a name more fitting, even after seeing me in the flesh. So I was Joey from day one, although legally I'm Josefine Noa Beckham. My middle name is for my dad, though they chose to use the Dutch spelling to honor my mom's side of the family.

All those years later, after my dad's death, it took months to find the perfect therapist, but the journey was worth it. Sora was everything I didn't know I needed.

At our last session, I cried tears of gratitude when she gifted me a mini plush kangaroo. I begged her to take on adult clients so we could continue our sessions. Then I asked her why she never asked me the dreaded *Do you want to talk about it?* question like the other therapists had.

Her response? That people who ask that question mean well, but the person they're asking may not be in the mental headspace to receive that question. She promised that, over time, those words would be less triggering.

Sora was right. Because for the first time, when Brooks asks if I want to talk about it, I say yes.

"I'm scared," I blurt out, surprising myself by diving right in. Usually I tiptoe around my feelings, testing the waters to see whether the person I'm considering confiding in can handle my emotions.

Brooks is unfazed. His deep brown eyes are warm with encouragement as he reaches across the table and squeezes my wrist.

Exhaling, I continue. "I feel so alone."

When I don't elaborate, he asks, "How so? Alone in what?"

Where do I even begin? I'm an only child, so I've carried at least a little loneliness around with me for as long as I can remember. Even though my mom is still part of my life, she hasn't been capable of giving me mental or emotional support in a long time. Tyler is a constant in my life, but even he can't be my everything. He hustles like mad at work, and when he's home, he's attached to his clients with an umbilical cord disguised as an iPhone. Don't even get me started on all the required nights out for work. Most days, I have to fight for his attention.

Every one of those answers swirls through my mind, but my writing and this book are what shove their way through to the front of the class, shouting, "Pick me! Talk about me!"

So I do.

Brooks removes his hat, fluffs his dark curls, and listens intently while I spill about how I can feel trapped in the quiet alcoves of creativity. He nods at the mention of feeling both blessed and burdened by my career choice. Wild ideas blossom out of nowhere, and I want to water and watch them grow, but sometimes loneliness settles like a thick fog over a meadow, making it impossible for me to tend to them.

Writing a book is like living on an island. Like being tethered to the shore of solitude but drifting in a sea of endless ideas with waves of self-doubt crashing against me, drowning me with impostor syndrome.

"I get it," Brooks says, resting his elbows on the table long after our coffees are drained. "We need the quiet and solitude to create, but we long for connection."

"Exactly," I whisper. "I need not only validation, but someone to share the highs and lows, the triumphs and struggles. But I don't want to be a whiny burden." I let out a sad laugh.

"I know what you mean. It's this delicate dance between isolation and connection."

"Mmm," I hum. "And I'm so wrapped up in what I create,

shoveling so much of myself into my art, that it's difficult to separate the writing from the writer."

Plus, my mind is constantly generating stories and drawing inspiration from my own experiences. It's exhausting.

"Sometimes I find more companionship in my characters than I do in people in real life," I admit.

Brooks laughs a hearty chuckle. "No truer words have ever been spoken." The café is bustling with chatty patrons, dishes clattering, and espresso machines whirring, but his voice is clear when he says, "You are not a burden."

My face heats, and I dip my chin. "Thank you, Brooks." His statement doesn't erase my struggles, but I can appreciate his sincerity.

"And hey," he offers, "maybe this vacation is what you need to clear your head. You can write, soak in some vitamin *sea*, relax on the beach, and have all the loud sex you want without your neighbors hearing." He punctuates that last item with a smirk.

I laugh at the memory of the time Tyler and I received a not-so-nice note stuck to the front of our apartment following quite the sex marathon. Since then, I've had to watch what I say—and how loud I say it.

Raj refreshes our coffees, then Brooks and I work in comfortable silence for a long while. After a quick loop around the block to stretch our legs, we hunch over our laptops once more. Surprisingly, we're only interrupted once by a pod of teenagers whispering words of wonder over whether Brooks is Penn Badgley. They look so devastated when he tells them he's not their favorite bad boy, but they perk up a little when he pulls the brim of his hat low and poses for a picture anyway.

After pounding away at my keyboard until well into the evening, my neck and shoulders are screaming at me to go home. Brooks and I stroll along the boardwalk, watching as dogs pull their owners from one item of interest to another, sniffing all the way. Older folks are out for their nightly walks, and kids on scooters with helmets so big they slide down their eyes zip by us. The Pacific air is still and cool, with a perfectly painted cotton-candy sky over the horizon.

    When Brooks and I part at the entrance to my building, he hugs me tight and says, "Remember what I said, Beck. You are not a burden."

Chapter 3

Cameron

"If we don't leave now, we'll be late," Hayden calls from the bathroom.

I'm the one waiting by the front door of my penthouse, but she's the one who's stressed about being late to dinner with her parents. *Penthouse* makes it seem glamorous and pretentious, but really, it's a modest three-bedroom apartment on the top level of my parents' hotel.

Hayden doesn't live with me, though by the looks of the place, one would think she's been living here for years. For months, she left so many of her things behind that I offered her ownership of the guest bathroom, where I wouldn't have to worry about accidentally mixing up her ten-step skincare routine.

Sometimes it's awkward living in a hotel, and other times, it's amazing. The unlimited access to room service is a nice perk, as is the nonexistent cost of rent. But working and living in the same building got old fast. My family has owned Hotel Connelly for three generations. The East Coast is sprinkled with dozens of our hotels, and we even have a few in California. We've been considering expanding to other countries in the near future as well. For the past several years, I've worked as the chief sales and marketing officer from the hotel's original location in Port Washington on Long Island, New York. Thankfully, my parents moved out of the hotel and into their own home. Only that house is also in Port Washington, but at least I no longer discover my mom sitting in my living room.

While being born into the family has come with a great deal of benefits, I've never ridden on my father's coattails. On my own merit, I earned a degree in hospitality management, with a minor in business. Though I would not have chosen to go into hospitality, it has been expected of me since the day I was born. When I was eighteen, my dad and I found ourselves engaged in a screaming match over my future, which sent my mom into a panic attack so severe she ended up in the hospital.

After that, my dad and I compromised. I'd go to college in preparation to take over the family business as long as I could choose the college. He wanted me to stay in the Northeast and attend an Ivy League, but I picked Florida. If I was being forced into the family business, I'd take advantage of the time away from my father. So I basked in the sun, surrounded by girls in bikinis. Best four years of my life.

Now, at age thirty, I've been back on Long Island for several years, and I'm dating my mother's friend's daughter. She and I attended different schools growing up, but would see each other sporadically at social gatherings. In our teens, we bonded a little, poking fun at the country club elitists we were forced to spend time with, but we fell out of touch after that. By the time I graduated from college and moved to Port Washington, she was working and living in DC with a boyfriend.

It wasn't until nearly a year ago, when she moved back, newly single, that our parents reconnected us.

"Remember Hayden?" my mother said in the limo on the drive into the city for a fundraiser.

"Draper?"

"Yes. Her mother said she had a nasty breakup with that boy in DC."

Where was she going with this?

Pulling her gaze from the window, she clicked her tongue. "She'll be at the fundraiser tonight. I hear she's looking forward to seeing you."

"She comes from a good family, you know," my dad added.

"I know." I knew all about the Drapers' status and reputation.

It was obvious what my parents were doing. I had just ended a casual relationship, and I'd allowed my parents to dress me like a Ken doll in a tux and drag me like a child to be pawed at by a bunch of stuffy rich folks. While I love a good philanthropic event, I despise the people I'm forced to interact with at each and every one. If they don't have their noses stuck halfway up my ass, asking questions about money, they're trying to set me up with their daughters, nieces, or granddaughters. As of that night, I could add my parents to the list of people trying to play matchmaker.

Upon arriving at the gala, I made a beeline for the bar. Before I'd even ordered a drink, I realized it was a mistake. As I waved for the bartender, I caught sight of Hayden, who was conveniently perched only a few feet away.

"Ah, perfect timing," my mother said as she sidled up beside me.

"Hayden, darling, you look wonderful." My father kissed her cheek. "It's so good to see you."

Her crisp blond hair was nestled at her shoulders. It was shorter than I remembered and complemented her face, letting her aquamarine eyes take center stage. Her lashes were long, likely fake for the event, but the rest of her makeup was subtle. My attention was drawn to curves I'd never noticed in any of our previous interactions. With our moms being as close as they are, I had never thought about Hayden as more than a friend; I figured she was off-limits anyway. My mom would have murdered me if I'd pursued her in high school. Her dad no doubt would have too.

But she was beautiful. Her floor-length emerald gown hugged her hips and exposed a strip of skin with a high but tasteful slit up one side. The cut of the neckline highlighted her cleavage, and if my mom hadn't been standing next to me, I might have needed to adjust myself in my dress pants.

No sooner had reintroductions been made than Dr. and Mrs. Draper appeared beside us, goofily shaking hands with my parents and exchanging kisses on cheeks.

"Oh, I see the kids have gotten together," Mrs. Draper drawled, the olives in her martini nearly sloshing over the side.

"Let's leave them to it, Flo," Dr. Draper remarked, plucking the drink from her hand. "Cliff, Stephanie, let's arrange a lunch at the club this week. You too, son." He nodded at me. With a shake of my hand, he escorted his tipsy wife toward the silent auction table.

My parents smiled at me, then at Hayden, before excusing themselves as well.

"Did you get dragged here too?" she asked.

Two days later, although I'd secretly hoped he would forget, I found myself having lunch with Dr. Draper, as well as Flo, Hayden, and both my parents. It was immediately clear why Hayden and I had been invited.

"Did you forget about your inheritance?" my father whispered at the table so only I could hear.

No, I had not. But truth be told, I'd hoped my parents had. Or at least were not going to follow through with the stipulations: *To be wed by thirty-two.*

My dad was set to retire in the next few years and had it in his thick skull that in order to inherit his title of chief executive officer, I would need to be married. Why my father believes I can't be a bachelor and run a company, I will never understand. He likes to spew words like "optics" and "standards" and "reputation."

Hayden, who sat across from me, had a willful look caked on her delicate face. Her eyes said *We have no choice. It could be worse.* While no one spoke the words aloud, what we were served during that meal—alongside overpriced lobster—was a modern-day arranged marriage.

I wasn't about to make a scene in the middle of the dining room, but I excused myself to the restroom. Rather than go into the men's room, I dropped into a winged-back leather chair in the lounge just outside the restrooms and hunched forward, knees on my elbows and hands through my hair.

That's where Hayden found me. She knelt beside me, adjusting the pearls around her neck. "Hey," she said. Her voice was barely above a whisper, though no one else was in the lounge.

"Hey." Heaving a breath, I sat back in my chair.

"Are you surprised?"

I shrugged. "I suppose not."

Her Rolex sparkled on her pale wrist when she placed her hand on my forearm.

Unspoken words passed between us. Life with Hayden would mean a life of security. It wasn't a death sentence. I liked her parents well enough. It wasn't the life I'd choose for myself, but what choice did I have?

And now that we've been together for nearly a year, we've found our rhythm. For the most part, life with her has been easy. Before her, I never once stopped to imagine what my future wife would be like. While I wonder whether there should be more passion in our relationship, I know it's the right thing to do for my family. Taking over as CEO is important to my parents, and I don't want to let them down.

After another fifteen minutes, Hayden finally finishes up in the bathroom, and we're out the door. Even though her parents stay in an apartment in the city the majority of the time, they've kept their house on Long Island—about a twenty-minute drive from us.

"You need a haircut," she says, but she's looking down at her phone.

"*Okay...*" I swipe my fingers through my hair and steal a glance in the rearview mirror before turning my focus back to the road. The top is getting a little long, but I keep the sides trimmed. I even styled it with the stupidly expensive pomade Hayden bought me, and I think it looks nice.

When we drive between the twin stone lions and pull onto the U-shaped drive, Hayden's mom is waiting for us. With one heeled foot still on a marble step, she pulls me in for a hug.

"Hello, Mrs. Draper." I squeeze back.

"Oh, Cameron, how many times do I have to tell you to call me Flo?"

Over Flo's shoulder, Hayden's dad is watching the exchange. His expression says *Don't you dare call me anything other than Dr. Draper.*

He offers me a friendly slap on the back when it's his turn to greet me, like he didn't just threaten me with his bushy brows. "Cameron, good to see you. How's the hotel?"

"Just fine, sir." I grin, despite how much I hate this question. I prefer not to talk about work when I'm off the clock. "How are the hearts of New York?"

Howard Draper is New York City's most infamous cardiologist. People travel from all over the world for his expertise. "Beating, thanks to me." He laughs at his own joke, and I feign a smile.

For the Plot

We take our seats around the dining table, and Maria, the Draper's longtime housekeeper, pours water into crystal glasses.

"Flo, how is the home and garden society?"

"Oh, it's just lovely. I keep trying to get your mother to join, but she says she's too busy these days." Flo waves a hand through the air.

"Did you make this?" I nod toward the giant floral centerpiece on the table, though I already know the answer. The gold vase towers over our wine glasses, and mini blue-and-white Greek flags play peek-a-boo among an abundance of white roses, peonies, blue hydrangeas, and olive branches.

"Yes, thank you for noticing." Flo side-eyes her husband. "I went with a Greek theme in honor of your holiday next week."

I restrain an eye roll when Flo uses *holiday* instead of *vacation*, like that's going to make me forget she's from the boondocks of Georgia.

"Very thoughtful of you."

"I hear the *Poseidon* ship is truly something. Are you excited?" Flo asks her daughter while sending me a knowing look.

A few months ago, when Hayden and I booked a cruise to the Greek Isles, I met Dr. and Mrs. Draper for lunch at their country club to ask for their daughter's hand in marriage. It's an arbitrary tradition, especially since this whole thing has been arranged, but our parents would be furious if I didn't follow through with formalities.

"Yes, Mother," she sighs, fumbling with her napkin.

Hayden's been looking forward to this trip nearly as much as I have until recently. When I asked her about why she's been a little off lately, she chalked it up to work stress.

She's an event coordinator in New York City and caters mostly to celebrities. She commutes from Long Island during the week, but her most recent client, an extra anxious bride, has demanded all her time. So she's been staying at her parents' apartment in Manhattan to make up for the extra hours she's putting in.

She and I both need this vacation. Lately, we've become complacent. Yes, we were forced into this relationship at first, but I do enjoy her company, and I think the feeling is mutual.

While our politics don't always line up, we get along well. We binge the same shows late at night and enjoy listening to the same music. Our friendship circles don't overlap, though, which is tricky when making plans. I like that she's ambitious at work and cares for her family. But I don't feel that fire with Hayden. She's pretty, and while the sex is good, we haven't had much of it lately, and I can't help but feel like we're missing an important connection.

In any case, Hayden's bridezilla got married yesterday, just in time to allow her to relax and unwind in Greece with me. And just in time for her to turn around and plan her own wedding.

Chapter 4
Josefine

SOUTHERN CALIFORNIA'S rainy season has finally received its eviction notice, and I'm all too eager to open the windows. The metal hinges protest with creaks and whines as I slide the panes up. Dust and spider corpses pool in the grooves. Writing from home has its perks. Like foregoing a bra. I'm in the middle of developing a difficult scene about a young girl navigating a world in which her mother is addicted to painkillers. When I woke up this morning, I knew it was what I needed to write. When I'm working my ass off on a particularly burdensome scene, I prefer not to be surrounded by people. I've made that mistake before. Unbeknownst to me, mascara was streaming down my cheeks, à la Taylor Swift in her "Blank Space" music video, in the middle of the coffee shop. According to Raj, he stood in front of me for a full minute, waving his hands like an air-traffic controller and asking if I was okay before I finally acknowledged him.

So yeah, I tend to sequester myself in the apartment some days. Scheduling self-care in anticipation of writing about heavy topics like this is vital. On days when I know my mental health will be drained due to the content of my writing, I take it a step further and call in a favor from a higher power: *Help me write whatever is meant to be written today.*

Additionally, I light my favorite candle—the one with hints of lotus blossom and aloe. I gather my emotional support drinks—water with lemon, peppermint tea, and black coffee—a box of tissues, pen and paper, a timer with a visible countdown, my hot pink Bluetooth keyboard (the *clickety-clack* sound is so satisfying), and my "Concentrate" playlist on Spotify. I swear I'm not usually this high maintenance.

Writing this book has been thoroughly cathartic. The act of writing fiction alone is healing me one small piece at a time. As an only child, I'm alone in the trauma of my youth. Losing a father at age ten and being left with a mother who didn't handle the loss well would make any person feel some shit.

I'm forever thankful to Aunt Rachel. She lived in San Diego as well, though she worked full time, which made it difficult to see her except on weekends. Those weekends, though, were my saving grace. When I visited, I could most often be found with my cousins Millie and Asher. They are two and four years older, thus wildly entertaining for me.

When Uncle Ethan's job relocated them to New York about the time I entered high school, and Millie, my closest friend and weekend lifeline, was suddenly on the other side of the country, I'd never felt lonelier.

My friends from elementary school didn't know how to act around me following my dad's death. I cringed at the way they'd walk on eggshells or pause mid-sentence with their eyes bugged out when they accidentally mentioned their own fathers. As if the word *father* would break me. It was even worse when they'd invite me over. Parents would ask me how my mom was doing, and I'd lie that she was "just great" when in reality, the last time I'd seen her, she was leaning over the toilet. And that was if she wasn't MIA.

In middle school, I was still the kid whose dad died. My peers would attempt to pair me up with the other kid whose parent died, as if that was a prerequisite for a special club. I kept my head down for those years, spending every spare moment in my English teacher's classroom, pouring poems and monologues into my notebook until it overflowed.

By the time I got to high school, I was no longer notorious for my dad's death. I'd become infamous for having the party house. My mom was rarely home (read: always out with a new boyfriend), and teens loved to congregate at the cool and unsupervised house. Those friends didn't stick around long, though. Once their parents discovered my mom was never around, they were forbidden from hanging out with me. Then there were the kids who befriended me long enough to steal prescription meds from my mother's medicine cabinet.

I used to dream about sneaking out in the middle of the night and catching a flight to New York City. I'd knock on my aunt and uncle's door and beg them to adopt me. But then guilt would claw its way in. Like if I left, then I'd be betraying my dad. If he were alive, he'd be devastated by the way my mom dealt with his death —prescription drugs, alcohol, and men. But then again, if he were alive, none of it would have happened.

No, I knew I could never leave her.

In my junior year of high school, my guidance counselor encouraged me to apply to colleges outside California. The notion of leaving the state frightened me, but I managed to distance myself from San Diego by choosing a school in Los Angeles. It allowed me to be far enough away to have the time and space to create my own life while being close enough that I could get home quickly in an emergency.

I've known Tyler since I was sixteen. He's a few years older than me, and before my move to LA when I was eighteen, we were nothing more than friends. After I had settled on a college and discovered I'd missed the deadline for housing and didn't think I could afford a place off campus, I called him. He lived in LA, and I thought he might know someone in need of a roommate or have advice regarding my situation.

Tyler insisted I move in with him, and so I did. It was impulsive and wild, but I had nowhere else to go. We've always had chemistry, though, early on, we strove to remain roommates and set boundaries. But before long, I found myself slipping under his sheets in the middle of the night. I claimed it was because his bed was like sleeping on a cloud. Not that either of us needed the excuse.

Four years later, we're still together.

Sometimes I wonder if I jumped into a relationship with him too quickly, like my mom with her men.

After my dad died, she couldn't stand on her own two feet. She was twenty when they married, and she hasn't worked a full-time job since. While we lived off a hefty life insurance payout in the beginning, I think she knew early on that the money wouldn't last forever. That's when she began throwing herself at well-off men. It was harrowing to watch, and if the way she numbed herself with pills and alcohol was anything to go by, it was painful for her too.

My mom quickly became a shell of herself. Sure, she is still fit and breathtaking to most, but there is a permanent hollowness behind her eyes.

Initially, when Tyler asked me to move in with him, I flat-out refused, despite not having a backup plan. I didn't want to leap into the arms of the first guy who propositioned me. It felt too much like something my mother would do. But Tyler assured me I was nothing like her, and because I was so tired of being let down by the one person who was supposed to love me unconditionally, having him show up for me was a huge blessing.

For the Plot

As a writer, the most splendid place to find myself is in the writing zone. A place where a character's soliloquy is so spellbinding it's hard to believe their words are actually coming from me.

Enchanted—that's how I feel right now, propped up against the headboard while a light breeze flows in from the open windows. My start was rough, though. I'd get fifty words onto the page, then delete forty-eight of them. Over and over until finally the ideas poured out of me like a waterfall, crashing and rushing, my fingers barely keeping up. At one point, the letter *R* ricocheted off my keyboard and I had to find a video on YouTube to figure out how to reattach it.

Because I'm in the zone, taking full advantage of the noise-canceling feature on my AirPods, I jump when Tyler slams the door.

According to the clock on my laptop, he's home much earlier than normal. I remove one earbud when he appears in the bedroom doorway and motions for my attention, but I don't catch what he's saying.

"Give me one minute. I'm in the middle of something." I nod at my laptop and pop my AirPod back in. I'm at the climax of a major scene involving a plethora of back-and-forth dialogue and I want to get it all down before I lose it.

Across the room, Tyler paces, huffing and puffing. He's obviously worked up, and the annoyance radiating from him is stealing my concentration. I'm trying my best to hang on to it, but he's doing an excellent job of distracting me.

He parks himself on the bed and yanks an earbud out of my ear, pulling a couple of strands of hair along with it.

"Ouch! What the—"

"I was fucking talking to you, Beck!" His eyes narrow and his nostrils flare. This combo has been making an appearance all too frequently these days.

"I'm working. You can't just interrupt me like that," I say, patting the mattress in search of my earbud.

"Working?" Tyler scoffs. "In bed?"

"Yes, in bed. I work from home."

"I've had a fucking hard day!" he spits.

"Okay, I hear you. I'm sorry about that, but it doesn't give you the right to interrupt my creativity." I sit a little straighter and pull my shoulders back. "Do you know how hard I've been chasing it all day? You come home and bark about whatever the fuck you're barking about, and now I've lost all the stuff swimming around in my brain."

He looks me straight in the eye. "You're fucking selfish."

"I'm selfish?" I jab my thumb at my chest. My ability to maintain an even tone is dissipating. "I spent the last two nights with *your* clients for *your* work, and now you won't wait ten minutes?"

This always happens. The life of a music producer is hectic. As the girlfriend, I'm expected to show up at parties and events on his arm. I've even been to the occasional award show, though I don't like being in the limelight on the red carpet and avoid that part at all costs. The last thing I need is to stumble upon an article from a still-lives-at-home-with-their-momma blogger about whether my stomach pooch is a food baby or a real baby. *I can assure them it's just a woman's body.*

Every time I turn around, we have to make an appearance at some event. Regardless of whether I want to attend or how busy I am with my own work, Tyler reminds me that it's important to him that I be there. I want to be supportive, I really do, but partying like that is exhausting. The nights start out promising. He sticks with me for a bit, showering me with attention, but after a drink or two, he ditches me for clients and other low-key celebrities, and I'm left making small talk with the bartender or calling an Uber so I can head home early. Then, when he returns just before the crack of dawn, he drunkenly slips into bed, apologizes, and makes it up to me with sex.

"Your job is different," he continues, kicking off his boots and letting them fall to the floor beside the bed. "You can write anytime you want."

Gritting my teeth, I work to keep my voice even. "That's not true. I can't control when creativity strikes. You should know that; you work with artists."

"Yeah, but they get paid hundreds of dollars a day," he says. "You're not even getting paid to write."

Oh, no he didn't. "You know that's not fair."

Regardless of how little he thinks of my writing, he doesn't even bother to consider the deadlines I have for my freelance clients.

Tucking my chin, so sick of this battle already, I close my laptop and return my AirPods to their case. I won't be writing any more today.

"And what about all the time you spend reading?"

Is he referring to me curled up with my Kindle before bed?

"It's for research," I sneer, slapping a hand on the mattress.

"How much *research*,"—he puts up air quotes—"are you going to do, Beck?" He hops off the bed and storms toward the tiny en suite bathroom.

"Do you think scientists ever stop searching for a cure for cancer?" I challenge him.

"This isn't cancer, Joey." He turns and stands in the doorway. "This is writing a book." With that, he spins on his heel and disappears.

I gape at the empty doorway, my stomach knotting.

"Are you going to write the fucking book or sit here all day and yell at me like you always do?"

The thrum of my pulse intensifies. "I don't always yell at you."

"You do. And it's getting really old," he calls from the bathroom.

I pop off the bed and stand in the doorway, blocking him in. "You wouldn't get it." I'm pushing it, but I can't help it.

"What?" He glares at me through the mirror, yanking at the handle of the faucet. "What wouldn't I get?"

"You didn't have to climb your way up in the industry."

His eyes are hard, cold, as he scrubs his hands under the stream of water. "What's that supposed to mean?"

Oh boy, I've really started it now. "It means—" *Don't say it, Josefine, don't say it.* "It means—" *Oh shit.* "You're only successful because you're a fucking nepo-baby."

"The fuck did you just say?" He whirls around so fast hygiene products go flying off the counter with a clatter.

I flinch, my heart leaping into my throat. I may have taken it too far, but he pissed me the hell off.

I can't party with him and his wild colleagues and clients "for work" nearly every night, then wake up with a clear, creative head. Though it may sometimes look like I'm staring off into space, in reality, I'm allowing my characters to work out their shit in my mind. Until now, I thought Tyler understood; he works with massively imaginative people every day.

He shoves by me and grabs his keys and boots. He doesn't bother to put them on his feet before he slams the front door with a "Fuck you, Joey."

My vision blurs and I wipe away my tears. I slump against the mattress and search the ceiling for answers. When I come up empty, I extricate my journal and a pen from the nightstand and pull the covers over my legs. There's so much power in writing things down, pen to paper, and I'm determined to work it all out before Tyler comes back. *If he comes back.* He doesn't always.

The room is dark when I open my eyes. A sole streetlight flickers outside.

"Wake up, Beck," Tyler whispers, nudging my shoulder.

I roll onto my back. "What time is it?" I croak.

"Late."

I sit up and pull my legs into my chest. "Listen—"

"No, me first," he urges. "I'm so sorry." He puts a hand on my knee and rubs circles against the sensitive skin on the inside with his thumb. "I shouldn't have said what I did. Your writing is important. I'm just so fucking stressed at work right now. The new crew we're working with is full of prima donnas and it's driving my whole team crazy. Our deadline is this week, and everyone is asking for more money. It's just stressful as hell right now." With a hand pressed to my cheek, he leans closer. "Please forgive me."

"I forgive you," I say, leaning into his touch. "I'm sorry too. It was shitty of me to say that stuff about your career. I didn't mean it." Though my words were true—Tyler's career is certainly attributed to nepotism—it was a low blow. He gets trashed for benefiting from his father's fame enough as it is. He doesn't need it from me too.

"Can we just forget about this stupid fight?"

"Yes. Please." I let out a long breath and close my eyes.

He kisses my forehead, lingering with his lips pressed to my skin.

The vacation we've had planned for months couldn't come at a better time. He'll have finished this project, and we'll both be able to unplug with the Mediterranean Sea lulling us to sleep every night for a week. It's exactly what we need to get back on track.

Chapter 5
Josefine

EXPECTING Tyler to unplug right away was delusional. The second we boarded the plane in Los Angeles, he was on his phone and his laptop. According to him, in order for him to step away from work on the cruise, he had to wrap several things up on the flight to Europe.

My dad always wanted to take me to Greece—the island of Crete, specifically—where his grandfather's family is from. But when he was diagnosed with brain cancer, he knew that dream would not become a reality. Instead, before he died, he set some money aside for the trip. It became accessible when I turned twenty-one and came with specific instructions that included a cruise to the Greek islands. He passed away twelve years ago, and I'm finally taking that trip on the anniversary of his death.

On the days leading up to my father's passing, I would crawl into his hospice bed. He'd whisper stories of visiting Crete as a child. Stories about his grandmother skinning a rabbit as casually as most people would water plants. And the time his sister pushed him off a cliff into the sea. Aunt Rachel, of course, denies the transgression. About the time a peacock chased him around the botanical gardens. His cousin's wedding when he was eleven; when his uncle let him drink wine, and he accidentally got drunk and threw up all over her wedding gown.

When I booked this trip six months ago, my mom had just checked herself out of rehab early. I hoped she would be better in time to accompany me, though, deep down, I knew she wouldn't. And as I suspected, my mother is in no condition to travel to Greece—nor do I want to spend time with her in her current state.

I wanted to bring my cousin Millie, but when I was scheduling, she had just signed a contract to play Nessarose in the national tour of *Wicked* and couldn't guarantee it would be wrapped up in time. Aunt Rachel couldn't travel halfway across the world either. Between working part time and helping Asher raise his young daughter, she's far too busy for an international trip at the moment. That left Tyler. It took some convincing, but in the end, he agreed it would be a nice break from work.

The *Poseidon* set sail from the Piraeus port in Athens and spent the first day and night at sea. We woke up at the island of Paros and spent several hours sightseeing. After another day at sea, we explored the island of Rhodes and a day on the island of Santorini. When we wake tomorrow, we'll be docked on the island of Crete.

Tyler and I compromised when it came to his phone. He leaves it in the cabin during the day, but he plays catch-up with notifications in the evening. I get it. It's hard to completely unplug when he's building a musical empire. He convinced me to upgrade to a balcony suite, and I'm glad he did. I can't imagine only having one tiny porthole to look out. I'm not typically claustrophobic, but excusing myself for fresh air (and a glass of wine) while he works from his phone on the bed has been wonderful. The view of the waves chasing the horizon settles my nerves.

Around the anniversary of my dad's death, I tend to feel off. I miss him in small ways every day, but May is excruciatingly brutal. This year, though, finally taking the trip he planned for me, I feel closer to him than I have in years.

We're on our way to dinner when a group of Americans recognizes Tyler. He politely poses for a few selfies so he doesn't get a reputation for being an asshole to his fans. Yesterday he got mistaken for Machine Gun Kelly, but neither of us had the heart to correct the ecstatic fan.

Dinner on the ship tonight is beautiful, romantic, enchanting. Tyler listens intently to several manic ideas about my book and only pipes in once or twice with advice. Having his undivided attention makes my insides fizz like the effervescent champagne we're indulging in. Our table is pressed against the floor-to-ceiling windows, offering us front-row seats to the world's most magnificent sunset.

Clinking his glass of champagne with mine, Tyler announces, "To us. To you, my love."

"To us," I repeat.

The restaurant is cozy and quiet, with only a few servers, since we preselected our course options using an app ahead of time.

A server has just placed salads in front of us when Tyler asks, "Have you talked to your mom lately?"

I set my napkin in my lap and let out a noncommittal hum as I bring my champagne to my lips.

Tyler runs a finger up and down the stem of his glass before taking a long swig. "Do you know if she's using again?"

My chest caves and I sigh. "She's always using."

"You know what I mean."

I do. What he wants to know is whether she's using more than normal. My mom's tolerance for pain medication is exceptionally high after years of abuse.

I shrug. "I don't think so?"

"When was the last time you saw her?"

Draining the lemon-infused olive oil from its tiny tin dispenser over my salad, I keep my focus downcast. "Just before we left, actually."

We visited my dad's grave together since I would be traveling over the anniversary of his death. At first my mom refused to accompany me, something she's never done before. That registered as odd, but I tried not to give the thought too much power. She could have had a million reasons for not wanting to go. But when I picked her up, she was simultaneously groggy and jittery. That wasn't totally out of the ordinary. What was, though, was her inability to string together a coherent sentence and the way she fussed with her hair obsessively on the drive to the cemetery—her tell. She was strung out.

I tried not to let her behavior affect my emotions at the cemetery, but our visit was cut short by her incessant need to talk about her newest fling. Frank *this* and Frank *that*. What he does for a living, where he's taking her on vacation next.

"Can you just shut the fuck up for one minute?" I blurted. Apparently my prefrontal cortex could no longer regulate my ability to keep quiet.

Mom stumbled back at my outburst, catching the heel of her shoe on a rock. She fell on top of another person's grave, crushing the fresh arrangement of flowers someone had left in their memory.

I helped my mom to her feet and dusted the dirt off her yoga pants. She couldn't even bother to put on real clothes.

"I'm sorry, Mom," I started.

"No, it's fine, Josefine." She used my full name. "You finish up. I'll wait in the car."

A wave of guilt washed over me for yelling. No matter how many years had passed, she was still a grieving widow.

"I can get her into that new rehab," Tyler says around a bite of salad.

A state-of-the art rehabilitation center recently opened in Palm Springs. The father of one of Tyler's clients owns the facility. How convenient for a person in the entertainment industry to have that type of resource.

"That's so sweet of you. I've brought it up to her, but she refuses to go."

If she isn't willing to do the work, then there's nothing I can do, no matter how desperately I want to. The more I push her to get help, the more strained our relationship becomes. But dang if it isn't hard to stand by and witness her crumbling brick by brick.

"Can we change the subject?" I plead, reaching for Tyler's hand across the table.

"Of course." He dips his chin. "What have you loved about the trip so far?"

"The water," I say without hesitation. "I can't believe how clear it is. And the sand. Just the beaches in general."

"You were the hottest girl on all the islands."

I blush at his praise. More often than not, his attraction is obvious in his actions, but he rarely compliments my looks, so I cling to the statement like a leech.

"Speaking of..." I cock a brow and give him an exaggerated perusal. "You look nice tonight."

Skinny black dress pants hug his trim hips. His pale pink dress shirt is unbuttoned at the top, creating a deep V that reveals his chest tattoos. His long fingers are adorned with silver rings, but he's removed his usual black leather bracelets.

"As do you." He tips his champagne glass my way.

I'm wearing a skin-tight gold gown, and my long hair is curled in big waves and pulled over one shoulder to showcase the exposed back.

"Thank you." I grin.

While the islands of Paros, Rhodes, and Santorini were far more beautiful than any image on the internet can convey, I'm most looking forward to Crete.

Sadly, the bed-and-breakfast my dad's family owned was torn down years ago. Though I'm still eager to stand on the island where my father spent most of his summers as a kid. My parents even honeymooned on Crete.

"For tomorrow—"

"Excuse me." Tyler interrupts me when a server places two desserts on the table. "We haven't gotten our main course yet."

"My apologies," the server says, fumbling for the dishes.

"It's okay, you can leave them," I say. We requested them, they just arrived out of order.

Tyler narrows his eyes on me.

"We're on vacation." I shrug. "Live a little. Eat dessert first."

The server looks from Tyler to me and back again until Tyler nods once. He leaves a plate of baklava with sprinkled pistachio for Tyler and watermelon and basil sorbet for me.

"Mmm," I moan, taking in the gorgeous presentation.

Tyler taps his fork on the table. "Don't do that."

"Do what?" I ask, peeking up at him.

Frowning, he leans in closer and grits his teeth. "Sound like you're having an orgasm at the table."

I huff. It's not like I'm imitating Meg Ryan in *When Harry Met Sally*. It's a tiny groan. "What's with you?"

"Nothing's with me. I just don't want you to embarrass yourself." He pushes his plate to the side. I guess he's going to eat his dessert last after all.

"*Okay*." I struggle to keep an even tone. "Like I was saying earlier, we're snorkeling tomorrow."

As I'm going over the itinerary, our dinners arrive—filet mignon with roasted vegetables and rosemary mashed potatoes for him, the fresh catch of the day with steamed vegetables and a citrus glaze for me.

"After snorkeling, the boat will shuttle us to shore to a traditional Greek taverna for lunch, then bring us back to the dock to board the ship. How does that sound?"

His responding smile doesn't reach his eyes. "Great, Beck."

After our out-of-order but delicious dinner, I collapse on the bed in our cabin. "I'm stuffed." I grunt and wiggle my way out of my gown, relieved to no longer be strangled by spandex.

Tyler tosses the room key on the table and kicks off his black loafers. Next, he goes to work unbuttoning his shirt. He leaves it open, displaying a collage of chest and stomach tattoos.

I sit up, thoroughly enjoying the view.

His gray eyes rove over me, paying special attention to my bare breasts. His knees hit the side of the bed, and he pushes my shoulders to the mattress. When I'm flat on my back, he straddles my hips. The ends of his shirt tickle my naked stomach as he hovers over me and plants a kiss on my collarbone. With my fingers tangled in the hair at his nape, I pull him to me and savor the taste of honey and pistachio that fills my mouth when he drags his tongue across mine. I nibble on his lower lip, relishing the connection, but pull back when there's a buzz against my leg. Either Tyler has something kinky in store for us or—

He digs his phone out of his pants pocket. The phone that was supposed to be left behind at dinner this evening. "Dammit, I've gotta take this."

I throw my hands over my face and huff. "Fine."

"Yo!" He steps around the bed. *It'll just take a minute*, he mouths to me. Then he retreats to the balcony to take the call.

For the Plot

Five minutes later, tired of making out pictures on the popcorn ceiling like I did as a kid, I roll off the bed and peer out the sliding glass door. Tyler is leaning against the railing and roughing his fingers through his blond hair. *A minute, my ass.* Whatever is going on can't be good, and I can't imagine he'll be happy when he hangs up.

Scanning the ship's schedule of events in the welcome packet we received, I find a description of tonight's entertainment: *Live Music at Muses Nightclub*. Perfect. I slip into a coral mini dress and slide my feet back into the nude heels I wore to dinner. Tomorrow I may regret the decision to wear them, but I'll look hot tonight.

By the time I've freshened up in the bathroom, Tyler has finished his call and come inside.

"Everything all right?" I ask, searching his expression.

Propped against the door, he shakes his head, his jaw ticking. "Just pissed-off clients."

"Oh no." I shoot him a frown and spritz the back of my neck with perfume.

"Yeah, really bad fucking timing." He swipes a hand down his clean-shaven face, then crosses his arms. "The team is losing their fucking minds without me."

"That bad?" I wrap my arms around his waist, forcing him to drop his arms, and press my chest to his. I thought he tied up all his loose ends before we left. Didn't he tell me this trip was coming at the perfect time?

He grasps my arms and pulls back. "Yes, it's fucking bad, Beck," he grouses, dropping onto the mattress.

The bite in his tone startles me. I'm doing what I can to be a sympathetic and supportive girlfriend despite the way his work keeps interfering with our trip, yet it feels as though I'm about to get my head chewed off for no reason.

I stand in front of him, eyes fluttering, waiting for his next move. "How can I help?" I try again.

The furrow between his brows relaxes a bit, but he ignores my question. "Why are you dressed again?"

Finally, he sees me.

"There's a dance club tonight. I thought we could go." I refuse to be in this tiny cabin if he's going to be cranky all night.

His eyes swim with hesitation, like he's in two places at once. *Come back. Be here with me,* I silently beg.

"Come on, it'll be fun." I bounce on my toes.

"Fine." He buttons his shirt, slips his bare feet into his loafers, and reluctantly follows me out the door and toward the elevators.

Muses is a social media influencer's dream. Backdrops perfectly curated for a digital square grid are hung every several feet, like a selfie museum. A white clawfoot bathtub filled with blue-and-white plastic balls sits under a neon sign that reads "Make a splash. Dive into life." Illuminated angel wings, complete with a floating halo, hang on the wall at just the right height for one to stand in front of for photos. On the other side of the club, a neon pink sign reads "Bad decisions make better stories." Below it is a bench constructed entirely of banned book spines.

Tyler immediately pushes through the crowd to the bar, dragging me behind him.

"What'll it be?" the bartender asks, throwing a rag over his shoulder.

"Two shots of tequila," he shouts over the music.

Just as I'm about to tell him I don't want tequila, he turns to me and raises a brow, silently asking for my order.

"Vodka water lime is fine."

He downs both shots of tequila before I've even reached for my glass, and he immediately signals for two more.

"Don't you think—"

For the Plot

    He brings a shot glass up and grits his teeth. "I don't wanna think tonight."

Chapter 6

Cameron

"I'll stay here with you." I run a hand along Hayden's flushed face.

She flinches almost imperceptibly at the touch and inches away.

An all-inclusive experience at Atlas Luxury Resort & Spa awaits us on Crete, Greece's southernmost island. Access to the pool and spa, lunch, snorkeling, and a private cabana with unlimited snacks and champagne. Today is the day I planned to propose. Mrs. Draper and my mother have even arranged to have the resort's photographer capture the moment as I get down on one knee on the shore. It's not my style, but our mothers could not be convinced otherwise.

"No, no, you go ahead," she insists against the fitted sheet.

"Okay, what's going on?" I sit on the edge of the mattress and put a gentle hand on her back.

She's been acting strange since we boarded the ship on day one. We haven't even had sex. Every time I've tried to make a move, she's complained of jet lag or a headache from too much sun, or she's sworn she's bloated from dinner. If we don't get off the boat, then what?

She remains silent, so I try again. "What time did you get back last night?"

When I left her, she was still dancing with a group of girls we met at Muses who are also, coincidentally, from Long Island. She was having the time of her life, and from the looks of things, her recent work stressors had been forgotten on the dance floor. I suggested she get some sleep and knew that if I stayed out any later, I'd regret it in the morning, but she waved me off.

Hayden sits up and brushes her tangled hair off her face, and for a full minute, she's silent. Finally, she turns to me with tears in her eyes and sucks in a breath. "I found the ring."

"What?" My posture stiffens, and a chill runs through my veins.

"The ring, Cameron. You're going to propose, right?" she asks, dropping her focus to the mattress between us.

Willing my heart rate to slow, I pull the box from the bag at my feet and hold it between us. "I don't—" I clear my throat. "I don't understand."

She swings her legs off the bed so we're sitting side by side. "I found the ring when I was looking for the spare phone charger."

"What are you saying?"

"I don't want to get married."

"What? But—" I rub the tension at my jaw.

"And I don't think you do either." Licking her lips, she turns. Her eyes are full of what looks like sadness mixed with guilt and maybe even a hint of pity.

My instinct is to retort, but I fight it, instead choosing to sit with the bomb she just dropped so I can process its implications. For the past year, I've tried so hard to make this relationship feel normal and natural. But the truth is, it's not. And until this moment, I haven't considered that she might be faking it too.

I study her face, looking for any sign of doubt. "What about your inheritance?"

"What about it?" She shrugs, her expression still full of pity, like she's surprised I don't understand her reasoning. "You really think it's worth marrying for money?"

Instead of answering, I throw the question back at her. "You don't?"

"At one point I did. In the beginning," she says, clasping her hands in her lap. "But is it really worth a lifetime of complacency?"

Even though I had the same thoughts, her calling our relationship complacent aloud makes me bristle.

"Sorry," she says, probably noticing the way I flinched.

"No, it's okay." I roll the velvet box between my hands. "You're right."

She raises a brow but doesn't respond.

"I don't want to get married either," I admit. "At least not right now. And not because my dad is dangling a hefty inheritance just out of reach."

Fuck, the repercussions of this may be brutal, but I'll deal with my dad later.

"I love you," she murmurs. "I just—"

"I know," I interrupt. "Me too."

Resting her head on my shoulder, she lets out a long sigh. "I think I'm still going to skip the excursion, though. We could both probably use some time alone."

As I hop off the van that shuttled a small group of us here, I feel lighter than I have in a long time. Hayden made the right choice, suggesting we take some time for ourselves. I need to process my thoughts after what just went down.

Our folks may lose their shit when they find out. They fully expect Hayden to come back with a shiny new adornment on her ring finger, not broken up from her boyfriend. But I suppress thoughts of that dreaded conversation and focus on what's right in front of me: a spectacular island.

I brought my camera along, eager to play around and capture the beauty Crete has to offer. Dodging giant cicadas—those fuckers are aggressive—I make my way to the front desk.

I'm escorted to a private cabana. A young man with a camera is not-so-discreetly lingering nearby, so I flag him down. Sure enough, he's the photographer my mother hired. His name is Aaron. He's American, too, and he's working at the resort for the summer.

I'm only hit with an inkling of heartache when I explain the cancellation to him. More than anything, I'm relieved. Luckily, his response doesn't hold even an ounce of pity like I anticipated it would. Instead, he notices my camera and changes the subject.

Come to find out, he's been traveling to Europe on a work visa for the last three summers as a luxury resort photographer.

After he promises to pass along more details about how he got involved in his work and we exchange contact information, Aaron excuses himself. I drop my bag at the cabana and sling my camera strap over my shoulder. Then I kick my sandals off and follow the path to the beach. I'm reluctant to leave my belongings behind, but the hotel assured me that they're cautious about the private property of their guests and that Crete is fantastically safe. The sand is like powdered sugar beneath my feet compared to the sand back on Long Island. Crystal-clear water laps against the shore, providing a peaceful soundtrack. Quickly, I find myself lost in a fantasy of doing this full time—photographing travel destinations for a living—and for once, instead of pushing it aside, I indulge in the dream.

Several boats anchored about two hundred yards out are bursting with eager snorkelers. Some are already in the water, splashing and chattering.

Using my camera, I focus on one person, then another, then another, until I zoom in on one woman in particular. Her neon pink bikini immediately seizes my attention as she waits her turn to slip into the water. The instructor is talking and gesturing with his hands beside her, probably giving her the rundown. With my finger trained over the shutter button, I pause, ready to snap a shot of her. But I rear back when she turns and pushes the guy behind her in the chest.

What was that about?

I peer over my camera, but they're too far away for me to see what's happening. Instead, I use my camera like a spyglass. I depress the shutter button just as she drops off the edge of the boat and into the Sea of Crete. When she bobs above the surface, I pull back and check my camera's display. *Got it.* Frozen in midair. Bold yet delicate, with the White Mountains in the background. Her long hair held captive by the wind and the biggest smile on her beautiful face.

After roaming the beach and climbing rocks to get the best shots, I return to the resort grounds. Damn, this place is incredible. The staff is attentive and friendly; the aesthetic is both intentional and practical. There is no shortage of images for me to capture, that's for sure. Almost instantly, I know I want to return to Crete just to stay here.

Putting a pause on picture-taking, I follow a narrow path to a small taverna that shares the resort's beach. Lunch at the resort is included, but I'd rather experience a little local flair.

"Sparkling or still?" the young server asks.

For the Plot

"Still is fine," I reply. "*Efcharistó.*" I thank her, stumbling over the one Greek word I've picked up since I arrived.

After eating the most delicious saganaki and grilled octopus, I wash it down with complimentary raki, a traditional after-meal drink my grandmother would probably say will put hair on my chest.

Full and even more buoyant as the hour passes, I go for a swim in the sea. When my skin is adequately caked in salt, I head back to the resort's pool deck, where I catch a flash of pink in my periphery.

The young woman in the pink bikini is disembarking from the boat along with her group, and she doesn't appear to be alone. A man with a towel draped around his tattooed torso jogs to catch up to her. He grabs at her wrist, but she swats at him. From where I'm standing, I can't hear their conversation, but it's hard to miss the way she rushes away, kicking sand in her wake. The man, a statue on the shore, doesn't even attempt to follow her as she hustles in the opposite direction of her tour group and plops herself in a hammock in the shade. For a heartbeat, I consider following after her, but then what? What would I even say? *Excuse me, miss, but I was watching you from my camera earlier and… well, was that guy bothering you?*

I shake off the ludicrous thought. She'd probably consider me just as bothersome, or worse, she'd think I was a stalker.

The champagne calls my name, and before I know it, I'm dozing off in my private cabana.

I wake with a start at the sound of a bang. Disoriented and a little drunk from the raki and the champagne, I take in my surroundings. Outside the cabana, rain falls in sheets. Rain? I clamber to my feet, ramming my shin into the metal chaise lounge.

"Dammit." I snag my phone from the lounger, only to discover the battery has died. "Shit." Sticking my head out of the cabana, I scan the area, looking for clues as to what time it is. The clouds have dimmed the sky and covered the sun, making it impossible to tell. The only people around are resort employees who are scrambling to strip the lounge chairs of their cushions. In a panic, I throw my things in my bag and secure my camera. Then I make a run for it to the lobby.

Inside, it's bustling with sopping-wet patrons hurtling around the lobby like ants searching for their hill.

"Excuse me." I stop an elderly man passing by. "What time is it?"

The man looks down at his watch. "It's nearly five, mate," he says, then shuffles to catch up with his family.

"*Five?*" I holler. Fuck. I was supposed to be on the cruise's shuttle at four. With long strides, I make my way to the concierge desk, nearly knocking over a toddler with a lollipop in the process.

"Excuse me." I smack the wooden countertop much harder than intended and inadvertently startle the woman behind her computer.

"How can I help you?" Her white teeth nearly blind me.

"Did the shuttle to *Poseidon* Cruise leave already?" My chances are slim, but I pray to the Greek gods, nonetheless.

She turns to her colleague and speaks in Greek before turning back to me, her brow furrowed. "I'm sorry, sir, but the shuttle departed an hour ago."

"Shit," I mutter under my breath.

"Excuse me," a feminine voice pants beside me. The young woman is just as soaked as I am. She's dressed in cutoffs and a wet tank top that's so transparent every inch of her bright pink bikini top is visible. If it wasn't raining, I'd think I was at a wet T-shirt contest on Daytona Beach during Spring Break.

"It's you," I stammer, stunned.

She digs her bright blue nails into the countertop and whips her head in my direction. "What?"

She's the girl from the snorkeling excursion. The one I captured midair.

"Sorry." I shake my head. I didn't mean to say that out loud. "Are you okay?" I ask, bulldozing forward in hopes that she forgets my first comment.

Her cheeks are splotchy and her eyes are red rimmed. "No," she whimpers. "Did I hear you say you missed the shuttle to *Poseidon* Cruise?"

I nod.

"I did too," she sniffles. "Well, not the shuttle. I was on an excursion on the water—"

"Snorkeling," I interrupt.

"Yeah," she continues, giving me a skeptical once-over.

I don't blame her. *See? I do look like a stalker.*

"They freaking left without me." She throws her hands in the air, dropping her phone in the process.

I crouch and retrieve it for her. She's lucky the screen isn't cracked.

"Thanks," she says when I hold it out to her. Her hand brushes mine in the transaction.

It's small and cold from the rain, and I shiver on contact. If I'm not mistaken, a ripple of goose bumps works its way up her arm too. I follow its path up until I'm locked on her bold brown eyes. Her lashes are long and her brows are lush. *I didn't even know eyebrows could be sexy, but here we are.*

"You're welcome." With a curt nod, I turn back to the woman at the desk, whose name tag reads Anastasia. "So what now?" I ask.

"I suggest you get a ride to the dock as soon as possible," she begins, her eyes glued to the screen in front of her. "With the way the rain is coming down, there's a chance they haven't left yet."

"Okay." I swipe a hand down my face, willing my heart rate to level out. There's no point in panicking yet.

"You should probably call the cruise line to let them know," she adds.

I turn to Hot-Pink Bikini Girl. "Can you call the cruise while I take care of transportation?"

Wetting her lips, she nods and unlocks her phone.

"Do you have taxis available?" I ask Anastasia.

"Of course." She picks up the phone and speaks in Greek again.

When she hangs up, she instructs us to wait outside for the car she's arranged. With a quick *"efcharistó,"* I nudge Hot-Pink Bikini Girl through the sliding glass doors.

"I can't believe this fucking happened," she mutters.

"Yeah, me neither," I agree. "Did you get a hold of the cruise line?"

The woman shakes her head. "It just kept ringing, and there wasn't an option to leave a message. Do you think we'll make it back in time?" She has to crane her neck to look up at me. The top of her messy bun is barely level with my shoulder.

"I hope so." I shrug. "I'm Cameron, by the way."

"Josefine," she replies, just as a black car with TAXI printed on the dash pulls up.

"To the port," I call to the driver once we're both situated in the back seat. "As fast as you can, please. We're in a rush."

Without a word, the driver tosses his cigarette out the window, letting the rain in as he does, and takes off.

"Where are you from?" I ask Josefine while I dig a portable charger out of my bag.

For the Plot

"California. You?" She uses the fabric of her giant beach bag to wipe the rain from her face.

"New York," I answer. "Are you here alone?" I ask, remembering the dude following her earlier.

The woman got into a taxi with me, a stranger, and I have the audacity to ask if she's here alone. Jesus, it's like the beginning of a *CSI* episode.

Josefine picks at the skin around her thumbnail. "I am now."

Frowning, I work to decode that statement but come up with nothing.

She eyes me, her lips pursed, then continues. "I came here with my boyfriend, but—" She drops her head back against the seat. "I caught him cheating on me last night."

"The fuck?" I practically shout. "That's shitty."

"Tell me about it." Her words are soft and her eyes are closed, like maybe she's holding back tears.

Before I can ask her what she's going to do, the car jolts so violently I almost hit my head on the headliner. "What the—"

"*Malaka!*" the driver shouts, motioning to a car speeding by.

"What happened?" Josefine's eyes are wide open now, and she's sitting ramrod straight.

The driver doesn't pull over. He puts the car in park and gets out to survey the damage. He walks around it once, being pelted by rain the entire time, before he climbs back into the driver's seat.

"Tire's broken," he says, his voice flat. "Pothole."

Josefine looks at me, wide-eyed, and I glance at my phone, which is charging at a snail's pace. I could call Hayden and ask her to track someone down in hopes of keeping the boat waiting for us.

"Is there another taxi?" I ask the driver.

He's already on the phone, and a moment later, he informs us that another driver is coming to pick us up.

49

While we wait, I tap Hayden's name in my contact list, but the call goes straight to voicemail. When I try again, the same thing happens, so I shoot off a text, letting her know what's happening.

For the next fifteen minutes, we wait. Electronic dance music plays through the speakers, and beside me, Josefine picks at the skin around her nails again. The car that finally arrives to rescue us is a tiny red island beater with the side-view mirror whacked off. There's no way we'll all fit, especially since there's already a woman in the passenger seat.

Our current driver shoos us out but remains where he is. *Okay, I guess he's not coming with us.* The two men exchange words through their respective windows and we're off. The leg room in this back seat is nearly nonexistent, so I'm forced to splay my left leg across the middle. As I get situated, I knock knees with Josefine. She's fingering the keychain on her bag and doesn't seem to notice.

"Uh, thanks for picking us up," I tell our new driver.

With a quick peek in his rearview mirror, he waves a dismissive hand.

The woman tilts closer to him and, in perfect British English, says, "You're going to have to pay extra for this."

Josefine jerks back, catching me already staring at her profile.

She blinks at me and says "is she a—" at the same time I mouth *prostitute?*

We tip our heads a little closer, sharing the space in the middle in hopes of picking up on the quiet words they're exchanging up front.

"You said one hundred euros." The driver throws a hand in the air.

"Yes. *An hour.*"

"Fuck it!" He throws both hands up this time.

For the Plot

The car swerves, causing Josefine to grip my light blue swim trunks to steady herself. She's dangerously close to my groin.

"Whoops." She bites her bottom lip and pulls her arm back in a flash.

I don't have time to process the shock of electricity that courses through me at her touch before our new driver and his, um, *friend* pull up to the port. They barely wait for me to throw down some cash before pulling away.

"Tell me, were we just in a car with a prostitute?" I hook a thumb behind me.

"Oh, most definitely." She bends over and presses her palms to her knees, her body shaking. "Although, I think the proper term is sex worker."

"What's wrong?" My heart lodges in my throat at the sight of her but quickly rights itself when I realize she's laughing. "Are you laughing right now?"

"I—I can't—" She giggles. "I can't help it," she finally spits out. "I can't believe this is happening to me. First, my boyfriend fucking cheats on me. With a blonde. How cliché." Hauling herself upright, she heaves a deep breath. "Then I get left behind. Did that bastard not even notice that I wasn't on the boat?" Throwing her arms in the air, she tilts her head back like she's seeking answers from the sky. "Then I get caught in the pouring rain and hitch a ride with a complete stranger, only to end up in a car with a fucking sex worker." A snort escapes her, and she slaps a hand across her face. "Now I'm back in the pouring rain with my tits glued to my shirt, still with a total stranger. Oh my god!"

Oh, she's delirious.

Adorable too. I should be just as put out after the day I've had, but all I can do is smile at her hysteria.

The lightness that hits me is short lived, though, because when I spin around, the boat that brought me to Crete is nowhere to be found.

"Dammit." *What the fuck are we going to do now?* I try Hayden again, but the call drops.

Josefine pulls her phone out and tries the number of the cruise line, but her calls keep dropping too. I try from my phone, but the same thing happens.

"Fuck!" I yell into the sky.

"Let's just calm down." Josefine puts a hand on my forearm.

With a huff, I shoot daggers at her, ignoring the way the rain pelts against my face.

"*Okay.*" She retracts her hand like I burned her. "Clearly a trigger. Noted."

The rain is coming down harder, and it's not safe for us to be standing out here without shelter. I scan the dock one more time for anyone who might be able to help us, but even the ticket booth is empty and locked up tight.

"Come on. I saw what looked like a hotel not too far back," I say. "Let's get there and figure out a plan."

Clad in our flip-flops and cheery beach wear, we tromp a quarter of a mile or so in the rain to Villa Aphrodite. Soaking wet and cold now that the sun is getting lower in the sky, we shuffle our way inside the quaint bed-and-breakfast. It's rustic, with paint peeling on the walls, but at least it's clean. Lots of concrete, pink stone, and pops of blue. Josefine's bathing suit and nail polish blend perfectly with the aesthetic.

Wearing what probably look like manic smiles, we greet the short, older woman at the front desk.

Josefine shivers next to me, making me wish I had something dry to offer her. Fortunately, we don't have to wait long because the attendant shoots us a toothy smile and declares, "Bravo, we have a room!"

"Only one?" I ask. "We need two. We're not together." I wave between us.

"*Po, po,*" the woman *tsks*.

"What does that mean?" Josefine mouths.

The woman's bright smile quickly transforms into a frown. "Only one room."

"You don't have anything else?" Josefine stands on tiptoe and angles her upper half over the counter.

The woman, Katerina, according to her name tag, shakes her head. "I am sorry. Everything booked. Lots of tourists. Busy summer." Her English is good, but her Greek accent is thick.

Josefine turns to me and worries her bottom lip. "I guess we don't have a choice but to share. With the way the rain is coming down, I'm not all that keen on heading back out in search of something else. It'll be fine, right?"

Is she saying this for my benefit or hers?

I cock my head to the side and shoot her a smirk. "How do you know I'm not a serial killer?"

"That question alone confirms it," she deadpans. "Plus, you're too clean cut." Pressing her teeth into her bottom lip, she gives me a once-over. "Serial killers are squirrelly and unkempt. Also," she adds, "they have tattoos and wear glasses."

We obviously watch different crime shows.

"How do you—"

"*Éla*! Come. *Páme*! Let's go." Katerina cuts me off much too enthusiastically.

With a nod, I extend an arm, motioning for Josefine to lead the way down the hall. I regret that decision when I'm confronted with the view of her toned calves and ass.

Outside our room, Katerina unlocks the door with a key that looks like it was found among the wreckage of the Titanic. "One key. One bed," she says.

One bed?

She points at the room through the open door. "Flip switch on wall for hot water. Dinner on other side of building." With that, she turns and leaves us standing there staring at, yup, one bed.

"Um." I gulp. "I'll go talk to her. Surely there's something else available." I turn toward the lobby, ready to demand Katerina find additional accommodations, even if it means I'm sleeping on a cot in a linen closet.

Josefine grasps my bicep to stop me before I can hoof it down the hall. "No, Cam."

Cam. No one but my sister and my best friend calls me Cam these days. "You heard her. The B&B is fully booked. It's a miracle this was even available."

"Look." She points to the open closet. "There are extra blankets. You can sleep on the floor, Mr. Serial Killer."

Chapter 7
Josefine

WE'RE HERE FOR DINNER, but the stranger I'm sitting with is looking like a damn snack. So far, Mr. Hottie-With-A-Backward-Ball-Cap is *not* a serial killer. *But the night is young.*

What luck that we're both passengers on the same cruise ship. Sure, I could handle this whole debacle by myself (cue Kelly Clarkson's "Miss Independent"), but this beautiful man with hazel eyes seated next to me is just the distraction I need. I won't make a move on him or anything, but I'll enjoy the view until we make it back to the ship. His bronzed face, symmetrical nose, and strong jaw are all bits and pieces of the world's best eye candy.

We were so starved we dropped our bags in the room and turned around for dinner without even bothering to change clothes. The taverna inside the bed-and-breakfast, which looks to be held up by plywood, is far from a five-star restaurant anyway. My white tank is almost dry, thus revealing only a hint of my neon pink bathing suit. Now that I'm not soaked, I'm no longer chilly, so my nipples have retreated for the night, *thank you very much.*

The wobbly table is outfitted with a basket of bread, olive oil, vinegar, napkins, and utensils. Katerina from the front desk drops off menus with Greek and English descriptions snuggled side by side. A prepubescent boy fills our water glasses, then leaves the plastic bottle on the blue-and-white checkered tablecloth. After a day like today, I'd love to stress-chomp some ice, but unfortunately ice isn't really Europe's thing. Though wine is Crete's thing. The boy returns with a carafe of local white that is supposedly known for being the best on the island.

Cameron and I clink our glasses and smile at one another. I don't know anything impressive about wine. My philosophy is if I like it, then it's good. The crisp, effervescent flavor is the perfect amount of sweet, which is to say, barely. The rain, while no longer coming down in fast and heavy droplets, offers a peaceful soundtrack against the tin awning. Plastic coverings hang perpendicular, protecting the surrounding tables packed with guests. With weather like this, the taverna is the main attraction.

For the first time in what feels like hours, I have a moment to think. So, naturally, my mind goes back to last night. Tyler and I fought recently, but we patched things up quickly, and that was more than a week ago. While I've turned a blind eye to rumors of him cheating in the past, I never imagined he'd sink so low as to cheat while on vacation with me.

On the anniversary of my father's death, no less.

What a dick. The dickiest dick there ever was.

How did it all go to shit?

Until yesterday, we were having a great time—sleeping in when we didn't have to be off the boat early, lounging around with cocktails on the beach or pool deck, holding hands while wandering the alleyways of the islands.

Then, at the dance club last night, we encountered a crew of people from New York who recognized him. Famous Tyler (read: inflated-ego Tyler) is my least favorite version of him, so I politely dipped out to refresh my drink at the bar while he schmoozed.

He's not so obviously famous that people recognize him wherever he goes, but occasionally, it happens. I was perfectly content fading into the background while he hung out with his mini fan club. For a while, I got lost in conversation with the bartender—also a writer—and before I knew it, an hour had passed. Ready to reunite with my boyfriend, I headed back to the last place I'd seen him, only he was nowhere to be found. Some of the New York folks said they saw him go into the restroom, so I headed that way, hoping to catch him on the way out.

At first, I thought there was just a long line outside the women's restroom, so I wandered closer to the wall to wait, but then I overheard a girl say, "Did you see who Tyler Jones went into the bathroom with?" followed by "I'd like a turn with him. Think I need to take a number?"

The hell? I broke out in a cold sweat and my vision blurred at my periphery.

Elbows out, I shoved my way through the crowd, wobbling on my heels. When I flung the bathroom door open, I think it smacked a girl in the eye. Not that I stopped to check.

Inside, I was assaulted by the last thing I would have expected. Right there in the club bathroom was my boyfriend. And he was getting his dick ridden by a chick with a butterfly tattoo.

"What the fuck, Tyler?" I yelled so loudly they could hear me on the mainland.

The blonde jumped and attempted to leap off his lap, but he held on to her by the back of her shirt, keeping his junk out of sight of the crowd behind me and the plethora of cameras trained on him.

He didn't even say anything, just hid his face in her chest. He knew. Whatever he was about to say was not going to dig him out of his premature grave. With both middle fingers in the air, I left him there with his pants around his ankles.

A girl stopped me on the way out and sent me a photo via AirDrop. "Just in case he tries to deny it tomorrow." She squeezed my forearm gently.

When I thanked her, she replied, "Don't mention it, honey. I've been there." The sympathetic look she gave me was the same expression I got all the time after my dad died.

From there, I rushed to my cabin and showered, desperately scrubbing his scent from my skin. With weak knees, I cried uncontrollably against the fiberglass wall. I was still crying an hour later when he came in, sloppy and stumbling and smelling like her expensive perfume. He tried to talk to me, but I wasn't having it. I ignored him until he eventually passed out on top of the bed with his clothes still on.

This morning, he insisted on coming along for the excursion. As much as I couldn't stand the idea of even looking at him, I sure as hell wasn't going to miss snorkeling off the coast of Greece. Whether he went, too, was his choice. I couldn't stop him.

On the short chartered boat ride that took us to a designated snorkeling spot, we really got into it.

"I'm sorry, Beck. I've just been under so much pressure from the record label." He grabbed at my waist and tried to tug me closer.

I swatted him away. "You said that last week. You promised this cruise would be a stress reliever for us both. What the fuck, Ty?"

"I got a little too drunk and made some bad choices. It's not a big deal, Beck. We can get over it."

"Not a big deal? How is cheating *not a big deal*? It's the biggest fucking deal there is."

"Keep your voice down," he gritted out, scanning the people nearby who were obviously listening in.

"Don't tell me to fucking keep my voice down." The audacity. He was trying to save face now? That only made me steam more.

"I was so drunk I didn't even know what I was doing. She doesn't mean anything." *She* meaning the preppy blonde he had his cock shoved up. "It doesn't count. It wasn't really me."

"That's the biggest load of horseshit I've ever heard."

"Come on, are you really going to throw away what we have?"

"*What we have*? Are you serious right now? From where I'm sitting, what we have is a whole lot of nothing. You're a cheating asshole, so yeah, I'm gonna throw it all away. Right in the fucking trash where it belongs. You're garbage. A real piece of shit. We're done."

God, I should have listened to those rumors.

He tried the we're-so-good-together-baby line once more, and I nearly kicked him in the balls in front of the whole excursion group. Call it compartmentalization to protect my emotions, but at that moment, I stuffed Tyler and his bullshit in a metaphorical dumpster and leaped off that boat with the biggest smile on my face.

Blessedly, it's virtually impossible to talk while snorkeling. Despite the drama that went down on the boat, I thoroughly enjoyed my time in the crystal-clear water.

Once or twice, those pesky problems found their way out of the dumpster, despite my best efforts to lock that shit up, and I nearly choked on my mouthpiece when the thought of Brooks saying, "But it's *for the plot!*" popped into my brain. Maybe someday I'll look back and agree, but not today.

When it was time for lunch, the charter boat collected our snorkel gear and dropped us at the dock, but I wasn't hungry. I grabbed my bag and hightailed it onto the beach, but Tyler was close on my heels.

"Go to hell. Do not follow me!" I yelled, striding away.

Before long, I found myself dozing off in a hammock. The sun and stress had worn me out. What felt like moments after I climbed in, though, I was startled awake by fat raindrops. I raced back to the beach, where I discovered zero boats left on the water. So I threw my hair in a topknot, and, looking like a drowned rat, I made my way to the hotel's lobby in search of help. I was mid-panic when a gorgeous man who had to be at least a few inches over six foot came marching up beside me.

I'm not going to lie. As terrible as it felt to realize I'd been left behind, this is a nice reprieve. And by *this*, I mean being separated from Tyler. If I never see his lying ass again, it'll be too soon. If only. Unfortunately, I'll have to collect my things from the ship and our apartment. But for now, I'll enjoy a fresh seafood dish and a glass (or two) of wine on this gorgeous island. The B&B may need a little TLC, but the view is delicious.

Chapter 8
Cameron

"Dammit!" I toss my phone onto the mattress and watch it bounce.

"Who are you calling?" Josefine calls from behind the bathroom door. I didn't realize she could hear me.

"Um, my—" *Girlfriend* is on the tip of my tongue, but then I remember I don't have one of those anymore. "My, uh, friend."

Josefine throws open the door and steps out, and my adrenaline spikes. I swallow, desperate to relieve the dryness in my mouth.

"What?" she asks, examining herself. "You look like you've never seen a woman before."

"I—I—have," I stutter, practically wheezing.

I've seen plenty of women before, just none as breathtaking as the one standing before me. Hayden's pretty in the traditional sense, but Josefine is just—*wow*.

"Is that all you have to wear?" I ask through gritted teeth. "Isn't there a robe or something you can put on?" Craning my neck, I look past Josefine, but I don't see anything but towels hanging in the bathroom.

"Excuse me?" she challenges, propping one hand on her hip. "What's wrong with what I'm wearing?"

"It's just that, um." Heat rushes to my cheeks. "That, um…"

Raising her brows, she lifts her chin and looks down her nose at me. "Yes?" She waves a hand, urging me to get on with it.

I sigh. "It's just that we don't even know each other, and you're wearing *that*."

That being the tiniest and sexiest lingerie I've ever seen. It's one piece and made of silk—or maybe it's satin. The lilac color is stunning against her sun-kissed skin. I can't see her backside, but I assume it barely covers her bum. The top is trimmed with lace and dips low between her braless breasts—the material makes that fact obvious.

"Why are you wearing lingerie?"

"What are you talking about?" She glances down at her body. Her *tight* body—that's how little her getup leaves to the imagination. "This is not lingerie. This is a bathing suit cover-up."

"It's definitely lingerie." Who am I trying to convince here?

"Nope."

"I think I know lingerie when I see it."

"You must not see very good lingerie, my friend, because this is a beach cover-up." She hits me with a blatantly fake smile.

"I've seen plenty of lingerie, thank you very much." I sound way too offended right now, but my pride is relentless.

"Whatever," she huffs, bending slightly to search for the outlet against the wall. "You can close your mouth now, darling," she drawls once she's plugged her adapter into the wall and connected her phone to it. "You're drooling."

I reflexively swipe a hand across my mouth, but it's dry. "Ha ha. Very funny. Get in bed."

"Ooh, so demanding," she quips. "Are you always this dominating in bed, or is it just for me?" She bats her lashes.

She actually fucking bats her lashes.

I bend over and rummage through my backpack. In truth, I'm not looking for anything, but I don't want her to see the semi she's got me sporting.

Josefine seemed so sweet and innocent on the dock, but now I'm wondering what I've gotten myself into. Maybe I'll go to the front desk one more time. There's a chance someone has checked out in the last hour, right? Or maybe they'll let me sleep in the lobby.

This girl intrigues me, though. She's the opposite of Hayden, who never asked me to be dominating in bed, despite my interest in it. She would always tell me to go slower or be more gentle. It's not like I wanted to hurt her, but I wouldn't have minded if she let me throw her around a little. Not that it matters anymore.

Was Josefine's comment a hint about what she likes? Does she like men to take control of her in the bedroom?

Blinking out of my trance, I stand upright. "Yeah, all good. Just trying to find my toothbrush."

"You carry a toothbrush on day trips?"

"Actually, no," I admit. "I don't remember what I was looking for." This girl has got me flipped upside down and I don't know a thing about her.

"There's an extra one in the bathroom," she offers, thumbing over her shoulder.

"Thanks." I stride across the room, giving her a wide berth, and close the door behind me.

Resting my palms against the chipped Formica countertop, I commence a staring contest with myself in the mirror. *Yes, the woman on the other side of the wall is beautiful, but you've got to pull it together.* It's one night.

I remove my contact lenses. Thankfully, I did bring their case and a travel-size bottle of solution. My eyesight isn't so bad that I can't see without them, but if I go too long, I get a headache. Even though I flipped the switch Katerina pointed out, the water comes out way too cold, forcing me to take the quickest shower of my life. For being a rundown B&B, the bathroom is surprisingly well stocked with basic hygiene essentials.

Thank my lucky stars I threw a change of clothes into my bag before disembarking the ship this morning. I exit the bathroom in gray sweatpants and a long-sleeve black cotton shirt and find Josefine sitting up in bed. I half expected her to be conked out, especially after two glasses of wine at dinner. But no, the duvet is draped around her waist and she's finger-combing her damp and tangled hair.

"You know, there's a plastic comb in the bathroom," I say, rounding the bed to where I left my bag.

Josefine looks up at me, her dark eyes filled with sadness. "I know. Nervous habit." She shrugs. "Did you figure out how to get us back on the boat?"

I get to work spreading a blanket out on the floor. It won't magically make this concrete ground comfortable, but I can survive one night.

"Yes, I did. As long as the storm has passed, a ferry is going to meet us at the dock in the morning."

She tosses me an extra pillow from the bed. "How much is that gonna cost?"

"Don't worry about it."

She opens her mouth like she's going to argue but snaps it shut again. Instead, she presses her lips in a tight smile and nods.

"All right, good night, Josefine." I flip the switch on the wall and park myself on the makeshift mattress. A curse escapes my mouth when I come down too hard on my elbow.

"It's Joey," she says.

"Huh?"

"My name." Her voice is soft in the dark of the room. "I go by Joey."

That's cute. "Okay, Joey. Night."

"Good night."

The bedding rustles for only a moment. I can't see her, but from the sound of things, she settles long before I do. I'm still tossing the sheets and blankets around like an Italian with pizza dough minutes later, but no amount of fluffing will make this situation pleasant.

"Are you sure you're okay?" she asks for the second time tonight.

"Uh, yeah."

She lets out a long sigh. "Why don't we just share the bed?"

"No, it's fine," I tell her, even though it's really fucking not.

"Cam." The way she says my name is full of authority. The way it rolls off her tongue like that makes me feel things I'm not sure I know what to do with.

"Come on, buddy. Get up," she demands. "It's not like we'll ever see one another again. It's just sleeping side by side. Not much different from drooling next to each other on a plane, right?"

I only hesitate for a minute before I give in and join her under the covers. But would she wear *that* on an airplane?

Flat on my back, I settle in. The mattress is surprisingly agreeable, though the sheets are about as soft as construction paper. I'll take it if it means I'm no longer sprawled on the floor. This situation would be a lot more complicated if Hayden and I hadn't just broken up. There's no way I'd even consider sharing a bed with a smoking hot woman if that were the case. Especially one with lush lips, slender and toned shoulders...

My semi is back, and I'm lying right next to her. I adjust my sweatpants beneath the sheets, praying she doesn't realize what's happening.

"You good over there?" she asks.

Dammit, she's no idiot.

"Mm-hmm, yup."

Her response is a chuckle.

"What?"

"You sure you can handle this?"

Does she mean *this* as in our situation, or *this* as in *her*? Oh, I could for sure handle her, all right. That silky long hair wrapped around my fist and her firm ass beneath my other hand. *I would devour you.*

"I have a girlfriend," I blurt. "Well, I did," I clarify. "We broke up this morning. Actually, I was planning to propose to her today."

She lets out a tiny gasp. "You were?"

Letting my head loll to one side, I survey her in the dark room. There's just enough light coming in from the window to make out her features. "It was sort of an arranged thing."

Joey rolls to her side so she's facing me head-on, her face pinched in confusion.

"Long story." Now is not the time to get into it.

"Do you have the ring with you?" she asks.

"Yeah, it's in my bag."

"Can I see it?"

"Nosy much?" I tease.

"Come on." She slaps the sheet between us. "Humor me a bit. It's the least you can do after you said you'd devour me."

Fuck, did I say that out loud? Cringing, I fold over the side of the bed to fumble for my bag on the floor. I don't even know why I carried it off the ship.

Joey sits up against the headboard and flips the switch next to her, bathing the room in dull light from the flickering sconce. As she's situating herself, her hand brushes against my ass. "Sorry," she says.

"S'fine." I kind of liked it.

Black velvet box in hand, I roll over and hand it to her.

"Hmm." Based on that sound, she's underwhelmed at best.

For the Plot

"Hmm, what? What does *hmm* mean?"

"Predictable is all." She shrugs.

"Predictable? It *is* an engagement ring. They all pretty much look the same."

"They don't have to." She ghosts a finger over the top of the oval diamond before shutting the lid and passing the box back to me like a hot potato.

I thought I was being creative by deviating from the typical round cut.

"Fine, then," I say. "Humor me. What type of engagement ring would you want?"

"That's presumptuous of you to think I'd want to get engaged." She scoffs, crossing her arms.

"You don't want to get married?" I ask, blindly tucking the box back into my bag.

Joey pulls herself up straighter against the headboard, and one thin strap of her cover-up slips off her shoulder. I resist the urge to hook my finger beneath it and slide it back up. I bet her skin is just as smooth and silky as her cover-up.

She eyes me, one brow lifted and her lips pressed in a straight line, and adjusts it herself. "After all the shit that just went down, I'm not sure I'll ever want to be in a serious relationship again." Her somber sigh fills the room.

I wrinkle my nose. "You can't really mean that."

Isn't it every woman's dream to get married? What else happened to make her feel this way?

"Oh, but I do." She squeezes her eyes shut. "But in an alternate universe, one in which guys are not dicks—no offense—I would want something colorful, vibrant, unique."

"Colorful? Like those birthstone rings I used to get from the treasure chest at the dentist?" I tease.

Joey throws her head back and guffaws. "Oh my god. I remember those. I haven't thought about those rings in years."

Her laughter is the most beautiful noise I've ever heard. Genuine. Pure. Hayden's laugh is calculated and proper. But Joey laughs without inhibition. My responding smile is so big my cheeks hurt, but I can't help it; it's infectious.

"Every time I went to the dentist, I'd pick one out and give it to my mom," I share. "Every six months for eight years. My sister would make fun of me for it, but I loved seeing the smile it put on my mom's face. She was…" I trail off, shaking my head. I don't need to recount my mother's struggles to a stranger.

"That's super cute." She gives me a small smile. Then, like she can sense my sudden unease, she steers us back on track. "I'd want something unique. Maybe something green."

"Green? Why green?"

"It's my favorite color." She shrugs. "And it was the color of my dad's eyes." That last part comes out as a whisper.

The way she says "was" makes me think her dad is no longer in her life, but before I can even consider asking, Joey continues.

"Yeah, I think I'd like something green. But not emerald green. More like green amethyst, you know?"

I nod, even though I have no idea what green amethyst looks like.

"And I'd want it with a yellow-gold setting—not silver or platinum."

Definitely unlike the ring I bought for Hayden.

"You've got pretty specific ideas for someone who doesn't want to get married." I poke her in the side.

She throws a pillow at my face but misses, and I catch it before it goes off the side of the bed.

"I'm sorry you've had such a shitty day," I tell her.

With a terse nod, she turns the sconce on her side of the bed off, and we settle under the sheets again. The room has cooled since we first arrived. When Katerina let us in, the air inside was stale, so after dinner, we cracked open the window, welcoming in the night air. In long sleeves and pants, I'm perfectly comfortable, but Joey's got to be chilly in that little getup.

"Thanks," she replies. "Have you ever been cheated on?"

My chest gets tight at just the thought of what she's been through. "Not that I know of, but I can imagine it's the worst."

"Totally," she sighs.

"How long were you together?" I ask.

"We met when I was sixteen. He was twenty-one."

"Oof," I say with a little more judgment than intended.

"Yeah, I was all googly-eyes for him, but he kept things platonic. We reconnected when I went to college and I moved in with him right away."

"You're living together?" Ouch. What's she going to do when she returns home? I suppose I should be thankful that Hayden and I have our own places. "Where in California do you live?"

"Santa Monica. What about you? In New York, I mean?"

"Long Island." Yeah, opposite sides of the country; we'll definitely never see one another again.

"What does your boy—ex," I correct myself, "do?"

"He's a music producer. You may know him, actually." She hesitates. "Tyler Jones?"

"As in Jeremy Jones's son?" They're a famous father-son music producing duo. I heard rumors he was on the ship but hadn't seen him. What a fucking prick for cheating on Joey.

"How did you two meet?" I guess knowing that we'll never see each other again makes it easier to ask personal questions.

"I snuck into a club with my friends with a fake ID, and he was scoping out talent that night."

"Really?" I ask.

"Yeah. I did a lot of crazy shit in high school. That's what happens when your mom is—never mind. That was a fun night." Her voice is soft, almost wistful. "He had no idea I was sixteen, of course. I can't even remember how he found out I was still in high school, but he was pissed. Especially after spending half the night showering me with attention. He punched his number into my phone and told me to call him the day I turned eighteen."

"Did you?"

"You bet your ass I did." She laughs, but it falls short. "Ugh!" She lifts both arms and smacks the mattress on either side of her. "Enough about him. Distract me," she begs, her voice breathy. "Help me get my mind off the last twenty-four hours."

"What did you have in mind?" For a second, I think she's asking me to distract her with sex, and my heart and my dick both leap. I shut that shit down quickly.

"Let's play a game." She pushes herself up again and fluffs the pillow behind her.

"A game?" I turn to face her and prop myself up on one elbow. "Are we five?"

She shoves my shoulder, and I fall back dramatically.

Then she lets out the most adorable laugh. "Come on. Don't be such an old man."

"Okay." I give in. "What game do you want to play?"

"Truth or Dare."

I groan. "Anything but Truth or Dare."

"What? Bad experience?"

"You could say that."

"Fine. How about Never Have I Ever?"

"Sure. How does it work?" I ask.

"You don't know how to play Never Have I Ever? Sheesh, you really are an old man."

I flick her arm. "I'm not *that* old."

"How old are you?"

"Thirty. How old are you?"

"Twenty-two."

I jolt upright. "You're only twenty-fucking-two?" I slap a hand to my face, feeling like a creep lying in this bed with her. I ought to return to playing "The Princess and the Pea" on the floor.

"Why are you being weird?"

"You're so young." My stomach ties itself in a knot when I remember all the times I've ogled her today. "I'm eight years older than you."

"It's not a big deal. Don't be weird."

Closing my eyes, I suck in a long breath and let it out again. Is it a big deal? Maybe not. We're just sharing a bed, and only because we're stranded.

"Come on," she whines.

"Fine." With a sigh, I settle on my side and prop my head up with my fist.

Joey switches on the small light again and runs through the instructions. "I'll go first," she says. "Never have I ever," she tilts her head to the side and pauses, "lived in New York."

"Hey!" I put down the thumb on my left hand. "I feel like that's cheating." I grin.

Joey rolls her eyes. "Your turn."

"Never have I ever had a fake ID."

She flips me off before putting down a finger. "Touché." She giggles. "Okay. Never have I ever cheated on someone."

Joey raises an approving brow when I don't put down a finger.

"Never have I ever worn lingerie." I smirk. I may be treading on thin ice with that one, but it's too late now.

She sticks out her tongue and puts another finger down. I kind of like this game.

"Never have I ever been to Greece until now," Joey says.

I don't put down a finger.

"Never have I ever been snorkeling."

Joey lowers another finger. "Never?" Her voice pitches in surprise.

"Nope. I've been on boats and have water-skied plenty of times, but I've never snorkeled. Weird, huh?"

"It's so fun!" She beams.

That look makes me want to show her the photo I snapped of her earlier, but I decide against it. Again, I'd probably come across as a total stalker.

"Your turn. Go," I redirect.

"Okay, hmm." She pauses. "Never have I ever gotten my partner's name tattooed on my body."

She sends me a look of approval when my fingers don't move.

"Hold up." I stop her, intrigued. "That's oddly specific. Explain."

Joey sighs, her lush lips pouting, like she's considering her words. "Last year, Tyler tattooed my name on his chest." The explanation lacks all feeling, like she's reciting a fact about US history. "I thought it was romantic at the time, but..."

We both know what she's getting at.

"Does he have a lot of tattoos?" I don't know why I ask. I saw him go after her on the beach earlier today.

"Umm?" her voice goes up at the end.

"I'll take that as a yes. Is that how you take your men?"

"Huh?" she asks.

"With tattoos?"

"If you're asking me if I think tattoos are sexy, the answer is always yes," she practically purrs.

"I see." Earlier, when I was shamelessly eyeing her in that bikini, I noticed that she had a tattoo, but now I wonder if she has any others.

"Moving on," she announces, forcing me to stop mapping her body in my mind. "Never have I ever," her pause is longer this time, "stolen anything."

Her jaw drops when I put a finger down. "What's the story there?"

"Nuh-uh," I say, shooting her a grin. "That's not part of the game."

"Hey. I told you my backstory."

I blink at her in response, but I don't budge.

"You play dirty." She furrows her brows, but I'm not buying her edge. "Fine." She rolls her eyes. "Your turn."

"Never have I ever gotten a tattoo of a bird." I wink.

She puts down a finger right away.

"Three, I should say."

"I'm only putting one finger down, mister." She smiles and lowers her pointer finger, leaving her middle finger raised on its own. Lucky for me, I still have three, formed in the sign for ok.

"You saw that, huh?" Joey asks, rubbing the back of her left tricep where three little birds reside.

"Yeah, what's the story there?" I ask.

"*Nuh-uh.*" She echoes my earlier response. "That's not part of the game."

"Fine," I huff. "Go on."

"While we're on the topic of tattoos… Never have I ever fucked someone with a butterfly back tattoo."

A sudden sense of dread washes over me and my heart rate picks up. "What the hell did you just say?"

"I said—"

Even though I asked the question, I don't give her time to answer. "Why would you say that?"

She frowns, scanning my face. "Because the girl Tyler fucked last night had a butterfly stamped on her lower back."

"What kind of butterfly tattoo?" My mind is racing and I can't sort through my thoughts fast enough.

"I don't know." She drops her chin and picks at an invisible speck on the sheet between us. "Why does it matter?"

"Because," I say slowly, "Hayden has a butterfly tattoo."

"Lots of people do." She peeks up at me, nibbling on her

bottom lip. "It's not very original. Does she *also* have blond hair and wear a fucking pearl necklace?"

My entire body stiffens; only my hands tremble, and Joey's mouth falls open.

"Shit."

Is it possible this is all just a misunderstanding? A coincidence? Hayden would never cheat on me. Especially not with someone like Tyler. From what I've seen of him in the media, he's way too messy. Hayden is classy, and the people she surrounds herself with reflect that, even if I don't fall under the stereotypical country club couture type. I certainly don't wear polos and plaid.

And again, lots of women have butterfly tattoos stamped on their lower backs. But how many of those women are on the same cruise?

I snag my phone from the nightstand and call Hayden again, but it goes straight to voicemail like it has all evening.

Letting out a long breath, I assure myself that it wasn't her.

No way.

But still...

My stomach twists. She did look awful this morning. I assumed she'd gotten too much sun or maybe ate questionable food from the buffet.

"Is this her?" Joey shoves her phone in my face.

Bile rises in my throat, and all the blood drains from my face. Joey has gone ashen too. I squeeze my eyes shut, hoping that when I open them, the image will have changed, but I'm shit out of luck.

It's Hayden.

She's in profile, but it's definitely her. Blond hair pulled back in a short, perky ponytail. Pearls wrapped snugly around her neck. A guy—clearly Tyler—clenching his fist around the back of her shirt, revealing a blue and purple butterfly just above her skirt; the one she got the day she moved out of her parents' house at eighteen. Her small act of rebellion. The white pleated skirt she was wearing when I parted with her at the club last night.

"That—"

"Bitch," Joey assumes for me. "I'm so sorry."

Following her hands to where she tucks the phone between her legs, my gaze burns a hole in the sheets.

I shoot off the bed and pace, clenching my fists and my jaw. "I don't fucking believe it," I pant.

"I'm so sorry," Joey says again. She hops off the mattress and rounds the foot of it. When she's close, she reaches for me, but she pulls back quickly before she can make contact.

"How? Why? How could she do this to me?" I knead at the tingling in my chest and pace across the cramped space like a tiger locked in its cage. "Why would she fucking do that?"

Wait. Maybe this is a misunderstanding. Maybe it just looks like Hayden's in a compromising position because of the angle from which the picture was taken. Those things can happen.

As if she can read my mind, Joey takes a small step closer, licking her lips. "I saw it with my own eyes. It's real. It happened."

I continue to pace back and forth, my heart pounding so hard against my ribs I worry it'll make its way right out of my chest. *How is this happening?*

"Cam."

"What the fuck?" Sure, we broke up this morning, but this happened last night. She cheated.

"Cam."

Sweat collects at my temples. My shirt is too tight at the collar and across my chest. I rake my hands through my hair and tug, my head woozy and my vision blurring around the edges.

"*Cameron*. Stop."

Joey steps in front of me, forcing me to halt my movement.

She grasps my forearms and pulls. Reluctantly, I release my grip on my hair. Sucking in short breaths, I scan her face, her dark eyes, her sad expression, my heart still racing and my vision still unfocused.

"Take a deep breath." She clasps my hands between us, her words patient. "You're spiraling. Deep breaths," she commands. "Come." Gently tugging, she ushers me back to the bed. "Lay down. You're having a panic attack."

Is that what this is? My mom had panic attacks when I was a kid. When it happened, her eyes would get as big as saucers and she would move her arms about like she was searching for an anchor—something to bring her back to earth.

Here, now, Joey is my anchor. She gently guides me onto my left side, and with one hand still holding mine, she turns off the light.

I squeeze my eyes tight and clutch at the sheets, praying the darkness washes away the image of Hayden and Tyler. Joey curves herself around me like a spoon and hooks one leg over my thighs, securing me in place. She wraps her arm around me and presses her hand against my pounding heart. Her nose nudges the back of my neck as she situates herself on my pillow.

"What are you doing?" I manage through ragged breaths.

"Match your breath to mine, okay? When I breathe in, you breathe in; when I breathe out, you breathe out. Got it? Focus on me. Nothing else." Her voice is so soothing I already feel myself gliding back to earth.

I nod.

"Inhale," she begins.

I desperately try to mimic her, but it's difficult when my heart is beating this fast.

"It's okay," she reassures. "You'll get there. Now exhale."

I release my tight grip on the sheets.

When Joey inhales again, I feel a tad more tethered to the moment.

I match her breath for breath.

Inhale. *Inhale.*

Exhale. *Exhale.*

"Again."

Inhale. *Inhale.*

Exhale. *Exhale.*

She's a miracle worker. It only takes a handful of breaths for relief to settle in.

She drags her breath out longer this time, challenging me to do the same.

Slowly, my heart rate returns to normal and the fog clouding my brain dissipates. Mostly clearheaded, I focus on my surroundings. On Joey's warm breath against my neck. On the way her body fits perfectly against mine. She paints circles on my chest, eliciting goose bumps beneath my shirt.

In moments, I've lost all sense of time and have given up on matching her breath. And from the sound of her breathing, she has too. In fact, if I'm not mistaken, her breathing has quickened. Or is that my imagination?

She continues tracing circles on my chest, her movements torturously slow. Then she works her way down my torso, only stopping when she reaches the hem of my shirt.

"What are you doing?" I croak.

She doesn't answer.

"Joey," I plead.

"Truth or Dare?"

"I told you I don't like that game," I say. This time, my words are smoother, more subdued.

"Answer me," she challenges, her tone fierce.

"Dare." I can't handle any more truths tonight.

"I dare you to fuck me."

Chapter 9

Cameron

Joey slides her hand lower, over the waistband of my sweats, and squeezes ever so slightly around my hardening cock. "Let's use each other." She groans. "Just this one night. What's the worst that can happen? It's not like we'll ever see each other again."

She's right. We live on opposite sides of the US. We've both been thoroughly fucked over—quite literally—by our partners in the last twenty-four hours; the least we can do is enjoy ourselves with the little time we have left on this island. Lord knows she's sexy as sin. It wouldn't be a hardship on my part.

"Is that a yes?" she purrs in my ear.

The second a *yes* escapes my lips, Joey has me pinned on my back. She straddles me, a knee planted on the mattress on either side of my hips, and wastes no time locking her lips to mine.

Without hesitation, I open, inviting her in. She nips at my bottom lip and swipes her tongue across it, soothing the prick of pain. I flatten my palms on her ass and groan when I'm met with smooth flesh beneath her risqué cover-up. She grinds her hips against mine and bites my lip once again. She's a fucking minx.

Delirium takes over. I'm no longer dizzy from my panic attack, but lightheaded from lust.

"Off," she demands, yanking my sweatpants down my thighs.

A gasp escapes her when my cock springs free of the fabric. I'm not wearing any underwear. She rubs her cunt across the thick head. Fuck. She's already soaked through her thong. The breathy noises she's making as she works herself back and forth over me are driving me fucking wild. With a hand between us, I fumble to find her clit, but when I do and I press my thumb to it, she jerks her hips forward.

"More," she begs, flattening her palms against my chest for support.

I shove her thong aside with one hand and suck on the middle finger of the other, then slide it inside her.

"Yes, Cam." Moaning, she rocks her body on my hand. "More."

Inserting a second finger, I work her clit with my thumb again, this time rubbing circles around it.

"How does that feel?" I ask, keeping a steady rhythm.

One-night stands are usually unexpected and feverish. There's no guarantee of chemistry, and there's almost no opportunity to discover what the other person likes. But with Joey, I want to know. Does she like having her nipples pinched? Her neck sucked? Her ass slapped? It's a gamble to try for the trifecta, but I'm overcome with adrenaline and desire. I want to experience it all with the woman writhing above me right now.

"It's not enough. I need your cock."

Holy shit. Is this the woman of my dreams?

For tonight she is.

Panting, she grips my shaft and tugs, but she freezes when she reaches the head.

"What's wrong?" My stomach sinks. *Please don't stop.*

"Nothing. I—I—" she stutters. Above me, her expression is

hard to read. It's dark, and her hair obscures her face, but she's got her lip caught between her teeth. "I just didn't expect you to be so big."

I grin into the darkness. "Think you can take it all, sweetheart?"

I swear she gulps in response.

"Condom. Now," she demands.

Twisting my upper half, I rifle through the front pocket of my bag.

With a quick tear, the foil packet gives, and I roll the rubber down my length. Above me, an eager Joey hovers as she shimmies out of her thong. When she settles herself again, she spits on my cock and strokes it over the rubber. Holy fucking shit. My balls ache and my chest goes tight at the sight of her lining me up with her entrance. My fingers dig into her hips as I carefully lower her down my length. She's warm and wet, and I have a suspicion this moment will live on in my fantasies for a long time.

"Fuck, you feel good," I whisper.

With a delicious moan, Joey slides up and down at a torturously slow pace, adjusting to my girth.

"How do you want it?" With my hands splayed, I explore her soft skin. I pull the straps off her shoulders and down her arms so her cover-up is pooled around her waist. Her breasts are the perfect size for my hands. Her already peaked nipples tighten as I rub circles around them with my thumbs. God damn. Her body is so responsive. Fire licks up my insides while I wait for her answer. I'm equal parts desperate to see where she'll let me take this and terrified that I'm woefully unprepared for the possibilities. Her heavy breasts sway mere inches from my face as she continues to work herself up and down me. If she keeps riding me like this, I don't know that I'll last.

"Rough," she says, her voice clear and sure.

That's all I need to hear. In one quick movement, I pull her off me and flip her onto her back.

I smother her responding yelp with a hard kiss, finally devouring her, then pepper kisses down her neck and suck on her collarbone. She raises her hips against me in approval, so I don't let up. I drag my tongue down to her breast and lock my lips around her nipple, swirling and flicking my tongue.

"Fuck, that feels good."

I move to her other breast and lavish it with the same attention before I make my way lower, pushing her knees apart so her pussy is on full display for me. We skipped dessert at dinner, but I think I'll finally have mine.

"This okay?" We don't know each other, so although her body language makes it pretty damn obvious she's all in, I don't want to misread the cues.

"Fucking do it," she commands.

Flattening my tongue, I lap at her clit. She bucks in response and grips my hair. I hum against her before fucking her with my tongue in earnest, dipping inside her wetness. Her back arches off the bed, and she cries out my name when I go back to sucking her clit and slide two fingers inside her.

"You like when I suck on your pretty little cunt?" I grin against her thigh, still working her over with my hand.

"You're so fucking good at this," she praises.

I suck again, this time with quick pulses, and in seconds, she's careening toward the edge.

"Fuck, Cam, I'm so close."

I know. I can feel it—her walls spasming and her thighs squeezing my head, keeping me pinned to her core.

"Come on my mouth," I demand, pulling her thighs toward me.

She rocks her hips faster, arching her back, and when I slip a third finger inside, curling just so, she lets out the sexiest primal scream I've ever heard. I gently rub on her clit until her arms and knees relax beside her.

"How was—"

"So... fucking... good."

With a laugh, I wipe her arousal from my mouth, then work my way up her body until my cock rests at her soaking-wet opening. Dipping low, I kiss between her breasts, where her heart rate is slowly settling. Then she's grabbing my cock and lifting her hips, her pussy nice and relaxed from her orgasm, and sliding me all the way in. I pause when I'm to the hilt, giving her time to adjust.

"What are you waiting for?" she says. "Fuck me."

With those words, I bury my face in the crook of her neck and slam into her. She smells like the hotel soap--rosemary, and eucalyptus. I lick at her sweat, suddenly regretting not ripping my shirt off. I wish I could feel her breasts against my bare skin, but I can't stop pounding into her. Her ass will be speckled with marks from my tight grip tomorrow, but I don't care. At least she'll have a nice souvenir to take home with her.

"You like when I'm rough with your pussy?"

She moans, arching and throwing her head back in response. Oh, she loves the dirty words I'm feeding her. She matches my pace, her cunt clenching around my cock with every thrust.

Our sex is hard and fast.

Messy and greedy.

Stealing and healing.

Taking and giving.

Perfect.

Chapter 10
Josefine

My body is throbbing with lust. Cam's words send shivers through my veins. I'm squirming beneath him, chasing my euphoria.

"You like my hard cock filling up your tight pussy, don't you?"

I moan against his jaw, his five o'clock shadow chafing my lips.

"Tell me," he orders.

"I fucking love your cock in my pussy." I grip his hair at the roots.

He slams into me harder and grinds his pelvis against my clit in a move that's so perfect it's hard to believe we didn't know each other before today. That familiar feeling swirls low in my belly, heat pooling in my core. Flurries form in the corners of my eyes, signaling another impending release.

With a hand between us, I slip a finger behind his balls, right to *that* spot. It's a risk, but this guy is giving off vibes that say he'd be down for a little ass play.

"Fuck, Joey." He stills, clenching his cheeks and trapping my finger in place. In the dark, his expression is hard to read. Oh shit, maybe I read him wrong. Has anyone ever done this to him before? I hope to god I just unlocked a new kink for him. Otherwise, I may have just blown up what's proving to be the hottest night I've had in a long time. The sexual chemistry I have with this man is unreal.

"Do you want me to stop?" I rasp into his neck.

"God, no." With a long breath out, he relaxes into me, then increases the speed of his thrusts. "But if you keep fucking doing that, I'm gonna come."

I love making a guy climax. Having that kind of power turns me on. With the way my wrist is trapped between us, I'll be sore tomorrow, but I don't care. I add a little pressure, then release before doing it again.

I almost never come twice in one night, but the guttural sounds coming out of his mouth have me chasing my next orgasm.

"Cam, I'm gonna—"

"Me too."

Fuck yes. He's there with me.

I press my finger to his entrance one last time, and he calls out my name. Between thrusts, I slip my hand from between our bodies, grab his ass, and pull him so there's no space between us. I greedily grind my clit against his body, desperate and feral, finding my own release in the friction.

Cam jerks above me, riding out his own climax. When he slows, he collapses on top of me, burying his face in my neck. His breaths are quick and his skin is damp. Still panting, he uses one large hand to brush my hair from my sweat-slicked face, then he plants a kiss at my jaw.

The move is gentle, almost grateful, making me bristle. What just happened was supposed to be raw and rugged, not sweet and charming.

For the Plot

"What is it?" he asks, pulling back and scanning my face in the dark.

"Nothing." I push the saccharine thoughts away. "That was so damn hot," I sigh.

"So fucking hot," he mumbles, pressing his face into the pillow beside my head, his dick still pulsing inside me.

I push at his arms, attempting to move his body off mine.

"What are you doing?" he groans, not budging.

"As much as I enjoyed that, the last thing I need to bring home with me is a UTI. Now up," I command, pushing against him again. Damn, his pecs are perfect under my hands. I should have insisted he lose the shirt.

Acquiescing, he pulls out and rolls off me. He swats my ass as I stand. When I turn to close the door to the bathroom door, he's on his feet, discarding the condom in the trash next to the bed. From there, he falls face-first onto the mattress with a groan.

I quickly rinse off, yelling a few expletives along the way when I remember there's a switch for hot water.

When I'm finished, I stumble through the dark room and climb back into bed. Cam replaces me in the bathroom, and when he returns, I pretend to be asleep. I don't want to know whether he's the snuggle-after-sex type. This is a one-time, hot as hell fling. He hovers over me, the heat of his body warming me even though we're not touching. But a moment later, and without a word, he settles on his back. When his breaths even out, I finally allow sleep to find me.

The summer sun heats my back through the open window as the room around me comes into focus. It takes me a minute to absorb my surroundings, but when I do...

Holy.

Fuck.

My face is pressed firmly against a rock-hard arm. Not just any arm, though. An arm covered with tattoos. From the top of his shoulder to the bottom of his elbow. I definitely did not see that last night.

Cam, his hair all askew, lowers his tortoise-shell glasses down the bridge of his nose and peers at me from where he's propped up against the headboard. "Think I'm a serial killer now?" He winks so gleefully it's like his wink even fucking winks at me.

He's fixated on my mouth, his hazel eyes warming to a heated gold.

My lips tingle at the attention and the memory of his kisses last night.

His focus drifts from my mouth and down my neck slowly. I follow the trail to my chest and—*whoops*! My tit is here for an encore.

Sitting quickly, I scramble to adjust myself. With a smirk, he snags a bottle of water and holds it out to me.

"Thanks." I twist off the cap and down half of it in one gulp. All the while, he's watching me. I can feel his perusal like a caress. With a deep inhale, I cap the bottle again and set it on the end table, then scurry out of bed. It isn't until I'm standing that I notice how bare my ass is. Looks like I never put my underwear back on. Crouching beside the bed, I grab my bathing suit bottoms and tug them on.

"What are you reading?" I ask, standing once all my parts are finally covered.

He blinks and drops his chin, holding his book up off his lap. "This?"

Now that his attention is directed elsewhere, I turn around and put on my bathing suit top, then quickly pull on my shorts and T-shirt.

"It's a travel photography guide."

"Are you a travel photographer?" I guess we never got around to talking about our professions last night. "I noticed your camera case." Sitting on the edge of the bed, I nod to where he left it on the desk.

"Umm." He lowers his gaze again and fiddles with his book. "Not really. I would love to be, but it's not my job. My sister Claire bought the camera for me."

"Why not? What do you do?"

He ignores the first question entirely. "I'm in the hospitality business." His tone is nothing but defeat and his lips are downturned as he says it.

"Wow, you sound super passionate," I deadpan.

He leans back against his pillow, hands behind his head, his biceps bulging.

I knew he was packing. Covertly, I wipe at my mouth to make sure I'm not drooling.

His lips turn up on one side and he cocks a brow. Dammit, I've been caught.

"Long story short," he begins, tilting his neck one way, then the other, "my family has owned a chain of hotels for a couple of generations. I'm expected to take over the business."

"But you don't want to." It's not a question. Everything about his demeanor tells me that.

"Right. While I love New York, I don't want to be stuck there full time. I'd prefer to travel, capturing and sharing images along the way." He sighs.

"Why don't you, then?"

With a long breath in and back out again, he studies me. "It's not that simple."

"Oh, don't go all Allie Hamilton on me," I tease.

That earns me a grin. "Did you just reference *The Notebook*?"

With a nod, I hop up and stand at the side of the bed.

"Fine, Noah Calhoun," he volleys. "If we're living in a fiction novel, then ask me what I want."

I gather my hair into a ponytail at the top of my head and go for a southern accent. "What do you want?"

He sits up high on the bed and twists so he's angled my way. "I want my dad to stop riding my ass about taking over the business. I want to pursue photography full time."

Rounding the end of the bed, I say, "Then do it."

"It's not that—"

I press two fingers to his lips, silencing him. "Before my dad..." I clear my throat and try again. "My dad once told me not to live my life for others. To do what makes *me* happy. He said life is more fulfilling that way."

Cam rears back and opens his mouth, ready to protest, I'm sure, but I shoot him a glare.

"He never said it was easier."

"Are you sure you're only twenty-two?" he asks, nipping at my fingers.

I pull away and give him a flirty smile. "What can I say? I'm mature for my age." Not by choice, but out of necessity. It's the kind of thing that happens to kids of addicts. After the age of ten, I was mostly on my own. I had no choice but to grow up.

He tilts his head and presses his lips together, contemplating me. But I ignore the scrutiny. Instead, I retreat to the bathroom, where I gather my remaining belongings.

"What about you?" he calls.

"What about me?" I ask, holding my toothbrush in front of my mouth.

"What do you do in LA?" He laughs, though it's the nervous kind. "Oh my god, please don't tell me you're a famous model or an actress and I'm an idiot who doesn't know who you are."

I finish brushing my teeth, grab my bag, exit the bathroom,

and think about fucking with him, then decide against it. "I'm a writer. Well, a wannabe writer." I frown. "And definitely not famous." Although I have been photographed by paparazzi while out with Tyler.

"What do you mean, *wannabe?*"

"I am writing. A book, actually. But that doesn't pay the bills. Not yet, at least. So I moonlight as a freelance editor. And I'll probably have to pick up another job when I get home." Even if I work two paying jobs, I'm not sure I can afford my own place.

"What is your book—"

"Hey." I cut him off. I'm not in the mood to get into the nitty gritty. "What time is it? We should get back to the dock, yeah?"

With a frown, he throws his legs over the side of the bed. "Yeah, sure." He strides to the bathroom, buck naked, and closes the door.

Cam's mood changes somewhere between the hotel and the dock. I barely know him, so it shouldn't bother me so much that he's gone quiet and contemplative, but it does. He owes me nothing. And wasn't I the one avoiding intimacy by faking sleep last night?

"Are you okay?" I ask, rolling and stretching my wrist. Oh yeah, it's definitely sore this morning. But hella worth it. "Are you worried about seeing your ex? At least there's only one more day left."

Thank fuck I only have to share one more sleep with Tyler. Hey, maybe Hayden and I can switch. Yeah right.

Cam shifts in the taxi until he's facing me, his lips downturned. "We shouldn't have done that." He drops his attention to his lap, fiddling with the hem of his board shorts.

Okay, I did not see that coming.

"We just broke up with our partners." Now he keeps his gaze averted and his voice low. "It was reckless. I kind of feel like I took advantage of you. We were both in shitty places last night. I'm sorry."

"Excuse me?" I ask, my voice a little too loud for such a confined space. Is this like buyer's remorse or something?

Sighing, he finally makes eye contact again, but the pitying look does nothing but fire me up.

"Joey," he tries again. "What we did last night was, um, completely gratifying, but we just—I just," he corrects himself, "shouldn't have jumped in so suddenly. We were angry and not in our right minds. Plus, we don't even know each other."

I grind my teeth and look out the window. I can't deal with another man directing my life right now. I have enough shit to deal with when I return to California. Cam and I slept together, sure, but it was a hot and impulsive hookup. That's it. Why is he making it so complicated?

We'll never cross paths again, so I should blow it off and move on, but his words irk me, nonetheless.

I turn to him. "You know what?" My nostrils flare. "Fuck you."

He jerks at my harsh words and his mouth drops open.

I said what I said. I've been a coward for too long, and I refuse to be that girl any longer. "Don't pretend like you're some goddamn gentleman now." My blood is boiling. "Not when you were pulling my hair and spanking my ass not twelve hours ago."

"Jesus—" he starts, eyeing our driver. His ears go pink and his eyes are wide.

I don't care. Lifting my chin, I stare him down, and when the cab pulls up to the curb in the next instant, I swing open my door. "Thank fuck I'll never see you again, *Cameron*. Good luck with your boring career and future pearl-wearing, vanilla wife."

Chapter 11
Cameron

THE FERRY RIDE to the cruise ship is uncomfortable as hell, and not because of the plastic seats or the choppy waves. Joey doesn't want me anywhere near her; she made that clear by dropping into a seat on the opposite side of the boat. Not that I can blame her after my speech in the taxi. I may not have handled the conversation as well as I could have, but apologizing was the honorable thing to do, right? Regardless, she's intent on giving me the cold shoulder.

In the grand scheme of things, it shouldn't matter. We'll never see each other again. It's too bad, though, because the sex was incredible. Beyond incredible, really.

Hayden hated when I'd go down on her—said it was weird and unnatural. And she never liked dirty talk, like it disgusted her. But Joey? She reveled in it. I haven't felt that good in bed in I don't know how long. Maybe ever? And it's not just because of the orgasm. We connected in a way I've never experienced. And maybe in another life—if she were older, if we lived in the same part of the country—we could have something. But that isn't the case, so it's time to let it go and focus on what's in front of me.

Joey's words worked their way into my skin like a tick. *Do what makes you happy. Life is more fulfilling that way.*

Under the awning of the ferry, mostly protected from the sun, I search the horizon. *What if?* What would my life look like if I did what I wanted for once? For starters, I'd have to find a new place to live. My father wouldn't let me stay in the penthouse if I quit my job. And my mom? She's waited so long for my dad to retire, and that'll only happen if I step up. She'll be devastated if I leave the family business.

I throw my pipe dreams overboard just as we pull up to the dock.

Hayden is waiting for me in our cabin when I return. I toss my bag on the floor with a thud, then carefully set my camera in front of the closet, breathing through the trepidation coursing through my veins at the sight of my ex-girlfriend.

"I'm so glad you're okay!" She shuffles close and cups my shoulders. The apples of her cheeks are pink and her eyes are bright. She looks much better than when I left her yesterday. Did she hook up with Tyler again? She leans in for a hug, but I push her away. I was so consumed with thoughts of my career and a certain leggy brunette on the ferry ride over that I failed to give much thought to what I might say once I confronted her. I was understanding when she told me she couldn't marry me, but that was before I knew she cheated.

"What's wrong, Cammy?" Jesus. I suddenly despise that nickname on her tongue.

"I don't know, Hayden. Why don't you tell me?"

She rears back, her blue eyes darting between mine. "What are you talking about?"

For the Plot

With a big step back, I cross my arms over my chest, like armor to my heart. "Where were you the night before last?"

She drops her focus to the floor for a heartbeat, and when she looks back at me, her face is pale. "I stayed at that club with those girls we met from Long Island."

I nod. This much is true. "And when I went back to the room? Then what?"

Her ocean eyes expand. "I...I don't know what you mean."

"Don't lie to me." Shaking my head, I dig my phone out of my back pocket, unlock the screen, and hold it up so she can see the image. Joey and I didn't exchange numbers or social media information, but she did send me the picture of Hayden and Tyler via AirDrop. If I didn't have it in front of me now, I might allow myself to believe it was a bad dream.

All the color drains from her face and tears well in her eyes. Dropping to the bed, she hangs her head. "I'm so sorry," she chokes out. The tears are already flowing.

This ought to be good. Without a word, I step closer, waiting for an explanation.

"How did—how did you find out?"

That's what she has to say? "His girlfriend."

"He has a girlfriend?" She gasps. She's sobbing now, a trail of mascara staining her cheeks. "I swear I didn't know."

Seriously? She's concerned that he has a girlfriend, not that she had a boyfriend?

"I can't believe you right now. Who are you?" I run my fingers through my hair.

She rises to her feet and grasps my wrist. "I'm so sorry, Cammy."

The girl before me is desperate, and it's pathetic.

"Don't fucking touch me right now." I yank so she's forced to release me, then I take a step back. Not that it puts much space between us in this tiny cabin.

I'm sure our next-door neighbors are getting quite the earful, but that's the least of my concerns.

"Why?" I plead, though I'm not sure I even want to know the answer.

She looks pained. Good. "I don't know." She ducks her chin and rubs the side of her arm. "I had too much to drink and my judgment was skewed, but that's not an excuse," she admits. "If I'm being totally honest, I think I just didn't feel like being the good girl for once."

My anger dissipates just a fraction with that confession. "What do you mean?"

"I'm so tired of feeling suffocated by my parents' expectations, and I'm sick of always doing exactly what they tell me to do. Aren't you?" She licks her lips and searches my face. "I mean, they freaking arranged our marriage without even considering how we might feel about it. That's crazy, right? I feel crazy right now."

Though I'd rather not touch her, I grasp her arm gently and guide her to the bed.

Sitting beside me on the mattress, she keeps her head bowed, not making eye contact. "What I did was shitty. I really am sorry. I feel so lost right now. Like I don't know what I want from life. Before you, I'd only dated one guy, and that didn't end well. I don't know. I just want the freedom to figure it out on my own without my parents breathing down my neck."

"I get that. I just wish you wouldn't have gone behind my back."

She turns to me, tears still streaming down her face. "I know."

My jaw loosens a bit. I'm tired. I don't want to fight over this when we've already decided not to be together. "Let's just get through the rest of the trip."

For the Plot

Though keeping things civil with Hayden feels like the right thing to do, I'd rather not look at her. The only face I want to see is Joey's, and with any luck, I'll bump into her on the ship today.

The pool deck is crowded with Brits who are all about an hour away from third-degree sunburns. I've set myself up on the lounge by the pool, praying my odds of catching her walking by this high-traffic area are decent. With a whiskey on rocks in my hand, I hold tight to the image of the prettiest brown eyes in my head.

Man, I really screwed things up. Why did I have to open my mouth and tell her I regretted our night together? It's the farthest thing from the truth. If the last twenty-four hours has taught me anything, it's that life doesn't always need to be planned to be beautiful. I may have just met the girl of my dreams, but I've royally fucked it up, and now I'll never see her again.

Chapter 12
Josefine
One Year Later

"Why would I ever go back there, Mills?"

"Because," she says, "your dad wanted you to have the time of your life in Greece and that fuckboy"—she throws her hands in the air—"ruined it. You have to go back and replace the bad memories with good ones."

My cousin is right. Tyler irrevocably ruined what I had anticipated to be the trip of a lifetime. Though I guess he guaranteed that I'd never forget it.

Before we even landed at LAX, I was coordinating with friends to move my stuff out of his apartment. Not only did I want to get the hell away from him, but from Los Angeles too. I needed a total rebirth—*Josefine's Version*, if you will—and zero distractions if I was ever going to get my life together and make it as a published author.

Lucky for me, my cousin Millie swooped in and saved the day. As soon as I called to tell her what *fuckboy* did, she bought a pull-out sofa from IKEA and a one-way ticket to Manhattan for me. When I made my way past baggage claim at JFK, she was waiting with a bottle of Macallan and a sign that read *Welcome back from prison, Joey!*

Our apartment in Washington Heights may be the size of a Barbie Dreamhouse, but we make it work. The light gray sectional that doubles as my bed is surprisingly comfortable, and the drum-shaped gold and walnut coffee table is an adorable place to store my bedding. Two large windows on one wall let in the most exquisite morning light, and most of my personal shit fits inside the television credenza on the opposite wall.

"There's no way we can book a last-minute trip to Greece," I say.

"That's what you think!" Millie jumps up from the black velvet captain's chair in the corner of her bedroom. Her obnoxious, faux-fur blanket falls to the ground in front of a gaudy, full-length mirror.

"What are you saying?" I squint at my cousin.

"Are you forgetting my landlord is also a travel agent, boo?" She grabs her phone off her nightstand. "I pulled some strings and *voilà!*" With a toothy grin, she unlocks the device and all but shoves it in my face.

"Please don't tell me 'pulled some strings' is a euphemism for 'sucked his cock.'"

She roars with laughter, and the phone slips from her hand and bounces on the black-and-white checkered rug.

"Bitch, why do you always think I'm slipping sexual favors to Gideon?"

"Because he's letting me live here without a sublease." I pick up her phone, then pass it to her. "If you're not sleeping with him, he's definitely trying to win his way into your pants."

"I can't help it if everyone wants a piece of this," she says, flinging her strawberry-blond hair back dramatically like she's Cindy Crawford in a Pepsi commercial. With a step closer, she brings the phone up so I'm forced to look at the screen. There, in bold colors, is an Instagram grid dedicated solely to an all-inclusive resort on the island of Crete.

"Even if I wanted to go back," I say, my attention caught on the pictures in paradise, "I can't afford it. I only took that trip because my dad left money specifically for it." Plus, moving across the country was pricey.

"Funny you should say that." Millie's eyes sparkle. "My mom mentioned recently that your dad left backup money with her."

"Backup money? What does that mean?"

"Apparently he left a chunk of money with my mom, along with a note that said *For a rainy day: In case my baby girl needs it. Keep it safe for her until she does.* Or something like that."

Tears flood my eyes, fogging my vision. My dad has been gone for thirteen years, yet he's still taking care of me, his baby girl, even from the afterlife.

"I'd say this qualifies as a rainy day, boo." She wraps an arm around my shoulder. "My mom agrees. She's going to wire the money into your account first thing in the morning. So pack your condoms and sluttiest clothes, bitch, 'cause we're about to fuck some Greek gods."

Chapter 13
Cameron

"Dude, where've you been?" I ask my roommate. It's been weeks since we've hung out.

"I'm sorry, man. Work's been so busy lately." Ezra shoots our server a flirty smile when she sets two glasses of whiskey in front of us.

She lingers a bit, batting her lashes the way women do when he's around. I call it the Bearded Effect. He's got that "I woke up like this" look. You know the one—tousled dark brown hair that hints at a late-night romp, paired with a beard trimmed to perfection like he has a live-in barber. Women crawl to him like they're cats in heat everywhere we go. Not that I can complain about my share of attention most days.

But lately I haven't bothered with the New York City dating scene. And by lately, I mean for the last two years.

I wish I could say the end of my year-long relationship with Hayden was the cause, but in reality, a single night with Joey is what broke me. I've gone on dates since the cruise from hell, but anytime I attempt to take things to the bedroom, all I see—and hear and feel—is Joey, and I back away before the belts even come loose. Ezra jokes that the women of New York are going to call me Chastity Cam if I don't get over my dry spell soon.

I raise my whiskey between us.

"Here's to new beginnings." My buddy clinks his glass against mine. "I'm proud of you."

"Thanks, man," I grin. "This last year has been wild. I couldn't have done it without you."

Rather than crawling home to dear ole Mom and Dad after my breakup, I channeled the peace and optimism that had hit me that day on Crete and quit my job. I hadn't even been back on American soil for three hours before I marched into my father's office and resigned. If I didn't do it right away, I might not have done it at all.

Naturally, my father canceled his meetings for the rest of the day, called my mother into the office, and tried to stage an intervention. It was shattering, watching my mom's dreams crumble, but I stood my ground. They chose this life; I didn't. And it wasn't fair for them to decide my future for me. I am my own person and I get to decide my career and path in life.

I choose photography.

Graciously, my mom talked my dad into letting me live in the penthouse until the end of the month. If it were up to my dad, he would have given me the boot that day. Ezra had been begging me to move into the city with him for years, so that's exactly what I did.

We've been best friends for more than half my life. For a year, we attended the same boarding school about an hour outside Manhattan and were thrown together as part of the school's senior-freshman mentoring program. Though he mentored me more on women than academics.

Ezra is my platonic soulmate and the one person I can always count on to have my back. After I quit my job, he was the first person I called.

When he shouted "It's about damn time, man!" into the phone, I could practically see his fist pump.

I stuck around and trained my replacement at Hotel Connelly for a couple of weeks, then hit the ground running. I busted my ass, sending my portfolio to every photography company I could find on the internet and scheduled meeting after meeting.

Through my contact with Aaron from Crete last year, I was connected with Atlas Luxury Resort & Spa. After submitting recreational photos I took around the resort, including the one of Joey jumping off the chartered boat, I accepted a seasonal photographer position.

I busted my ass in local workshops to hone my skill, but freelance photography is competitive. It's exhausting combating impostor syndrome and not selling myself short.

Fake it till you make it.

With the last year of hustling to build my online portfolio, this job is just what I need. I get to live on Crete for a month with guaranteed income. The fifty percent discount for staff accommodations is a perk, too, and exactly what I used to convince Ezra to join me for a week. While I'm there, I'll spend a handful of hours each day taking engagement and family photos as well as photos the resort will use for marketing. That will leave me with ample time to relax and explore the island. And in a couple of days, I'll be on my way.

One Month Later

"Damn. This has been your home for the last month? Smells so much better than the city," Ezra laughs.

"Just wait until we drive through the villages," I say as I pull out of the airport. "You'll be missing the smells of the subway in no time."

Beside me in my little island rental, Ezra's hair is losing its battle with the wind, so he ties it back in his infamous man bun. "I'm stoked to be here." He rests his tan arm halfway out the window. "Enjoying hotel life again?"

To be honest, there's no comparison. This place is nothing like Hotel Connelly. "It's like I'm on an extended vacation."

Most days it doesn't feel real. While I've had plenty of ridiculous encounters with clients (a puking mother-in-law, a blowout diaper incident, a very touchy-feely bachelorette party), this job is cush. I've only had to capture one surprise engagement, and rather than triggering, it was confirmation that Hayden and I were not meant to be.

Eating my weight in souvlaki, bureki, olives, and fresh seafood is my new religion, as is spending my free time exploring the island and staying up way too late to drink with the locals. Life is good.

"Have you talked to your parents lately?"

Gripping the steering wheel a little tighter, I force my shoulders to relax and let out a breath. "My mom, yeah."

"Your dad still not speaking to you?"

Behind me, a car inches closer, so I drive on the shoulder lane to let them pass. Driving on the island is intuitive. Slower drivers use the shoulder to allow faster cars to pass, and no one is upset over the encounter. People only honk to say hello. That would never happen in the States—especially New York City.

"He's speaking to me—*kinda*." I check twice for motorcyclists before catching up with traffic. "If you count a few sentences every time my mom forces him to get on the phone."

For the Plot

My dad is still bitter. He doesn't think I can make a living "taking pictures." In his eyes, I swear my only purpose in life is to take over the family business. He doesn't hold Claire to the same standard. Though she chose medicine. Of course he'd be supportive of such a respectable career.

"Anyway." I give my head a shake. "How are you?" Fathers are a sore subject for both of us, so he doesn't call me out when I redirect the conversation. "Are you still seeing that chick from work?" I ask. "What was her name? Lemon?"

"Lennon." Ezra rolls his eyes.

"Are you saying *Lennon* or *Lemon?*" I tease.

"Are you saying *Pan* or *Pam?*" He quips. This routine is one of our favorites. We've probably watched *Stepbrothers* more than a hundred times together throughout the years.

I laugh. "Crete sort of reminds me of Catalina Island." Years ago, he and I took a trip to the small island off the coast of Southern California when we found out it wasn't just a fictional one mentioned in a movie.

"I can see that," he replies, scanning the scenery.

Out here, we're surrounded by mountains peppered with Venetian-style architecture. Brick castles carved into mountains can be seen in the distance, as well as unfinished concrete rooftops with laundry hung on clotheslines.

"So, Lennon," I try again.

"Oh, yeah. No, that's not going to happen."

"Why not?"

Ezra doesn't look away from the scenery for another moment, but when he does, he huffs. "She told me she was separated from her husband. Turns out she lied, and I didn't catch on until he walked into their apartment looking as clueless as ever."

I gasp. "No way."

"Yup." He covers his face and mumbles into his hands. "I never want to be caught with my pants around my ankles again."

"Metaphorically speaking or—" I snap my mouth shut when I peek over at him. His face says it all. "I'm sorry, dude."

"No worries. Who knows, maybe I'll find a Greek goddess and ditch your ugly ass," he chaffs.

Chapter 14
Josefine

"Kalimera." A big, burly and hairy man with a handlebar mustache tosses our luggage into the back of the shuttle van.

"*Kalimera.*" I repeat the Greek phrase for *good morning*. After two hours of messing around on my Duolingo app, I can officially say "the purple carrot" and "drama in the mini market." Both should be super handy when I order cocktails at the bar.

"What's the name of the hotel again?" my cousin asks, examining her freshly painted nails.

"Atlas Luxury Resort & Spa."

"It's the place you stayed at last time, right?"

I shake my head. "No. That was a bed-and-breakfast. Atlas is the resort where I fell asleep in the hammock."

"Oh, that's right. Where you met Mr. Serial Killer," she says, scanning our surroundings.

So far, our view is just a runway of white rental cars. I can't wait to witness her face when the real scenery is revealed.

"Ugh, don't remind me," I sigh. If I said I haven't thought about Cam over the last year, then I'd be a big fat liar. For weeks, I carried him with me. Not only did he bury his very large dick inside me that night, but he buried his soul inside me too. I let myself mope around for precisely one month before I shoved the memory of him in the metaphorical garbage disposal. There was no point in pining over him. After I decided to put him out of my mind, grieving the loss of my long-term relationship with Tyler and building a new life for myself in New York City mostly kept me from thinking about Cam's perfect pecs and toned ass. Even if I wanted to look him up, I wouldn't know how. We didn't share last names or exchange contact information before he made it very clear he regretted our one-night stand.

As we hit a switchback and the city center comes into view, Millie gasps. "Oh my god!"

"I told you."

Side by side, we admire the expanse of turquoise water. The lighthouse is in the distance, and thousands of colorful buildings are sprinkled in every direction. It's truly picturesque. And with my best friend and partner in crime by my side, I know this will be an unforgettable experience.

"Feels... so... good," Millie moans.

"Don't lay down!"

But it's too late. She's already sinking face-first into the mattress.

"I know you're exhausted, babes, but let's dig up the last bit of adrenaline we have and push through the rest of the day. We've gotta beat the jet lag before it beats us." I'll share my melatonin later.

"All I heard was *beat*," she mumbles against the white duvet.

"Up." I smack her ass.

For the Plot

"Hey!" Millie sits up and straightens her romper. "The only one who should be smacking my ass is Adonis at the front desk."

"Is that really his name?"

"I have no idea." She chuckles. "But he was giving off major book boyfriend vibes. Did you see his corded forearm veins? I'd like to drag my—"

"Easy there, killer. I thought you were into that chick. What's her name again?"

"Who, Samantha?" Millie joins me in the bathroom and sits on the counter, popping the top of the complimentary shower gel and unleashing the scent of orange blossom and rosemary. "Sam's hot as fuck and cool as shit, but I don't think she's into me." She frowns.

"Why do you say that?" I spray a cloud of dry shampoo before running a brush through my hair.

"Because," Millie grabs the brush from my hand and drags it through her shoulder-length hair. "She hasn't made a move."

"Well, have *you*?"

She shrugs.

"Amelia. You haven't made a move yet? Hasn't being a voice narrator for a spicy audio stories app taught you anything?"

She dips her chin and twists her fingers in her lap, then she jumps off the counter. She catches my eyes in the mirror. "Sam's way out of my league, Jo. Plus, I don't even know if she's into girls."

"Hey." I soften my tone and grasp my cousin's hands. "Remember when you didn't know if you were into girls?"

She nods and drops her gaze. "That was a really confusing time."

"Maybe Sam just needs more time or a friend she feels like she can talk to."

"Thanks, boo." She squeezes my hands three times, our silent way of saying *I love you*, before releasing.

"Now..." I dig into my cosmetics bag, giving her first dibs on the concealer. "Dab this under your eyes and let's go find Adonis!"

"You look like you need the caffeine." Nik, the bartender, places two tall glasses on the counter in front of us. He talked us into trying Freddo cappuccinos, but they look more like failed attempts at Frappuccinos.

"What the hell is this?" Millie scoffs.

"You Americans think you know coffee." Nik tosses his head back. "But us Greeks? We invented coffee."

"Is that true?" I sip from a paper straw, savoring the bitterness.

"We invented everything." Nik smacks the bar, a wide smile plastered across his sweaty face.

Millie spits her drink back into the glass like a fucking toddler, her face curled in disgust. If there's no sugar in her coffee, she doesn't want it.

Nik laughs and hands over packets of sugar before we take our coffees to the cabana and settle on the blue-and-white striped chaise lounges.

"What do you want to do tonight?" she asks, stirring the sugar into her drink with her straw.

"I one thousand percent plan on sleeping."

"Oh, come on." She swats at me. "Don't be such a buzzkill."

"Says the woman who was making out with the mattress earlier."

"That's before I had this freaky Freddo drink. I'm wired. What the fuck do they put in their coffee over here? I feel like I'm going to have a heart attack. I'm too young, Joey!" She brings the back of her palm to her forehead, overly dramatic as always.

I chuckle. "I doubt it's the jitter juice. You put like forty packets of sugar in there."

"I'll let you be lame for one night," she huffs. "Then I don't want any excuses, missy. This is a trip of a lifetime and shouldn't be wasted in a hotel room."

"You're making it seem like I'm no fun. I'm hella fun, Mills. I'm just exhausted from traveling. I swear I won't hold back tomorrow. It's just you and me, boo."

True to my word, I wake bright and early, ready to take on Greece. We pop into the only Starbucks on this side of the island so Millie can get her sugar fix. I opt for an Americano, and with our drinks in hand, we roam the never-ending shops of Old Town.

We turn a corner down a cobblestone alleyway, and I gasp at what's laid out before us. "Oh my god. Look."

Four vending machines are tucked into a hole in the wall. The first contains ice-cold drinks, the second is filled with a host of European snacks, the third with medicine, toiletries, vapes, and baby products. But it's the fourth machine that intrigues me. It's stocked with lube, condoms, and sex toys. Who knew a variety of vibrators, dildos, and anal plugs could be bought like a bag of chips?

Millie squeals, snapping a picture with her phone. "Now there's something you don't see in America."

"See anything you like?" I laugh.

"*Actually.*" She drags a finger over the tempered glass and pauses at B4. "You, right there."

Once she's inserted twenty-five euros, a hot pink rabbit drops from its shelf.

"I can't believe you bought a sex toy from a vending machine." I cackle, inspecting the box. It looks legit.

"When in Greece."

"How much more time do you need?" Millie asks, applying another coat of mascara to her lashes. Her cheeks are dewy, courtesy of our outing earlier today.

I'm in the middle of curling my hair, towel still wrapped around my body. "Another ten or fifteen minutes?"

"I'm going to head down to the lobby and book a reservation for that excursion we talked about while you finish up. Let's meet at the fountain I pointed out on our way in."

"Sure. See you there."

Earlier at dinner, the people at the table behind us were talking about getting caught in the rain on the beach yesterday, and it instantly catapulted me to last May. *To Cameron.* I swore I wasn't going to think about him while I was here, but I can't help it. I couldn't stop the image that sprung to mind first. The one of him wearing a wet shirt that clung to his broad chest and shoulders when I noticed him in the hotel lobby. He was flustered and angry about missing his connection to the cruise ship, and maybe I'm romanticizing our interaction, but it's almost as if that all floated away when he saw me standing next to him.

And the look on his face when I stepped out of the bathroom in our little room at the B&B? I'd never admit it, but I *was* wearing lingerie. I'd been so out of sorts that morning that I must have tossed it into my beach bag by mistake. The look he gave me when he saw me come out of the bathroom? Damn, what I wouldn't give to have someone look at me that way again.

I saw him on the ship that last day. He was lounging on the pool deck with a drink in his hand. It took the mental strength of a Navy SEAL not to rush over and demand a redo of our morning-after conversation. When the ship made it back to port, did he go back to his perfect little prepackaged life, or did he have the balls to go after what he wanted?

Chapter 15

Cameron

THE LAST THING I ever expected to delay our return to the resort was a pile of logs strewn about the coastal highway. It was a scene straight out of *Final* fucking *Destination*. Thank fuck we weren't the stars of that reenactment. Only one side of the road was blocked, and workers were already directing traffic, so the holdup was a short one, but now I'm in a mad rush to make it to my photography session in twenty minutes. Ezra heads to his room, and we make plans to meet up at the bar later, so I dump my bags in my room, shower and change, and take the shortcut through the lobby.

Halfway across, I stop dead in my tracks.

It can't be.

There's no fucking way.

Three little birds, inked on a woman's tricep. My brain has malfunctioned, and before I know what I'm doing, I'm grasping for said tricep and twisting its owner toward me.

"Oh!" The woman's green eyes widen, and she sucks in a breath.

"Oh, I'm so sorry." I hold up my hands and take a step back, too disappointed to be embarrassed. "I thought you were someone else."

She drinks me in. "That's okay. I'm happy to be someone else," she purrs.

Definitely an American on vacation. It's not against hotel policy to fraternize with vacationers, and while she's a beautiful woman, she's not *the woman*.

Damn if her tattoo isn't identical to Joey's, though. Birds are a common choice, sure, but in that location, and that precise configuration? This is too freaky.

The strawberry blonde shrugs when I don't respond and turns to whatever she was doing before I interrupted her with my delusion.

I round the activities desk and head to my office to grab my name badge. Heading back out, I clip it to my shirt. My standard uniform could be worse. The off-white linen shirt goes well with the resort-issued cerulean blue shorts. And after a memorable encounter with goat poop my first week here, I now exclusively wear sneakers instead of flip-flops.

As I approach the fountain where I typically meet with my photo clients, I catch sight of the blonde from the lobby.

"Hello again." She extends her arm, a dozen gold bracelets clanking. "I'm Millie."

I shake her hand, and instead of greeting her like a normal person, I ask, "How did you get that tattoo?"

"Excuse me?" Her brows pinch together.

"Your three birds tattoo. How—"

She pops up on her toes and cranes her neck to look around me. "Here's our girl!"

Following her line of sight, I turn. You know how in movies, time freezes?

Yeah, that just happened.

"This is Joey," my new client says. I think. My ears are

buzzing too loudly to be sure. My body is coiled with too much energy, like an animal stalking its prey.

She taps my shoulder, but my sole focus is the ghost in front of me. Tan legs on display below the hem of her mini dress. Strong calves and toned thighs. Perfect hips that taper to a narrow waist. Ample breasts beneath shimmering gold material.

"Oh, you wouldn't believe the trip she had to Greece last year…" Millie goes on, shuffling around me.

She's here. Fuck. *Please don't let this be a hallucination.*

The woman is still talking. Something about a sleazy ex-boyfriend and getting stuck in the rain. About a taxi ride with a sex worker and the best sex of someone's life. I don't catch any more than that because I'm entranced by the gorgeous woman beside her.

"Okay, that's enough, Amelia!" Joey, eyes wide and cheeks flushed, slaps a hand across the woman's face.

"No, no, Amelia, please continue," I say, finally pulling myself out of my stupor.

Joey grabs her arm and tugs. "I've changed my mind. I don't want to take pictures." She doesn't look at me when she adds, "Thanks for your time."

"What? No." Millie yanks free of Joey's grasp. "My mom already paid for the session and demanded I send them to her ASAP. Plus, you look fucking hot." *Agreed.* "We're doing this." She ducks close and whispers, "What's your deal, Jo?"

Yeah, what is running through your mind right now, Josefine?

Chewing her bottom lip, my gorgeous blast from the past looks from her friend to me to the lobby doors, clearly in fight-or-flight mode.

"Will you excuse us one moment?" She finally turns those beautiful eyes that only visit me in my dreams my way, and it's like a punch to the gut.

Swallowing thickly and giving her a silent nod, I step back. I don't go more than a couple of yards. It's all I can manage now that I've found her. I take her in again. There's no way she'll be able to walk in those stilettos on the beach. I can't help but imagine bending on one knee and removing one, then the other, brushing my fingers against her smooth skin as I go.

I'm far enough away now that I can't hear what they're saying, but the "holy shit!" that flies out of Millie's mouth can be heard all the way to Mykonos. Then she click-clacks her way over to me, her arms flailing.

"*You're* Cam?" She shoves a finger in my chest. Apparently she doesn't do personal space.

Pointing to my name tag, I hit her with an award-winning grin. "Cameron," I correct her. "Nice to meet you, *Amelia*."

She bounces on her toes and clasps her hands in front of her. "Well, if this isn't the perfect Crete cute, I don't know what is."

"The perfect what?" Joey and I ask at the same time. Her eyes dart to mine, then away as fast as lightning.

"A Crete cute. Like a meet cute, but we're on Crete."

Joey pushes Millie's arm. "Oh my god. You're ridiculous." The smile she cracks is like an instant hit of dopamine.

Her friend's responding expression is one of pure elation. She's eating this up. It's obvious by the way Joey's avoiding even looking at me that she'll be hard to crack, but Millie here might be my perfect accomplice.

I turn to the woman I've been dreaming about for a year and give her another long look, starting at her toes and working my way up over that sparkling gold number that shows off all her curves. When I get to her face, I catch her sizing me up, too, her plump, glossy lips pursed and her eyes somewhere between curious and guarded.

Unbelievable. My Joey is here. On this island. Standing in front of me.

Figuring the best way to keep from scaring her off is to do

what we're all here for, I clear my throat and revert to professional mode. "Are we ready to get started?"

It was all I could do not to get a hard-on during our sunset session. Every time I looked through my lens, I was reminded of the night we shared last year. Zooming in on her flawless skin instantaneously brought me back to the way it felt to have my hands on her.

After thirty torturous minutes of looking but not touching, I thanked Millie and excused myself, but not before whispering to Joey that I'd find her at the bar later. I didn't give her an opportunity to object before I strode in the opposite direction.

Now, I close the door to the office I share with the other resort photographers and breathe a sigh of relief when I find it unoccupied. I immediately upload the pictures to my work laptop. Enthralled, I toggle between the images. Sure, I got plenty of the girls together, but then Millie stepped away, insisting Joey take center stage.

I click from one image to another but freeze when one in particular pops up. The light island breeze swept up her hair, and Joey raised her arms to tame it. In that instant, I captured her with her hands buried in her hair, her elbows wide, her sculpted biceps flexed, and a spontaneous smile on her face.

Without a second thought, I save the image and send it to my phone.

This one's for me.

Ezra better have drinks on deck because he's not going to believe it when I tell him.

I'm approaching the bar when I feel her. I halt in my tracks and give her another appreciative once-over, only to realize she's looking at me too. Conveniently, Ezra is standing next to her. I take a step forward, ready to introduce the two of them, but stall when Joey leans in close and speaks to my best friend.

She sets her delicate hand on his forearm and glances over at me so quickly I nearly miss it. My legs are like lead, holding me in place, and the blood in my veins heats. What is she up to? If Ezra knew who she was, he'd shut this shit down, but he doesn't, so I give it a moment to see how this plays out.

With a laugh, she tosses her head back, and in that instant, I know exactly what she's trying to do.

Chapter 16
Josefine

Do I feel just a little bad about roping the man beside me into being my unwitting accomplice? Sure. But it's too late now. I'm committed. As soon as I caught Cam coming my way, I panicked.

When I came face to face with my long-lost one-night stand earlier, my heart not only stopped, but it packed its bags and left without notice. His hair is a little longer on top than I remember, and it's definitely been a day or two since he's shaved. Not that I'm complaining. His olive skin is tanned to perfection, like maybe he's been on the island for more than a few days.

Is he the jealous type? I guess we're about to find out. He's either going to stride over nonchalantly or bend me over his knee.

And if he *is* the *bend-you-over-my-knee* type?

Heat blooms in my core at just the thought.

No, Joey! Stop it. No getting bent over. Not by him, at least. Ugh, what is happening to me right now? I was completely over him. Sort of. I'd at least made peace with the idea that I would never see him again. Though any time I've hooked up with a guy in the last year, the encounter has fallen short because I couldn't help but compare the guy to *him*.

And now we're here. At the same resort. How is this even possible?

I train my attention on the poor pawn beside me. What did he say his name was? Isaiah? I swivel on my barstool so I'm facing him, my bare knee swiping the dark hair on his thigh. Tipping forward just a tad, I proudly display my girls. I'm only half listening to his story about a road trip with his buddy and logs on the highway, but I throw my head back and laugh, nonetheless. And that's when Cam waltzes over and not-so-subtly knocks my knee away from Isaiah's leg with his hip.

With his hands in his pockets, he stands close, cool and collected.

"May I help you?" I tilt my head and eye him. Terrible idea. He's so damn close I can see the flecks of gold shimmering in his irises. There's a slight scar I didn't notice before running through his left brow, marring the perfection of his face in a way that somehow only makes him look sexier.

"Hey, man. There you are," Isaiah says when he notices Cam standing close.

What the heck? Mr. Beard-And-Man-Bun is supposed to be on my team.

My accomplice hands Cam a glass of amber liquid with an orange peel garnish—no doubt an old-fashioned, my father's favorite. They clink glasses, and Cam peers down at me with a wink. "I see you've met my buddy."

I oughta wipe that shit-eating grin off his face right now.

"Oh, yes," I say, using my knee to push him back a bit.

His eyes dart to the gap between my legs.

"Isaiah here was just telling me about how beautiful the east side of the island is and suggested we go sometime."

Cam's jaw ticks, and he turns to his friend, who's wearing a look of confusion.

"*Ezra*," he says, "meet *Joey*." By the way he says my name and the way his buddy's eyes bug out, I know my little ruse is over.

Ezra throws his hands in the air and tips his head back. "This is your Joey? I had no idea, I swear." He brings his glass to his lips and finishes his drink in one gulp.

"We're cool, man." Cam tosses back his drink, too, then leans over me to set his glass on the sticky counter. The sweet scent of orange lingers between us when he doesn't immediately pull away. "I ought to bend you over this bar and teach you a lesson for trying to make me jealous like that." His breath is hot against my ear.

I knew he was the bend-you-over type, dammit.

Before I have time to process the comment Ezra made about me being *Cam's* Joey, Millie arrives. It's impossible not to be entranced by her presence. She's got that glow about her. Yeah, she was absolutely made for theater. On occasion, the gals at FrenchSHEs—the drag and cabaret club where Millie bartends between tours—pull her up on stage and give her space to do her thing. And just like on those nights at the drag club, every eye in this place is on her. She's wearing a two-piece set she bought in the city center during our shopping excursion this morning. The flowy skirt is blue and white with gold threading throughout. Her hair is pulled up in an intentional messy bun that accentuates the skin the backless crop top exposes.

Oblivious to the attention she's pulling, she slams her clutch on the counter to the left of me.

"Hey, boo." She looks from me to Cam and back again. "Oh shit," she says under her breath, clearly picking up on the hostile energy. "What did I miss? Do I need a shot for this?" She waves over the bartender. "Three shots of tequila, please."

"Make that four," Ezra interjects.

"Who's he?" She peers over my shoulder, checking out the new guy.

"Ezra." He holds his hand out.

"Nice to meet you." She presses her palm to his. "I'm Millie. I take it you belong to him?" She nods to Cam.

"I guess you could say that," Ezra laughs.

"All right," I say. "Now that the introductions are over, we'll be on our way." There's got to be more than one bar at the resort.

"What?" Millie yaps, holding out two of the shot glasses the bartender slid her way. "We just got here." Head held high, she hands both shots of tequila to Cam.

"Millie," I urge, unsuccessfully trying to catch her eye.

Either she's not picking up what I'm putting down or she's deliberately ignoring me. Knowing her, probably the latter.

"Yeah, Joey," Cam says. "We just got here." He undoes the top button of his shirt, showcasing a smattering of dark hair, then rolls up his sleeves. The move reveals a collage of tattoos on his corded forearm that did not exist last year.

Fuck, this cannot be happening.

"Plus," he adds, "it's karaoke night."

Millie squeals beside me. Shit, that's it. I'm never getting out of here. I don't wait for anyone to make a toast before I throw back my shot.

The four of us relocate to a table near the stage where the staff is setting up for karaoke. After two more shots of tequila, I order a vodka tonic with lime, feeling much more at ease than I was thirty minutes ago.

"Easy there, sweetheart." Cam drapes his left arm over the back of my chair.

Sitting next to him means I can avoid making eye contact for the most part, but the proximity and the heat radiating from his body are dangerous for my libido. It's said that energy isn't exchanged from one person to another during sex, but that's hard to believe when I'm this close to this man. We exchanged something a year ago, and it's still trapped inside me. The question is, how do I get it out?

"Don't tell me what to do," I sneer. I dig through my clutch for a hair tie, then secure my hair in a low ponytail.

"If I recall correctly, you liked it when I bossed you around," he whispers, gently tugging at my ponytail.

Thankfully, Ezra and Millie are locked in a heated discussion about which songs are best for karaoke and aren't paying us a lick of attention.

"The best ones are the crowd pleasers," Millie states. "People want familiarity."

"I disagree." Ezra crosses his arms. "The best are the unexpected ones. People want to be wowed."

"And you would know this because?"

I tune them out and turn my attention back to Cam, keen to change the subject. "How's Little Miss Pearl Necklace?" Sure, I'm prying, but I don't care.

He shrugs. "Last I heard, she's back in DC. We didn't keep in touch after…"

Despite my best efforts, my heart aches just a little for him.

"What about you?" He shifts in his seat. "Please tell me you didn't take that asshole back."

"Don't call my husband an asshole." I sit straighter and square my shoulders. "Our daughter would be very offended."

His jaw drops so far I worry it'll detach completely. "Wha—"

"I'm kidding!" I snort loud enough for Millie and Ezra to stop arguing. "You should see the look on your face right now."

"You jerk," he teases, leaning back in his seat. He takes a swig from his second old-fashioned. "How's LA, then?"

"Actually..." Should I tell him I relocated?

I'm still pondering the implications when Millie pipes in. "She's living in the city with me now."

Guess we're telling him, then.

"What city?" He turns his head and watches me as he brings his lowball glass to his lips again.

"*The* city," Millie answers so very helpfully. "Manhattan."

Cam rocks forward and nearly spits out his drink. "For how long?"

"It'll be a year next week," I say, lifting my chin and brushing a stray strand of hair from my face.

"You've been in the city this whole time?" His eyes are wide, and there goes that slack jaw again. "You've been in the city this whole time and never told me?"

"Oh, I'm sorry. How was I supposed to contact you to let you know? Telepathically maybe? Or via carrier pigeon?" I deadpan. "It's not like we traded digits or handles."

He huffs. "You're right." With his focus still locked on me, he digs his phone from his back pocket. "What's your number?"

"Nah, I'm good," I say, shaking my empty glass in the air to signal to the passing server that I'd like a refill.

"What?" He puts a hand to my forearm and lowers it. "Why not? We're practically neighbors now."

I take a deep breath and collect my thoughts before speaking. "Look, I don't know why the hell we're back on this island at the same time, but you made it pretty clear what we had was a one-time thing."

"Joey," Millie interjects. "It might be good to have his number. You never know when you might need it. Like for an emergency." She sounds reasonable, but the glee in her eyes tells a different story.

"Exactly." Cam smiles at her with a similar level of excitement. "Thank you, Millie."

Before I can come up with an excuse for why I won't give him my number or social media info, she snags his phone, holds it up to his face to unlock the screen, and punches in my number.

"Traitor." I stick my tongue out.

When she hands him back his phone, he says my full name for the first time. God, it sounds good coming from his lips.

"Josefine Beckham," he murmurs. He gives me a long, thoughtful look, then sucks in a breath and changes the subject. "So, what's with the matching tattoos? Was that like a drunken best friends' Truth-or-Dare thing?"

My heart leaps at the mention of Truth or Dare and the memories that flood my mind.

"More like a pair of cousins honoring their dad and uncle sort of thing," Millie responds.

It's so subtle I almost miss it, but his fingertips tenderly caress the top of my shoulder. I squeeze my arms to ward off the goose bumps threatening to erupt across my skin.

"Ah. Cousins. Makes sense," he says, rotating toward me. "How old were you when your dad died?"

"Ten." I keep my answer short and rack my brain for ways to roll this conversation into something more chipper.

But he tips closer, his irises swimming with anguish and his lips downturned. "I understand big losses like that at such a young age."

My expression must morph from *can we just change the subject* to *I'm confused, tell me more,* because he continues. "My sister died when I was ten."

"I thought—" I drop an elbow to the table and shift so I'm looking at him head-on. Last year, he told me his sister had gifted him the camera he'd brought along.

"I was ten, Claire was six," he explains, lowering his head. "Our sister Chloe was two weeks old when she suddenly died in her sleep." He brings his drink to his lips but holds it there. "My mom was never the same after that. I did everything I could to make her happy, but it was never enough to fill the void left behind when Chloe was gone."

The story Cam told me about bringing his mom rings from the dentist takes on a deeper meaning now. He spent his childhood desperately striving to make his mom happy. I know the feeling all too well.

"Why birds?" he asks, clearly ready to move past his revelation.

I laugh, and my heart lifts just a little. "My dad was terrified of birds. Like, would walk out of his way to avoid them. It made trips to the beach and zoo quite interesting." I peer at him from beneath my lashes. "When he died…" I pause when his fingers dance down the back of my arm. "Three birds circled above for the entire funeral service. One bird shit directly on his grave, like a giant metaphor for the day."

"Seriously?" His brow—the one with the scar—raises, along with the corners of his lips.

I nod, finding it impossible to hold back a full-on smile. The memory is too precious.

"All right, boo." Millie claps, knowing full well if I start to talk about my dad whilst drinking, I'll be on the fast track to ruining our night. "What are we singing? Our usual?"

Ezra perks up and plants his forearms on the table. "Oh, there's a usual?"

"Hell yeah!" She pulls out a tube of lipstick, a stunning Taylor Swift red.

"How often do you do karaoke?" he asks.

Millie shrugs. "With Joey? Maybe once a month."

Cam arches a brow, probably wondering where in the city this takes place. FrenchSHEs puts on karaoke once a week, but I accidentally became a once-a-month regular not long after I moved to the city. The energy the crowd puts out is addictive.

The best kind of karaoke night is the kind that leaves a person dabbing a cocktail napkin between their boobs the moment they jump off the stage.

Ezra tilts his head and eyes me, then turns back to my cousin. "And by yourself?"

"Oh, all the time, honey." She winks.

"She's a pro," I add.

"So the usual?" Millie finishes applying her lipstick and drops it back into her clutch.

"I think I'm going to skip this one," I sigh. No amount of alcohol could get me on that stage in front of Cam. He's seen me naked, but right this minute, this feels a lot more vulnerable.

She pouts. "But who's going to be the Danny to my Sandra Dee?"

"I'll—"

"Fine!" she huffs, cutting Ezra off. "I'll just have to go with the next best thing."

"And what's that?" He keeps inching closer to my cousin.

"Prepare to have the *time of your life*," she croons. And with that, she's out of her seat and gliding toward the emcee, shoulders back and flowy skirt swaying.

"Please don't tell me she's doing the song from *Dirty Dancing*," he says to no one in particular.

"Nope. Just you wait." I beam.

If karaoke were an Olympic sport, Millie would be dripping in gold.

Minutes later, with her Pilates-toned midsection on full display, she's got the entire bar convinced she's Meryl Streep in *Mamma Mia*.

Then we've all got our hands in the air as we shout along with her to the last refrain.

On the verge of floating off the stage, she waggles her index finger at Ezra. "I told you! The crowd-pleaser always wins." She flops into her seat and blots at the sweat beading at her hairline with a napkin.

There's a sensuous flame burning in his eyes when he watches her. "It was an exceptional performance, although it would have been better if you had an actual tambourine rather than the tiara you ripped off that poor bachelorette's head."

"I did her a favor." She waves him off and brings a glass of water to her lips. "Like you'd do better."

"Oh shit." Cam brings his fist to his mouth and bites down on his knuckles.

"What?" I spin to face him. "What's happening?"

"You'll see," is all he offers.

"Up next," the emcee calls, feedback screaming from the mic. "From *Dancing* Queen to *The* Queen. Give it up for Ezra from New York City!"

He stands, his man bun bouncing, and straightens his broad shoulders. "Watch and learn how it's really done, *honey*."

The crowd is frozen in wonder as the iconic opening strains of Freddie Mercury and David Bowie's "Under Pressure" blast from the speakers.

Millie flinches in her seat and her mouth falls open. But she quickly crosses her arms and sucks in her cheeks. She's doing everything she can to keep a smile from spreading across her face.

As if rehearsed, the audience screams *"Let me out!"*

But not my cousin. For the entire performance, her brows are drawn together. She's going to need Botox to smooth out the creases between them. I wave a hand in front of her face, but her expression doesn't falter.

After the roar of the crowd dies down, Ezra drops beside her and leans back in his chair with a grin.

I sit silently, watching them, waiting for the bomb she's about to drop.

But it's Ezra who speaks first. "See, I told you," he gloats, tucking stray hairs behind his ears.

Without a word, she jerks to her feet and storms out of the bar, and a second later, Ezra is hot on her heels.

"I should probably go after her," I say, rising from my seat and snatching my clutch from the tabletop. The two things Millie hates most in the world are being wrong and being upstaged. It's going to take a while to calm her down.

Cam grasps my forearm. "Stay." While his fingers are strong, his eyes are gentle and contemplative and filled with a curious longing.

Chapter 17
Cameron

Joey shudders beneath my fingers when I clasp her arm, her eyes full of a somber curiosity. The two of us are connected, frozen, and while the noise level of the bar rivals that of New York City on any Saturday night, I hear only the beat of my heart.

"I need to leave." She tugs her arm back, but the move is half-hearted.

"I'll go with you," I say as I rise from my chair.

She doesn't object when I follow her out of the bar. The cool island breeze is refreshing against my skin, but in Joey's tiny dress, it's got to be downright chilly. God, that fucking dress. The champagne color complements her golden skin perfectly, but it's the plunging neckline that has a choke hold on me. No, wait. I change my mind. It's the way the dress hugs her ass. And her hair? It's already in a ponytail, and it's so long I bet I could wrap it around my fist a few times.

Fuck, I need to pull myself together.

On the sidewalk outside the resort bar, she peers over her shoulder and gives me a once-over, her eyes twinkling, and lets out a throaty laugh.

"What?"

"You may need to adjust your pants, darling," she drawls, turning and pointedly staring at my crotch.

Stopping short before I bump into her, I peer down, but nothing is externally obvious. "*Ha ha.* You caught me." I shrug.

"Caught you what?"

She's playing dumb, but I'll indulge her. "Checking you out." I give her body another long, luxurious perusal and pause at her plush lips for a couple of breaths before locking in on her eyes.

Satisfaction purses her lips, and she shakes her head. "What—" she begins. "How—How are we even back here? Together."

My heart flips at the way she says "together."

"I don't know, but don't you think it's a sign?"

"A sign?" She scoffs and takes a step toward me. "Do you really believe in signs?"

"I don't know." I scratch at my jaw and scan the quiet space around us, easing my way closer to her. "But I think this is too wild to be a coincidence. Don't you?"

Of their own accord, our fingers lazily lock together between us, but only for a heartbeat before she withdraws and steps to the side, making room for a family coming down on the path.

With a groan, she tips her head back and surveys the night sky. "I don't know what I think. Or what the hell the universe is trying to do. What I do know, though, is that one year ago, you made it perfectly clear that hooking up with me was a huge mistake."

"I—"

She holds up a hand, and I snap my mouth shut. If only that hand were holding mine again.

"You were an asshole to me, remember? Am I just supposed to forget and climb onto your lap again?" She pulls her bottom lip between her teeth and scrutinizes me, her brow furrowed.

With a long sigh, I let my shoulders drop. "You're right," I begin. "I was an asshole. I never should have said what we did was a mistake." I run my fingers through my hair. "It didn't take me long to realize that I said those things to protect myself. Finding out Hayden cheated on me fucked with me. But holding on to the memory of you—of us, our night—for the past year and knowing I'd never see you again fucked with me even more."

She steps closer, her heels clicking on the concrete. Her eyes are glowing beneath the moonlight, her mouth parted with anticipation. And for the first time tonight, I catch a handful of hope.

For a moment, I'm confident she's going to kiss me. Fuck. Lord knows I want her to, but not here.

"Can I show you something?" I ask, shoving my hands in my pockets to prevent myself from reaching out for her. "Please."

She watches me, her dark eyes a mix between curious and wary.

"Okay," she says, her voice just above a whisper.

With a hand on her lower back, I lead her down the path. A few slap-happy teenagers nearly bump into us, causing me to step in so close I get a whiff of Joey's perfume. I swipe my keycard to unlock my office and hold out an arm, silently signaling her to walk inside ahead of me.

The shared office space isn't much to look at. Four desks set up in two pairs, all with laptops and matching ergonomic chairs. I make my way to my mostly clutter-free station near the back of the room. Joey follows, and when I stop, she props a hip on the edge of the desk next to me.

Besides a few pens and a stack of sticky notes, the only other item on display is an 8x10 photo in a frame. With a deep breath in, I pick it up and pass it to her.

She gasps. "When—"

"I didn't know it was you when I took it," I say, watching her expression go from confusion to shock to a little awe as she absorbs the image in the frame. It's a photo of her, reckless in midair, pure, unadulterated joy plastered on her face, right before she plunged into the sea.

"But why—" She lifts her head and meets my gaze, blinking.

When she turns her full attention on me like this, it's like a hit to the solar plexus. It knocks the air from my lungs. "Why did I frame it?"

She nods, dipping her chin to examine the photo again. The reminiscent smile that forms on her lips grows the longer she studies it. Thank fuck the image elicits happiness rather than bringing up bad memories of a shitty time in her life.

I take the frame from her and set it back where it's been sitting for the month since I arrived, then prop myself up against the desk, mirroring her. "It's the image that urged me to pursue photography full time. It's the image I submitted to apply for this job."

"It is?" Joey fiddles with the gold rings on her fingers.

One small shift in her direction and we'd be touching. Just being this close to her ignites a low flame of desire inside me. "Do you remember when you told me not to live my life for others? To do what makes me happy?" I ask.

She nods again, rolling her bottom lip with her teeth. Without thinking, I press my thumb against the plump flesh, releasing it. She lets out a barely audible sigh, and when she doesn't pull back, I drag the pad of my thumb down her chin, then her throat, along her clavicle to the top of her shoulder. I take a moment to relish the smoothness of her skin, then drop my hand, but only so I can grasp hers and intertwine our fingers.

"You saved me from my boring life. As soon as I got back to New York, I quit my job."

"You did?" Her voice breaks with a surprised sort of charm.

"I did." I let out a husky laugh. "I've busted my ass for the last year, but I've never looked back. A couple of months ago, Ezra encouraged me to reach out to this resort and see if they were hiring for the summer. It was this picture," I point to the frame, "that I submitted along with my resume. You got me this job. So no, I don't know how it's possible that we're both here but—"

She presses her lips to mine, cutting me off, and loops her arms around my neck.

With one arm around her waist, I drag her to stand between my legs.

Pulling back just a little, she tips her chin and scans my face, searching my eyes, but a second later, she's diving back in. Our kiss is urgent and exploratory, like we're making up for lost time. In a way, I suppose we are.

I bend to kiss the hollow at the base of her throat, eliciting the kind of moan I've dreamed about for months. It sends blood rushing straight to my dick. She trails her fingers up and down my arms while I caress the smooth bare skin at the small of her back and work my way up to capture her lips again.

With a hum, she buries her face in the crook of my neck, her eyelashes fluttering against my skin. She's got her arms draped around me like a necklace, so I use the opportunity to pull her even closer.

"Tell me you've thought about me," I whisper, my heart drumming rapidly.

She rakes her fingers through the hair at my nape, sending a warm shiver through me. "I have," she says into my skin.

"You've what?" I lean back for a better view. I need to hear her say it.

"I've thought about you," she admits, loosening her hold on me just a little.

My shoulders relax, and I let out a long exhale. I cup her face with both hands so I can soak in all her lovely features. The face that's overpowered my dreams for the past year.

Her laughter breaks the silence, and she rests her palms on my chest. "I can't believe you framed my picture."

"I can't believe I found you again."

Chapter 18
Josefine

His words reverberate in my brain.

I can't believe I found you again.

Neither can I.

The emotions coursing through me are like waves, buffeting me one after another with so much force they threaten to drown me if I don't act on them.

Fuck it.

The urgency to take Cam, to take what I once had and claim it as mine, is all-consuming. The validity of his statement, coupled with the flames of desire blazing in his eyes, draws me in like a moth to a flame. I'm so captivated I don't know where to start.

Throwing all caution to the wind, I plunge for his lips. As if he can read my thoughts, he's ready, mouth open and eager for me. Our teeth clash, but it only takes a moment to find a rhythm, giving and taking, sharing the air between us. With Cam still leaning against the desk, I sink into him, allowing him to support my weight. The growing bulge beneath his shorts only spurs me on and sends a bolt of electricity straight to my core. With my mouth still fused to his, I work the button on his shorts blindly, though I slow our pace, matching it to the speed at which I delicately palm his hardness over his underwear.

He lets out a groan against my lips and throws his head back, giving me the perfect opportunity to sear a path down his throat. I nip and suck, then pause at his Adam's apple, relishing the way it bobs when he swallows.

He grips my hand over his fully hard cock, signaling me to continue. Pulling back, I give him a wicked grin.

I've been with other men since our one-night stand, but none of them has come close to pleasing me like Cam.

Though I don't want to break our connection, I release my hold on him so I can ease myself to the floor, but just as I bend to my knees, the office door clicks open. Cam jumps up fast, taking refuge in his chair behind his desk. I push myself back against the wall, panting. Two employees step into the room, deep in conversation. They don't notice us at first, which gives me a moment to gather myself. I feel like a teenager getting caught in the act. Before either employee can even acknowledge us, I hightail it out of the office and into the cool night air.

What was I thinking? My heart pounds against my ribcage and my legs wobble. I've spent no more than a couple of hours with that man, and I nearly let my hormones take over again. Though I'm shaking, I quicken my pace, my head down and my stomach rolling, and speed walk toward my hotel room, where I pray my cousin is waiting.

Instead, I turn a corner and run smack into what feels like a brick wall.

"Oh, I'm so sor—" the brick wall says. "Joey?"

"Ezra?" Saying his name sends a wave of embarrassment rushing over me. God, I sounded like an idiot calling him Isaiah earlier. "Sorry, I didn't see you."

I take in the large man in front of me. His shirt is wrinkled, and the buttons are done up wrong. "What happened to your shirt?"

He glances down, and when he looks back up, a mix of trepidation and challenge swims in his eyes.

"Where's Millie?"

He looks over his shoulder, then turns back to me. "She, uh—"

Before he can form a coherent sentence, his accomplice slips out from behind a door labeled *Staff Only*, her messy bun looking even messier.

"Amelia Greer!" I stumble forward and shake my head.

"What?" She tries to play it off with a shrug, but her eyes are the size of saucers. "I'm on vacation."

Millie, with her skin flushed—most definitely not from the Mediterranean sun—saunters over to me just as Cam catches up.

"Joey, there you—" He halts when he sees Millie and Ezra and the state of their disheveled clothing. "What's going on?" he asks.

I don't have time for this. I cross my arms in front of me, ready to bolt. I almost let myself get involved with him all over again.

He thinks it's a sign that we've found each other again, and here, of all places.

Even if I believed in signs, I swore off relationships. For most of my life, I've watched my mom get wrapped up in one man after another, only to be dumped faster than a contestant on *The Bachelor*. And because I'm my mother's daughter, I followed suit, putting all my eggs in a man's basket, only to find myself cheated on and homeless. Nope. Nope. And more nope.

I had a moment of weakness, that's all. But I'm good now.

Not bothering to wait for anyone's response, I spin on my heel, ready to make a hasty exit.

"Wait!" Cam leaps in front of me, blocking my path. "What happened back there? We need to talk."

"I'm good." I step around him, but he blocks me again.

With his thumb and index finger, he lifts my chin, forcing me to look at him, and for a second, I forget how to breathe.

"There you guys are!" Nik, our favorite barista-slash-bartender strides over. "Mr. Connelly!" He grabs Cam around the neck. "*Éla!* Come."

"That's okay, I'm going to call it a night," I say, holding up a hand.

"*Po po,*" Nik replies. "Nonsense!" He grasps my wrist and tugs me toward the bar, with everyone else following close behind. "The night is just beginning."

I have no idea what's happening, but I obey the instructions, nonetheless, and before I know it, he's set a platter of shot glasses and a carafe of clear liquid on the table in front of us.

"Oh no," I groan, slumping into one of the chairs.

We were introduced to this Cretan tradition in the taverna earlier today. Raki, also known as lion's milk, is an alcoholic drink made of twice-distilled grapes. According to our server, it's supplied at nearly every meal for basically every occasion and is a symbol of friendship and nobility. And according to Google, it's forty to fifty percent alcohol.

Nik slides a shot glass my way and smiles. "I promise you will like this one. We add local honey."

I'm not so sure I believe him, but my Google search also told me that turning down the drink can be considered rude, so I slap a smile to my face and raise my glass along with everyone else.

"*Yamas!*" We shout the Greek equivalent of *Cheers!* then throw back our shots.

"Woo!" I huff, dabbing the corner of my lips.

"Well?" Nik raises his brows, his eyes bright.

"Not bad," I admit. "The honey really takes the sting away."

"Bravo." He smiles wide. "Stay. I bring you rose-infused raki this time. And orange cake!"

I could leave now, and I probably should. But I can't walk out on a Greek man who's bringing me cake. Instead, though I know I'll regret it in the morning, I pour myself another shot of lion's milk.

Chapter 19
Josefine

My body's best efforts to remain in slumber are no match for the rays of the sun streaming in through our window. Millie's obsessed with her blackout shades in the city, so a brightly lit room is the last thing I expect when I finally crack one eye open. Damn. I slam it shut again. My mouth is as dry as the Sahara Desert, and as I lift my head to reposition myself, a bolt of pain shoots down my neck. When I settle again, my nose rubs up against something hard. Maybe my phone? Did I forget to plug it in last night? I use my fingers to walk my hand toward the object, but I'm met with the corded veins of a forearm instead.

What the—

I blink my eyes open, though my left lid is glued shut, so it takes a moment for it to cooperate.

"Good morning, gorgeous," a dreamy voice croons.

That's it. I'm definitely dreaming. Why else would I be lying next to *him*? Maybe if I doze off again, I'll wake up later and find myself in my own hotel room.

I bury my face in my pillow, refusing to peek at my surroundings, but the feel of the bed dipping next to me proves I'm not dreaming.

Motherfucker. *Not again.*

Keeping my eyes closed, I run through the events of last night.

Pictures with Millie.

Karaoke.

Kissing Cam in his office.

Running out of his office.

Bumping into Millie and Ezra. (I'll revisit that one later.)

Nik.

The raki. *Damn that Grecian elixir.*

If I'm in his bed, that must mean...

I bolt upright and throw off the covers, slapping my palms to my chest and abdomen. Okay, not naked. That's good. Only I'm not in my own clothes. I pull at the soft black fabric clinging to my damp skin. I pat my thighs. No pants, but I'm still wearing underwear. That's good too.

"You okay?" Cam taps my knee.

Am I? I rub my eyes and lick my lips, trying to reactivate my salivary glands. What the hell does my face look like right now? I need to find the bathroom.

I tumble out of bed, nearly dragging the duvet with me. The abrupt movement sends pain slicing through my head.

He calls my name, but I ignore him and make a beeline for the bathroom. Once I'm safely hidden in the tiled room, I throw the lock and step up to the mirror over the sink.

I look surprisingly *not repulsive.* Huh. Though the red-rimmed eyes and smudged mascara aren't exactly a good look. I moisten a washcloth under the faucet, then gently wash my face.

From there, I do something I'm not proud of. I borrow Cam's toothbrush. Once I've brushed the grime from my teeth, I run my fingers through my hair, then toss back two full glasses of water from the tap. Feeling fifty percent more refreshed, I investigate *downstairs*, rubbing a hand along the apex of my thighs. While there are no obvious signs of funny business, one can never be too sure.

Next, I pee, then rub a little soap under my armpits. I'm examining myself in the mirror again when Cam knocks on the door.

"Joey? Are you okay?"

Stomach roiling—from the raki, yes, but also because I freaking woke up in his bed—I open the door.

The sight before me makes my knees wobble. I throw my hands out to steady myself on the doorjamb and focus on breathing. Damn. He's dressed in nothing but a pair of athletic shorts that sit low on his hips. His bare chest is toned, and he's got that damn V that points right to his—

My mouth is the opposite of dry now.

"Hmm?" is all I can muster up, though I do steady myself enough to take a step back. Standing so close to this man when he's half-naked is nothing but dangerous.

His eyes glow behind his glasses. This is a sight I never thought I'd see again. And it's one I should not be seeing right now. He props his elbow against the doorframe and rests his head against his hand. The move makes his tattooed bicep flex in a way that makes my core clench and my blood heat.

"Here." He holds out his palm. "Thought you could use some ibuprofen."

"Thank you." I force a grin. When the tips of my fingers brush against his palm, a memory of those calloused hands gliding across my body in the dark assaults me, followed by another. This time it's an image of him pinching and tugging on my nipples. The next is a flash of him cupping my ass and holding me tight against his body.

I throw back the pills and snatch the bottle of water he's also holding so I can wash them—and my memories—down.

Brushing past him, I fumble for words. "Umm." How the hell do I even phrase this question? If I flat-out ask if we hooked up, will it make me look like a slut? Will he be offended if I can't remember having sex with him? Holy crap. I should grab my stuff and go. But where is my stuff?

I scan the room but come up empty.

Without a word, Cam shuffles to the closet and pulls my dress out.

"Oh, thanks," I say when I grab the hanger. "I, um..." *Just ask.* "Did we, um..." I wag a finger between us.

"Did we...?" He scratches at his jaw, his brows raised.

That bastard's going to make me say it, isn't he?

Collecting my hair over one shoulder, I stand tall. "Did we hook up last night?" I gnaw on the inside of my cheek and close my eyes. This vulnerability will eat me alive if he doesn't answer right away.

He takes a step closer. "Call me old-fashioned, but one doesn't have sex with women who are unconscious."

"I was *uncon*—Wait. Did you just quote *The Holiday*?"

The playful smirk that tugs at his lips tugs at my core too. He shrugs. "It's my favorite movie."

"No." I toss my hair behind my shoulder, annoyed by the way he affects me. "It can't be your favorite movie because it's my favorite movie." I dig a thumb into my chest for emphasis.

"You can't call dibs on a favorite movie," he says, crossing his arms, making his pecs flex in the hottest way.

All of a sudden, I'm acutely aware that I'm not wearing a bra. Damn my traitorous nipples. They've been painfully hard since I opened the bathroom door and came face to face with his chest. I cross my arms in front of me, too, the clothes hanger scraping against my skin in the process. "Well, I just did. *The Holiday* is *my* movie. I watch it on Christmas Eve every year, then again on New Year's Eve. Why do you like it so much?" Usually guys go for action movies like *Die Hard* or *Top Gun* or something set in World War II.

He lifts his chin and inspects the ceiling, as if summoning an answer. "I may be sentimental, but there's something about second chances that gets me. The possibility that anything can happen." When he says those last couple of words, he homes in on me, his eyes heated and his expression serious.

The air around us crackles with energy in a way I've never experienced as he holds me hostage with just that look.

That was not the answer I was expecting. I sway on the balls of my feet a bit, and Cam takes a step closer, his toes brushing against mine. He towers over me, giving off major Daddy Jude Law vibes behind those tortoise-shell glasses. God dammit. Is he hiding two adorable little girls with British accents, too, because my ovaries will not be able to take it.

I'm still holding my dress between us like a shield, as if the silky fabric could protect my heart from beating out of my chest.

He takes the dress from my grasp and hangs it on the doorknob behind me. Then, featherlight, he skims his hands down my arms until his thumbs rest on my pulse points. I duck my chin, avoiding the way he's staring into my soul. But there's no hiding the goose bumps he just set off.

"Hey," he rasps. "Look at me."

I can't. I have the sudden desire to flee, but my feet are glued to the floor.

"Joey." He tries again, squeezing my wrists.

I try not to inspect his happy trail on my way up, but it's impossible. It's just begging to be appreciated. At least I resist the urge to run my fingers through the dark hair. When I finally look him in the eye, he hits me with a dazzling, devastating smile.

I push away the spark that arcs between us. Far, far away. Fuck, I need fresh air. And coffee. Stat.

"Come get coffee with me," he says, surprising me with his mind-reading abilities. It's not a request.

"I can't get coffee in this." I tug at the hem of the shirt that hits me mid-thigh. "Or that," I say, nodding at the dress I wore last night. If I showed up for coffee wearing that, every person I passed would gawk and make assumptions about how my night went.

"Then I'll walk you to your room and wait for you to change." Again, his words are not a request. "What's your room number?" he asks, tugging a T-shirt over his head. He looks at himself in the mirror, then swipes a hat off the counter.

Fuck. Me. He puts the damn thing on backward.

"Yup, okay, let's go!" I say, my heart rate spiking instantly at the sight. If I stay in this room—with this man; with that hat; with this bed; with no pants—we're going to have a major problem.

I pluck my dress from the chair, then spin for the hotel door. Cam's standing beside it, cradling my shoes and clutch. I take them from him and search for my phone and room key.

"Dammit, my phone's dead. Millie's probably so worried."

"Nah, I texted her," he says, sliding his feet into a pair of leather sandals.

My spine goes ramrod straight. "You texted her? How do you have her number?"

"She added it to my contacts when she gave me yours last night." He saunters to the door and holds it open with a warm smile.

I suck in a breath as I pass him, trying hard as hell not to make any contact whatsoever.

This is a walk of shame if I ever saw one. Cam, looking way too effervescent and put together, even without a morning shave, next to me, barefoot and clothed in a man's shirt.

"What room?" he asks again.

"Umm, 6206."

"What?" he asks, catching the toe of his sandal on the carpet and stumbling.

"What?" I side-eye him.

For a second, I swear a flicker of disbelief, or maybe amazement, crosses his face.

"Nothing." With that, he picks up his pace a little and leads the way to the elevators.

Thankfully, we don't pass a soul as we stroll to the end of the hall. I place my card against the sensor on the door, ignoring the *Do Not Disturb* sign hanging on the handle, and push my way into my room.

Chapter 20
Cameron

I'M CURSING those two *malakas* (a Greek expletive I learned from my boss) for interrupting Joey and me in my office yesterday. Everything went downhill after that. I finally had her alone, and I was convinced she was settling into our reunion. At least that's what her body was telling me when she claimed my lips. And when she had her hand on my cock while she bent those knees like she was going to drop to the floor in front of me.

We're here. Together. In some wild twist of fate. So I've pushed away the questions and chosen to accept it as the gift it is. Joey's back, and I'm not willing to let her go. How can I go about my life not seeing her or speaking to her when I know she's here on the island?

This morning, I'm keeping my movements slow and tempering my words. The woman is in flight mode, and the last thing I want to do is send her running. The metaphorical running shoes are already on her bare feet. She's just one Lululemon outfit away from making her great escape.

I need to tread lightly, not come on too strong. But fuck if I don't want to drag her back to my room and confess how I've been carrying a piece of her everywhere I go for the past year. For months, I beat myself up for how I left things between us, for the way I dismissed our hookup as a mistake. I was worrying out loud, processing my thoughts and emotions and speaking before I had them sorted. Never have I ever had sex like that until her. Like my life could be better than I've ever imagined.

"Millie?" Joey calls out, setting her phone and bag on the narrow table in the foyer.

"Holy shit!" she gasps as she rounds the corner. "What the fu—" She spins and collides with my chest. There's no mistaking the owner of the bare ass on display over her shoulder. Ezra's notorious *Your Name* tattoo is *right there*. The words—yes, *Your Name*—are printed in goddamn Comic Sans on one cheek. He got this particular tattoo one drunken night the summer after he graduated from high school. Why? According to him, so that he can tell women "I got your name tattooed on my ass."

My best friend is face down on the mattress. Beside him is a second lump, this one fully covered in the white sheet.

Still pressed to my chest, Joey shakes so hard her movements vibrate through me.

"Are you—" I take a step back and examine her face. "Are you laughing?"

She slaps a hand over her mouth, in the process dropping her dress to the floor between us, the hanger clattering against the tile.

"What the hell is happening right now?" She snorts, her eyes filled with tears of laughter.

Unable to stop myself from laughing right along with her, I smother a fucking giggle as I collect her dress from the floor and lay it over the back of a chair.

When Ezra lets out a groan and rolls onto his back, I slide a hand over Joey's eyes and shout, "Dude!"

I don't need her seeing my friend's massive dong.

He sits up in bed like he's not conscious enough to process that he's got an audience, but knowing him, it's more likely that he just doesn't care.

"Hey!" Joey bats at my hand and sucks in a sharp breath when she's met with the sight of his—

"Whoa, Millie!" She gallops to the other side of the bed and practically climbs onto her cousin's lap.

Millie's bare shoulders peep out from under the sheets as they bow their heads and whisper.

Trying like hell to avert my gaze from my stark-naked friend, I snatch a pillow from the floor and toss it at him. I have to take a quick step back to keep from stepping on a bright pink vibrator on the floor.

"Hey, man," he says, swinging his legs over the side of the bed. "What's up?" Thank fuck he's casually got the pillow tucked under one forearm so it covers his junk.

"Anyone care to explain what's going on?" Joey asks, wearing a wicked smile.

"Yeah." I stand a little straighter and cross my arms over my chest. "Let's address the elephant in the room."

"Which one?" Joey sends herself into another fit of giggles.

I roll my eyes at her innuendo, and Ezra reaches across the bed to give her a high five.

"All right, out, boys!" Joey announces, bouncing a little on the bed next to Millie, whose fair hair is wild and tangled.

"What about coffee?" I pout, my heart sinking.

"Raincheck?" She gives me the world's cutest puppy-dog eyes. "Millie and I have *lots* to catch up on." She boops her cousin's nose, her expression morphing to a mischievous one again.

"Sure," I sigh, tamping down my disappointment. I don't want to pressure her and scare her off, so we'll play this her way. I pull out my phone and check my work schedule. I'm not on the clock until six tonight. "I'll text you."

She nods and shoots me a smile. "Sounds good. Sorry."

"Dude, what the hell was that?"

When the server brings us two steaming cups of coffee, I can't help but wonder how Joey takes hers—if she even drinks coffee.

Ezra brings his mug to his lips and takes a slow sip. "You saw. Not much to explain." He shrugs. "Unless, of course, it's been so long you need a lesson," he teases.

He can be a real pain in my ass when he's being elusive.

"What about you and Joey?" he asks, spinning the arrow to me.

My heart rate speeds up at that phrase. *You and Joey.* Like we're a thing. "What about us?"

He cocks a brow that screams *I'm not taking your shit.*

"Fine." I set my coffee down and take a deep breath. Talking this out might be exactly what I need, and who better to do that with than my closest friend?

"Nothing happened. She was drunk, so I brought her back to my room so I could make sure she was safe. That's all."

She would have been safe in her room, too, but when I offered to keep an eye on her, Millie winked and said that was an excellent idea. At the time I thought she was doing me a favor, but after what we walked in on this morning, I'm rethinking that assumption.

"She woke up disoriented but recovered quickly. She wanted to run back to her room to change. Then," I stretch my arm to the side, "we find your ugly ass—*literally*—this morning. We were supposed to get coffee together and talk, but she bailed on me."

For the Plot

"I can't believe she's here. That's like some psycho-fate shit," Ezra says, snagging a croissant off the plate our server set between us. He watches me, obviously waiting for me to spill more details.

"Tell me about it." I take a sip of my Americano, relishing the way the warm liquid coats my throat. "I just feel this pull toward her, you know?" I flex my fingers around my mug.

Whether or not Ezra understands, he gives me a nod of encouragement.

"A year ago, I was planning a life with Hayden. Then, in an instant, that blew up in my face. But when the smoke cleared, this drop-dead-gorgeous girl was splayed out before me, and I haven't been the same since." Damn, it feels good to get that off my chest.

Joey burrowed her way under my skin, and I'm not ready to tweeze her out.

"What are you going to do?"

I pull the hat off my head and run my fingers through my hair. "Charm the fuck out of her."

Ezra gives me a nod and digs into his breakfast. He refuses to kiss and tell about his night, so I let it go. He says he's planning on a solo hike today. Whether it's to clear his head or for my benefit, I don't really know, but I'll take the opportunity to try to connect with Joey regardless.

During a break in conversation, I pull out my phone and shoot her a text.

ME
Hey, it's Cam. How are you feeling?

Her response is almost immediate.

JOEY
The meds kicked in. Thank you 😌

> ME
> My pleasure. Can I see you later?

I hold my breath when *Joey is typing...* appears at the top of our WhatsApp chat, trying to convince myself not to get my hopes up.

> JOEY
> Want to go to the beach?

THIRTY MINUTES LATER, we're slipping into a taxi together. I can't help the grin that splits my face at the memory of the first time I was in a taxi with this woman. Beside me, Joey's biting back her own smile and her eyes are dancing. Yeah, I'm pretty sure she's thinking about the minor car accident and the sex worker too.

"Which beach should we head to?" I ask.

While the hotel has a private strip of beach, Joey insisted we get off the resort and explore a different part of the coast. She turns to the driver. "What do you suggest?"

He names a beach, then winks in the rearview mirror.

Joey catches the exchange and leans in close. "What?"

"Nothing." I try my best to hide my grin. "It's a great beach."

When the driver pulls off the road, I hand him a wad of cash, then snag her beach bag and help her out of the car. She doesn't put up a fight, and when she's standing beside me, she dips her head, but not before I catch the smile beneath the brim of her sun hat.

We make our way down a small hill, dodging short, spiky bushes that have probably been here since biblical times. Joey stumbles a bit and instinctively grabs my forearm, and she doesn't let go again until we reach the stable bottom.

"There are so many rocks," she observes. Rocks of different heights—from one foot to over six feet—hug the shore.

"It's perfect for privacy," I tell her. I haven't been here before, but I've heard about it from some of my coworkers.

"Privacy? What do you—" We clear one of the larger boulders, and the beach area comes into view. "Oh." She stops in her tracks when she spies a pair of nude beachgoers. "Is this a—"

"Nude beach?" I finish. "Yeah." I chuckle under my breath.

"You knew, didn't you?" She swats at my chest and scans the shore, her eyes wide and her lips parted.

Damn, she's cute. I can't help but watch her take in her surroundings.

She throws her head back and laughs. Thank god she's not pissed. "That's what that silent conversation with the cab driver was about, huh?"

Going with his suggestion was a gamble, but so far, it's a win.

I usher her to a small alcove. It's still early, so only a handful of people have set up for the day. Joey drops her bag in the sand. I follow suit and lay out my towel as well, then remove my shirt. When she shimmies out of her blue-and-white striped cover-up and pulls at the strings of her black bikini, my lungs seize.

"When in Greece, yeah?"

Is she really going to ditch her clothes? And do I want her to? I mean, hell yeah, of course I do. But do I want her naked in front of strangers? A surge of possessiveness rises in me, making my blood heat in my veins. *She's mine.* Only, she's not. Not yet at least, but that'll change soon if I have anything to say about it.

The Greek gods certainly gifted us the perfect beach day. Unlike the murky waters on the East Coast of the US, the sea is a brilliant blue so clear the bottom is visible even far from the shore. The horizon is dotted with white sails and kayaks and paddle boards.

It's taking all my willpower not to ogle Joey, because in this moment, it occurs to me that I've never really *seen* her body. A year ago, even when she was naked and in my arms, the room was dark. And that next morning, she made quick work of getting dressed, so all I got was a peek at the smooth skin beneath her cover-up. But now, with the Mediterranean sun acting as her personal spotlight, I have a front-row seat to the most beautiful show in all the world.

And fuck if it's not an entrancing show. She squirts a dollop of sunscreen into her palm, then rubs her hands together. Fuck. Me. Now. Because the next thing I know, she's got her hands on her breasts and she's massaging the milky lotion into them.

I cannot sport a hard-on at a nude beach. I'd be a total cliché. With a groan, I pull my hat over my face.

"What?" she giggles. "I can't have burnt tits. That's not a good look."

Sliding my hat to one side, I peer around it but keep my attention trained on her face. "I love barbecue. I'll gladly pour a little sauce over and devour them for dinner."

"*Gross!*" She snickers.

I can't help but join her. Oh, how I love that sound.

Without overthinking it, I tug my swim trunks off.

"Are you going to do something about..." She motions to my lower half.

"If you're suggesting I rub a white substance over my dick in public, you're delusional." I throw my hat at her and blast her with my best shit-eating grin before walking backward to the beach.

"Where are you going?" she asks, still rubbing lotion onto her golden skin.

I pause when my feet hit the water. "For a swim." I can't sit here and not touch her a minute longer. "You coming?" Without waiting for her response, I turn and wade into the sea.

Though she's still behind me, I can feel the burn of her attention on my skin, and fuck if it doesn't make me walk a little taller.

Like what you see?
Come and get me.

The water is still a little chilly from the snow melting off the mountains this spring, but I welcome the initial bite as I lunge forward. Lord knows I need to cool off.

A moment later, Joey is beside me in the water. She purses her lips, making me want to lick the saltiness off them, then tips back until she's floating, perfectly peaked nipples bobbing above the water. I float next to her, and water laps at my face as I watch her search the sky.

She must feel me gazing because she lifts her head to look at me.

"Are we going to discuss what's going on here?" I ask.

"What do you mean?" She doesn't look my way.

I let out a huff in response. She's going to make this difficult, I can tell.

Dropping my legs, I face her full-on, but with a grin, she spins and swims for the shore.

"Hey!" With a deep breath, I duck below the water and follow her.

Halfway back to the beach, she stands on the sandy bottom, her shoulders barely above the water, and spins back to me. "Listen..."

How I'm going to listen with her tits practically floating in my face, I don't know. But I'll try.

"Distraction is the last thing I need right now. I know you believe we've been put on this island for a second chance or whatever, but to me, it's nothing but a massive coincidence, all right?"

Her words are resolute, but the furrow between her brows contradicts the declaration.

I nod, placating her for now.

"Clearly, we have major chemistry, and I'm on vacation, so..." She sucks in air. "So, I think we should have sex."

Damn. Normally women are not so forthcoming, but I can't say I mind it. And neither does my dick.

"I'm here for five more days." She shrugs. "If you're down, I think we could have a lot of fun. But," she adds, "we leave it all on the island."

I choke on my saliva. "Excuse me?"

"You heard me. What happens here stays here. We're not bringing whatever this is," she waggles a finger between us, "back to New York. I don't want any strings. Are you in or not?"

Am I in? God, I want to be all the way in with this woman. But not just physically. She's already in my soul. It's wild, I know, and I can't explain it. I want all the strings, but for now, I'll take anything she's willing to give me.

"Okay." I keep my voice neutral, calm. "If we're going to do this, is there anything else I should know?" I ask.

She licks her lips and surveys the horizon for a moment. When she looks at me again, her dark eyes are molten. "Yeah." She squares her shoulders and lifts her chin. "I have a major praise kink. And I like to be thrown around, but I also like to be in charge. That cool with you?"

Fuck. Her words hit me like a punch to the gut.

Without waiting for my response, she turns and heads for the shore. When her body comes into view, her dark hair is plastered to her back and her bare hips sway.

Is this my dream woman?

Well, shit. There's no way I can get out of the water now.

Chapter 21
Josefine

CAM DOESN'T FOLLOW me out right away, but he keeps his attention fixed on me while I dry off in our private little alcove. If the way he's blinking so rapidly is any indication, then the wheels in his head are spinning as fast as mine.

Did I really just proposition him for sex? I feel like Natalie Portman in *Friends With Benefits*. Or is that with Mila Kunis? Who's the one in *No Strings Attached*? I always get the two movies mixed up. Anyway. Not only did I proposition him for sex, but I dispensed my top kinks like bubblegum from a machine.

For a heartbeat or two as I made my way back to the beach, I thought my pounding heart might beat right out of my chest, but I shook off the sensation. I refuse to cower.

Women should feel empowered in the bedroom, not ashamed. And life's too short to have terrible sex. While there is nothing wrong with the vanilla variety, I'm more of a rocky road with rainbow sprinkles kind of gal.

I didn't intend to embrace my brazen side in the middle of the Mediterranean, but I can't resist our chemistry. Call EMS, because I nearly died whilst floating nude next to the man. And a man he is. The way the muscles of his legs flexed as he sauntered into the ocean should be illegal. And those dips in the sides of his glutes? I'd lap milk out of them like a kitten if he'd let me.

After we walked in on Millie and Ezra this morning, she and I had a little heart-to-heart. My cousin, who's normally an open book, kept the door closed on the scene that unfolded last night.

But if there's one thing Millie is good at, it's helping me see through my bullshit. She pointed out that this thing between Cam and me doesn't need to be a big deal. Therefore, I'll embrace the joke the universe is playing on me, put on my casual overalls (metaphorically speaking), and get some good dick out of it. But I refuse to fall in love like Natalie or Mila. In the end, he will not be my Ashton or my Justin.

This is strictly physical. No feelings involved.

Easy.

Following my breakup last year, I swore off relationships. In retrospect, I can see how I was following a pattern my mother had modeled for years. When I needed a place to live, I let Tyler dangle shiny things in my face. (And I'm not talking about his Prince Albert.) Offering a desperate eighteen-year-old an apartment steps away from the Pacific Ocean? That was a major red flag, though I wasn't old enough or wise enough to see it then. From where I'm standing now, I'm not even sure he loved me. Maybe he liked the companionship, the sex, the convenience, but he never valued me the way I deserved.

I'm long overdue for a therapy session. This I know to be true. But I refuse to be like my mother and permanently rely on a man.

Aside from ending a toxic relationship, moving to New York City has been the wisest decision I've ever made. But dang, has it been an arduous adjustment. Thank fuck for my cousin. While Millie has declined my numerous offers to pay rent, she did agree to let me take care of groceries and cooking. Shout out to cooking tutorials on social media, or else our diet would consist of smoothies, grilled cheese, and Hot Pockets.

For a split second, I'm hit with an image of cooking for Cam and the kind of reactions I could elicit from him. But I quickly suppress that picture. Nope. Stuff that image right down the garbage disposal I wish our NYC apartment had. I shall not be cooking for any man anytime soon, thank you very much.

Cam, now sliding his shorts up his thick thighs, grins at the sound of my stomach rumbling and picks up his phone to call a cab. Thank fuck. After my mini declaration in the water, it's been next to impossible to keep my hormones in check, and I can't blame the sea water for dampening the towel beneath me.

"So, you survived your first nude beach experience. What did you think?" Cameron's body is tucked in close behind me in the resort's revolving doors. The salt from our skin feels like sandpaper when his bare arm brushes the back of mine.

"Honestly?" I giggle. "I kind of loved it. No tan lines."

"I'll have to inspect later to be sure," he growls in my ear.

"Speaking of later," I begin, hiking my bag up higher on my shoulder when we've stepped into the lobby, "I'm going to take a shower and then..." I trail off. How does one say 'and then come over for some sex'?

"Why don't you shower in my room?" he suggests, his eyes ablaze with anticipation.

The idea is intriguing. Showering in his room would be more efficient. And when was the last time I showered with a man? It's been so long I can't remember. While he didn't precisely propose we shower together, the heat in his expression makes it pretty damn clear he wouldn't object.

"Let me shoot Millie a text." I pull my phone from my bag, absolutely not relishing the way Cam steps closer and the warmth radiating from him.

ME
Hey boo. Back from the beach. What are you doing?

MILLIE
About to take a nap. Do you need in the room?

ME
Nope. That's perfect. I was going to shower with Cam's

*at Cam's

MILLIE
I think you were right the first time <winking face>

ME
😏

Maybe...

MILLIE
Have fun and make good choices

ME
I'm always good...

MILLIE
I'll let Cameron decide that 😉

ME
Enjoy your nap love u

MILLIE
Enjoy your 🍆👀

Love you too boo

"All good?" Cam asks when I slip my phone back into my bag.

It isn't until that moment that I realize I've blindly followed him to his room. Like daydreaming while driving. One moment, I was in the lobby, and in the next, I'm standing outside his room, without any recollection of the journey.

"All good."

Joey-o

Stupid grin-1

"Bath or shower?" He eases my bag from my shoulder and sets it on the table next to his. I slip out of my flip-flops by the door, leaving behind a dusting of sand on the tile.

As much as I'd love a bath, I think I'll save it for after. "Shower." I saunter to the bathroom, ditching my linen cover-up in the process, and peek over my shoulder. "You coming?"

Wearing a devilish smirk, Cam strides across the room like he may burst if he has to wait one more minute and pins me against the counter from behind. My hip bones sting at the abrupt contact.

Cocking a brow, I shoot him a challenging look in the mirror. *What's your next move?*

With his arms wrapped around my torso, caging mine at my sides, he pulls me in tight, and I grind my ass against his growing erection.

"Fuck. See what you do to me, baby?" he breathes against my neck, sending goose bumps dancing down my arms. Slowly, so damn slowly, he pulls at the strings on one side of my bikini bottoms, just enough to loosen them. "When these come off, what am I going to find?"

My cheeks heat, and warmth unfurls low in my belly as he sucks at the spot where my neck and shoulder meet. Damn. How does he know exactly how to turn me on? My knees buckle, giving away just how incredible that small action makes me feel.

"Oh, you like when I kiss you here?"

With a moan, I reach behind his neck and pull his head closer. Sand collects in my fingernails when I dig into his scalp.

"You didn't answer my question," he whispers, kissing behind my ear. He's two for two when it comes to my erogenous zones. I feel like Monica Gellar in *Friends*. I can hardly wait for him to get to number seven.

"What was the question?" This man makes me dizzy.

"I said," he tugs on the other side of my bikini bottoms, leaving the fabric suspended between our bodies and the counter. "What am I going to find between these legs, sweetheart?"

Sweetheart? The word pings around in my brain like a bouncy ball for a minute before I decide I like it.

"This," I pant, tearing at the fabric and tossing it to the floor. Once I'm bare, I grasp his hand and guide it between my legs.

"Just as I suspected." He smirks over my shoulder, cupping my pussy. With his eyes locked on my core in the mirror, he runs a finger through my slit. "Fucking soaked."

God, how I've missed his filthy mouth.

"Now be my good girl and bend over for me," he growls.

Damn. I love to take control in the bedroom, but a guy who knows what he wants is hot as hell.

Resting my forearms on the counter, I fold in half, leaving my bottom eager and defenseless.

Ghosting his palms down my back and to my ass, he asks, "You like it rough?" He heard me at the beach, but he's asking for consent, nonetheless. Another total turn-on.

The second I lift my chin in approval, he pulls back and smacks my ass with a satisfying *whack*. An instant later, he caresses the tender flesh and squeezes. Then he smacks it again. God damn, the contrast is arousing. I'm writhing with need already, so turned on it takes a moment to realize he's stopped and he's now on his knees on the hard tile behind me.

"What are you doing?" I startle, my heart leaping in my chest. "I need to shower. I'm all salty."

Before I can stand up and pull away, he grasps my cheeks and spreads them like he's reading his favorite novel. "A little salt is good for my health."

A shiver sprints along my spine. Never have I ever been in this arrangement. It's maddening and so fucking hot. I widen my stance in anticipation.

Reaching between my legs from behind, he collects my arousal and rubs at my swollen clit. I buck my hips, but he stills them, pressing his fingertips into my skin. At the first swipe of his tongue, I'm transcended. The juxtaposition of *hell yes, I'm so glad we're doing this* and *oh shit, I'll never recover* sends a contradictory blast of heat through me.

The sound of Cam devouring me is obscene. The rhythm at which he's fondling my clit and plundering my pussy with his tongue makes me dizzy.

In a matter of moments, I'm perched on the edge of ecstasy. I'm only a couple of flicks away from rocketing into the abyss. But when I push against Cam for relief, he stills.

What the fuck?

He keeps a firm grip on my hip, but he backs away, and in his place, a rush of cool air greets me.

Oh no, I will not be edged right now.

"Cameron, *please*." I'm not above begging. The heat licking up my insides is like magma, ready to erupt.

"I'll tell you when you can come. Right now, I wanna revel in this pretty little pussy." He spreads my lips, his thumbs framing and teasing my entrance.

"Please," I attempt again, my breath shallow and strained.

He plunges two fingers inside me and drags them out with expert intention, then pushes back in—again and again.

"Yes!" I'm panting like an animal in heat; his touch is intoxicating. I'm hanging by a thread, my pussy clenching around his fingers.

When he replaces his fingers with his tongue and tenderly taps my clit with a single finger, I lose it. I come, crying out his name like a prayer.

With delicate kisses planted against my ass, Cam grounds me. And as my heart rate begins to even out, he rises and curls against me like a question mark, his chin resting on the top of my head. His mouth is coated in a layer of my arousal so thick it's visible in his reflection, yet he doesn't make a move to wipe it away.

"That was..." I force my breath steady, but I'm shivering through the aftershocks of my orgasm.

In one quick movement, Cam whips me around to face him and pulls me flush against him. Only when we're face to face does he swipe at his mouth. Then, with a tenderness so at odds with the way he just manhandled me, he drops his lips to mine.

The remnants of my release passed back and forth on our tongues fan the flames still burning inside me, but eventually, I find the strength to tear my mouth from his so I can extricate myself from my bikini top. Without breaking eye contact, I loosen the knot at my neck, then along the center of my back, keeping my eyes locked on Cam's the whole time. When the fabric tumbles to the tile, he drags a hand down his face and groans.

"Like what you see?" I quirk one brow.

Cupping my breasts, he bows his head and takes my nipple between his teeth. Fuck. The way he tugs sends bolts of desire shooting straight to my core.

"Shower. Now," I order.

When he pulls back, I drag him by the waistband of his swim trunks across the bathroom, then release them with a snap.

He shucks out of the shorts and follows me into the stall. The initial chill from the rainfall showerhead startles me, and I jolt back, but he's there to catch me, steadying me around my waist. His hardness juts against my lower back, and an ache beneath my ribs cries out with need.

A need for more.

Pivoting to face him, I rest my hands on his broad shoulders and tip my chin up to soak him in. The water cascades between and around us, and as it heats, steam billows, fogging the glass enclosure. His eyes, hooded and hungry, pause at my lips before trailing down my body, drinking me in.

"Do you know how gorgeous you are?"

Besides Millie and the gals at FrenchSHEs, no one has complimented me in such a blatant, heartfelt way in a long time. Come to think of it, I can't remember a man ever calling me gorgeous. It was always "hot" or "sexy." Occasionally "beautiful." Don't get me wrong, every one of those adjectives is flattering, but being referred to as *gorgeous* feels a thousand times more gratifying.

Chapter 22
Cameron

I CAN STILL FEEL the weight of Joey's wet hair when I worked shampoo into it. The suds rode down her bare skin, some disappearing with urgency and others sliding in slow motion, as if, like me, they were enjoying every second they caressed her silky skin.

She was wide-eyed when I looped my arms through hers and pulled her off her knees. Embarrassed, even. As much as I've been dreaming about those long, slender fingers and that smart mouth wrapped around my cock, all I wanted was to worship her.

Her voice has haunted me for months, and her words today will haunt me for the rest of my life. *I think we should have sex*, followed by *I have a major praise kink. And I like to be thrown around, but I also like to be in charge.* The way she asked if those things were cool with me like she was suggesting we split a sandwich at Subway left me shaken.

I'm determined to make the most of every encounter with her. I'll squeeze and scrunch each one till there's nothing left to wring from them.

But damn, am I spent. Joey absolutely paid me back for edging her against the bathroom countertop. She teased me, dragging her tongue along my shaft, only to pull back when she reached the head. And the way she told me I could come down her throat if I wanted? Shit, I almost called the paramedics, certain I was having a cardiac episode.

She had dinner plans with Millie, so I begrudgingly let her go. I walked her to the door and kissed her on the forehead. So subtly I'm not sure she realized she was doing it, she leaned into me and sighed. I nearly wrapped my arms around her waist and threw her back onto the bed. But she came to Greece to spend time with her cousin and replace memories from her disastrous trip from last year with new, happier ones. The last thing I want is to stand in the way, but fuck if I don't wish I could have her all to myself.

Chapter 23
Josefine

I KICK my cousin beneath the table. "Put your phone away."

"Sorry." She types furiously for a few seconds, then places her phone face down on the tablecloth.

"Who are you texting, anyway?" I ask, peering over my menu at her. "Ezra?"

"Nope. Not him." She straightens her shoulders and picks up her menu without another word.

"What excursion did you sign us up for? And will it just be the two of us, or are we going with a group?"

The resort's Asian fusion restaurant was a must tonight. Though I love Greek food, we agreed we could use a break from olive oil and tomatoes. Our server sets a pear Moscow mule in front of each of us, then takes our order. Millie chooses a teriyaki salmon dish, and I catch her peeking at her phone while I order two shrimp tempura rolls. The restaurant is covered, but three sides of the space are open, allowing the cool night air in. The orange textiles complement the white and Grecian blue outfits many of the vacationers here are dressed in.

"It's a monastery hike," she says once the server steps away.

"With caves and a small gorge. It's just us," she clarifies. "The hotel said we didn't need a tour guide."

"How long is the hike? What do I need to bring?"

When we were kids, my dad took Millie, Asher, and me hiking regularly, but there's not a lot of opportunity for hiking in New York City, unless walking along the Hudson River counts, so it will be fun to do it again.

"Um." She picks up her phone and uses a finger to scroll. "It says here that it takes about an hour to hike down to Katholiko Bay. The ladies at the front desk said to wear closed-toe shoes and a bathing suit because the water is surrounded by rocks and there isn't an accessible place to change."

"All right, I can handle that." I take a sip of my mule and relish the bite of the ginger beer. "What time do you want to leave?"

Turns out we'll have to be up far too early for what's supposed to be vacation. Millie swears it'll be worth it, especially if we beat the heat and the other tourists.

"I guess we better make it an early night if you're going to force me to get up at an ungodly hour."

Cam is working this evening, but that doesn't stop me from shifting in my seat and searching for him on the path outside the restaurant. The sun is at its picture-perfect peak, so I assume he's busy, but the urge to text him hits me hard. I really didn't want to leave him this afternoon, but I didn't come here to do nothing but have sex. I want to explore and enjoy the island the way my dad would have wanted.

"Whatcha looking at?" Millie asks, draining the last of her cocktail.

"Hmm?" I bring my glass to my lips and follow suit.

"Don't *hmm* me. You're looking for him, aren't you?"

Slipping my fingers beneath the elastic of my tube top

romper, I wiggle it just a little higher over my breasts. "I don't know what you're talking about."

"You like him," she says, placing her elbows on the table and resting her chin on her fists.

Leaning back in my chair, I fold and unfold the cloth napkin in my lap. "Sure. He's hot as sin."

"That's not what I mean," she says, angling in closer. "It's okay to like him."

"It's just sex," I murmur, careful to keep my voice low.

"It doesn't have to be." She sits up straight again and clears her throat. "I know your ex screwed you over, but Cam isn't anything like that fuckboy."

"You're right," I sigh. "But still—"

Millie puts her hand up between us. "I'm not done," she says. "Between Tyler and your mom's history with men, I don't blame you for having your guard up, babe. But..."

"But what?" I ask, lowering my gaze to the table and stirring the ice in my glass.

"I see the way he looks at you."

That gets my attention. It's my turn to prop my elbows on the table. "How does he look at me?"

"Like you've changed his life."

After a delectable dinner and no sign of Cam, we snag a couple of bananas and apples from the lobby to snack on in the morning, then head back to our hotel room. We left the windows open, and as we enter, the white drapes billow in the breeze.

In tandem, we remove our makeup and brush our teeth. When I'm finished and in my pajamas, I settle under the sheets, set my alarm, and plug my phone into its charger beside me.

For the Plot

Then I set two backup alarms that'll go off in ten-minute increments, just in case, and flip off the light over my nightstand.

Alone in the quiet, dim room, I can't help but let my mind wander to our conversation at dinner. Millie thinks Cam looks at me like I've changed his life? Doubtful. I'm pretty badass, but not that badass.

"It's okay to like him," she said. And I do like him. But do I *like* like him?

What we have is just sex. That's all it can be.

And damn, was it fantastic sex. Just the thought makes my blood heat and my pussy pulse. Refusing to overthink it, I grab my phone off the nightstand and prop myself up against the headboard. With my cousin still in the bathroom, I tug the front of my negligee—coincidentally, it's the "cover-up" I wore the night we met—until just a peek of areola is visible through the lace trim. I wrap my right arm around my torso and lift. One strap falls off my shoulder in the process, but I don't fix it. With my free hand, I swipe open my camera app and angle it so my face is hidden (rule number one of taking nudes: never show your face) then snap a few shots. Sinking lower again, I examine each one and then open my text thread with Cam.

ME

How were your photoshoots tonight? Anything like this?

When there's no immediate reply, I switch to my Kindle app. The world may be scary and weird and overwhelming at times, but I sure do love living in an age where I have access to books on my phone.

I'm two chapters into Hannah Bonam-Young's latest release when Millie crawls into bed, bringing with her a wave of orange blossom. I must remember to snag the travel toiletries from the bathroom before we leave. They're heavenly.

171

"What's wrong, boo?"

She knows me too well.

I'm about to shrug off the question when a text notification appears at the top of my screen. I tap the banner, and my thread with Cam opens.

"Let me see," Millie squeals.

I tilt the screen away, but she shuffles closer and twists my wrist so she can get a better look. Nosy bitch.

"Don't you dare," she scolds playfully when I try to pull away.

> CAM
> My dirty girl. I knew it was lingerie

He remembers what I wore a year ago.

> ME
> 😏

> CAM
> Come over

> ME
> Can't 😔 Waking up early for a hike with Millie

> CAM
> I want you in my bed tomorrow

> ME
> So demanding. What happened to saying please?

> CAM
> I will not be the one begging, Josefine

> ME
> And I will?

For the Plot

> CAM
> Yes. While you're gagging on my cock

I completely forgot Millie was wedged against me until she gasps and throws her hand in the air in triumph.

"Jesus!" I yelp. "You scared me."

But she just laughs.

I nudge her with my elbow. "Go sleep on your side of the bed."

"Not a chance," she says. "This is just getting good."

"Mills," I plead.

"Fine." With a *humph*, she scoots over and switches off the light.

When I turn back to my screen, I'm met with a picture of Cam.

Holy. Fuck.

I tap to enlarge it. He has one hand inside his black boxer briefs. It's obvious he's hard and that he's gripping his girth. The waistband of his underwear is slightly pushed down his abdomen, revealing a light smattering of hair.

> CAM
> That's what you do to me, baby

Baby.

> ME
> You're distracting me. I need to go to bed

> CAM
> Fine. But I *will* see you tomorrow, gorgeous

Gorgeous.

ME
Yes, sir

CAM
Fuuuck

The notification at the top of the screen signals that he's typing, but I need to end this conversation if I plan on getting adequate rest, so I send a quick *good night* with a kiss emoji, then silence my notifications.

As I settle into the mattress, all sorts of thoughts bubble to the surface. Does he really think some bigger power is at play here? I don't believe in stuff like that, do I?

My mom is Christian and my dad is Jewish, so I grew up eclectically religious. My parents would cherry-pick holidays. Sometimes we'd get dressed up and go to church for my mom, and sometimes we'd go to synagogue for my dad. But after he died, it was hard to believe an entity like God really existed. How could such a powerful being take away a person I loved so much?

In Jewish tradition, when a person dies, their loved ones sit shiva—a weeklong mourning period following their burial. It's meant to be a time for mourners to come together for spiritual and emotional healing. At ten, I didn't understand the meaning behind it but relished the weeklong sleepover with my cousins. I didn't understand why mirrors had to be covered with cloth or why candles were constantly burning, but I appreciated the delicious spread of tuna, kugel, brisket, and bagels with cream cheese and lox from my dad's favorite delicatessen.

People loved to pat me on the head and say things like "your dad was such a good man" and "he's in a better place now" and "everything happens for a reason." Even now, I hate that last phrase. There should be a law against uttering those words to a person who's just lost a loved one.

For a long time, I was convinced God took my dad from me to

punish me for some unknown sin. It took years of therapy to understand that wasn't the case and that his death didn't serve a bigger purpose.

When it comes down to it, bad things happen to good people all the time. Searching for a reason won't change the facts. *It's what we do next that matters most.*

That all leads back to my question about Cam and me. Is this happening for a reason? Is it fate? Destiny? Or is this just life?

I sit up straight when my alarm goes off, cursing myself for not choosing a gentler tone for such an early morning. Snagging my phone off the nightstand, I paw at the illuminated screen to silence the cursed thing and catch sight of the time. Shit. It's 6:25 already. I unlock the screen and discover that I set the first alarm for six fifteen *p.m.* Because of course I did.

"Ugh, Millie, we overslept. It's time to get up."

When she doesn't even groan in protest, I swat at her, only to hit the cold sheets where she should still be snoozing.

What the heck? If she's already up, why didn't she wake me?

With a huff, I roll out of bed and open the drapes, then make my way to the bathroom. It's also empty.

"Millie?" I shuffle back to the bed to grab my phone so I can call her, and that's when I notice the folded piece of paper on the nightstand.

Went for a run. Meet you at the front desk – xo, M

A run before a hike? She loves her fancy Pilates classes, but this is a little overboard.

Sitting on the patio with a coffee in hand, I open my text thread with Cam. My traitorous facial muscles contort into a goofy grin the second our exchange appears. Damn, I wish I'd gone to his room last night. I'm only on this island for a few more days. I want to soak up as much of him as I can, because when we get back to the other island—Manhattan—there will be no more soaking. I made that perfectly clear.

Getting cheated on fucked me up, and I refuse to go down that path again. The path where I lose a part of myself in a guy. I need to focus on my career, and I cannot have any distractions.

Our driver is meeting us out front at seven, so I quickly drain my coffee and get ready for the day. I scarf down a banana and toss an apple into my foldable nylon backpack.

Slathered in sunscreen and with my hair thrown up in a messy bun, I head downstairs and swipe a complimentary bottle of water from the lobby, then scan the open space. *Where the hell is she?*

I've got both thumbs poised over the screen of my phone when a puff of warm air hits my neck and a familiar voice rumbles in my ear. "I couldn't sleep at all last night. You fucking tease."

Cam's stubble tickles my cheek, sending goose bumps down my arms and a shiver down my spine. I spin, and when he comes into view, decked out in a backward hat and fitted white tee, my phone slides out of my hand and clatters to the floor.

He bends to pick it up, deliberately dragging his fingertips along the outside of my bare leg on the way up.

"What are you doing here?" I survey the lobby, but besides the concierge, we're the only people here this early. On the other side of the glass doors, a black car pulls up to the curb and idles. "Where's Millie?"

"About that." Cam adjusts his backpack on his shoulders. "I'm taking her place."

"What?" I take a step back and whirl in a circle. "Where is she?"

"Let's walk and talk. Our ride is here." He motions to the

door with his chin, and while I'm utterly confused about this little switcheroo, I let him press a hand to the small of my back and guide me to the car.

We settle in the back seat, and after the driver confirms our destination, we turn toward each other, knocking knees in the process.

"Well? Explain to me why you're here and Millie is not," I demand, tugging at the hem of my white tank.

"Because I asked her to trade places with me."

I rub at my forehead and search his face for answers.

"Joey," he exhales, tucking a loose strand of hair behind my ear. "You said this thing, whatever it is, between us—"

"Sex."

"Okay, sex." He lets out a beleaguered sigh. "It can only last this week, right?" He frowns, then goes on. "As far as I'm concerned," he caresses the inside of my thigh, right below my cutoffs, "it's not enough time. So I asked Millie if I could steal you for the day. She mentioned you were going on a hike, so we switched places."

"You Parent Trapped me?" I gasp.

"Sorta," he laughs.

"Why didn't you say anything last night or just ask to tag along?"

He drops his chin and cocks one brow.

Yeah. He and I both know I would have objected.

"Are you mad?" His voice is low, almost hesitant. "I can ask the driver to turn the car around if you don't want me to come."

Damn, this man is thoughtful, even if he's a little conniving. And he's gorgeous, even at seven a.m. His sturdy jaw is tight and his eyes are pleading. He toys with the fray of my shorts, peeking up just a little while he waits for my response.

I trace the top of his hand. "No. I'm not mad."

I'm sure my cousin is perfectly fine, but I text her anyway.

ME

Are you Annie or Hallie in this scheme of yours?

MILLIE

You know I'm Meredith. You've seen Daddy Nick Parker 🫠

"Did you put on sunscreen?" Cam asks.

Our driver takes a switchback up the mountain too quickly, and I'm launched into Cam's side. Instinctively, I grasp for purchase and find it when I dig my fingers into his thigh. With a grunt, I pull back like it's scorched me.

"You can touch me, you know."

"I know," I mumble. "And yes, I put on sunscreen."

He grasps my hand and sets it back on his thigh. "I like it when you touch me."

A surge of warmth flows through my veins, so I lean in, bringing my lips to his earlobe. "Where do you like me touching you?" I capture his lobe in my teeth and tug for emphasis.

He groans when I pull away. "Don't fucking start what you can't finish, Josefine."

"Who says I won't finish?" I wink.

Adjusting his shorts, he clears his throat. "It looks like we're here."

The taxi comes to a stop next to a brick wall in an empty dirt lot.

"Are we sure this is the right place?" I ask.

"*Nai*," the driver says, the Greek word for *yes*, which trips me up every time.

Cam grabs my bag and climbs out, and I follow. Once we've paid the driver, we drop several coins into the donation box, then follow the paved path.

We pass the Gouverneto Monastery, and a broad man,

presumably a Greek Orthodox monk, walks past as we peep through the open door.

"Want to go inside now or after the hike?" I ask.

"After," he decides, clasping my hand and pulling me down the path until we're met with a rickety wooden gate.

He holds it open for me, and when he lets it go, it slams shut with a sharp clatter. "Oops," he chuckles.

The world is so quiet this morning. The only sound is the gravel crunching beneath our shoes. When the path at the top of the mountain opens to a clearing, we're met with an expansive view of the Sea of Crete. The magnificence of the scenery pulls all the air from my lungs.

"Wow," we gasp in unison.

I dig my phone out of my pocket and spin so I can take a selfie with the sea as a backdrop.

"Here," Cam says, holding out his hand. "Let me."

I hand it over. He is the professional, after all. He swings an arm around my shoulder and snaps a selfie of the two of us. Our smiles are wide, and the water is unbelievably blue behind us.

"After you?" He motions toward the path.

"I'd say you're a gentleman, but you just want to stare at my ass, don't you?"

"I'm not even going to try to deny it," he says with a devastating grin.

A few beats later, the gravelly path morphs into slick, wide stones. Cam grabs my elbow occasionally to steady me as we go. Nature's barbed wire, these short, thorny bushes, are the only things stopping us from going over the side of the mountain. We remain quiet in our descent, taking in the harmonizing symphony of goats, bees, and cicadas.

After about ten minutes of doing my best to avoid a sprained ankle, we arrive at the Arkoudospilio Cave, or Bear Cave, named for the huge stalagmite that resembles a bear bent over a well, and Cam finally breaks the silence.

"Some say this cave was used to worship Artemis and Apollo." With a grin, he steps inside. "Watch out for goat poop."

I follow closely, using my phone's light to take in my surroundings, then follow him back to the trail, where wind-bent trees keep us company, alongside the Cretan goats (a.k.a. *kri kri*) that scale the mountains.

Now that the sun is rising higher in the sky, Cam pivots his ball cap so the brim shields his eyes. Beads of sweat collect at his temples. While my back is warm from the friction of my backpack, the rest of my body is comfortable.

That is, until he speaks next. Just the tone of his voice is enough to stoke the low flame that's been burning inside me since I saw him in the lobby this morning. "Can I ask you a question?"

The path is wide enough now that we can safely walk side by side. "Mm-hmm," I reply.

He side-eyes me. "What's your book about?"

Ah, the question every writer loves as much as they hate it. While I'm flattered when people show interest in my craft and passion, there's no possible way to formulate a coherent summary and keep it under three minutes. I once spent two hours spilling my brains out to Brooks when he asked what I was writing, diving into the backstories of my backstories in fear that he'd think my idea was unappealing. So with all that in mind, I give Cam the most condensed version.

"It's fiction." I take a deep breath in, willing my heart to steady. It's always daunting baring my soul like this. "Wait." I stop dead in my tracks and frown. "How did you know I'm writing a book?"

"You mentioned it last year and Millie may or may not have sent me your Instagram," he admits with a wide smile. Damn, his teeth are so white he could be in a Crest commercial.

For the Plot

    I curse my cousin under my breath. Of course she did. I step away from him so I can focus on the path rather than him while I explain. "It's a coming-of-age novel about a girl. A *woman*," I correct, "who was raised by a mother who's addicted to painkillers and how she struggles to find her way in life."

    Cam is silent, studying the ancient steps beneath us. When I don't offer more of an explanation, he speaks up. "And does she?"

    "Does she what?"

    "Does the woman find her way in life?"

    "I don't know." I bite my bottom lip. "I haven't gotten that far."

Chapter 24

Cameron

Joey's eyes practically bugged out of her head when I told her I'd looked her up on Instagram, so I didn't mention how far I scrolled back or how long I spent studying each of her images. She probably would have thrown me off this cliff if she knew. Jealousy bubbled up inside me, hot and ugly, when I scrolled back far enough to see that her grid still included pictures of her with her ex from more than a year ago.

The most recent image was one she took at the nude beach yesterday. I had to zoom in to be certain, but sure enough, my bare back was in the frame, sticking out from the water. If I hadn't been there, I wouldn't have known it was me. The caption, *Not a bad view,* made me smile.

Joey made a comment about her mom last year, so when she explained the premise of her book, it was easy to assume that it was at least partially based on her experience.

As we journey down the ancient stairs, blanketed with shade from the mountain, she's got her lips pressed together and her brow furrowed in concentration. In this moment, I want nothing more than to be the person she leans on while she finds her way.

For the Plot

"Do you have siblings?"

"Nope," she huffs, reaching for my hand at the same time I hold it out to help her navigate around a giant rock. Nobody warned us this hike was so treacherous.

"No siblings. It was always just my mom, my dad, and me." A delicate grin slips out.

"The Three Musketeers."

"There you go quoting *The Holiday* again." Her eyes crinkle at the sides.

"What was your dad like?" I keep my tone light, going for nonchalant, but I ask anyway.

She purses her lips and ducks her head, likely unused to being asked about him. Just as she lifts her head and opens her mouth (probably to tell me to fuck off), we turn a corner and are met by the Katholiko Monastery, a church carved into a rock and nestled alongside a breathtaking bridge built of orangey-red bricks.

"This is one of the oldest monasteries in Crete."

"You're like a walking encyclopedia, aren't you?" she teases.

With a laugh, I lean into the spiel, hoping I don't sound too much like a dull history teacher. "This monastery is from the eleventh century, but six centuries later, the monks abandoned it due to frequent pirate attacks."

"Stop it before I feel like I have to pay you for this kind of knowledge." She nudges me with her shoulder.

Oh honey, I can think of several ways you could pay me.

Together, with our sneakers firmly planted on the ground and my hand secured around Joey's waist, we peer over the edge of the bridge. Per my quick Google search this morning, there was once a river below. Now, though, a collection of olive trees grows.

"How do we get down there?" She backs up and spins in a circle, scanning our surroundings.

"Over here," I call out when I spot two small red and white dashes painted on a rock, signaling the trail.

I descend the rocky path first. Though it turns out to be pretty stable, I pivot to help Joey anyway. Because of her shorter legs, she has to face the rocks and scale down like she's descending a ladder at one point. Her foot slips, and I instinctively reach out to guide her. As I do, I end up palming the back pocket of her cutoff jeans.

"Cameron," she reprimands, her tone full of mirth.

"Yes, Josefine?" I feign innocence.

"You can take your hand off my ass now."

"I think I should make sure you get down safely first." I give her bum a good squeeze. "It's the gentlemanly thing to do."

She snorts. "I'd hate to disrupt the patriarchy, Mr. Connelly."

She gets a smack to the ass for that one.

Once we're on flatter ground, she eyes me up and down over the top of her water bottle, chest heaving from exertion. "How are you in such good shape?"

"Excuse me?"

"How are you in such good—" She groans when she sees the smirk I'm sporting. "You heard me, you jerk." Water dribbles down her chin when she can't contain her wide grin behind her bottle.

I do work hard to stay in shape, but more than that, working out does wonders for my mental health. "I hit the gym most days, and Ezra and I play basketball when we can." I shrug. "What about you?"

"What about me?" She tilts her head to the side and leans back against a boulder.

"You're gonna make me say it, aren't you?"

Playing her little game, I stalk up to her and drag a hand from the top of her shoulder to her wrist. Dipping low so my mouth is at her ear, I cup her ass and squeeze. "How do you keep this ass so fucking tight?" I croon.

Without missing a beat, she sings right back. "By fucking hot guys like you."

I'm hit with a burst of pride, but it's immediately followed by an urge to possess her. "There's only one hot guy, Joey," I growl. "And that's me. Got it?"

The spark that arcs between us any time we're close is so damn electric it can't be ignored. There's no way she doesn't feel it, too, especially with the way she presses her breasts against me.

The tingling sensation in my stomach that appears in her proximity intensifies when she pulls back and licks her lips.

Bold and seductive, she brushes her fingers down my arm. "Yes, sir."

Heart lodging in my throat, I grasp her hand and hold it close; I would permanently glue it to my chest if I could.

"You drive me fucking crazy, Josefine," I say into the pulsing hollow at the base of her throat.

I drag my lips along her jaw and ghost them over her lips, teasing her for a moment before sinking into them.

She tugs on my bottom lip with her teeth and releases, then slips her tongue inside my mouth. The heat behind her kiss singes through my veins. I let my water bottle fall to the ground with a *clang* and grasp her waist. Her shirt is damp with sweat and her kisses are salty. With her arms draped around my neck, she devours me, shattering me and putting me back together at the same time. Yet I still demand more.

There's a dizzying current racing between us, but after a moment, Joey breaks the spell and pulls away. I stumble forward, eager to share the same breath with her again.

"You should stay hydrated." With a wink, she bends to pick up my water bottle.

I take it from her and adjust myself with my free hand.

Knowing if we don't move on to other topics I won't be able to keep my hands off her, I take a long pull of my water, then a couple of deep breaths. "What was your dad like?" I try again.

She draws her sunglasses from her backpack and puts them on like she's using them for more than just protection from the sun.

I anticipate a generic description. Something along the lines of "He was kind… had a good job and supported our family…" The stock description for the middle-class father figure.

But with a vulnerability so out of character for the fierce woman I've spent the last couple of days with, she says, "He was the best," choking over the words.

I toss her a microfiber towel from my backpack, and though I thought she could use it to wipe her welling tears, she stubbornly pats at the sweat on her neck and brow before giving in and dabbing at the corners of her eyes.

"He loved surprising me. One day, on the way to school, the radio DJs announced that a local band I loved was doing a meet and greet at a record store nearby that afternoon. I nearly broke my seat belt as I wiggled so spastically in my seat. I wanted to meet them so badly, but I didn't dare ask to skip school, and Dad had a big showing scheduled for that day. But just before the lunch bell rang, I was called to the school office." She tosses my towel back and takes a long swig of water, eyes closed.

I steal those few seconds to study her. The flush in her cheeks, the way her neck elongates when she drinks, the sweat glistening on her chest and disappearing behind her shirt.

She swallows and wipes her lips with the back of her hand. "I thought for sure I was in trouble, although I'd never done anything to warrant a visit with the principal. Kind of like how, as an adult, I'd never even consider transporting heroin—hell, I've never even seen it—yet when I'm at the airport and spot a police K-9, I instinctively pat my pockets *just in case.*" She laughs.

For the Plot

"I do that too," I snicker. "As if today is the day I forgot I'm smuggling drugs up my ass."

"Right?" She slaps a hand on her knee.

For a heartbeat, I can't do anything but stare at her toned thigh. So badly, I want to run a hand up her leg, tease the frayed hem of her... I clear my throat to shake away the fog of lust I can't seem to escape. "So, the principal's office?"

"Right. I get there, and my dad is standing by the front desk. My first thought was that something happened to my mom or my aunt, and I started to panic, but then I really looked at his face, and his enormous grin calmed me. He grabbed my backpack, thanked the people in the office, and led me out the door. He ignored my incessant questions, and it was only when we were in the car that he told me we were headed to the meet and greet. I've never screamed so loud in my life."

The pure joy on Joey's face makes my chest feel tight. Damn, seeing this side of her only makes me want to keep her more.

"What about your mom?" I dare to ask.

All at once, her expression falls. She swallows thickly, then returns her water bottle to her bag, slings the strap over her shoulder, and heads down the trail. "What about her?"

Weighing my words, I hustle to catch up. The last thing I want to do is push her away, so I ask the simplest question I can come up with. "Is she still in California?"

"Yup." She pops the *P* and leaves it at that.

For a long moment, the only sounds are our footsteps on the rocky trail and the mountain goats in the distance.

I'm having an internal debate about how to get our day back on track when Joey lets out a long breath.

"Okay, fine." She says it like she's admitting defeat. "I was ten when my dad died. I think I told you that."

I nod, even though I'm behind her.

"For a whole year my mom handled things okay. I only saw her cry twice—the day he died and at the funeral."

She goes quiet again, but I let her work through her thoughts.

"That's so weird, right?" she finally says, her attention focused on the trail ahead of her. "I cried every freaking day for months. Anyway," she continues, tightening the elastic in her hair, "a year later, on the anniversary of his death, some switch inside her flipped. A light went off. Hell, all the lights went out that day."

Joey's somber mood, her flat tone of voice, and her expression are in stark contrast to the lightness and joy that radiated from her when she spoke about her father only moments ago. Where a smile once flourished, it now has withered.

I squirm with the earnest need to reach out and touch her.

"For a whole year, she fooled me and everyone we knew—probably even herself—into thinking she was okay. She got me to school on time and went to work like she always had. She didn't hang out with friends like she had in the past, but she started going to the gym a lot. On the anniversary of his death, though…" She wipes her mouth with the back of her wrist and sniffs. "She broke. All of a sudden, she'd spend all day in bed. She'd forget to pick me up from school. Wouldn't eat anything but toast and a banana for days at a time.

"My Aunt Rachel—Millie's mom," she clarifies, "took a couple of weeks off work to take care of us. When she had to return to her own family, she made arrangements with the mom of one of my friends so I'd get to school and back, and she set up a meal train. When the meal train ended a month later and my mom still wasn't better, Aunt Rachel convinced her to check into a psychiatric hospital."

A shudder shakes me to my core as memories bounce in my mind and I gasp.

"Wild, right?"

"It's not that." I drop my head and run a hand up and down the back of my neck. "My mom was *also* in a psychiatric hospital when I was ten."

Joey's sneakers kick up dirt when she halts in front of me. Because my focus is still downcast, I nearly collide with her.

She turns and blinks at me, her mouth agape. "Are you serious?"

"Yes. After Chloe died, my mom was sad all the time. Anyone would be in that situation, but she couldn't get out of her sadness. It's like it was pinning her down, suffocating her. She couldn't eat or get out of bed, let alone care for two young children. After she'd gone a week without uttering a word, my dad took her to the emergency room. The ER doctor referred her to psych, and she was admitted to an inpatient program."

Eyes wide and soft, Joey steps into me and wraps her arms around my waist. I drop my cheek to the top of her head and squeeze her back like I never want to let her go.

"We have a lot more in common than I thought," she says into my chest.

There's an ache in my throat for the both of us. *Does she feel it too?*

A bleating mountain goat interrupts the silence, spurring Joey to extricate herself from my hold. "When do you work today?"

A hollowness forms in my chest at the loss of contact. Desperate to fill that void, even just a little, and prolong the tender moment, I tuck a strand of hair behind her ear and cup her jaw. "I need to edit photos from yesterday before my session tonight. Tonight's group is a big one. A family reunion. Those are always interesting."

"Why's that?" she asks as we continue hobbling over rocks through the gorge.

"Nine out of ten times, the mother and daughter or mother-in-law and daughter-in-law are locked in some kind of showdown because neither wants to give up control. Then there's the sibling who hates wearing white. The kids are usually hungry because their parents wouldn't let them have a snack once they were dressed for photos. Or they come with bribery chocolate, which is a melted nightmare waiting to happen."

"I take it you don't like working with families."

"You'd be correct. I'd much rather work with nature. It doesn't insult or argue."

For the first time since I asked about her mom, she laughs. It's a small one, but I'll take it.

"Not that I don't like kids." Despite my comments, I'm not a total dick.

"No, I get it. Millie's brother Asher has a daughter, and dang if that kid isn't a handful."

Does that mean she doesn't want kids? Not that it's my business. I don't even know if *I* want kids. I've always just thought of it as another step in life. College, a good job, marriage, kids. My parents and Hayden's were always making comments about grandchildren. Like procreating was expected. I didn't even question it. But now...

Over the past year, I've questioned so much. My job. My passion. Where I want to live. Who I want to marry.

"I can hear you thinking." Joey turns, one brow raised. "Care to share with the class?"

I blow out a long breath, considering how to put into words the inner workings of my brain. If only I could just blurt *I want more than just sex. Stay on this island with me. You can write and I can take pictures and we can forget about everything else.*

If I did, she would be out of here in a heartbeat.

Thankfully, I'm saved by the beauty of Crete. Steps ahead is a majestic view. Emerald water glistens, hugged between a collage of silver and copper rocks.

For the Plot

"Holy—" She abandons her words at the spectacle before us. "Have you ever seen anything as beautiful as this?"

Soaking in the wonder in her smile and the reverence in her eyes as she takes in the view, I yearn to scream *Yes, actually, I have.*

"Turn around," I say, pulling my phone from my pocket.

Joey leans against a rock, and I snap a few pictures. She isn't even looking at the camera for most of them because she can't take her eyes off the view.

"Come." I lace my fingers with hers, and we make our way down the rocks. A platform big enough for two is the only thing separating us from the sparkling sea.

She makes haste in stripping down to her bikini. I remove my shirt, hat, and shoes just as quickly. With a snorkel mask I brought along for the occasion looped around her arm, she lowers herself onto the rocks below us. It wasn't easy getting here, but it's absolutely worth it.

"*Shitmotherfucker!*"

"What?" I shout, hurtling myself into the water after her.

Oh, I get it now. Air is sucked from my lungs when the icy water hits my waist. Quickly surveying the rocks below, I pull her under the water with me. When we break the surface, gasping for air, Joey climbs up my body like a koala, desperately trying to escape the chilly water.

"You asshole," she purrs, locking her arms around my neck and her ankles at the base of my spine. She dips in, and for several heartbeats, with the taste of the salty sea on our lips, we get lost in one another. Eventually, we find the strength to pull away and put on our snorkels.

"Do you need a tutorial?" she asks, sliding the strap over her head.

"Huh?"

"Or have you been snorkeling since last year?" She slides the mask over her face, unhooking the hair that gets stuck over her ears.

She remembered.

"I went with a few coworkers last week." I pull my mask down. Once it's in place, I lean in to kiss her, but the goggles clang together and prevent our lips from touching. "But thank you."

A wave of gratitude washes over me when I lower my face below the water. This is the kind of experience most people only ever dream of. For a while, we weave between one another and circle schools of black and silvery-blue fish. When Joey swats at my shoulder, I turn to where she's pointing below us, and sure enough, tucked between two rocks is a fucking octopus. Its dusty-colored tentacles retreat and blend in with the rocks so quickly I question if I truly saw the mystical creature in the first place.

We pop up to the surface and rest the masks on our foreheads.

"Did you see that?" she shouts, treading water a couple of feet away. She's like a five-year-old who's just jumped off a swing and wants to make sure her parent was witness to her antics.

"Sure did." I can't help but grin right back.

"That was so fucking cool." She drops back and spreads her arms wide, her perfect breasts bobbing above the surface.

God, is she gorgeous. All I want to do is watch her every move when she's this carefree. "I'm having the best time."

"Me too," she says up to the brilliant blue sky.

She wraps her legs around my waist again, her breasts pressed against my bare chest.

With an arm around her back, I balance on a rock anchored to the sea floor.

"What's your sister like?"

"Claire's creative like you, though watercolor is her preferred medium. And when she's not slammed at the hospital or painting, she's at spin class."

She tilts her head. "I like spinning too."

"I think you'd get along." I'd introduce them, but since she's adamant about not continuing what we have once she leaves the island, I don't know that I could handle seeing her around if they hit it off.

We stay like that, teasing and splashing and flirting. Flirting turns to kissing, which turns to petting, until we're interrupted by a throaty cough that is definitely not coming from one of the mountain goats. We pull apart and spot a man holding tight to a child near the edge.

"Looks like that's our cue." I grasp Joey's hips and pull her away just a little.

She unwraps her legs from my waist willingly, although not without a little pout. Then we make our way to flatter land.

"Ready to head back?"

With a deep inhale, Joey eyes the steep climb. "Ready as I'll ever be."

Nearly an hour later, at the top of the stone stairs, we pull out our phones and take a few selfies, then survey the glorious horizon one last time in a comfortable silence. My phone finally has service, so I call for a car. By the time we make it back to the monastery, we're too beat to go inside. Feet dragging and shoulders slumped, we head to the parking lot, where the driver is waiting for us.

Chapter 25
Josefine

"Good morning, gorgeous."

"Jesus!" I jump, and my coffee sloshes dangerously close to the rim of my mug. "You scared me." It's been two days since our hike, and my glutes are still sore.

"You look like you were deep in thought." He's fishing for information, but there's no way I'll tell him I was lost in memories of him.

"What are you doing?" I change course.

"Hoping I'd catch you. I missed you in my bed last night," he says as he ghosts circles over my exposed shoulder.

"I will admit, your snoring is much more tolerable than Millie's thrashing about," I chuckle.

"I do not snore." Feigning offense, he tugs on a strand of my loose and unruly hair.

I didn't even brush it before leaving the room—just came straight to the breakfast buffet.

"Look who I found." Ezra strides up to the table, my cousin reluctantly trailing behind him. She's balancing juice and a towering plate of pastries that I hope she plans to share.

For the Plot

"Morning, Ezra. What did you boys get into last night?"

He steals something chocolatey from Millie's plate before she can swat him away. "We went for a night swim with some of the staff and learned how to make raki."

"Only Ezra here did more drinking than learning." Cam smacks his friend's back and barks out a laugh.

Two women passing by gawk openly. One even bobbles her cappuccino. The men together are enough to send anyone stumbling.

"We'll leave you ladies to it," Ezra says, lowering his chin. "Enjoy your breakfast."

Cam bends to press a kiss against my cheek before following his friend outside. I may or may not ogle his ass as he strides away.

"What do you want to do today?" I ask Millie now that we're on our own.

Her response is garbled by the mouthful of sweets she's talking around. "I'm not sure what I'm going to do, but I think *you* should write."

"Write? But I'm on vacation," I protest, picking up the other half of the mystery pastry. It's flaky and sticky and tastes faintly of figs.

She downs the rest of her freshly squeezed orange juice. "Yeah, but look at this place. You can't tell me you don't feel inspired."

"Of course I feel inspired. This has been the best people-watching week of my life." I cackle.

"What's the thing you and Brooks are always saying?" she asks.

My chest expands and warmth unfurls when I think about Brooks and our writing sessions. *"For the plot?"*

"Yeah, that." She waves a hand like Vanna White at the vacationers milling around us. "How much *plottier* is this?"

195

"True." I split a smile. "But 'for the plot' is typically reserved for turning inconvenient moments into positive experiences. Like the subway unexpectedly shutting down or breaking a heel on the sidewalk."

She steals a piece of bacon from my plate. "Why can't it be about whatever the fuck you want it to be about? 'For the plot' could be used to describe any juicy-ass shit, don't you think?"

Huh. She's not wrong.

"Take Cam, for example."

"What about him?" I can't help the shiver running through my veins just thinking about him.

"The two of you together are definitely some juicy-ass shit." She winks.

Yeah, it's juicy, all right.

I roll my lips and school my expression. This is why I love this woman. She helps me see things from other perspectives. Everyone deserves a Millie.

Maybe a day *for the plot* is exactly what I need.

After breakfast, we return to the room, where I pull out my laptop—a first since we arrived on the island.

She changes into a bathing suit and cover-up, then snags my Kindle off the nightstand.

"Don't you dare judge my smutty books or the stickers on my case," I call over my shoulder.

My newest sticker, from a niche romance bookstore in Brooklyn reads *Begging for a Pegging*.

"Oh, we both know you wear them like badges of honor." She cackles on her way out of the suite.

I fluff the blue-and-white striped cushion of one of the

For the Plot

balcony chairs and dust the surface of the wooden table with a towel before placing my laptop on it. The most opulent panoramic view unveils itself from my vantage point. Fronds from flourishing palm trees frame the resort's private beach. Workers scramble below to secure umbrellas in the wind. Sailboats and luxury yachts kiss the horizon while paddle boards and jet skis sprinkle the cerulean coastline.

I snap a panoramic picture of my dreamy office space and text it to Brooks with a message that reads: *For the plot* before remembering it's three a.m. in LA. Oops. When I moved to New York, I was worried our friendship would suffer. While it has changed due to our geographical circumstances, we still communicate regularly and make a point to be available for one another for encouragement and support.

Just as I connect to the hotel's Wi-Fi and set a timer on my phone, there's a knock at the door. I consider ignoring it. Housekeeping has already been here, and Millie should have her key card.

Another knock, louder this time, sounds.

"Coming!" I hustle to the door and throw it open. When I do, my heart leaps in my chest. "Cam," I breathe. "What are you doing here?"

He's dressed in a tight sage green tee and navy blue shorts that hit his thighs a third of the way down. Just how I like them. And that damn backward cap. How the hell am I supposed to be productive now?

As if he can read my thoughts, he holds up a hand. "I ran into Millie, and she mentioned you were going to write."

"Mm-hmm." I take a small step back, hoping that if I can avoid his intoxicating smell, I can keep my hands off him.

He holds up his laptop case and camera bag, his eyes shimmering with hope. "I thought maybe we could share an office space?"

Biting my lip, I step aside.

There's no way I'll get any work done with this perfect specimen of a man in my hotel room. I'm not even going to fight the temptation of his chiseled jaw and perfect stubble. We're just going to have to get it out of the way; clear the space for a productive writing session.

He slips out of his flip-flops and regards me, still clinging to his bags. "I promise I'm not here to distract you." His words are earnest, but his quirked brow says otherwise.

"Right." Grinning, I shake my head. "You are not the least bit distracting." I wave a hand in front of his chest. "Fine. I think we should get this *distraction* out of the way."

"What?" He gently places his bags on the floor.

Orgasms release endorphins and oxytocin. Endorphins and oxytocin are good for cognitive flexibility, therefore... "Orgasms are good for creativity."

In one fluid motion, Cam pushes off the dresser and pulls me by the waist until the backs of my knees hit the edge of the bed. He buries his face in my neck, sending goose bumps skittering down my arms. "I think I remember you saying you like to take control."

He gasps when I grab his arms, spin, and throw him onto the bed.

I straddle his hips. "Think you can handle it?"

Chapter 26
Cameron

I swear this is not why I came.

After breakfast, Ezra and I parted so I could get a little work out of the way. My colleagues were much too loud, so I swiped my belongings and made my way to the resort's main entrance. Millie spotted me along the way and, with a mischievous look, suggested an alternative office.

Did I imagine Joey would be straddling my lap within two minutes of my arrival? Of course, but I swear I wasn't anticipating it. What I told her was true; I figured that since we were both working remotely this morning, we could do it together.

But now, the most beautiful girl on the island is taking the reins, and I'm ready.

I toss my hat onto the floor and lie flat against the mattress. Just as my hips shift upward in greeting, Joey hops off and scurries into the bathroom.

"What the—" I groan and slap my hands against the sheets. I'm ready to haul myself up and chase her down when she returns. She's got her hair pulled up in a messy bun and a belt from one of the complimentary robes in her hands. With her lip caught between her teeth, she glides the white cotton fabric between her fingers, then tugs it tight.

"Do you consent?"

I nod.

"I need to hear you say it."

"Y-yes. I consent." I can't spit it out fast enough. What is this vixen up to? And what did I do to deserve her?

"Undress. *Now*." Her irises are molten and her chest is flushed with desire.

Never have I ever shed my clothes so quickly—not even in college when playing strip poker.

With deft fingers, she drapes the soft sash over my eyes, then secures it with a knot off to the side of my head. While it doesn't block out all the light, if I close my eyes beneath it, I can't see a damn thing.

Without my sight, all my other senses are heightened. The symphony of tourists outside is muffled when she closes the sliding glass door, and the soft padding of bare feet against the tile takes center stage. The room quiets like she's stopped beside the bed, so I drag one arm out over the sheet and find the hem of her sundress. The sight of her cleavage on display in this tiny piece of fabric at breakfast almost did me in. I don't know what she has in store for me, but I better get a taste of those tits today.

I work my fingers beneath the hem until she backs away. The rustling that follows leaves me hopeful that when she returns, she'll be naked. The bed dips, and she straddles my waist. The heat of her has my dick ready for duty in an instant. In the next moment, her arousal is coating me. A shudder runs through my body; not knowing what may happen next is both thrilling and terrifying. Petite hands squeeze on either side of my neck, massaging circles down to my shoulders, then to the tops of my biceps.

"Relax," she breathes into the silence. "I promise I'll take good care of you."

The duvet rustles as she shifts to settle between my legs. I expect her to go straight for my cock, but I should have known better. My toes curl on instinct when she drags her nails up the insides of my legs. She starts at my ankles, then pauses mid-thigh.

With my left hand, I squeeze my shaft, desperate for release. I'm already aching.

Joey grasps my wrist and tugs, forcing me to let go. "Do I have to tie your hands too? Or will you be a good boy and behave?"

No? Yes? I thrash my head from side to side, so out of my mind already I can't think straight.

"Will you? Be my good boy?" She drags the words out.

My mouth is dry and my ears are ringing, but I swallow and nod obediently.

"Oh, sweetheart, I need to hear you. Speak. *Now*," she commands, and I don't think she's talking about Taylor's Version.

This is *Josefine's Fucking Version*.

"Yes," I mumble.

"Yes, what?"

My whole body jerks when she expertly wraps her fingers around my cock. But just as abruptly, she releases it, and I'm left bereft of her touch.

"Yes, I'll be your good boy," I utter with a shaky breath.

Fingers ghost across my chest, phantom touches on my quads, my biceps, my shoulders. I never know where she'll land next. When she plants a kiss along my waistline, my hips jerk again. I draw my heels up to anchor myself and quell this maddening sensation. She doesn't protest. Her only response is to rake her nails into the tops of my trembling thighs and drag them toward my knees. I squeeze against her, and she counteracts by pinning my legs to the bed.

I'm spread out before her, one hundred percent exposed and vulnerable, and I fucking love it.

"You're doing so good, baby." Her voice, laced with sensuality, sends a ripple down my spine.

"Joey." I fist the duvet. Fuck, do I need to touch her.

She drags the tip of her tongue from my navel down to my pubic hair, intentionally avoiding contact with my cock.

"*Fu-u-ck.*" I'm the hardest I've ever been, and she hasn't even touched my dick.

She hovers over me, still careful not to come into contact with me where I need her most. "If you ask nicely, I may just suck your cock," she breathes against my lips. She pulls away quickly when I arch up for a taste.

With my hands still tangled in the duvet, I rasp, "Joey, baby, will you please suck my cock?"

"Thatta boy," she praises. I can practically feel her smile floating in the air between us.

The mattress dips as she gets comfortable between my legs. She caresses my balls, her touch featherlight, and my stomach contracts in response. With her fingers digging into the sides of my glutes, she sucks the head of my cock, expertly lifting it off my abdomen with only her mouth.

She takes me to the back of her throat and holds. Saliva slides down my sensitive skin, and with a deep inhale through her nose, she releases her grip on my hips and grasps my cock, stroking in time with her tongue.

Cool air washes over me as she pops off and clambers up my body. The next thing I know, her tongue is in my mouth, but before I can react and kiss her back, she's gone, wrapping those lips around my dick again, sucking and slurping.

"Holy—" I'm cut off when her tongue tangles with mine once more. Her tongue in my mouth after it's been on my cock is a kink I didn't know I had.

She returns down below, and when I'm confident she's there to stay, I thrust my hips once, testing to see what I can get away with. When she doesn't protest, I thrust again. This time, though, she releases me, and my dick hits my stomach with an obscene smack.

"Don't you fucking dare," she snarls, pulling my shaft back like a joystick before letting go again.

The back and forth is driving me wild.

"On your side," she commands.

I do exactly as I'm told and roll to my left. I adjust the knot of the sash for comfort, but I don't dare peek.

I refrain from reaching for myself again, though I desperately want to. It needs to be stroked. Badly. The sound of her breath mixed with her skin sliding across the duvet is all I hear.

"I want you to gag me with your cock while you eat my pussy."

Kill me dead.

With searching hands, I can't grab at the soft flesh in front of me fast enough.

Voice delicate, she urges, "Easy, baby. I've got you." Then she settles her lower body snuggly against my face.

Hooking my arms around the backs of her thighs, I nuzzle her core, inhaling her heady scent. When she yanks me into her mouth, I take that as permission to devour her.

Sixty-nine is truly underrated. Though some claim multitasking dulls the enjoyment, the juxtaposition of giving and taking lights a fire inside me.

When I lick, she hums.

When she sucks, I blow.

Moans are exchanged for groans that turn to grunts before becoming moans again. Round and round, a tug-of-war of pleasure. Though in this game, we'll both be winners in the end.

Leaving one hand on her ass, I slip the other between her legs and find her clit. Her mouth goes slack on my cock and my tip rests against her lips.

I slide my middle and ring fingers inside her wet heat and work them in time with my tongue while she sucks me lazily, humming her enjoyment around my cock. It's difficult to resist thrusting my hips for my own pleasure here and there, but I'm mostly focused on getting her to the finish line.

It doesn't take long for her hips to buck wildly. Her movement slides the sash right off my face, but I keep my eyes closed. I'm not about to ruin my first sensory-deprivation experience.

Every noise I pull from her brings me a little closer to the edge of my own orgasm. *Come on, baby*, I beg with my tongue.

"Right there. Do that again," she demands.

I happily comply, flicking her clit with the tip of my tongue while curling and pulsing my fingers deep inside her.

She grips my cock with both hands now, muffling her moans with my girth.

"I'm gonna come," I say into her pussy, warning her of my imminent release.

"Let's go, baby," she says around me.

Thighs tighten around cheeks, noses are pressed to damp flesh, and pure bliss passes between us, until the tug-of-war rope we've been pulling on goes slack and we collapse in flawless ecstasy.

Joey swallows around my dick, taking every drop of my release while her pussy pulses against my tongue.

"Holy shit," I pant, finally opening my eyes.

With a giggle, she peppers kisses against my inner leg.

Sitting up, I pull her into my side. As I do, just a hint of hesitation flickers across her face.

"What's going on in that brain of yours?" I ask, shifting on the bed to get a better look.

For the Plot

Her cheeks are flushed and her hair is all askew. "It wasn't too much, was it?"

"Baby," I plant a reassuring kiss on the top of her head. "You're a fucking queen."

Chapter 27
Josefine

BABY, *you're a fucking queen.*

The giant smile that splits my face can't be tamed. With an audible exhale, I relax into Cam's embrace and loop my arm around his waist, my bare breasts resting against his hard abdomen. "Good," I whisper.

He swirls lazy patterns along my heated skin, teasing the side of my tit. Then he pulls back a little and reaches for the phone on the bedside table.

"What are you doing?"

"Calling room service. You need new sheets."

He cleans up in the bathroom while I slip back into my sundress and wait for room service. Thankfully he comes out just as they knock, and I replace him in the bathroom. I do not need to see the look on the housekeeper's face when they replace our sex-damp sheets.

When I return, Cam—with his hat returned to his head—is sitting on one of the chairs on the balcony, lean legs stretched out in front of him. His laptop is open on the table.

As I approach, I take in his background image. It's from our hike the other day, but it's a picture I haven't seen before. A panoramic view of the abandoned monastery, with the sea peeking above the rocky horizon. My back is to the camera and I'm off to the side a bit, but my head is slightly turned and my smile is visible. This so doesn't make me feel things deep in my belly. *No sirree, not at all.*

I snag two water bottles from the mini fridge before plopping down in the vacant chair at the outdoor table. Thank goodness the balcony is shaded, because when Cam showed up, I abandoned my phone and laptop completely in favor of our little *endorphins-inducing creativity boost.*

When I check my phone, I find three notifications. All texts from Brooks.

> **BROOKS**
>
> Yo, Beck! Good to hear from you
>
> Thought you might have run off with a Greek god
>
> Now *that* would have been good 'for the plot'
> 😏

I chuckle under my breath.

"What's so funny?" Cam asks, eagerness flashing in his eyes.

Damn, this man is beautiful from every angle. Above me, below me, beside me. I'll take him any way I can get him.

I set my phone in my lap and shift so I'm looking at him head-on. "My writing partner, Brooks."

His brow, the one with the scar, raises in question, and his jaw ticks, but he doesn't say anything.

"He lives in LA."

At that comment, his shoulders visibly relax, as if knowing Brooks lives thousands of miles from me is a relief. "How long have you two been..."

"Writing together?"

"Yeah." He exhales and scratches at the scruff on his jaw.

"A couple of years. We met through Tyler."

It's subtle, but he bristles at the sound of my ex's name.

"Brooks was working as a songwriter then, but he's been trying to break into screenwriting. He's really the only writing friend I have. We used to meet at a coffee shop not far from my apartment and write side by side. We'd proofread for each other, bounce ideas back and forth, or just commiserate."

"Sounds like a really great friend," he says, his expression soft and warm.

I shoot off a text to Brooks, hinting at the plot twist of my own life I can't wait to dive into with him, then set my phone on the table.

Cam clears his throat and removes his hat. For a moment, I'm dumbstruck watching the way he rakes his fingers through his hair.

"How are you so confident in bed?" He nods at the open patio door. "That sensory-deprivation shit was one of the hottest things I've ever done. But—and please don't take this the wrong way—you're so young. How are you so…"

"Were you going to say *experienced*?"

Kind eyes meet mine. "Maybe?" His voice quivers with uncertainty. "Have you been with a lot of guys? It's okay if you have. I'm not judging."

Wow, a guy who isn't judging my count. That's refreshing.

Not that he deserves an explanation, but he's evidently earned it.

"Not really. I had sex for the first time in high school. Then I was with Tyler. Then you last year." An easy smile plays at the corners of my mouth. "I hooked up with a couple of guys not long after I moved to New York, but I haven't been with anyone in several months."

Cam lights up in a smile, but he quickly tries to cover it up by swiping a hand down his face. "Really?" he asks. "So how are you so confident?"

My cheeks heat, but I let out a laugh. Confidence or not, that answer is easy. "Life's too short to be having terrible sex. Did I tell you Millie works as a narrator for a spicy audio stories app? I get a lot of my ideas there. And to be honest," I thread the ends of my hair around my fingers. "I've never done what we just did either."

"Seriously?" he sputters. "Damn."

I lift my chin just a little. Maybe I'm more confident than I give myself credit for. "Can I tell you something without you getting all weird or judgy or cocky about it?"

"Of course." He drops an elbow to the tabletop and rests his cheek on his fist.

"I thought I was having good sex when I was with Tyler."

To his credit, Cam doesn't flinch when I mention his name this time.

"I climaxed some of the time. For a long time, I felt like that was enough. Every woman's experience with orgasms is different, so I didn't think much about it. And when I didn't get off with him, I'd get off by myself later. But when I met you? That night?" I press my lips together and drink in the man beside me. "I realized what I was missing out on."

He sits up straight, his face alight and his lips tipped up.

"Hey, I said not to get cocky." I laugh.

He leans in and nudges me with his shoulder. "I didn't say anything."

"Something primal took over that first time we were together," I continue. "I felt bold, brazen. You didn't know who I was, and for the first time, I realized I could be anyone I wanted to be. So I went for it. I chose to channel the woman buried somewhere inside me who asks for what she wants in the bedroom. The woman who calls the shots, who presses buttons." What I don't tell him is that our first night together felt natural, and with every encounter with him since, I'm discovering more about my authentic sexual self.

    I swallow thickly, choking back the fuzzy sensation coursing through me. The one I fear means that this may be more than about sexual freedom. I can't go down the relationship path again. This has to be solely about sex. And sex that doesn't breathe past this island. But damn if I don't melt a little when Cam, with hands locked at the back of his neck, elbows pointing out with those juicy biceps on display, exhales. "You're like a dream come true."

Chapter 28

Cameron

Working parallel to Joey yesterday was as natural as walking on solid ground.

Despite her proximity and the temptation she always brings, I accomplished all my work for the day. When it came time to edit Ezra's professional headshots, she paused her own work to laugh with me over his outtakes. The scent of her shampoo would hit me when her hair dipped into my lap like a waterfall. The way she rubbed my forearm after droplets of spit flew from her mouth when she laughed at a picture of Ezra purposefully picking his nose was ridiculously endearing.

When Millie arrived shortly after lunch, slightly wet and disheveled, I excused myself. While I wanted to ask Joey to stay with me last night, I want to give her the space she needs to enjoy the vacation she planned. I'm greedy, sure, but I'll take what I can get.

Even if it breaks me in the end.

Ezra and I ate our way through the city center—the perfect distraction. Local beers by the lighthouse, pork gyros from a hole-in-the-wall restaurant, more beers down a random alleyway, fresh-caught fish at a traditional taverna, then an off-the-grid gelato place recommended by an Italian colleague. A taxi brought us back to the resort, where we sat at the bar, though we were too stuffed to eat or drink any more. I'd be lying if I said I wasn't slightly preoccupied with situating my stool for a better vantage point, praying Joey would walk by.

I obsessed over our text thread for longer than I care to admit in bed last night, thumbs hovering over the screen while I debated whether I should contact her. In the end, I opted not to and paid for it with a fitful night's sleep, even after rubbing one out in the shower.

This morning, I woke to a notification from Joey. She and Millie plan to laze by the pool today, but they want to know if we will join them for dinner for their last night.

I button my salmon-colored shirt, leaving the top few undone, then I fix my hair one last time before stuffing my phone and keycard into my charcoal slacks.

Mild anxiety courses through my veins like a current. Because this is her last night on the island, and I still have a week left of my contract before I fly back to New York.

We arrive at the resort's upscale restaurant before the girls do. The walls are painted white, with textured lines that look like someone dragged a rake through the plaster. The waiter leaves a pitcher of water on our table after filling our glasses, and when he walks away, my eyes nearly bug out of my head like those of a cartoon character.

As if she's walking down a runway, Joey, in nude stilettos, saunters through the front doors. She's wearing the champagne-colored mini dress from the first night I saw her. Karaoke night.

For the Plot

The night we kissed in my office. When she got so drunk off raki I had to help her undress. I was a gentleman that night, but at this moment, that's the last thing I want to be. The desire to rip that shiny fucking fabric to shreds and worship her body all night long is overpowering.

"You okay?" Ezra chuckles and slaps my back.

"All good." I wave him off. My sole focus is on the leggy bombshell walking my way. Her dark hair is curled in loose waves, and her skin glows beneath the dim restaurant lighting.

I rise and give Millie a peck on the cheek. The kiss I plant on Joey's cheek lingers while I inhale her rosemary and citrus scent. I could eat her, she smells so good.

When I breathe "You look gorgeous" into her ear, goose bumps ripple across her soft flesh.

We settle quickly, but almost immediately, her leg bounces beneath the table like a drumbeat. I slide my hand across her exposed thigh to steady her.

Four servers in black place shallow royal blue glasses at each of our place settings.

"What's this?" Millie asks.

"An olive oil tasting," I answer. "It was Ezra's idea."

After a brief lesson in the history of harvesting olives and the differences in types, a waiter pours about a tablespoon of oil from an amber-colored glass jar.

We're instructed to swig and swish the olive oil around in our mouths before slowly letting it fall down our throats.

"If it burns, that's how you know it's the good stuff," the waiter says.

Unprepared, the girls immediately choke and sputter, their eyes watering.

When I lean into Joey's neck and croon, "C'mon gorgeous, you take my cum better than that," she practically needs an inhaler to calm down.

The remaining oils are equally robust, though the women don't down such large samples this time.

"That was fun." Joey pats her lips with a napkin, leaving traces of her blush pink lipstick on the cloth.

"Yes, very cool. Thank you," Millie adds.

When the staff removes our glasses and replaces our placemats with fresh ones, Joey shifts in her seat so she's facing me. "What will you do when you get back to the city?"

"For work, you mean?" I ask.

"Yeah."

"I applied for a job based out of Austin, actually. I'm waiting to hear back."

She rests an elbow on the table, cupping her chin in her hand. "Is it still freelance?"

I nod. "If I get it, I'll be traveling a bit."

"Mmm," she hums, studying me. "I hope you get it." Her genuine smile fills me with more warmth than whiskey.

Chapter 29
Josefine

"Are you left-handed too?" I rub the sleep from my eyes and sit up.

I didn't spend the night with Cam after dinner last night, but we did visit the nude beach together one more time this morning. Afterward, he brought me back to his room and ate me in the shower before properly fucking me in bed. Then he fed me lunch and put me down for a nap.

He sets the pen on top of the hotel's stationary and makes his way to the espresso machine across from me. "Coffee?"

"Please."

"*Too?* Does that mean you're a leftie?"

When I nod, his eyes light up behind his glasses.

Motioning to the desk with my chin, I ask, "What are you writing?"

The espresso machine whirs to life, spitting out liquid fuel in a cup the perfect size for an American Girl doll.

The bed dips when he scoots in next to me. "Just something." He holds the porcelain cup and saucer out to me but carefully pulls it back before I can take it. "Wait. I don't know how you like your coffee."

"Black. Like my soul." I laugh.

He presses a kiss to my forehead. "Trust me, sweetheart, there's nothing black about your soul."

Like his compliment, the first hit of liquid warms me from the inside out.

With the cup to my lips, I watch as Cam saunters back to the desk. He doesn't sit again, but he crouches over the page, scribbles something at the bottom, then folds the paper, slides it in an envelope, and seals it with a swipe of his tongue. *I'd like to be that envelope right now.*

Millie insisted I spend time with him this morning, even though it's our last day on the island. Oof, am I glad she was cool with it, because the things that man did to me in the shower... Maybe he'll let me take a snapshot of his tongue and show the salesperson at a sex shop. I have to stifle a laugh when I imagine marching into the shore, and demanding *do you have anything that resembles this?*

"What are you smirking about?" he asks. The tattoo on the inside of his forearm—a circle with a line drawing of clouds, mountains, water, and a path cutting through—snags my attention. It's simple yet complex all at once.

"Nothing." I pull my lips between my teeth to hide my smile before draining the last of my espresso and setting it to the side. "Come here." I pat the mattress next to me.

Cam concedes and drops onto the bed with a groan. Praying my coffee breath overrides my napping breath, I kiss him with more intention than I've ever had, then pull back to study him like he's a work of art.

"What was that for?"

Letting the duvet fall to my lap, I tug at his biceps until he's flush against my bare chest. I'm going to miss the warmth of his skin against mine; the friction from the heat of our flesh.

He wants to bring *us* back to New York, like a souvenir. He may have mentioned it a time or two. But I made a commitment to myself. To my writing career. And I won't let a man distract me. No matter how big his dick is.

"One more O before you go?" His voice is soft, the opposite of his erection, which is now digging into my thigh.

I groan into his lush lips. He smells of mint and coffee. "I can't."

He grinds against me in protest.

God, how I wish he could tuck himself between my thighs right now. I'm so wet he'd glide right in with just one thrust.

"Please, Josefine," he breathes into my neck, causing a cascade of goose bumps.

Just like earlier, when he licked the length of my leg, from my ankle to my hip, and blew over my core through pursed lips.

If it weren't for the screaming of the cicadas outside our open window, he would hear the pounding of my heart.

"I have a flight to catch and I still need to pack." I place a kiss on the tip of his nose. "Thanks for getting us an extended check-out, by the way."

He rests his forehead on mine. "I wish I could keep you just a little longer."

"What the hell is this?" I guffaw, casting shade at my cousin.

"Oh, that?" Millie's eyes twinkle.

I shake my head. A mini wooden penis keychain painted with flowers in varying shades of blue hangs from my carry-on bag. All the kitschy tourist shops sell them, along with wooden penis bottle openers of *all* sizes. I assume the popularity has to do with fertility, like the Penis Festival in Japan, but wouldn't wooden vulvas make more sense?

"Just a little something to remember your time on Crete." She winks.

"I don't think that's what my dad had in mind when he imagined this trip." Though I try to fight it, a snort sneaks out.

My bag slips off my shoulder, and Ezra catches it before it hits the ground.

"Thanks," I say. "I can't believe we're on the same flight back to New York."

Not wanting to draw out our departure, I said my goodbyes to Cam in his hotel room. A clean break is what I was going for, although by the ache in his eyes, it looked like I trashed his heart. When I returned to my room, my cousin was waiting for me with outstretched arms.

I make it through security before Millie, who gets selected for a random pat-down. *Yes, please* she mouths, paired with an eyebrow wiggle, when the hot TSA agent approaches. I chuckle when I notice his name tag. She sort of got her Adonis after all. When we meet up, carry-ons in tow and shoes on our feet, she's homed in on her phone, with a scowl glued to her face.

"What's wrong? Was Mr. Sexy Security's inspection not thorough enough?" I tease.

Instead of grinning like I expect, my cousin shoves her phone in my face instead. "Look."

There's an email from Gideon, our landlord, on the screen.

RE: *Urgent Evacuation Notice for Critical Concern*

Shit. I scroll down.

The safety and well-being of our residents are of the utmost importance to us, and as such, we must take necessary action.

I dart a glance at Millie, then continue reading. Something about "structural engineers" and "building's infrastructure."

"What does this mean?" I ask, just as my eyes land on *The evacuation is scheduled to begin on Sunday and is expected to last for approximately—*

My stomach drops to the floor. "*One week?*" I screech. Starting tomorrow.

Ezra takes hold of the phone and scans the email himself. We're blocking the path of restless travelers, so we shuffle to the side, where he murmurs phrases like "leave your apartment" and "relocate to temporary accommodations" and "secure your personal possessions during the evacuation period."

"Where the hell are we supposed to go?" My heart pounds so hard against my sternum I'm worried I'll crack a rib. A week away to relax, and this is how I'm welcomed home?

While my IKEA pull-out sofa isn't as luxurious as the bed (okay, *beds*) I've been sleeping in for the last several days, I was looking forward to the comfort of my own home. Drinking tea out of my favorite mug and lazy weekend mornings with my best friend nursing our hangovers. Even listening to Peg and Fran next door argue over which Campbell's soup flavor is superior. (Peg: classic tomato; Fran: New England clam chowder.)

Millie's frantically texting when Ezra speaks up. "You can stay with me."

"Absolutely not." She doesn't even look up from her phone.

"Amelia," I reprimand.

"Sorry," she tries again. "What I meant was, thank you for the offer, but I'll be staying with Sam."

Her face is still buried in her phone, so she doesn't see the way he flinches at Sam's name.

"Sorry, boo," she goes on, "but Sam says accommodations would be too tight for both of us. I'll text Stevie at the club, but—"

"Joey will stay at my place." Ezra pipes up again, giving me a soft look. "Cam's away for another week."

I look to Millie for assistance. *Do you see a flaw in this plan?*

Her silent response: *Sounds perfect to me.*

"You're sure you don't mind?"

"Not at all," he grins. "I wasn't looking forward to going back to such a quiet apartment. You'd be doing me a favor."

Feeling a tad resigned, I shrug. "All right." Why the hell not?

"Are you shitting me?" My eyes practically pop from their sockets when Ezra sends me his address outside baggage claim. "You live four blocks away?"

I've been living this close to Cameron for a year?

After our geography surprise, we share an Uber into the city. Ezra offers to help me collect my things, but after catching him yawning for what has to be the twentieth time, I send him on his way with the promise that I will head over to his apartment later.

On the outside of the building, the only sign that things aren't business as usual are a couple of orange cones, but inside, a sea of yellow caution tape floods the walls. While Gideon assures us it's safe for us to enter, the elevator has already been disabled. That means we have to climb four stories with our luggage. After traveling for the past eighteen hours, I'm not confident my legs won't give out. Maybe I should have accepted assistance after all.

Gideon gives us thirty minutes to collect our things. We're too jet-lagged to do more than just gather our shit and leave.

On the curb outside our building, we say our goodbyes, and then I'm off. The differences between New York City and Greece bombard me, one after another, on my trek to Ezra's—*Cam's*—apartment. The aromas of thyme, sage, and rosemary are replaced by gasoline, hot dog water, and garbage. The symphony of cicadas is traded for the cacophony of New York City's urban melodies—cars honking, construction trucks crooning, and sirens wailing.

I can do this. It's no big deal. Cam isn't even on the same continent, and I will be back in my apartment before he returns.

As I approach the building, a jaunty older man, who introduces himself as Hector and is obviously expecting me, greets me by name and ushers me into the elevator. Thank goodness, too, because the apartment is on the sixth floor.

"How long will you be staying with us, Ms. Beckham?" His smile shines bright. He keeps his eyes locked on mine even when I discover my shirt is askew from schlepping my luggage four blocks. I like him.

"Just a week. Maybe less." One can hope.

He carries my duffel down the hall of the sixth floor while I follow like a timid puppy being brought home for the first time. It hits me, suddenly, that I'm intruding on Cam's personal space. My heart lodges in my throat. Shit. This was a terrible idea.

"Here we are, Ms. Beckham. Number 6206," Hector announces, just as Ezra opens the door.

6206? *Oh my—*

"Hi," I squeak, bewildered. No wonder Cam was all squirrelly about my room number at the resort.

"I've got it." Ezra takes my bag.

I shuffle into the narrow entryway behind him, shouting "Thanks, Hector!" over my shoulder.

"See you around, honey." He salutes, then turns on his heel and strides back toward the elevator.

I kick off my shoes and add them to the basket in front of what I presume is a coat closet. To the left is a narrow, updated kitchen. Directly in front of me is a large wooden desk in a beautiful chestnut color. A Mac desktop rests on top, and on the wall above are two exquisite photographs.

"Are these—"

"Yup," he responds. "He took them in Greece last year."

Chapter 30
Josefine

I FELT WILDLY uncomfortable sleeping in Cam's bed last night, but Ezra refused to let me crash on the sofa. Snuggled between clean sheets, I laid awake most of the night, heart aching no matter how many breathing techniques I tried. Laser focusing in on every inhale and exhale to calm my pulse and my mind only led to more thoughts of *him*.

Cam on the precipice of a panic attack; me soothing his tense body from behind. When I was sure he was calm, whispering "I dare you to fuck me" in his ear.

But today is a new day, and I'm determined to situate my head straight. No more fawning over alluring men, with their forearm porn and tortoise-shell glasses. I am a strong, independent woman with one goal: finish writing a goddamn book.

Ezra was kind enough to make breakfast, and I offered to clear the dishes.

Like a boxer battling an opponent, I fight the jet lag by powering through. I know if I stay within the confines of the apartment—especially anywhere near Cam's cloud-like mattress—none of my tasks will get accomplished.

I could walk to one of my regular coffee shops, but why not switch things up a little? I google cafés nearby and head to one with great reviews.

The baristas at the Black Hole café are the nerdy-on-purpose kind, and a sign on the exposed brick wall over the bar reads *I licked it, so it's mine.* Wallpaper made to look like the pages of books covers the remaining walls. All the drinks are named after fictional characters, so although I typically drink my coffee black, I treat myself to a Mr. Darcy—a half-caf soy latte with whipped cream.

I connect to the café's Wi-Fi. (Password: *ilikebigbooksandicannotlie*)

When I fish for my blue-light blocking glasses, two stickers fall from my laptop case. Cam bought them at the hotel's gift shop after he noticed the collection covering my MacBook Air the day we worked side by side on my balcony. Just like I wanted to ask about each of his tattoos, he questioned my stickers.

I bought the *Reading is my foreplay* sticker for myself.

Millie gifted me the *Am*bitch*ous* sticker when I told her I was finally writing a book.

Working hard or hardly working came from Tyler. I need to take that one off; I thought it was funny at the time.

A cartoon pigeon from Poland reminds me of the time Millie got shit on after we visited Auschwitz-Birkenau during my senior year of high school. (There's a dark metaphor somewhere in there.)

Remember your why is also from my cousin.

There's a sticker made to look like a library card, with the face of Matilda in the little rectangle window.

And now I can add two more. I run my fingers along the vinyl surface of the first. It's the outline of a Greek goddess on a calming blue background. *Aphrodite* is printed beside the long-haired woman. The second sticker, in the same style, is of *Atropos*.

A quick google search explains that Aphrodite is the goddess of love and beauty, while Atropos is the goddess of fate and destiny.

Hmm.

After applying both, I snap a picture of my laptop to send to Cam. I stop, though, with my finger frozen over his name. When I switched out of airplane mode yesterday, there was a text from him waiting. I let him know I'd arrived safely but left it at that. There was no mention of sleeping in his bed last night. I bet he'd appreciate a picture of the stickers' new home, but then what? Sure, we're technically friends, even without the "with benefits" part, but what does a friendship with him post-Greece even look like? Will we hang out when he's back in the city? We didn't talk about it before I left.

Deciding against messaging him for now, I prop my phone against the small floral arrangement on the table, set a three-second timer, and snap a picture of myself holding my Mr. Darcy, keeping the new stickers on display in the foreground. Then I navigate to Instagram and post the picture along with a caption that reads *Cozy vibes & caffeinated inspiration with Mr. Darcy*, and tag the Black Hole.

After a few minutes of mindless scrolling, a notification pops up.

@click_it_with_cam started following you. Then *@click_it_with_cam liked your post*, followed by *@click_it_with_cam commented on your post.*

I slap a hand over my mouth when I literally snort at his punny handle, then I tap on the last notification.

@click_it_with_cam: Bird by bird...

Did he just reference every writer's bible? Who is this guy?

Before I can dissect that, a banner appears at the top of my screen, alerting me that @click_it_with_cam has sent a direct message.

CAM
Ask Iris for the Andalusian Dream next time. It's part of the secret menu
😉

ME
What's that?

CAM
Please tell me you've read The Alchemist

ME
No... 🙈

CAM
I should spank you for that

Yes. Yes, you should. While I love his playful side, I can't let this convo go there.

ME
😊

I pull up my web browser and search for *The Alchemist*, then zoom in on the orange cover with a yellow circle in its center. The drawing inside the circle is familiar. Where have I seen this design before? I sit back and survey the ceiling while I rack my brain. It only takes a moment to place it.

Cam's tattoo. Specifically, his forearm tattoo. I feel like Sherlock Holmes solving a mystery. (*Sherlock Holmes* also happens to be what the Black Hole calls their black coffee.)

I switch over to Instagram again.

For the Plot

> **ME**
> Is that your favorite book?

CAM
Yes

What's your favorite book?

I don't even hesitate.

> **ME**
> Maestro by Auden Dar

CAM
Never heard of it

> **ME**
> I should spank you for that

I couldn't help myself.

CAM
You'll have to tell me all about it when I get back

Whether he's trying to guarantee we see each other when he returns or not, there's no way I can resist talking about my favorite book.

> **ME**
> You may change your mind once I get started. I could talk about it for hours. Days, maybe. How long do you have?

CAM
For you? All the time in the world

Chapter 31
Josefine

IT TURNS out Iris knows more than just the secret menu at the Black Hole. After making small talk and learning that I'm a writer, she introduces me to her fellow barista, Ari, who invites me to tag along to a six-week creative writing workshop that begins tonight. I'm terribly jet-lagged and want nothing more than to sleep for a solid week, but when Ari mentions there's only one spot left, I seize the opportunity.

With a cup of Winnie the Pooh (honey latte with condensed milk), my AirPods in, and my favorite "Get Shit Done" playlist cued up, I reply to every email I received while on vacation and even complete a project I left unfinished before Greece. Then I head back to the apartment to freshen up.

At a quarter till five, I meet Ari outside the Black Hole.

"Aren't you a sweetheart?" I warble when the adorable man hands me a to-go cup of coffee.

By the time the bus spits us out in front of the arts and education building in West Harlem, I'm well versed in Ari's life story. The small-framed man, also twenty-three, looks like Timothée

For the Plot

Chalamet, with his mop of black hair, sharp cheekbones, prominent jaw, and crystal-blue eyes.

He grew up on Long Island with his Jewish-Italian family, but like me, he moved to the city last year. We instantly bonded over our Jewish dads. He works at the Black Hole part time to supplement his income as a social media manager.

"You're going to love Talulah!" Ari trills, taking and tossing my empty coffee cup by the door.

Talulah, I learned on the ride over, is our instructor. She's also Ari's grandmother.

The classroom he leads me to smells earthy, and the walls are covered in paintings. A handful of people are already seated, with a mix of notebooks and laptops scattered across tabletops.

I settle into a navy blue plastic seat like the ones from school, and suddenly, I'm hit with memories of a high school English class.

I've wanted to be a writer—an author—since I was seven years old. As a child, I would sit in front of the TV and copy dialogue into my Lisa Frank notebook as quickly as my chubby little hands could keep up. By the time I got to high school, I had more notebooks than my desk could hold. But stringing together words and scenarios became especially therapeutic following my dad's death.

When given a creative writing assignment in freshman English, I dove in wholeheartedly. Only I messed up the due date. I was mortified when I was called to the podium to read my paper before it was ready. Believing I had one more week to work on the assignment, I was forced to read my shitty first draft to a room of judging classmates.

When I sank into my seat, hands clammy and my heart racing, a guy behind me leaned in close and whispered that it was the worst thing he'd ever heard.

I willed my sticky plastic chair to swallow me whole on the

spot. I was humiliated that the one thing I loved more than anything was put on display in its ugliest form. No dancer wants to be forced to perform a triple pirouette in front of a live audience before they've had time to practice and polish their technique. The same is true for writers. We have to fill a page with some pretty ugly shit before we trim and prune and cultivate the words into something magnificent.

My memory is interrupted when a very loud—and colorful—woman saunters through the door.

She has a silvery-lavender bob, purple glasses perched on her button nose, and aquamarine Converse sneakers that match her cotton coveralls perfectly.

When she passes Ari, she playfully flicks his ear.

"That's your grandma?" I gape at the eclectic woman poised at the front of the classroom. Ari said she's in her seventies, but she doesn't look a day over fifty, and she oozes an infectious charisma.

"Yup. That's my *bubbe*," he beams.

"Now." Talulah claps, commanding our attention. "Most of you are here because you have dreams of becoming a published author, correct?"

Not a soul speaks, but many of us nod.

Talulah leans a plump hip on the desk behind her. "Over the next six weeks, we will cover a variety of topics, beginning with grammar and punctuation. While I consider this the least important part of creative writing"—she rolls her eyes like a teenage girl whose mother is giving her a stiff lecture—"it seems to have a chokehold on my students. I've learned it's best to get it out of the way."

Talulah continues, explaining all the topics we'll cover—expanding vocabulary, improving flow, understanding sentence structure, and writing concisely.

For the Plot

"We will not have any flappy sentences." She flaps her arms like a chicken, garnering a round of laughter from the class.

"We'll cover plot, story arc, and character development, then get into how to spot plot holes and how to fix them."

Talulah goes on to explain that when the six weeks are over, she offers a two-week extension for those who wish to embark on a little *spicy* challenge.

When that topic comes up, Ari shifts in his seat and gives me a knowing wink.

He introduces me to his grandmother after class, then we all hug and part ways.

I cross the courtyard and pull out my phone to check my notifications, only to run smack into a petite body. Papers go flying and a steel water bottle rolls into the busy street with a clang.

"Shit!" I yell.

The woman I knocked into bends at the same time I do.

"Are you okay?" I ask, assessing her.

I'm met with a perfect dark brown bun situated on top of her head. "I'm fine," she says, swiping her bangs off her gold wire-frame glasses.

With a long breath out, I help her collect the pages strewn around us. Once they're collected, she sticks them back into her portfolio.

We rise and I apologize again, insisting I'll buy her a new water bottle, as it's currently New York City roadkill. After learning that she will be at the education center again next week, I wish her a good class and tell her I'll be waiting outside.

Chapter 32
Josefine

THE AIR IS WARM, and the world around me is vibrant and alive. From the cheerful geraniums in neighborhood planters and window boxes, to the climbing roses and lush peonies, June in New York City is my new favorite.

"I can't thank you enough for letting me crash with you the past week," I tell Ezra over Chinese takeout. We're sitting at the dining table while the sounds of the city seep in from the open windows.

"Don't mention it." He slurps his lo mein and smiles.

"This week has flown by," I say, more to myself than to him.

The writing workshop is incredible. Ari is a riot and has filled the writing-partner void that opened inside me when I left Santa Monica. While Brooks and I still share our latest works-in-progress through email and text, the distance and time difference make it difficult to give the immediate feedback we both need. Plus, there's nothing like in-person accountability. After only two classes with Talulah, the literary fire inside me is blazing, invigorating me to focus on my writing.

Between clients and my book, I haven't climbed out of my

For the Plot

metaphorical cave much. I've barely talked to Millie. She's been busy with work, too, and with whatever is happening between her and Sam, whom I've yet to meet. I'm looking forward to cracking open a bottle of Sauvy B and pinning her down until she catches me up on all the details of her week.

"Are you excited to have Cam back?"

Ezra tilts his head to the side and assesses me for a moment. "Do you know he only lets his family and me call him that?"

"Call him what?"

"Cam."

Heat floods my cheeks, and I duck to hide my embarrassment. "Oh shit, am I not supposed to call him that?"

The night we met, he introduced himself as Cameron, I suppose. But when I shortened his name, he didn't correct me. He's *never* corrected me.

Ezra shakes his head. "That's not what I meant."

"So," I hedge when he doesn't elaborate, "when does *Cameron* get back?"

"Tomorrow. Around one, I think."

Great. I'll have more than enough time to change the sheets and restock the fridge after Ezra leaves for work. I'll drop my bags at my apartment before heading to the Black Hole, then to West Harlem for Talulah's writing workshop. No Sunday Scaries here!

From the kitchen, he hollers, "Do you mind finishing cleaning up? I'm heading out for the night."

"Sure thing," I reply, standing to collect the remaining takeout cartons. "Will you be back later or—" I snap my mouth shut. Maybe my question is a little too intrusive.

Ezra wanders out of the kitchen and pulls me into a hug. It's not unwelcome, but it surprises me. We just met, though we've quickly become friends. "I'm going to Brooklyn to see my mom. I won't be home." He presses a chaste kiss into my hair. "It's been nice having you around, kid. Don't be a stranger now that Cam's coming back. We're neighbors, after all."

I return the hug and force a polite smile, because, truth be told, I don't know what's going to happen when Cam—uh, *Cameron*—returns. I don't plan to actively avoid him, but I also don't see myself going out of my way to have a friendship with him. Or do I? There's no reason we can't be friends moving forward, right? I'm a mature adult. Okay, I'm an adult. I can be friends with a guy I've had sex with once or ten times and not be weird about it. Yes. Yup. Totally.

I triple-check the lock behind Ezra before emptying the remaining contents of the bottle of wine we shared with dinner into my glass. With my laptop in tow, I settle in one of the twin leather captain's chairs in the living area and turn on *The Office* for background noise. I get lost in the clicks of the keys on my keyboard as my fingers struggle to keep up with the sheer number of ideas erupting from me.

When my neck and hips ache, signaling that I've been sitting for too long, I check the time. It's after midnight. How long has *Are you still watching?* been frozen on the television screen? Standing, I drain the pale liquid from my glass and take it to the kitchen. I'll finish the dishes in the morning.

I turn off the lights as I move from the kitchen, through the living area, and into the bedroom.

In the bathroom, I open his medicine cabinet one last time, even though I've memorized its contents: Motrin, eye contact solution, Benadryl, a travel-size Crest toothpaste, floss (good boy), a disposable razor I may or may not have used because I forgot mine, deodorant, and expired cold and flu medicine that I'm tempted to throw out. I decide against it. I don't want him to know I snooped, after all. But doesn't everyone snoop inside people's medicine cabinets?

I climb into the queen-size bed for the last time. Either the mountain-fresh scent of the dark gray sheets has faded, or I'm immune after a week. Turning off the main light with the remote control, I exchange my phone for my Kindle, and before I know it, I find myself downloading *The Alchemist.*

By the time I get to the part about the boy finding the courage to tell his father he'd rather travel than become a priest, I understand why Cameron likes this book so much. I read a little more—about Santiago and his dreams and the secret to happiness, before my mind wanders to the man whose bed I'm sleeping in. Besides his comments on my posts and briefly texting about our favorite books and the secret menu, we haven't chatted.

What did he do after I left Greece? Did he go on any more hikes? Hang out at the nude beach again?

I clamp my eyes shut, but images of him on that beach are permanently painted against my lids: thick thighs and a toned abdomen. Ass cheeks flexing and contracting with every step on the shore. The sand peppered across his hard chest. How I licked the saltiness off his nipples in jest.

Dammit. I squeeze my thighs together, but it's too late. My panties are already soaked. I roll onto my stomach and bury my face in the pillow, releasing a frustrated groan. It doesn't appease the ache at my core, though. If anything, the friction caused by the movement intensifies it. With a deep breath in and out, I drag my hand down my body. I stop when I reach my clit and rub light circles over my underwear. It's instantly obvious that my own touch won't be sufficient tonight, so I reach for my vibrator, temporarily perched on the bedside table. I absolutely cannot forget to pack it tomorrow morning.

The silicone device whirs to life when I flick the switch, and a low buzz joins the white noise of the city outside.

Let's try this again.

I slip my underwear down my legs and kick them off, then I let the vibrations take control. My body relaxes, and I sink into the mattress. With the apartment to myself, I let out a moan. I drag the vibe through my slit, collecting my arousal, then slide it inside me an inch or two. It's a tight fit, so I repeat the action once, then again. Deep pulses arise, signaling ecstasy is just around the corner. I snake a hand up my shirt so I can twist and pull at my nipple.

A clatter sounds on the other side of the apartment.

My heart leaps into my throat, and all signs of climax dissipate like smoke.

Footsteps sound on the floor, drawing closer. I jackknife up in bed and mentally flip through all likely scenarios.

Could it be Ezra?

Did he change his plans?

If it's him, though, he's being kind of loud for after midnight.

Oh my god!

Someone is breaking in! That has to be it. All sense of logic and reasoning flies out the window, and I'm one hundred percent sure there's a criminal in the apartment. With my vibrator gripped tightly in one hand, I fumble around for the remote on the nightstand with the other. If I flip on the light, maybe make noise and signal to the intruder that someone is home, they'll get spooked and take off, right?

Shadows move in the sliver of light between the door and floor, and the sound of feet on the hardwood grows louder. Just as I locate the proper button on the remote, the door flies open. Afraid for my life, I throw the items clutched in both hands at the intruder.

"What the fuck?"

This is it. This is how I die. I couldn't have gotten one more orgasm before my demise?!

"What in the—"

A smacking sound echoes through the room, and a moment later, the overhead lights blaze, illuminating the figure in the doorframe.

"*Cameron?*"

"*Joey?*" he shouts, his face pinched in surprise.

On the verge of hyperventilating, I clutch at my chest and will the drumline pounding against my ribcage to ease up. "What the hell?" I pant. "I thought you were an intruder."

He throws his head back and guffaws.

"It's not funny!" My damn heart is still lodged in my throat, and my hands are trembling. "I thought I was going to die!"

"And you thought *this*," Cameron crouches and swipes my weapon from the floor, "would save you?"

Wearing a shit-eating grin, he dangles my vibrator next to his face. He couldn't have picked up the remote instead?

Suddenly, my heart is racing for another reason.

Cameron, in those damn gray sweatpants I love to hate, a black tee that hugs his biceps, and a backward cap, is holding my most intimate toy, fresh off the press.

When did I slip into literal hell?

Mortified, I sink into the mattress and pull the covers over my head, praying to the Egyptian cotton gods to swallow me whole. Forget that last orgasm—*take me now*.

Pulling back the covers and looking like a damn midnight snack, Cameron looms over me. "You thought this would protect you?"

Sitting up, my back smashed against the pillows, I cock a brow and inspect the way his large fingers are clutching my vibrator. "I mean, it is pretty big."

With a lopsided smirk, he says, "It's not as big as—"

"Don't finish that sentence!" I shout, covering my face with my hands.

He tugs at one of my hands until I'm forced to look at him. "Why not?"

"I don't need your head any bigger than it is."

A devilish glint flashes in his eyes. "Which *head* are we talking about?"

"Oh, dear god, make it stop!" I toss a pillow at his smug, pretty face.

Uninvited, he sits at the edge of the bed. His hip bumps my knee, so I shimmy over, making room for him. It is his bed, after all.

"What are you doing here?" I ask, my cheeks still warm from embarrassment.

"What am *I* doing here?" he asks. "This is my apartment. My room. What are *you* doing here? In my bed."

"Uh." The warmth in my cheeks turns to a full-on flame. Is he teasing me? "Didn't Ezra tell you?" I'm hella confused.

He scans the room. I can practically see his brain collecting the clues—my large weekender bag leaning against his closet, a small collection of shoes on the floor. "Tell me what?"

Sitting a little straighter, I lift my chin. "That I'm staying here."

"What do you mean, you're staying here?" His jaw is practically unhinged.

I take in a deep breath, then let it out, willing my body and my mind to calm. "Before we boarded our flight back home, Millie was notified that our apartment complex was being evacuated to fix some structural issues."

He blinks rapidly and remains quiet.

"Ezra said he cleared it with you," I add. "But by the look on your face right now, I'm going to assume he did not."

"You would be correct." He rubs a hand over his jaw. It

doesn't look like he's shaved since I last saw him, and I'm kind of digging it.

"He told me you wouldn't be home until one."

"Yeah, one *in the morning*."

"That bastard." I curse his best friend under my breath. "Well, this is awkward."

And what's even more awkward? The way he's still holding tight to my vibrator.

Chapter 33
Cameron

AFTER THE LONG TRIP HOME, the last thing I imagined coming home to was a beautiful woman beneath my sheets. And her, um, toy. A very impressive toy, I might add. Joey's eyes ping back and forth, following along with the game of Hot Potato I'm playing with her vibrator—her *still slick* vibrator. Just the thought of her sliding it inside her pussy makes my dick twitch.

Shifting on the mattress, I scan the gorgeous girl before me. Her long hair is tousled and tangled at the ends, just how it looks post-sex.

"Is that my shirt?" The sheet has pooled at her waist, but even in the dark, it's obvious it is.

She dips her chin and surveys herself but doesn't respond.

I lean forward, closing the distance between us. "Why are you wearing my shirt, Joey?"

Still averting her gaze, she pulls her bottom lip between her teeth and worries it.

"Fine. Next question." I twirl the vibrator between us but pull it away when she makes a grab for it. "What were you doing with this in my bed, Josefine?" I draw out her formal name like a song.

She gulps, but she still won't look at me.

"Eyes on me."

Obediently, she drags her focus up my chest, then my neck. She pauses on my lips for a beat before meeting my eyes. Does she feel what I feel? Heat radiating between us like the warmth of the sun we left behind in Greece.

"I—I—" she stammers. "I couldn't sleep."

If I had to guess, that's not the whole truth, but I'll leave it for now.

"So you thought you'd, what? Relax a little?" What's got her so tense?

She nods. "Mm-hmm. But then someone interrupted me." She pouts. She fucking pouts.

Damn, I want to nip at those pillowy lips.

"So you didn't get to finish?" I duck my head and inch closer.

Dropping her attention to the sheet covering her legs, she shakes her head.

"That's a pity. What are we going to do about it?"

"We?"

"I'm here now." I sit a little straighter. "This is my room, and you're in it. So, yes—*we*. I can't very well let you go back to bed unsatisfied. What kind of host would I be?"

She's already trembling with anticipation, and her breathing has sped up.

Steadying her with a hand at the back of her neck, I ask, "Did you miss me, sweetheart?"

She locks those dark eyes on me now. I lean in, lips so close to hers that her minty breath breezes over them with every pant. She licks her lips, and the tip of her tongue grazes my mouth— whether on purpose or accident, I'm not sure. All I know is I want to claim her.

She gasps. "No."

No?

A pit forms in my stomach and I pull back.

"I mean, we can't. I can't." She places a hand on my chest, then immediately retracts it, like I've stung her. "Cameron..."

Cameron? What happened to Cam?

Her posture is so rigid that if I were to touch her, I'm afraid she'd poke me with poisonous quills.

"Look," she sighs, drawing her legs underneath her. "What we had in Greece was..."

Amazing. Incredible. Sexy. Hot. Sexy. Hot as fuck. Magical.

With a faraway look in her eyes, she wrings her hands in her lap. "That has to stay in Greece. We agreed, remember?"

We agreed? No. I only went along with it because I was desperate to have her in any way I could. I cover her hands, stopping her fidgeting. "Joey."

She pulls away quickly and swings her legs over the edge of the bed, her brows drawn low, like it pains her to turn me down.

I'm right there with you.

I want to tell her that I haven't been able to shake my thoughts of her. That I burned with jealousy when I pictured another guy holding her at night. That I can't shake the ache behind my ribs each time I think about wrapping my arms around her and holding her until morning. I want to tell her that I get drunk on dreams of her every night and wake up feeling hungover.

I can't get you out of my fucking brain, I want to scream.

Instead, I keep my words under lock and key. I'm not giving up, but I won't push her. Not right now, at least.

Standing, I pull in a deep breath, will my dick to calm down, and change the subject. "It's late. I need to shower."

"I'll sleep on the sofa," she says, dragging a pillow and throw blanket off the bed.

For the Plot

"No." I cup her elbow, halting her. "Go back to bed. I'll take the sofa."

"But this is your room," she protests, narrowing her eyes on me.

"I'm hungry," I tell her. "I'll probably eat something before I go to bed, and I don't want to keep you up." It's not a complete lie. I am hungry, even if what I'm craving isn't food. "Please." It's not a suggestion.

I step away, my body buzzing with lust and defeat all at once, and shuffle into the en suite bathroom.

Chapter 34
Josefine

DAMN, that should have earned me a gold star. More like five hundred gold stars. Turning Cameron down was no easy feat. If my pussy could talk, she would have told me to lie on my back and shut the fuck up. In fact, she's screaming at me right now, throbbing with want. Wanting the man on the other side of that door, the one who's stark naked with water dripping down his chiseled body.

Even after a day of traveling, he looks better than I remember. A Mediterranean tan highlights his dreamy features and accentuates the sinewy muscles of his arms. I shut down the traitorous quiver my body unleashes at the thought and drag the covers up to my neck.

When Cameron steps out of the bathroom, he's met with a view of the back of my head. Squeezing my eyes closed, I will him to hurry. I feel bad that he's going to be stuck sleeping on the sofa in his own home, but the determination etched on his face told me I wasn't going to win that round. A drawer near the foot of the bed slides open, then another. I feel his gaze on me like a hot, intense spotlight. A sigh, then the soft click of the door.

Rolling onto my back, I throw my arms across my face. What am I doing? Is it too late to go somewhere else for the night? Is it too early to go back to my apartment? The email said we could return on Monday. Technically, it is Monday. I swipe my phone from the nightstand.

> ME
> Guess who came home early???

I will Millie to respond. I need a pep talk. But no message. It is the middle of the night, after all.

My body's circuiting with fitful electricity. There's no way I'm sleeping now. So I tap on the Instagram icon, well aware that scrolling on my phone is the last thing that'll help. I notice Cameron is online. Great. Here we are, under the same roof, doing the same thing but separately. That is not weird at all.

My phone buzzes a few seconds later. A DM from *@click_it_with_cam*.

> CAM
> What are you doing awake?

I contemplate just silencing my phone and rolling over, but my fingers have other plans.

> ME
> Can't sleep

> CAM
> I'm sorry. I feel like that's my fault

> ME
> It's not. You didn't even know I was staying here lol

> **CAM**
> True. Ezra is gonna hear it from me tomorrow
> 😂

Rather than respond, I stalk his Instagram grid. Yeah, I'm a glutton for punishment. I swipe in a swift upward motion, and pictures fly by in a blur like the wheel from *The Price is Right*.

The fifteen-photo grid displayed when it stops is full of photographs of places and things—hotel lobbies, a meadow of wildflowers, specialty cocktails and an artisan charcuterie board next to a luxury pool. There are a couple of featured people too. There's one of Cameron and Ezra at a baseball game. Another I recognize instantly. It's me, but this photo wasn't taken recently. It's the picture he had framed on his desk in Greece. The one of me jumping off the side of the boat in my pink bikini. The date beneath it shows he posted it more than a year ago. And the caption? *The most beautiful view I've ever seen.*

My pussy is no longer screaming. No, she's got a full choke hold on me now. A relentless ache tugs behind my heart. I don't have time to think about what this means, though, because another message comes through.

> **CAM**
> You still there? I can't sleep...

> **ME**
> I'm here
> Why can't you sleep

The man traveled across an ocean today. He's got to be exhausted.

Three dots appear, then disappear. Then reappear.

For the Plot

> **CAM**
> Truth?

> **ME**
> Truth

I grin at the memory of the night I tried to get him to play Truth or Dare at the bed-and-breakfast.

> **CAM**
> I can't stop imagining how you were grinding against my mattress before I interrupted

Yup. Pussy, meet choke hold. *Help.*

> **CAM**
> When you leave tomorrow, will the scent of your pussy be branded on my sheets?

Dear Lord, the man's lewd. I fucking love it.

> **ME**
> You're making this really hard for me

> **CAM**
> I could say the same about you...

I snag my vibrator and twirl it. He's right about one thing—there's no way I can go to bed in this state. I'm way too pent up. Why does it feel like the man's sexual energy has a force field over me?

An idea strikes me then. One that'll leave me satisfied and won't have me going back on my word...

Mere seconds after I text *Come here*, the bedroom door flies open and a shirtless Cameron skids across the hardwood floor.

When I turn on the bedside light, I can't help but revel in the merriment brightening his stupidly handsome face.

"I have a proposition," I say, sitting up higher against the headboard.

He takes a hesitant step closer, his brows jumping. He regards me, then my toy, then me again. Oh, I've piqued his interest, all right.

It's more than a force field of sexual energy.

With a deep breath in to ease the ache in my chest, I push that thought away.

"Neither of us is falling asleep anytime soon," I begin.

A nod, then he's positioned in the middle of the room, hands clenched into fists at his sides and his chest heaving.

I stand by my decision. I won't have sex with him, but I have needs—and dare I say kinks? A little voyeurism could satisfy us both without crossing the line.

It's the perfect loophole. I'm metaphorically patting myself on the back for having come up with it.

Cupping the long, slightly curved vibe in my left hand, I continue. "How about this? You can look, but you can't touch me."

Cameron, hair still wet from his shower, drags a hand down his face. A faint "fuck" falls from his lips.

I quirk an eyebrow, silently asking, *Are you in?*

Without a word, he closes the space between us, only stopping when his knees bump the side of the bed. He yanks the sheets, eager and impatient, like a kid with wrapping paper on Christmas morning.

"Spread your legs, gorgeous."

He snags two pillows and settles them halfway down the bed, and without needing direction, I swivel so my upper body is propped against them. I plant my feet on the edge of the mattress and spread my legs. Then I tug on the hem of his T-shirt I'm still wearing, pulling the fabric up my abdomen until it rests just below my breasts.

I never answered when he asked why I was wearing his shirt. My first instinct was to lie and say because my clothes were already packed, but neither of us would have believed that. The truth is, I haven't been able to shake thoughts of him. Our time in Greece has left a stain on my soul. So when I found myself sleeping in his bed, I swiped a shirt from his drawer and wore it like I had on the nights we were together in Greece.

"Let me see that pretty pussy." He pulls me from my reflections.

His eyes are glued to my core, where I'm exposed and vulnerable. I never did put my underwear back on. "Doesn't look like you'll need lube," he says. "You're already fucking soaked."

I swirl my favorite toy through my wetness and drag it up my slit. I've never pleasured myself with an audience before, but I'm instantly a fan. Putting on a show, I'm discovering, turns me on more than if I were solo.

I dip the vibrator into my entrance, then trail up to my clit, *slo-o-o-wly*, several times over. Cameron's eyes are locked between my legs; mine are locked on his. When I finally turn on the device, he startles. A laugh bursts from my lips, making him scowl at me. But the laughter dies and is quickly replaced by a moan as the vibrations stimulate my clit.

With a curse, he grips the bulge in his sweatpants.

"I said you couldn't touch," I reprimand, when he rubs his length through the fabric.

He gulps. "You said I couldn't touch *you*."

Touché.

I don't argue. Watching him touch himself is only speeding along the momentum building inside me. Like live-action porn. With one elbow, I prop myself up for a better view. He takes my silence as permission, and when he drags his pants down his thighs and lets them drop to the floor, I fucking whimper.

He snickers. The man's no idiot—he knows exactly how to get me going. Damn, I love how in tune he is to my needs and desires.

Fuck, I cannot be using *love* in reference to this man.

"Where'd you go?" he whispers.

See? He just knows.

Shaking my head, I focus on what's in front of me. The way he strokes his length and swirls his precum at the tip with his thumb forces a whimper from me.

He huffs out a laugh in response, and I shoot him a glare. But my grudge doesn't last long. Between the vibrations and the sight of this gorgeous man throwing his head back in ecstasy, I'm perched on the edge. Watching him jerk himself is torture. Why did I make the stupid no-touching rule?

"Let me see you slide it inside," he rasps.

I obey, arching off the bed and finding a rhythm.

"Thatta girl," he croons. "You like being filled up. You wish it was me fucking you right now, don't you?"

My groan is confirmation enough.

"Eyes on me."

When I force my attention to focus on him, he's leaning over me with one hand planted by my side and the other gripped tightly at the head of his cock, like he's fighting not to spill himself all over me. Still, he's not touching me.

When I mutter, "I'm close," he spits in his hand and coats his cock and matches my pace, stroke for stroke.

I can't look away from him. I say his name like a prayer.

"That's it. Don't slow down now, sweetheart."

I drag the vibrator over my clit, relishing the rumble that works its way through me.

When he grits out "Come for me, baby," I'm a goner.

Without constraint, I squirm and shiver, conceding to ecstasy. My eyes are shut tight when the first warm droplets hit my belly. Fuck, I don't want to miss this. When I open them, the image above me is magnificent. Cameron, quivering and grunting through gritted teeth.

"*Fu-u-ck,*" he howls in pure bliss.

With one final shudder, he collapses onto the bed to my right, hand lightly wrapped around his cock.

The aftereffects of my orgasm are subsiding, the heat in my core banking just a little, but there's still a faint pulsing sensation inside me.

Next to me, Cameron props himself up on an elbow and assesses my body, now sprawled out on the bed. "Shit," he sighs, taking in the cum pooling in my belly button. "I'm sorry."

Still riding my high, I dip my finger into the milky warmth and drag it over my lips, then lap it up with my tongue.

"Fuck, Joey," he pants, his hot breath caressing my cheek. "Are you trying to kill me?"

I stifle a predatory laugh, then heave myself up on both elbows.

"Wait." He sits and snags a few tissues from the nightstand, then wipes at my stomach with a flourish. He surveys me, his breaths slowing. We stay like that for a heartbeat too long, but before I can muster the energy to back away, he excuses himself and strolls to the bathroom. He turns on the water for a moment, and then he's back, crossing the room in full birthday-suit glory and scooping his sweatpants off the floor.

He holds out my silicone toy. My clean, dry silicone toy.

"Did you just clean my vibrator?" I ask, dumbfounded. I hadn't noticed he swiped it from the bed.

He nods. "Consider it the sixth love language."

Love language. He can't be saying shit like that. Not when I'm trying to put distance between us. *Yeah, because letting him jerk off on your stomach is "distance."*

I'm so fucked.

"Well, good night," I blurt out, quickly looking away from the longing look in his eyes.

"Good night." With that, he's gone, quietly closing the door behind him.

After rinsing his stickiness off my body, I settle into his bed and pull the sheets up to my chin. Though I got the orgasm I was in such desperate need of, an emptiness settles in my soul. Fear forbids me from finding out what it means.

Chapter 35
Josefine

I MUST HAVE FORGOTTEN to set my alarm this morning, because I wake to a sunlit room and the smell of bacon and coffee, then discover it's already ten. Shit. My plan was to get up at eight and be out of here shortly after. And I still need to run by the store for a replacement water bottle for the woman I bumped into last week before tonight's writing workshop.

After brushing my teeth, I secure my hair with a gold claw clip and take the world's fastest shower. I don't even bother to wait until the water is warm. I guess a little bit of Greece came home with me after all. I pull on a short yellow sundress I bought in the resort's boutique, then pull in a fortifying breath, straighten my shoulders, and venture to the kitchen.

Cameron is standing over the hot stove, wearing his glasses, and he's got a cup of coffee pressed to his lips.

"Morning," I announce, reaching into the cabinet for a mug of my own.

"Morning," he echoes, pulling on the waistband of his gray sweatpants. Fuck, I really wish he'd take those off. No, not like that. I mean wear something less sexy. It's a well-known fact that women can't focus when in the proximity of men wearing gray sweatpants. If *Scientific American* hasn't published an article on it already, they're sure to release it any day now. The sight of his shirtless chest and abs aren't helping either.

I utter a thanks when he pours me a mug of freshly brewed coffee from the French press and shuffle behind him to get to the fridge, careful not to brush up against him in the narrow galley kitchen. I want to take a mental inventory of what I need to replace.

"What the—" I pause when the cool air hits me. Inside, the shelves are exquisitely stocked. The display before me would put The Home Edit to shame.

I stand up straight and spin. "Did you—"

"I went shopping this morning." He shrugs, laying the last strip of bacon on a plate just as the oven timer goes off.

"You didn't have to do that. I was going to wake up early to replace everything this morning, but I guess I forgot to set my alarm."

By "forgot," I mean that I was too distracted by our matching orgasms.

With a grin, he dons an oven mitt and pulls a Michelin-worthy quiche from the oven. "*Thank you, Cam,* is acceptable."

"*Thank you, Cameron,*" I mock, bringing my mug to my lips. There's nothing like the first sip of coffee in the morning.

Once the quiche is resting on the stovetop, he props himself up against the counter and folds his arms over his chest, putting his perfect pecs on display. "Since when am I Cameron?"

I shrug, hiding behind my mug. "Ezra may have mentioned that only family and close friends call you Cam."

Pushing off the counter, he picks up his own coffee, then he takes a step in my direction. "I've been inside you, Joey. How much *closer* can two people get?" He taps his porcelain cup against mine with a wink. "Call me Cam."

My body breaks out in a shiver as I'm once again assaulted by images of our little mutual masturbation session last night. Not that there was anything little about it. He hovers close and opens the cabinet above me. Desperate for a hit of air that doesn't smell like him, I scurry to the sink and fill the water glass I left there last night, then chug its contents.

"Listen." I swipe at the water that dribbled down my chest in my haste, and shit if he doesn't home in on the movement. "What happened last night...it—it can't happen again."

"I think I've heard that before." He rolls his eyes as he pulls silverware from the drawer.

"I'm serious," I say, making my way to a stool at the bar.

He plates the quiche. It's filled with tomatoes, onions, spinach, and sweet potatoes, and it looks incredible. Then he sets the plate of bacon on the bar and drops into the stool beside me.

"Joey."

"No, wait."

He snaps his mouth shut and regards me with a patient expression.

"I don't know what came over me last night."

Actually, I do know what *came over me*. And he does too, if the smirk on his face is any indication. I drop my chin and sigh. "I was frustrated and—"

"Horny."

I roll my eyes. I really hate that word. "*Aroused.*" (Though is that any better?) "And you were there." I drag my hand down my face and let my shoulders slump. "But if I'm going to be serious about writing my book, I need to avoid distraction. For so long, I was in a relationship that I didn't realize was toxic. I can't go down that path again. I need to do this myself, and I can't let anyone get in the way."

He drops his fork to his plate with a clatter. "You done?" he asks, his tone even.

I nod, peering over at him.

Cracking his knuckles under the table, he exhales deeply. "With all due respect, I'm tired of the bullshit."

I wince.

"Just tell me what's really going on. I know you feel this thing between us."

I open my mouth, ready to argue my point, but he raises a finger between us.

"Wait." He picks up his napkin and wipes his mouth, then spins so he's facing me. "I don't know what to call this thing between us, but whatever it is, it feels good, and I want more of it. Don't give me bullshit excuses about independence. You can do whatever the fuck you set your mind to. That's been obvious to me since the moment I met you. I don't want to be your knight in shining armor. You don't need one. And I'm nothing like the dipshit you wasted all that time with. I will not hold you back. I will support you in whatever capacity you need. Didn't you read my letter? I want to be your hype guy. Please, let me be that for you. Don't you want to see where this goes? I'm not asking you for forever; I'm just asking for right now."

Chapter 36
Josefine

"What did you tell him?" Millie asks, now that I've caught her up on Cam's morning truth bomb.

The second I walked into our apartment, she knew something was up. And honestly, I need her advice. The short walk home wasn't enough to work through the shit between Cam and me. *What letter was he talking about?* He didn't give me a letter before I left Crete, and I've checked my mail a couple of times over the last week.

"I told him I need time to think."

She embraces me in a tight hug. "Fair enough," she agrees. "But he's right, you know."

"Hmm?"

"He's not like Tyler," she calls from her closet, where she's unpacking.

That's obvious, but it doesn't mean he won't hurt me. Look at all the men my mom has dated. They started off as good guys too. Most of them, anyway.

As if she can read my mind, she yells, "You're not like your mom. Cam is a good guy. And if there's a time when he does treat you poorly, you'll kick him to the curb like the badass bitch you are. You're self-aware as shit, and you have no problem standing up for yourself. As shitty as Tyler was, your breakup taught you a lot about yourself and what you want moving forward. Didn't that fuckboy at least teach you there's *good* in goodbye?"

"I think that was Taylor Swift," I tease, despite the dull ache in my heart.

Millie sticks her head out of the closet and rolls her eyes. "While your ex may have dragged your dreams through the dirt, it doesn't sound like Cam would do that."

"But how do you know?" I plead.

"I don't. You gotta have faith."

Faith. Huh. Every type-A control freak's nightmare.

Mumbling a dismissal, I head to the living room to unpack my own bags.

After our unfinished breakfast conversation, Cam and I fell into an oddly companionable silence while we ate. I helped him clean the kitchen, and he gave me space while I finished collecting my belongings. When he popped in to check on me and saw me fingering his copy of *The Alchemist*, he offered it to me to borrow.

"Nonsense," he scoffed when I told him I'd already downloaded the e-book. "There's nothing quite like holding the physical copy in your hands."

As I unpack my suitcase, I discover a white envelope tucked under a cover-up. The blue stamp at the top left corner reads *Atlas Luxury Resort and Spa*; my name is scrawled in the middle. I turn the envelope over in my hand. Written on the back is a quote, one I already recognize from his favorite book. The one that says that everything that happens once can't ever happen again, but if it happens twice, it'll happen a third time.

My heart stutters. We met last year. That's one. Then we

For the Plot

were thrown together a second time. And last night? That was our third. Or am I stretching to make truths out of nothing?

Carefully, I tear open the envelope, remembering then the moment I realized Cam is a leftie. When he was hunched over the desk in his hotel room writing on a piece of resort letterhead.

Five minutes later, after having read the most encouraging letter of my life, and wiping the tears from my eyes, I reach for my phone.

> ME
> Hi. Thanks again for breakfast. It was delicious 😊
>
> Also… my answer is yes

After I tuck my phone into my laptop bag, I add my laundry to Millie's pile. She's a saint, offering to take care of it since I've got a busy day ahead of me. I shout a goodbye, then make the trek to the Black Hole. There's a little extra pep in my step as I pass Cam's place along the way.

"An Andalusian Dream?" Iris asks when I walk in.

I laugh. "How did you know?"

She shrugs, her jet-black hair swaying at her shoulders. "I had a feeling."

As it turns out, my new favorite coffee shop has a selection of aluminum water bottles for purchase. Knowing nothing about the woman I knocked over last Monday, I choose one with a purplish-blue Milky Way design. The pages that scattered on the sidewalk were full of sketches, and this bottle looks artsy to me.

As I'm paying, my phone buzzes from inside my laptop bag, so I wedge the bottle under my arm and dig it out.

> CAM
> Can I take you out tonight?

> ME
> Sounds great

I make my way to my new favorite table at the back of the café, where Ari is already typing furiously on his laptop.

"Hey," I say, brushing by the table. "What are you doing?"

Removing his earbuds, he turns his laptop so I can see the screen. "Working on the assignment that's due today." He frowns. "Don't tell my bubbe."

"Don't worry." I wink. "Your secret is safe with me."

We work side by side in silence for hours, only breaking for lunch. It's an introvert's dream.

Just before five, we pack up and head for the bus stop. When we arrive and step up to the education building, we have to dodge a collage of sidewalk chalk art. The concrete is flooded with four-by-four squares of rainbow-themed scenes, likely in preparation for a Pride Week celebration.

We settle in our seats, and moments later, Talulah saunters in. She's as captivating as ever, but I struggle to focus; my mind is adhered to my date later this evening. *What am I even doing?* I was adamant about avoiding distractions, but I can't deny that Cam and I have a connection. He called it cosmic, and maybe he's right. Millie certainly thinks I should give him a chance. Admittedly, I'm notorious for second-guessing myself.

Should I leave home for college? Should I finish college? Should I write a book? Should I get bangs? Should I order extra queso with chips? (Okay, so I'm never indecisive when it comes to queso.)

Decision fatigue and the constant questioning game my brain plays are exhausting. Sometimes I wish I could crawl out of my own head and take a nap in someone else's. With a weighted blanket.

Mentally shaking off that train of thought, I sit up straight in my chair, determined to put Cam aside for the time being and focus on writing.

After class, I situate myself against one of the twin pillars at the entrance of the education building and wait for the dark-haired woman to appear. I pull up my text thread with Cam to confirm we're meeting at my apartment.

Just as I'm sticking my phone back in my bag, she steps out of a taxi in front of the building. Her white V-neck shirt is tucked into a pair of high-waisted acid-washed jeans, and black Birkenstocks hug her feet. She's got her hair pulled up in a bun again, although it's messier than last time, and her bangs frame the same circular, gold-rimmed glasses she wore last week. She pauses at the edge of the sidewalk and hunches over one of the chalk drawings. As she does, a man steps out of the taxi and sidles up to her to examine the artwork.

A man who, not even nine hours ago, was cooking breakfast for me in his kitchen.

A man who, not even eighteen hours ago, was coming on my stomach.

My chest tightens like a balloon inflating against my lungs, and I clutch my hand to my heart. *What the fuck?* Time needs to speed up, and I need to get the hell out of here.

The woman who, a moment ago, I could see myself striking up a friendship with, elbows Cam in the ribs. He stumbles back, feigning injury, causing them both to break into laughter. The joy in the sound and the glee in his expression are so familiar. This morning, they brought a welcome hunger. Now, though, they cause a pit of dread to form in my stomach.

She hands her phone to him, and they turn to take a selfie,

being sure to catch the chalk art in the background. When he returns her phone, he swings an arm around her shoulder and guides her toward the building, all cozy and shit.

The pit in my stomach cracks open, and pain leaches into my extremities. I want to run.

No, I want the concrete below to open wide and swallow me whole.

How could I have been so stupid? Typical. I peel back the tiniest of layers and let him in, and instantly, he tears a hole in my heart. Just like my mom. Just like my ex.

The concrete below me doesn't grant my wish, and now, two feet in front of me, is the star of my next therapy session.

Cam nearly trips up the stairs when he catches sight of me. "Hi." He drops his tattooed arm from around the woman's shoulders and leans in to kiss my cheek.

Hell no, jackass.

I rear back like his touch alone might singe my skin. In an instant, his bright expression morphs into one of confusion. In response, my nose burns, but I force the tears threatening to well in my eyes to abate.

"Cam," I say through gritted teeth. If I open my mouth any wider, I may just throw up. Wouldn't that be grand? Then he'd carry this gorgeously adorable human beside him home in his pocket, wash and worship her in his shower, and then make love to her in the bed I slept in last night. After, they'd surely cuddle like otters and laugh about the girl on the stairs who vomited all over them.

"Did you hear me?" he asks. He's wearing a white V-neck—as if they coordinated outfits—army green chinos, and cognac-colored leather sneakers. His face is freshly shaved, and even his hair has been trimmed since this morning. He looks like he walked right off my Pinterest inspo page, and I fucking hate it.

"Huh?" I grunt. Rude? Maybe, but I don't care.

For the Plot

"Are you okay?"

The woman looks from him to me and back again, no doubt assessing the situation. Does she suspect her boyfriend has been playing her like a chessboard? Well, checkmate, darling, because I'm about to end this game.

Behind a forced smile, I turn to her. "Here." I hold the brand-new water bottle between us. "I'm sorry about last week."

With an outstretched hand, she accepts it. "Thank you." Her smile is gracious, beautiful. I want to knock in her perfect teeth. But she's not who I'm angry with.

Careful not to make contact with Cam, I take a step to one side. But a strong hand grasps my wrist. When I yank, attempting to free myself from his hold, he towers over me, practically pinning me against the pillar.

"What are you doing, Joey?" His deep voice is crisp and urgent.

"*Joey?*" I must be hearing things, because I swear there's a hint of wonder in the woman's voice.

"Yes?" The word wedges in my throat, and my voice goes up an octave too high to sound sane.

"*This* is Joey?" she asks. Now I'm confused. Her tone is far too pleasant for what's happening here. If I were her, I'd be wondering about the identity of the mystery woman my boyfriend is trying to kiss on the cheek.

"Oh my god!" She pushes him out of the way and nearly knocks me over with an awkward hug.

My arms are superglued to my sides, and my shoulders are basically stuffed into my ear canals. "What's going on?"

Cam puts one hand on the woman's arm, signaling her to step back.

"Joey," he says, his voice so frustratingly soothing, "this is my sister, Claire. Claire, this is—"

"Your Joey!" she cuts him off, bouncing on the balls of her feet.

Claire? The woman he took a selfie with is—

"Oh my god, your sister!" My body ignites in a flash fire of mortification.

I offer a redo introduction. This time I embrace her with genuine gratitude, sighing into her tiny frame. Thank fuck he isn't just another fuckboy in my life.

When I face him, he asks, "Did you think—" He doesn't finish the question, no doubt because the answer is written across my face.

Relief courses through my veins, but radical emotions are crawling their way to the surface. My cheeks are still flaming, and tears well in my eyes. I guess relief has to go somewhere.

"Oh, baby," he says, pulling me into his chest and clinging to me like a lifeline.

I sniff back my tears as quietly as possible, then inhale deeply and relax against him when the familiar scent of his detergent hits me.

When I pull away, I turn to Claire. "I'm so sorry." Wringing my hands, I let out a nervous laugh. Now that the confusion and fury have fled, I take her in more closely. How did I not notice the resemblance? Not only do they have the same hazel eyes and dark brown hair, but their smiles take shape in the same crescent curve.

"This is so embarrassing," I accidentally say aloud.

"Forget it," she assures me, embracing me again. *Okay, I guess we have a hugger.*

Not that I'm complaining. I'm back to imagining this classy hipster as my BFF.

"I'm so glad I'm finally meeting you after all this time!"

All this time? It's only been a couple of weeks.

"My brother hasn't shut up about you for like a y—"

"That's enough, sis." He smacks a hand across her mouth.

Her eyes are full of spirit and secrets. What has he told her?

Cam releases her, then places his hand on the small of my back and rubs circles with such delicacy I shiver. "Are you okay now?"

My lips tremble, but I smile and nod.

"Where are you two going tonight?" She inquires, doing her best to clear the air.

"It's a surprise," he croons.

"You don't know yet, do you?" I call his bullshit.

"Nope." He closes the last few inches of space between us and brushes his cheek against mine. His breath is hot in my ear when he whispers, "But I promise to make it worthwhile."

"I heard that!" Claire gags at her brother's comment. "I'll be going now. It was lovely to meet you, Joey." She hugs me once more and lingers for a moment. "Give him a chance."

When she pulls away, she jogs up the stairs with a backward wave and a "good to have you back, big bro."

When she's out of earshot, I throw my hands over my face. "That was definitely not a great first impression."

Pulling my hands down, Cam intertwines his fingers with mine. "I hate that you thought she was someone else. I would never." Still holding tight to me, he brushes his fingers against my hip. "I'm a one-woman kind of guy and..." He ducks his head. And if I'm not mistaken, his cheeks go the slightest shade of pink.

Oh, wow. Are we having the "exclusive" talk already? Here? Right now? We *have* been sleeping together. Our friends-with-benefits relationship was my idea and was only supposed to last on the island. But now?

A muscle clenches along his jaw, and I push back the lock of hair that's fallen across his forehead.

"I'm not seeing anyone else," I confirm.

His posture slackens. "Good. Because I don't want to share

these"—he pulls a scrap of lace from his pocket and dangles it between us like a pocket watch—"with anyone."

My cheeks rush with heat. "Have you lost your damn mind?" Yanking the black lace that got lodged in his sheets last night, I panic-stuff them down the front of my dress, between my breasts, giggling the whole time.

Cam tucks a strand of hair behind my ear. "Come on, gorgeous." He grabs the strap of my laptop case and guides me down the stairs with a hand at my back. "Since I'm here now, let's take an Uber. We'll have to drop your stuff and run if we want to make our reservation on time."

"But I thought you didn't have a plan."

He pulls up his ride-share app as we wander to the end of the block. "If I told my sister where we were going, her crazy ass would follow us there."

"Clever boy," I laugh.

When we step through my apartment door, I'm acutely aware that this is the first time Cam has entered my personal space. I mean, my *physical* personal space. Dang it. I mean my apartment.

"Do you want anything to drink?" I offer, tucking my laptop below the television in its designated resting spot.

He shakes his head, taking in the open kitchen to the left before he joins me in the main living space. A basket full of folded laundry sits on the sofa. I could kiss Millie for taking care of my least favorite chore. I remove my thong from my cleavage and toss it onto the pile.

The heat radiating off Cam hits my back before his breath

wafts over my ear. Then he's looping his arms around my waist. "Where do you sleep?"

"Here," I squeak, motioning to the sofa before us, positive he can feel the pounding of my heart against my ribs.

He releases me and plops onto the gray sofa, swiveling his hips for emphasis. "Does it fold open to a bed?"

I nod.

"That's cool," he murmurs, though the sentiment falls flat.

I'm right there with you, buddy. I'd love to have my own room, let alone a real bed, but that's not in the cards for me right now.

Cam stretches his arms across the back of the sofa and spreads his legs wide. He looks like a fucking GQ model. The temptation to crawl on my knees between his legs is as strong as a magnetic force. But tonight is our first official date. I cannot saturate it in sex. I promised I'd give us a chance, and I meant it—no matter how nervous it makes me. Courage is being scared and doing it anyway, right?

Chapter 37
Cameron

THE FIRST THING Joey thought when she saw me with my sister was that I was seeing someone else. Fuck. How can I make it any more obvious that I'm into her?

I was just as shocked to see her at the education center, though without the dread she probably felt when she saw me with Claire. After Joey left my apartment this morning, I made plans to meet up with my sister. Luckily, she wasn't working at the hospital today—a rarity—and fit me in.

The two of us are close. When kids experience tragedy together at a young age, it either bonds or breaks them. Fortunately for us, it tied us together. It could also be attributed to how I took on the caregiver role when our mom was hospitalized.

I've never resented being forced to care for her back then. I take pride in being her big brother, and I'm proud of her for pursuing medicine. Though she's never spoken it aloud, I've always assumed her choice has to do with Chloe's death.

The only point of contention that has come between us was when my parents withheld my inheritance because I didn't take over the family business. We never argued about it, but for a

For the Plot

while, this unspoken tension lingered between us. Our parents have never held Claire to the standard at which they hold me. She was never expected to be involved, yet she'll still receive her inheritance.

Regardless, we moved on from the awkwardness quickly. She played no part in the decisions our parents made, so I had no right to hold any of it against her.

Once Claire and Joey get to know each other, they're going to be thick as thieves. I was tempted to tell her about our plans tonight to get a second opinion, but if I told her I planned to take Joey to Under the Summer Stars, the temporary outdoor theater overlooking the Hudson River near the George Washington Bridge, she would follow us like a puppy seeking adoption.

When I found out *The Parent Trap* was playing tonight, I instantly purchased tickets and made sure to reserve two inflatable chairs. My favorite deli is on the way, so I figure we can grab food to-go.

I planned to pick Joey up tonight and assumed she'd meet me outside her building. At every turn, I have to be patient and give her time to warm up, so I was under no misconception that I'd see the inside of her apartment. Now, I'm sitting on her sofa-slash-bed, and it's taking every ounce of my willpower not to pull her onto my lap and confiscate another pair of panties.

"Should I change?"

Her question pulls me out of my fantasy. Tilting my head, I give her a once-over. As much as I love the way that dress puts her perky tits on display, she'll probably get chilly.

"Yeah. The forecast says it's going to get down into the low sixties tonight."

"Oh, will we be outside?" she asks, thumbing through the clothes in her laundry basket.

She retrieves a long red dress adorned with tiny white flowers from the pile and excuses herself. When she returns, she's added a white T-shirt that says *Kind people are my kinda people* in red letters. The shirt is cinched in a knot at her navel. She's still wearing her white Chucks, and she has a denim jacket draped over her forearm.

"You look beautiful." I stand and follow her to the door.

She rummages through the purse hanging on a hook in the entryway until she pulls out a bottle of pink gloss and a black scrunchy, then she steps in front of the small mirror mounted on the wall.

"Wait." I pull her close. She smells like she did in Greece: citrus shampoo, mixed with her light floral perfume. "Before you put that on," I capture her chin with my thumb and forefinger and tilt her face so she's looking at me, "can I kiss you?"

"What? Pink not your color?" she teases, tugging on my bottom lip.

I nip at her thumb, and even though we're alone in the apartment, I whisper, "Oh, sweetheart, pink is my favorite color. But the only place I want to be marked with it is my cock, when your lips are wrapped around it." It's not a joke.

Biting her bottom lip, she pops up on her toes and presses her plush lips to mine. I barely have time to drink in the sweetness of her kiss before it turns feral, like heat on metal, soldering us together. I open my mouth in invitation, and she gladly accepts. Damn, I'll never tire of this. But her stomach grumbles, and my innate need to take care of people assumes control.

When I step back, she stumbles forward, and a whine escapes her lips, all pink and swollen from my kisses. See? She doesn't need lipstick after all.

"Hungry?" I ask.

The way her eyes blaze tells me she knows I'm not talking about food.

Once outside, we cross the street and walk the couple of blocks to Bubbe's Nosh Pit, my favorite delicatessen. The aroma of the place--the combination of chicken broth, potato, and onion--reminds me of Ezra's mother's house.

"Joey, my love!" Mark calls from behind the counter as the bell chimes over our heads, and an instant later, he follows it with "Cam? My man!"

She turns around, just as astonished as me. "You know Mark?" we say in unison.

Mark, the owner of the deli, is a middle-aged man with a round belly. Though he's bald, his arms are covered in a thick layer of dark hair, and the glasses he wears are constantly slipping down his nose.

Before we make it to the counter, he's holding a black-and-white cookie wrapped in a napkin over the counter to Joey.

Beneath a clear encasement lies a display of traditionally Jewish foods—potato pancakes, potato salad, lox, bagels, several flavors of cream cheese, chopped liver, matzo ball soup, pickles, and so much more.

Accepting the cake-like cookie covered in chocolate icing on one side and vanilla on the other, she smiles. "Thank you. How's your bubbe?"

"Wait, how do you know about his grandma?" I ask. "And how come she gets a cookie and I don't?" I cock a brow at Mark, feigning offense.

He pulls another cookie from the display case and winks as he passes it over.

With a shit-eating grin, I accept the treat. "Thank you. But yes, how's your bubbe?"

"She's bossing us around, so I'd say she's made a full recovery," he huffs, pulling on a new pair of plastic gloves. "She says to say thank you for the flowers and the puzzle."

Peering up at me, Joey laces her fingers with mine and squeezes. I squeeze once in response and shoot her a smile.

"What'll it be?" Mark inquires.

She steps closer to the counter. "I'll have half a pastrami on rye."

"With extra pickles?" he assumes correctly. "What else?" He looks at me, then back at her.

"Two potato pancakes and a side of fruit. Oh! And a Dr. Brown's Black Cherry."

"Make that two cherry sodas, six potato pancakes, and a *bowl* of fruit," I pipe up. "Plus, a corned beef sandwich and an assortment of *rugelach*." I love the flaky pastries. Especially the ones with dates and cinnamon.

I guide Joey to the side, hands still intertwined, while Mark puts together our order. "How do you know Mark so well?"

"Sounds like you know his grandmother pretty well," she says, bumping my shoulder.

"This is my go-to place for comfort food."

She arches a brow. "Jewish food is your comfort food?"

"It is," I laugh. "Ezra's Jewish. Did you know that?"

She shakes her head.

"I've spent a lot of time at his mom's house. She loves to cook."

"Huh." She shrugs. "My dad was Jewish. Millie is too."

"Yeah?"

"Yeah. My mom is Christian, so I grew up both and neither at the same time, I guess. But we celebrated all the holidays," she says. "Mark and his wife live in my building." Dropping my hand, she leans in and loops her arm around my waist like it's the most natural thing in the world. "They bring us food all the time, so I don't come into the deli often. They're like our surrogate parents, I guess." The smile that lifts her cheeks is bright and full of genuine adoration. It makes me want to kiss the soft flesh.

Mark spots us in the crowd that's forming and motions for us to meet him at the checkout counter.

For the Plot

Joey reaches for the large brown paper bag just as I reach for my wallet.

"So what's happening here?" Mark questions, waggling a finger between the two of us.

"It's our first date," I say, lifting my chin and maintaining eye contact.

"You don't say." He beams. "Well, then, my friends, it's on the house."

"What?" I look at Joey, who's biting back a smile. "No—"

He shoves two extra black-and-white cookies in the bag and announces, "Next!" effectively dismissing me.

"Thank you," we say in unison.

He puts his hands over his heart, and when we're halfway to the door, he calls out her name. He points to me. "He's one of the good ones!"

With blushing cheeks, she nods and blows him a friendly kiss before stepping onto the sidewalk.

The streets of New York City are alive tonight. The diverse population, the cultural richness, and the urban dynamic make it the greatest city in the world. The greenery is lush this time of year, with dogs and children rolling in the open grass spaces. A gentle breeze carries the city's fragrances: one second, the acute scent of blossoming flowers, and the next, the aroma of a nearby pretzel stand. By the time we arrive at the park and have been led to our reserved seating, the sun has nearly set, and a canvas of pastel hues paints a backdrop for us.

When *The Parent Trap* toggles on the giant screen, Joey nearly catapults out of her green inflatable seat in excitement. We lay our food, plastic utensils, and sodas on the small circular table positioned between our chairs and eat our sandwiches straight from the paper wrapping.

When we arrived, there was a black blanket wrapped in plastic, much like those on an airplane, resting on each of our seats.

And about the time Chessy figures out Hallie is Annie, we unwrap our polyester blankets and Joey climbs onto my lap. With her butt flush against my hip and her legs draped over my lap, she snuggles into the crook of my neck.

"You smell good," I whisper.

"Shh," she scolds. "This is my favorite part." She quickly kisses me on the cheek. "And you're a liar. I smell like pickles."

"Shh," I tease. "Pickles smell good." I steal a kiss, smacking my lips against hers for dramatic flair, and someone to the left shushes us.

The movie ends, and Joey slips her arms through her denim jacket. "That was really fun." She stands and helps me throw our trash away. "Thank you."

"I'm glad you enjoyed it." I release the pieces of her long hair that are still tucked in her jacket.

Just as I reach for her hand, she spins around on the pavement to face me and walks backward. "Wanna grab a drink?"

I absolutely don't want this night to end, so I take her hand in mine and drop a kiss to it. "Sounds great."

She leads me to a bar I've never been to about halfway between our apartments, and we snag a high-top by the window.

"Old-fashioned," I tell the server before we've even had a chance to look at the drink menus.

"Make that two," Joey adds.

When our drinks arrive, garnished with oranges and maraschino cherries, she spins her glass on the sticky surface. "This was my dad's favorite drink," she admits, nostalgia caught in her throat. "He used to ask for extra cherries, then give them to me."

Lifting my glass, I raise a brow, and when she follows suit, I clink mine against hers. "He sounds like a solid man."

"Did you give Ezra hell about his little mix-up?" She uses air quotes, then drops her elbows to the table and tucks her fists beneath her chin.

"Yeah, he heard it from me, all right."

He called this morning to make sure I'd made it home, and when I questioned him about not telling me that Joey was sleeping in my bed, his response was along the lines of "are you kidding me? You would have been up my ass for a play-by-play, or worse—you would have flown home early."

He's not wrong.

"Too bad he and Millie didn't work out," she says, bringing her drink to her lips. "I think he could be good for her."

I take a sip, too, relishing the way the bold bourbon slides down my throat. "He's on a date with someone tonight, actually."

"Oh?"

"Yeah. Her name is the same as one of those American Girl dolls Claire used to have. Kirsten or Molly or something like that." I laugh. I can't keep up with my roommate and his women.

Joey sighs. "I'm sure going to miss your bed tonight. Not looking forward to my pull-out sofa."

"Spend the night, then." The words are out of my mouth before I've even considered them.

"What? No, that's not why I brought it up." She swirls a finger in the condensation on her glass, then wipes it on her cocktail napkin. Her cheeks are tinted pink, like maybe she's embarrassed. She finishes her drink in two long gulps.

"I know," I assure her. "But I'm actually going to be gone for work for a couple of weeks."

She's chomping on a piece of ice now, but she freezes when the words register. "You are?"

"I got that job I was telling you about. The one in Austin."

Her eyes widen with genuine glee. "That's great!"

"Thank you." I grin. "So, my bed needs someone to keep it company."

"Oh, it does, does it?" She leans closer, playing along.

I pluck the cherry from my glass and hand it to her, then take the remainder of my drink back. Her eyes twinkle and she grins at my gesture.

"Yes, if no one sleeps in it, it will lose its lived-in shape."

"You goof. It's Tempur-Pedic." She lets out a loud laugh.

"Okay, fine, you got me. But still. I think you should stay at my apartment." My gaze is steady. "I already know how much you love my bed."

Chapter 38
Josefine

THE COUCH'S springs squeak when I roll onto my back. Flopping a hand over my face to block out the light filtering in from the gap between the curtains, I curse myself for not going home with Cam last night. I did accept his offer to stay in his apartment while he travels for work, but he doesn't leave until this weekend. We've technically only been on one date. Staying overnight so soon didn't feel right. I refuse to repeat the mistakes I made with my ex and jump into things too quickly.

I reach for my phone on the side table and check my notifications, noting the sound of clothes hangers clanking on the other side of the wall.

> **CAM**
>
> Morning, beautiful
>
> FYI Claire may text you. She begged me for your number and I couldn't say no. I hope that's ok

Just then, a *ding*.

UNKNOWN NUMBER

Hey Joey! It's Claire. Cam gave me your number. Hope that's ok. I go to spin class on Wednesdays at 8am. Wanna join tomorrow?

I reply to Cam first.

ME

Morning, gorgeous 😊 Yes, it's fine. She's already texted me

Then I reply to Claire.

ME

Sounds great! see you tomorrow

An eight o'clock workout is perfect. It'll give me the energy I need for a full day of work after. Just as I'm about to set my phone down and crawl out of the bed so I can fold it back into itself like a reverse bunny in a magician's hat, my phone rings.

"Hello?"

"Hey. How are you?" Cam's husky morning voice is so damn sexy.

"I'm good," I reply through a yawn.

"Are you just waking up?"

"Mm-hmm." I hoist myself off the bed and stumble into the kitchen to boil water for the French press. "How are you?"

"I didn't sleep very well," he answers.

"Oh? Why not?"

The velvet edge of his voice sends shivers down my spine when he responds. "I was missing a certain someone."

"Oh, you were, were you?"

"Mm-hmm," he breathes. "When are you moving in?" The words are serious, but his tone is light and teasing.

"I'm not moving in!" I retort, pouring the hot water over the coffee grounds. I dig a spoon out of the drawer and give them a stir.

"I know, I know," he says. "But I leave for Austin on Saturday. Want to spend the night Friday? That way I can help you haul stuff over."

"I'm quite capable of carrying my own things," I say, though warmth blooms in my chest at the offer.

"Oh, I know. I've seen those biceps. I'm just trying to make myself useful."

Millie exits her room, catching my eye. I suppose staying with Cam for one night before he leaves isn't a big deal.

"Okay." I hip check Millie and mouth *morning boo*.

"Okay." His tone is so chipper his happiness seeps through the phone. "I'll let you go. Have a great day."

"You too."

"Oh, and have a great time at spin with Claire tomorrow."

"H-how'd you know?" I stammer.

He laughs. "She already texted me."

I can't help the smile that spreads across my face. "She seems like the type of gal who will dish all your embarrassing moments to me."

"Oh god," he buzzes. "What have I gotten myself into?"

"It'll be fine!" I assure him, though I make sure to add a hint of mischievousness to my tone just to mess with him. "Goodbye, Cameron."

"Goodbye, *Josefine*."

Millie slowly slides the plunger of the French press down, trapping the grounds at the bottom, then pours us each a cup. She hands one to me before pouring a ridiculous amount of sugar into hers. "How was your date? You were already asleep when I got in last night. I hope that doesn't mean it was terrible."

"It was really sweet." I slide into a seat at the little table off the kitchen, and she follows. With my knees tucked into my oversized shirt and my feet flat on the chair, I take my first sip. "Cam's leaving for Texas, and I think I'm going to stay at his place while he's gone. What do you think?"

Her face remains passive. "How long will he be gone?"

"Two weeks, I think."

She rubs her lips together in contemplation, and by the sparkle in her eye, I think she approves.

"Sounds good, boo." She pops up and grabs two cartons of yogurt from the refrigerator, then two spoons from a drawer.

I honestly thought she might have more questions. I tear open the foil top and give it a good lick. "What will you do without me for two weeks?" I tease.

"First of all, I can record a scene without being interrupted."

"That was one time!" I cry. "I thought you were being attacked!"

"Sometimes it be like that." She laughs, and so do I. Yeah, so I may have burst into her room thinking someone was strangling her, only to find her with giant headphones on, moaning into the mic.

"Plus," she continues around a mouthful of yogurt, "I don't know. Maybe I'll invite Sam over while you're gone."

"Oh?" I scoot forward in my chair. "What's the story there?"

"No idea." She shrugs. "She's giving me whiplash. Things were cool when I stayed at her place, but I've barely heard from her since."

She stands and tosses her spoon into the sink, signaling that the conversation is over, and heads to her room to work.

I stay in for the rest of the day, taking breaks from writing to help

For the Plot

Millie practice her audio recordings for the LULU app. I play the male role opposite her and do my best impression of a man climaxing, but we end up in hysterics, and I nearly crack a rib falling off my chair. It's safe to say she will not be asking for my assistance again.

Spin with Claire on Wednesday is a blast. Our instructor, Paul, reminds me of Ted Lasso. While he doesn't have the infamous mustache, he has the motivational speeches down to a T.

"I want you to turn up that resistance! And while you're at it, turn up that love for yourself!" Then, "Time to sprint! But this time, we're sprinting for our dreams!" and "Life's a lot like riding a bike. As long as you keep pedaling, you'll keep moving forward!"

I tend to prefer instructors with more of a Roy Kent vibe—the kind who grunt and yell controversial things like "Pain's just weakness leaving the body!" and "Turn up the resistance. Life's full of fucking hills. You either climb 'em or get left at the bloody bottom!"

Although it's farther from my house than the place I normally work out, the studio's atmosphere is incredible. The locker rooms are cleaner and the staff is friendlier too. Plus, Claire is a member, and I really like her. She doesn't have much time before her shift at the hospital, but we grab a couple of açaí bowls in the gym's café and chat.

The second we sit down, her mouth split into a wicked grin. "My brother really likes you."

Heat creeps up my neck and into my cheeks, and I duck my head, at a loss for what to say. I've never been friends with the siblings of any man I've dated.

"I'm not trying to embarrass you," she says, giving me a real smile this time. "It's just, I haven't seen him this happy in a really long time."

That gets my attention. "What do you mean?"

She sets her spoon on a napkin next to her bowl and clears her throat. "Has he told you much about our..."

"Chloe?" I ask. "Yes. I'm so sorry. That must have been so awful."

"Honestly, I don't remember much other than following my big brother around like he was the coolest guy in the world. He always made sure I was safe and happy." She presses her lips together, and her eyes go glassy. "That's backfired a little now that I'm older, because I don't know how to sit with some of my emotions, but I'd never tell him that. We were so young, and he did what he thought he was supposed to do—care for me."

I nod, envisioning a little Cam taking on a huge role at such a young age.

"My brother likes to care for people. It's in his nature. I just wish someone would take care of him."

It's Friday, my kinda-sorta-but-not-really-move-in day. Cam is coming to "help" me carry my bags to his apartment. It's evidence of the truth of Claire's comment. He's always caring for others. I hope I can find a way to reciprocate. I say I'm a feminist, and *fuck the patriarchy* and all that jazz, but if someone offers to carry my bags, I'm going to pack extra shoes and shout, "Here you go!"

"Ms. Beckham, it's so lovely to see you again." Hector greets us at the door to his building.

"You too." I match the intensity of his smile.

"Staying a while, are we?" He nods to my small rolling suitcase, then looks to Cam, who's carrying my duffel.

Cam's eyes crease at the sides when he grins. "Yes. She's staying here while I'm in Austin."

"Delightful!" Hector sings, corralling us into the elevator.

For the Plot

"You ran this by Ezra, yeah?" I'm suddenly nervous that he "forgot" to mention to his roommate that I'd be crashing here for the next couple of weeks.

He unlocks the door to his apartment and holds an arm out. As I step through, I'm hit with a reminder of the last time I was here. It was the day he called me out for being chickenshit. The day I left him hanging. Crossing the threshold now feels like a new beginning.

"Yes," he chuckles. "Of course I ran it by him."

"And he doesn't mind?" I ask, kicking off my shoes.

Ezra pops his head out of the kitchen doorway. "Mind what?"

"Mind sharing whatever it is you're cooking!" It smells delicious: garlic and onion, with hints of rosemary.

The hairs on my neck stand when Cam whispers against my ear. "Don't worry, baby. I promise you're welcome here."

If I weren't a totally monogamous girlie, tonight could have been a real "why choose" moment, because the boys of apartment 6206 can cook. Between Cam's quiche and Ezra's homemade focaccia, I may never leave.

We share a bottle of Shiraz while the guys regale me with all kinds of entertaining stories. They've got a seriously adorable bromance going on.

"Remember the time you got caught stealing condoms from the drugstore?"

Cam shoots a glare at Ezra but can't keep a straight face. "It was the first and last time I played Truth or Dare." He gives me the side-eye, though, because we both know that wasn't actually the last time. But for the sake of this conversation, I don't correct him.

"It was sort of this unspoken initiation between seniors and freshmen in this mentorship program at our high school," Ezra adds, "and I dared him to steal a box of condoms."

"What happened?" I ask.

"I got caught," Cam admits. "The owner wanted to press charges, but Ezra convinced them to call my parents instead."

"Which might have been worse," Ezra laughs, dragging a hand down his face.

"Why's that?" I love the dynamic between these two.

"Because my parents grounded me for a month and made me watch this sex education video—circa 1970. For nearly a year after that, I believed you could get a girl pregnant just by kissing."

I can't help the snort that escapes me. "Aww, babe, I hope you've learned a little more since then."

He leans in and whispers, "Oh, baby, I've learned more than a little."

"And on that note!" Ezra rises and gathers our dishes.

I insist on cleaning them since he cooked, and Cam helps me while Ezra excuses himself to the building's basement to finish his laundry.

In the bathroom, he hands me a clean towel and shirt, then leaves me to freshen up before bed. When I'm finished, we switch places, and when he comes out, he's wearing nothing but a pair of black boxer briefs. I turn so I'm facing him as he slips under the sheets and gets settled. I can't see him in the dark, but I hear his labored breathing; feel it against the bridge of my nose.

His fingers graze against my wrist, spurring me to sputter, "I don't think we should have sex."

"Okay…" He draws out the word, but there's no accusation behind it.

I loop my fingers in his. "It's just," I huff. "We jumped into things so quickly. And I want to make sure this…this "—*Relationship?*—"thing between us is about more than sex."

For the Plot

He presses a chaste kiss to the back of my hand and holds it there. "Oh, Joey," he murmurs, smiling against my skin, "it's more than just sex."

I sigh, shifting so close our noses brush.

The air between us is thick and heavy. My heart thunders in my chest, and my stomach is all twisted up.

Cam, probably sensing the way the moment is consuming me, lightens things. "What about over-the-shirt stuff?" he asks, his tone full of mirth. "Maybe some heavy petting?"

"Oh my god," I laugh into him. "Do not say heavy petting."

"No?" He tickles my waist. "That doesn't do it for you?" He eases back a fraction. "A little dry-humping never hurt anyone."

I snort out a laugh, and it takes me a solid minute to calm myself.

When I do, he pecks at my nose. "Fine." He drapes an arm over my midsection and pulls me in tight. "What about kissing?"

"As long as there's no hip thrusting involved," I breathe.

"Got it. My hips shall not thrust." He presses his mouth to mine quickly, but drags out the release, like he's inflating my lips.

I hold back a moan, eager to sink my lips into his. But this man is so damn thoughtful. He's hesitating, waiting for permission. So I part my lips, my way of saying *yes, kiss me more*, and swipe my tongue along his, slow and delicate, soaking him in. We communicate that way, an unspoken understanding, a silent language of our connection.

Mini promises being passed between us—of a future filled with passion and desire:

I don't know what's going to happen, but I'm here with you now.

I'm here too.

Chapter 39
Josefine

ME
Have a safe flight. Text me when you land xx

CAM
Landed and headed to my hotel now

Clean shirts are in the bottom drawer on the right 😌

ME
I know…

CAM
Josefine MIDDLE NAME Beckham, did you snoop through my drawers?

👋🗑️

ME
Maybe lol

BTW my middle name is Noa. What's yours?

CAM
No middle name

For the Plot

> **ME**
> Really??

CAM

Seriously. My parents couldn't agree on a middle name, so they decided not to give me one at all

CAM

How's my bed?

How many pairs of panties will I find tangled in my sheets when I get home?

> **ME**
> First of all, don't say panties 🤢
>
> Second of all, you perv 😏
>
> How's the job?

CAM

It's solid. I just follow real estate agents around and take pics for their listings. I've seen some outrageous homes

My chest swells when I read his text. In another life, maybe Cam could be the photographer for my dad's company.

CAM

How was your weekend?

> **ME**
> It was nice. Hector's dog sitter was sick, so I took Puffin today

I snap a selfie with the gray French bulldog and send it to him.

CAM

Cute

He is too

ME

Iris and Claire say hi

I send a selfie of the three of us at the Black hole.

CAM

Hanging out with my sister now, huh?

ME

She's much cooler than you

CAM

I beg to differ

ME

All I read was "I beg"

CAM

😇

CAM

You didn't tell me Maestro would make me cry like a baby

His text is accompanied by a selfie. The man has tears in his eyes.

For the Plot

> ME
> WAIT
> DID U READ MY FAVORITE BOOK????
> R U OK??!!

CAM

I may never recover…

> ME
> Jerk 😣

CAM

Ok fine, I'll recover. But those tears are real!

Wish you were here

> ME
> Me too
> But don't worry. Puffin keeps me warm at night

CAM

Josefine Noa Beckham, did you let that dog sleep in my bed?!

> ME
> 😬
> It was one time! And I changed the sheets

CAM

You will pay for that

> ME
> Can't wait…

Katie Van Brunt

ME

Thanks for calling. I was having a really shitty day, but hearing your voice helped

CAM

Of course, baby. I'm glad you're feeling better. Get some rest

Call or text me in the morning

ME

🩶

ME

Just a few more days…

CAM

What's a few more days?

ME

Until you're back!

CAM

Back where?

ME

Back in your bed

CAM

Will you be in my bed when I come home again?

This time, sans flying vibrator

ME

But he's already charged and ready for an encore

CAM

I'll take one ticket to that performance, please

Chapter 40
Cameron

Two weeks away from Joey felt like a lifetime. And the video chats were nothing more than a tease. I was set to leave Austin this evening, but I managed to hop on an earlier flight.

Maybe I should have given her a heads-up about my early arrival, but it's too late now. I'm already in the elevator and on my way up. Will she consider this a good surprise? Or will she be annoyed? To be honest, I didn't want to give her an opportunity to run. Catching her this way means she hopefully hasn't had time to pack up and return to her apartment.

According to Hector, she left this morning, but she returned shortly thereafter with a bag of groceries and hasn't come downstairs since.

Inside my apartment, I kick my shoes off and hang my keys. Ezra's hook is empty, signaling that he must be out. The faint scent of chocolate floats in the air and the sound of clanging echoes in the otherwise quiet space, followed by a *"Motherfucker-shitdammit."*

"Joey?" I call, abandoning my bags in the hall. In the kitchen,

I find the beautiful brunette with more flour on her face and countertops than in the bowl off to the side.

"Whatcha doing?" I peer at the ingredients strewn about. "Are you making cookies?"

"I was trying to!" she huffs, causing her hair to float around her face.

I bite back a smile. Now doesn't seem like the appropriate time to tell her how adorable she looks. She's dressed in tiny sleep shorts and one of my old white university T-shirts, which she's cinched at her navel. Figuring I'll help, I sidle up next to her at the sink, where she's washing a bowl, and brush my hands with hers beneath the water.

I dry my hands on a towel sprinkled with flour, then tuck a strand of hair behind her ear and cup her cheek, anchoring her.

"Hi," she whispers, her eyes softening and her shoulders relaxing.

"Hi."

It's been two weeks since I kissed this gorgeous woman, and there's no way I can wait a second longer. With one hand cupping the back of her neck, I drop the other to her lower back. Regardless of how desperate I am, though, I pause an inch away and ask, "Can I kiss you?"

In answer, she loops her arms around my waist, rises on tiptoe, and parts my lips with her tongue. Her kiss sends a wild swirl straight to my core. For several moments, we make up for lost time. Our tongues tangle and breaths mingle while I explore the velvety flesh beneath her shirt.

Pulling away to catch my breath, I bury my face in her neck and press more kisses into the pulsing hollow at the base of her throat. I want to devour her softness.

She loosens her hold on me and takes a step back, her focus returning to the countertop. "I thought you weren't coming home for another few hours."

For the Plot

I swiftly kiss the top of her head and inhale a hint of my shampoo. "I changed my flight. I couldn't wait to see you."

Her eyes flutter shut, sending a shot of fear coursing through me.

"Is that okay?"

"Of course." She shrugs. "It's your home."

The way she says *your home* doesn't sit right with me. Coming home to find her in my bed a few weeks ago, and now, in my kitchen, wearing my shirt again, makes two words flash in my mind: *Our home*.

"Hey," I begin, "what's wrong?"

"For starters," she waves a hand across the mess on the counter, "I was supposed to have this all cleaned up before you got here. And I think your oven is on child lock. I can't figure out how to switch it off." Her brow furrows and her voice goes up at the end.

She stabs at the button on the panel of the oven, over and over again, like she has a vendetta against the appliance. "How the fuck do you turn this thing off? And why is the child lock even on? It's not like there are kids in this apartment!"

Pressing my front to her back, I steady her wrist. "You have to hold down the button."

"I did! I was. I pushed the button, like, a million times!"

She's riled up and I love it.

I slide my index finger over hers and press, making sure my tone is slow, relaxed, soothing. "You have to be patient and gentle with the button, baby."

She drops her head back against my chest. "Oh, is that so?" she inquires, nothing but suggestion.

"Yes. See?" The red light next to *Child Lock* flickers off, and I swirl the pad of my finger on her knuckle, around and around. "You have to wait."

"What if I don't want to wait?" Her voice breaks with a sort of huskiness.

Caging her between me and the stovetop, I sigh into the top of her head.

She turns and loops her arms around me, then she's gripping my ass and pulling my hips into her.

"Seems like you don't want to wait either." She angles back and looks down, where the bulge in my pants is growing.

"The cookies can definitely wait," I say, peppering her lips with kisses.

"You don't like cookies?"

"Hate 'em. Worst food ever," I tease into her mouth. Dipping my hand down the back of her shorts, I reach between her ass cheeks and tease her entrance, eliciting a yelp from her. "They're not what I want to taste right now."

She nips at my bottom lip in approval and squeezes my glutes again.

Without letting up, I tilt to one side and dip a finger in the cookie dough next to the stove. I bring it to her lips and just about come in my pants when she sucks it deep into her mouth and hollows out her cheeks.

"Mmm, tasty," she purrs, eyes hooded.

Breaking our seductive seal, I remove my hand from her pants and take a step back.

"Where are you going?"

I exhale a long and strangled breath. "First, I'm going to shower. Next," I narrow my eyes on her, assessing my prey, "I'm going to fuck you with my fingers. Then you're going to suck your cum off them and tell me which is sweeter—you or the cookie dough."

Chapter 41
Josefine

THE MAN STANDING before me is hungry. And not for the cookies I abandoned in the kitchen precisely two minutes after he walked away to shower. The second the water was running, I joined him in the bathroom, where I stripped out of my clothes at lightning speed.

Cam's hair isn't even fully wet when I step in behind him.

He sighs my name like a prayer on his lips.

His abdominal muscles flex under my hands, and he wraps his own around mine. We stand in silence for a moment, skin to skin, swaying beneath the waterfall showerhead. Painstakingly slow, I drag my nails down the hard curve of his thighs and lower to my knees. I knead his ass cheeks and silently declare his butt my favorite part of his body. Playfully, I bite one smooth cheek, and then the other, before he rotates to face me. He leans against the white subway tiles, widening his stance so his cock is lined up with my mouth. Ignoring the way my knees ache pressed into the tile floor, I inch forward, gripping him. The water from above sluices over us both as I pump up and down.

Looming over me, he hisses, head tipped down and water dripping from his hair.

Despite the heat of the water, goose bumps rise on my skin, an outward sign of radiating pleasure. I lick my lips and inch closer, though I keep my focus trained on his face, silently asking for permission.

With a nod from Cam, I swipe my tongue across his swollen head, pulling a guttural groan from him. When I slide his length inside my mouth, he grasps the back of my head and holds himself to the hilt. I swallow around him, and he jerks back.

"*Fu-u-ck.*"

I sputter at the water splattering against my face, and he eases back, angling the showerhead away.

With two hands, I tug him by his cock until his head brushes my lips. Slowly at first, I swirl my tongue at the tip, then suck, hollowing out my cheeks. I alternate the actions a few times, relishing the grunts and groans echoing off the tile.

"Stop," he gasps. "You're going to make me come."

"That's the point," I argue around his cock.

With a breathy laugh, he slides his arms under mine and pulls me up until his hardness rests at my ribs. "There are so many things I want to do to you," he whispers.

He lowers his head and presses a kiss between my breasts. Cupping one and teasing its nipple, he laps at the other, sucking it into his mouth and tugging at it with his teeth.

"Fuck, that feels good," I groan.

Now he's the one kneeling. I drop my head back, expecting his tongue or fingers at my cunt, but instead, he slides his hands down my abdomen and thighs until they're at my knees. Tenderly, he massages my kneecaps, soothing the places imprinted with tile marks. He bends to kiss the raised skin on one, then the other.

This man.

For the Plot

Pinning me against the wall, he rocks back on his haunches and throws my leg over his shoulder, then hooks his arm around my thigh. He teases the perimeter of my pussy with one thumb, causing the nerves at my center to short-circuit. He flattens his tongue and drags it up my pussy, finishing with a puff of air against my clit. My knee wobbles, and I slap my hands against the tile behind me as he shoves a finger inside me so deep he nearly lifts me off the ground.

"Cam!" I yelp.

"Is it too much?" He extricates his finger and searches my face.

"No," I pant, blindly searching for the faucet handle. A dizzying current is racing through my body, and if I don't turn down the heat, I may pass out. "I need more."

"Is that begging I hear?" The skin at his temples crinkles when he smiles, and I want to bury myself in those beautiful lines.

But I'm too desperate to answer.

Taking the cue, he presses a delicate kiss to my clit, the water-saturated stubble on his jaw brushing against my thigh, and gets back to work. This time, he slides two fingers inside me, rotating and scissoring, stretching me in the best way. With one more glance up, he descends, licking and lapping around my clit in time with his fingers.

A pulsing, a beating, floods my core as he quickens his perfect choreography. My orgasm breaks through with such ferocity that he has to scramble to keep me stationary.

I'm panting and struggling to suck in air and spewing expletives, and all the while, his fingers are still locked inside, my pussy pulsing around them. It's only when he stands that he steadily slides them out and brings them to my lips.

"Open up, gorgeous."

Holding his gaze, I obey. The taste of my own obscene release instantly ramps up my arousal all over again. When he tries to pull away, I bite down on his fingers gently and suck the final traces of myself from them.

In one fell swoop, he hoists me off the ground and shifts us so we're under the water. I snag a bottle from the cutout shelf in the wall and squeeze a generous amount of the liquid onto his chest. A subtle pine scent mingles with the steam, sending another bolt of need to my core. I'm surrounded by this man in every way.

With Cam supporting my back, I massage the suds into his chest, over his shoulders, and up his neck. With my nails, I work it into his scalp, then massage behind his ears before I make my way back down his neck and shoulders and arms. He sets me on my feet and takes a step back, giving me full access to his body. With a reverence I've never experienced before sinking into me, I wash every inch of his firm body, paying close attention to all my favorite virile parts.

He steps under the spray to rinse the suds away, kissing me with veneration and gratitude. He turns off the water and steps out, only to turn back around with a towel outstretched for me.

With his cock still at full attention, he slings his own towel around his shoulders and demands, "You. Bed. Now."

I wring out my wet hair and rush to hang my towel on the hook. On my way out of the bathroom, he gives my ass a firm smack.

Not even bothering to slip beneath the sheets, I prop my upper back on his pillows, leaving my naked body on display. A moment later, Cam glides in on long, sturdy legs, his beauty magnified by the afternoon light filtering in. Then he's hovering over me, his knees on either side of my legs, drops of moisture still clinging to his damp forehead.

"You're so beautiful," he breathes against my ear. Before I have time to absorb his sweet words, he captures my lobe between his teeth and tugs. "Now, get on your hands and knees so I can fuck the shit out of you."

Stunned into ecstasy, all I can do is gape.

"Don't make me tell you twice," he commands when I don't move.

Immediately, I obey, rolling over and pushing up onto all fours. Hands flat on the mattress, I eagerly grind my ass against his hard length, not even a little embarrassed by the desperate mewls escaping my lips.

"I need you," I beg.

Craning my neck, I drink him in.

With his focus locked on my ass, he strokes his length.

The move sends liquid heat surging in my core. I don't know how much longer I can last without him inside me.

He collects my hair and wraps it around his hand. The way he tugs makes my scalp sting in the best way. With the head of his cock, he collects my dripping arousal, then slides his length between my cheeks. This teasing is maddening.

"Fuck me," I cry. *Destroy me.*

In one fluid motion, he obeys, pushing inside me. But a second later, he stills, then pulls back out. "Shit."

I drop my head and curse at the sudden emptiness.

"What's wrong?" I question, lowering my hip to the mattress so I'm facing him.

"Condom," he murmurs, swinging his legs over the side of the bed so he's sitting on the edge.

Oh. I can't help but examine his cock, the vein pulsing along his impressive *bare* length.

"I've—" I swallow past the lump that's formed in my throat. "I've never had unprotected sex before."

"I haven't either. I'm so sorry." He drops his head between his shoulders and caresses my thigh.

"No." I put a hand on top of his. "I meant that I've been

tested recently, and my results are negative." My heart pounds hard against my ribs, but not for the same reason it did moments ago when he was teasing me. I worry my bottom lip and pull in a deep breath. "And I have an IUD."

He lifts his head and scrutinizes me, his expression full of curiosity. "I haven't been with anyone since Greece."

"I should hope not." I let out a nervous laugh. "That was only a few weeks ago."

"No." He stares at his hand and squeezes my leg, then looks me in the eye. "I mean that I haven't been with anyone since Greece *the first time*."

My chest tightens and my already pounding heart takes off in a gallop. "Fuck. Me. *Now*," I growl.

With a tick of his jaw, his inherent confidence comes flooding back. "Get that ass in the air, baby. Show me that tight hole," he demands, grasping my waist and flipping me over.

"Yes, sir."

I yelp when he smacks a cheek but mewl in the next second when he rubs at my tender skin. Swiveling for a better view, I drink him in. He's got one hand on my hip and his head bowed. Then the man fucking spits on his cock. My pussy quivers in response. With his eyes on me now, he strokes his length and notches his head at my entrance.

"You sure?"

A wild storm brews inside me, sending pure desire running through my veins. I'm feral for him. "If you don't fuck me right now, Cameron," I pant, "I swear to g—"

He slams into me, knocking the breath from my lungs.

"God!" I scream, reveling in the sensation of being filled up.

"That's not my name, baby, but I love that you think so highly of me."

I match him push for push, calling out commands like *Faster!* and *Harder!* and *Please don't stop!* between gasps for air.

He lets go of my hips and runs his hands deliciously over my back, then he curves his body flush against mine. "You're doing so good, baby," he breathes into my cheek. "Taking my cock like the good girl you are." That praising comment alone nearly sends me over the edge.

Instinctively, I bring a hand to my clit, desperate for relief.

Cam yanks my arm away. "Uh-uh," he *tsks*. "Not yet."

He pulls out of me, and I collapse onto the mattress with a frustrated groan, pressing my forehead to the sheets.

"Roll over, sweetheart. I wanna watch your face when you come all over my cock."

Fuck, I'm a goner.

I do as I'm told, and he wastes no time devouring me. He sucks my swollen clit while he simultaneously finger fucks my pussy and rims my ass with a thumb. It's all too much. My vision blurs and stars dance in my periphery. A tingling heat crawls from my shoulders, across my chest, and straight to my heart.

I scream his name and tear at his hair, anchoring myself through the explosive release.

He doesn't stop until my muscles relax. Then he kisses my inner thigh, the move sending a shiver through me. "I've got you."

When the stars have disappeared, I raise my head and take in the most glorious sight—Cam, still positioned between my legs, watching me. His caramel eyes are filled with lust and pride.

"How do you feel?" His voice is full of wonder, tenderness.

I cover my eyes with my arm and sigh. "Amazing." Truly.

"Good." He climbs up my body until his hardness rests against my core. "Because I'm not done with you." It's subtle, but his brow twitches, asking for permission.

Legs spread wide, I welcome him.

"Tell me you want this."

"I want this," I cry.

On one long thrust, he slams into my still-wet core. "Give me one more, baby. Let me hear those pretty little moans."

With his arms trapping me on either side, he expertly drags his length against my inner wall. My name falls from his lips like an incantation, and I'm a whimpering mess. He doesn't hold back, slamming deep, over and over again. His unrestrained grunts and groans alone are enough to get me off. God, I wish I could bottle them up to replay later.

"Joey," he breathes against my lips, stealing sloppy kisses between moans. "Your cunt feels so good gripping my cock. I'm—"

"Me too." I'm on the edge, somehow already hurtling toward a third release. I rake my nails down his back until I reach the top of his glutes, then I direct him so he's grinding against my clit.

"Come with me," he insists.

And with those words, we let go. Together. He jerks and I contract. Our bodies naturally know how to support one another through such powerful ecstasy. He fills me up like I'm the perfect home for his release. Our hearts converse with one another, beating in their own language.

I want more, his says.

You're so good to me, mine says back.

He collapses on top of me, his sweat mixing with mine in beautiful triumph. When he pulls out, he dips his fingers into my sensitive center, then brings them to his mouth and sucks the cocktail of our release. I nearly die from the eroticism in the way he brings his lips to mine and shares the flavor of *us* on his tongue.

"Mmm," he moans against my lips. "We taste sweeter together."

It's only when his warm, labored breath blows against my face that I sense cool tears sliding down my cheeks.

God damn. This is so much more than just sex.

Chapter 42
Josefine

IN HIS BATHROOM, Cam cracks the tiny window to let out the steam, then wraps a towel around me for the second time today. Once I've secured it around my damp body, I dig my hairbrush out of my toiletry bag. My hair is so tangled I'm tempted to chop it all off.

He removes his contacts, then props himself up against the countertop, watching me, those damn glasses perched on the bridge of his nose. At least I have something pretty to look at while I undo these stubborn knots.

"Stay with me tonight." His voice is hushed, barely audible over the sounds of traffic filtering in from the streets below.

Eyeing his reflection, I worry my lip, still working out a tangle.

"Just one night," he urges.

Shifting closer, he gently pries my fingers off the handle of my brush and sweeps my hair back before dropping a kiss to my bare shoulder. Goose bumps skitter down my arms—whether from the kiss, the chill of my wet hair on my back, or Cam brushing it, I'm uncertain.

"Don't look so shocked." He grins in the mirror. "I have a little sister, remember?" His face falters, and the corners of his mouth turn down. "I brushed my mom's hair when she was really sick too."

"How's your relationship with her now?" I watch his reflection, note the way some of the sadness in his expression dissipates. "You saw her before you left for Austin, yeah?"

"I did." He balances the brush on the sink's edge so he can work through a knot with deft fingers. "Our relationship is pretty good. Right now, though, she's in a tough position between my dad and me."

"What do you mean?"

Having worked out the biggest tangles, he picks up my brush again. "My parents don't see eye to eye when it comes to my inheritance. My dad is withholding it because I don't want to take over the family business. She doesn't agree. But she's also ready for him to retire." He says all of this with his eyes cast down and his shoulders a bit slumped.

I turn and grasp his forearm gently, silently giving him support.

"I don't see my dad very often, and only if my mom or Claire is around," he supplies. "But my mom comes into the city to meet for coffee or lunch pretty regularly. I think she'd really like you."

"Me?" I can't imagine an upper-class woman from Long Island who owns a hotel chain and frequents the local country club liking me.

"Of course you." He boops my nose and returns the brush to my bag, effectively ending the conversation.

I dance my fingers up his chest and link them behind his neck. With my face pressed against his heart, I find the answers I'm looking for between each beat. "Okay."

"Okay what?"

For the Plot

I raise my head. "Okay, I'll stay."

In the morning, I turn down Cam's offers to make me breakfast. I'm anxious to get home and fill Millie in. Before we went to bed last night, I sent her a text and told her, in all caps, that we needed to talk.

Her response: *Coffee or mimosas?*

Both.

Cam, being the annoyingly handsome gentleman he is, walks me home.

"What are your plans for the weekend?" I ask, dodging dog poop on the sidewalk.

"To the Statue of Liberty, believe it or not," he chuckles. "I've never been. Claire is off tomorrow, too, so we're going to a whiskey distillery in Brooklyn with Ezra and his mom."

"That sounds fun," I say. "Claire and Ezra aren't—"

"No. No way." He guffaws. "And it's not even a *stay away from my little sister* thing. It's more like a *zero-chemistry* thing."

"Gotcha. Is she seeing anyone?"

"If she is, she hasn't told me," he replies. "She's so damn busy at the hospital that I doubt she has much time for dating."

When we approach the door to my building, he waits for me to fish my keys out of my purse before handing my duffel over.

"Thank you. And thank you for letting me stay at your apartment while you were away. And thank you for..." I trail off, shoving down all the affectionate words fluttering to break free from where I've got them caged behind my ribs.

"The best sex of your life?" he supplies, quirking a brow.

Heat rushes to my cheeks, and I scan my surroundings,

hoping a random passerby hasn't overheard our conversation. Grasping the fabric of my sundress at my hip, he tugs until my sneakered toes bump into his. He wraps one arm around my waist, and I bury my cheesy smile deep in his chest. When I pull back, he drops a kiss to my forehead, and we both linger, unspoken sentiments passing between us. Only when someone exits the building do we break apart.

I step to the side for them to pass, and Cam catches the door with his foot.

"When can I see you again?"

"I'll text you." With a smile over my shoulder, I step into the building.

"Hey." He rests a foot on the doorstep. "I'm not trying to push you," he says, rubbing a hand against his cheek. "If you feel like things are moving too fast, I can—"

"I don't," I interrupt. "At least I don't think so."

That's what I need to talk to Millie about. We've only just begun dating, and I'm already staying at his place for days on end. Even if we have technically known each other for more than a year.

"I just—" I exhale and search for a way to explain my confusion. But words escape me. "I'll text you. I promise."

His eyes are filled with hope, despite his terse smile. "Have a good weekend, Joey."

True to her word, Millie is waiting with fresh coffee and a bottle of chilled champagne. She's wrapped in an emerald green robe, and her hair is loose.

"Hey, boo," she sings, sweeping me up in her arms.

"I missed you too," I laugh, kicking my sneakers off.

For the Plot

When the oven beeps, she scurries into the kitchen and pulls out a tray of cranberry-orange scones.

"Did you make these?" I gasp, inhaling the zesty scent of my favorite pastry.

"Fuck no," she scoffs. "Peg and Fran dropped them off last night. I just tossed them into the oven so they'd be warm when you arrived."

"Oh, good. For a second, I thought you turned into Martha Stewart while I was away."

"Me? Domesticated? That'll be the day." She transfers the scones onto paper plates and drizzles vanilla frosting from a plastic package on top. "Sit."

I follow instructions, and she joins me at the table. Though I could use a cup of coffee, we skip straight to the mimosas and dive in.

I tell her everything. "We clearly have chemistry," I share, picking at my scone.

"Duh." She rolls her eyes. "You two are wrapped in this aura." She swipes a hand in a wax on, wax off kind of motion. "I can feel it a mile away."

"And the sex is..." I drop my forehead to the table and mumble, "Fucking incredible."

"What's that?" she asks, kicking me under the table.

Lifting my head, I repeat, "Fucking incredible."

"I'll drink to that." She raises her glass in the air.

"Do you think we're moving too fast?" More than anything, that's what I want to know.

"Do *you*?"

I blow a raspberry at her. "C'mon," I whine, fully embracing my inner brat. "I need my best friend to tell me what to do."

She puts her hand on top of mine and squeezes. "You know that's not how this works."

After I drain my mimosa, she pours me a refill. This time it's strictly champagne. "Now tell me what you're really afraid of."

I lick the sweet frosting from my lips and dust the scone crumbs off my dress while I collect my thoughts. "I'm scared, Mills. I'm scared of what might happen between us. When I think about a partner, Cam's everything I'd want." I lift my glass to my lips and savor the way the dry bubbles sting my throat on the way down.

"Love can be scary, babes. But it can also be beautiful and transformative."

"Who said anything about love?" I bristle. The four-letter word makes my stomach sink.

My ex used to tell me he loved me, and we all know how that turned out. The word feels tainted now.

My cousin chews on the tip of her thumbnail. "Sounds like you're afraid of getting your heart broken."

"I'm fucking terrified." The words tumble right out of my mouth. Relationships come with far too much risk of vulnerability and potential for heartbreak. Do I want to bare my soul to another? Share my fears and insecurities? My imperfections?

"I built up walls after my breakup. Even with my mom. I keep her at arm's length for fear of disappointment."

"And you think Cam will disappoint you too?"

I nod. "He's too good to be true. What if I lose myself in him like I did with my ex? What if I become so wrapped up in his dreams that I forget about mine? What if he shatters my heart?" I'm spiraling and I know it.

"Worrying about things going wrong won't make things go right."

I scoff. "Did you get that from a fortune cookie?"

She responds with a one-fingered salute, and we both giggle.

"I don't want to lose my independence." My heart aches. Because no matter how I feel about Cam, that's what it comes down to. I've worked so hard to be where I am, and I can't risk backsliding.

"Does he make you feel like you would?"

"I guess not, but what I've been doing—sleeping in his bed while he's gone, even though we've only started dating—is a little too reminiscent of the way I moved in with Tyler when I didn't have a place to live."

"You know you always have a place with me," she says, dipping her head and catching my eye. "And who knows? Maybe I'll nail that audition next week. Then I'll be traveling for months, and you can keep my bed warm." Narrowing her green eyes, she teases, "Just be sure to change my sheets after all the *fucking incredible* sex you're gonna have."

I exhale a laugh, grateful for the bit of comedic relief.

Through a mouthful of scone, I admit, "It's like I'm headed toward a tunnel. It's pitch black, and I can't see the other side."

Her eyes light up and she straightens. "Remember when I visited a few years after your dad died, and you had that really amazing therapist?"

"Sora." Out of habit, I glance at the kangaroo plush that sits on our kitchen windowsill. Sora gave it to me years ago, and I always keep it close.

"What was that thing she said about headlights? It was a metaphor."

My chest tightens at the memory. It's been so long since I've thought about that session. "She said that when we're driving toward our destination in the dark, even with the headlights on, we can only see a few yards in front of us."

Millie's genuine smile encourages me to continue.

"Anything beyond the headlights is dark. We can't see whether there's a bridge ahead, and we can't tell if the road will be closed. We don't know yet. But despite the uncertainty, we keep driving."

"That's right," she agrees. "We don't know what's at the end of the road, but we look out our window and embrace the journey. One step at a time, boo."

Over the last couple of weeks, Cam and I have fallen into a sort of groove. He signed up for a photography course taught by a New York Film Academy legend, so he's been busy. My writing workshop wrapped up, and Ari and I have decided to stay on for the two-week extension.

Cam and I continue to see each other regularly, though I've only spent the night once more. The fear that getting involved with him will pull me away from my writing career has yet to come to fruition. If anything, he's intentional when making plans, and he's always sure to check in about my availability and whether I have the mental capacity to hang out. He didn't even seem upset when I canceled on him last-minute because I was deep in my metaphorical writing cave. Instead, he had Mark hand-deliver food from Bubbe's Nosh Pit, with extra black-and-white cookies.

I've reread the letter he stuck in my suitcase the day I left Crete multiple times now. I keep it tucked between the pages of my tattered copy of *Maestro*.

He copied down a quote from *The Alchemist*. The line about fear of failure preventing us from achieving our dreams. I used to think the fear of failure was only reserved for one's career. But Cam is showing me that there's more to life than just what I do. Who I do life with is just as vital. I think about my dad and how he would hate seeing me hold back because I'm afraid.

"Embrace the journey," Millie said. *One step at a time.*

Maybe this thing with him is worth the risk after all.

For the Plot

Millie nailed her audition like I knew she would. Yesterday, she hopped on a bus to Syracuse, where the touring company is rehearsing. She will be gone for several months, and I already miss her dearly, even though her absence means I've taken over her bedroom.

I'm between editing projects for the next couple of weeks and beyond thrilled to devote the hours I normally spend working for others to my own manuscript.

Cam texted before his photography class started to see if he could pick up dinner and bring it over to my apartment after. I couldn't respond in the affirmative fast enough. The idea of christening the space already has my blood pumping. I may have to buy my cousin an entirely new mattress, but it'll be worth it.

I'm jotting down notes in my notebook for a writing exercise Talulah assigned yesterday when I grab my phone to check the time. I thought he would be here by now.

> CAM
> Hey baby. I'm downstairs. I don't think the buzzer is working. Can you let me in?

The time stamp shows the message arrived three minutes ago. I hop off the couch and slide my feet into a pair of Birks. With my keys in hand, I throw open the door, ready to hustle downstairs. Instead, I rear back when I come face to face with Cam, his fist in a knocking position.

"Hi," I gasp. "How did you—"

He tilts his head to one side, so I lean over the threshold and peer down the hall.

When I catch sight of my neighbors, Peg lifts the back of her hand to her forehead and mock-swoons. Fran waves a hand in front of her face and whistles. "Whew, that one's a looker."

"You staying the night, sugar?" Peg asks.

Eyes wide, Cam looks to me for an answer.

I shrug and shoot her a smirk. "If he's on his best behavior, maybe. Why?"

"Give us a warning so we can turn down our music," Peg says.

"I think you mean *up*," I laugh.

"I meant exactly what I said," she deadpans.

"Ignore the old bird." Fran shoves her wife into their apartment, but not before Peg calls out, "Be sure to annunciate, kids! The batteries in my hearing aids are on their way out."

With that, their door slams closed.

Once we're alone, we fall into a fit of laughter. I can't live here forever, but when I finally have enough saved for an apartment of my own, I'll miss those two.

"I'd say I'm sorry about them," I tease while ushering him into the kitchen, "but that was them being mellow."

He sets the bags of food on the counter and kisses the side of my head in greeting. "They seem delightful."

Unsatisfied with the peck, I tug him by his shirt and pull him into me. I tease at the waistband of his chino shorts, then drag my hands up and down his back and slide them into the back of his shorts.

With a groan, he brings his lips to mine and hovers there. I drink in the air he exhales and continue my tactile examination of his body by moving on to his biceps, relishing in the way they bulge. I've never seen Cam at the gym, but the selfie he texted from the locker room the other day may or may not be the wallpaper on my phone.

My knees weaken during a series of slow, quivering kisses.

When his lips leave mine, I groan in protest, but he placates me by dropping a line of kisses along my jaw.

"As much as I don't want to stop doing this," he whispers in my ear, "I'm starving." With one final peck, he releases me and rounds the small kitchen island. "And if we're to give Peg and Fran a show later," he waggles his brows as he digs through the takeaway bag, "I need fuel."

He sets the to-go containers on the counter, next to my pen and notebook. I bought it at the Athens airport and almost refused to use it; it's so pretty, with its thick golden spiral and a hard cover hand painted by a Greek artist.

"Were you working on something?" he asks with a nod at it.

My eyes widen and my heartbeat quickens. Horrified, I snatch it up and clutch it to my chest. The contents are for my eyes only.

"What?" He gapes. "Is that for your rated-R writing class?"

"It's not rated R." I snigger. "It's a course on writing mature material."

The extension Talulah offers is for writers who want to explore and experiment in writing more "explicit content." (Okay, it's smut. We're writing smut.) Talulah did not hold back in the first exercise whatsoever.

"Tell me," he says, his voice low and smooth. "What are you writing about?"

I suck in my cheeks, stifling a sheepish grin. "You don't want to know."

"Now I'm intrigued." He abandons his dinner and crowds my space, leaning his hip against the counter.

I slap my notebook to my face to hide my blushing cheeks, like a kid discovering her father's stash of *Playboy* magazines.

"Joey," he croons. "What was the assignment?" He crooks a finger over the top of the pages and pulls back the corner of the front cover.

Exhaling a long breath, I clutch the subject of this little discussion to my chest. "If I tell you, you have to promise not to laugh or get all weird about it."

"Scout's honor." He holds three fingers high in the air.

"That's the volunteer sign from *The Hunger Games*, not the Cub Scouts' sign, you nerd," I laugh. Dropping my work-in-progress on the counter a little harder than intended, I gather my courage and dive in. "You remember how quirky my instructor is, right?"

"Yeah, Ari's grandmother."

"Yes." I shake my head at the memory of her excitement over this exercise. "She created an assignment where penis-owners have to write about what sex would be like if they had a vulva. And those of us with a vulva have to write about what sex would be like if we had a penis. It's a personal exercise only, thank god. Standing up and sharing this with the group might be a little too far out of my comfort zone."

He raises a brow.

"I think the point is to get outside ourselves, see things from a different perspective."

Cam steps in closer. "And how do you expect to do that?"

I roll my lips between my teeth. "I was trying to imagine being *you*... fucking *me*."

His Adam's apple bobs, and he dips so close the heat of him warms me. "Did it work?"

A shiver runs down my spine. "Did what work?"

"Imagining you're me... fucking you?" The way he emphasizes the *-ck* in "fuck" causes pinpricks of painful pleasure along my skin.

"Yes and no." I lower my chin and consider how detailed I want to be.

Beside me, Cam's breathing picks up.

"I don't have a dick, so I can't *really* know." I press a hand to the notebook, guarding the embarrassing words I wrote only moments ago.

"I have an idea." He pushes off the counter and towers over me.

"Hmm?" My heart lodges in my throat at his proximity and the suggestion framing his words.

With his lips against my ear, he rasps, "What if we gave you a dick?"

"Come again?" I choke, my lungs seizing.

"You know, like a strap-on."

I search his face, expecting him to break into a grin, but all I find are twin flames of desire blazing in his eyes.

"You would—" I swallow, desperate to knock my heart loose before it cuts off my breathing completely. "You'd let me do that to you?"

It's a fantasy I've never spoken aloud. One I never thought would be possible.

Cam pulls himself up to his full height, like maybe he's about to shout, "Just kidding! No way!" But he doesn't. Instead, he tugs me to him, locking my hips against his so I can feel how hard he is.

He slips a hand under my shirt and swirls patterns on my bare skin with the tips of his fingers. "Why not?" Tucking a strand of hair behind my ear, he regards me with blatant yearning. "It could be really hot."

I gaze into his bronze eyes. Would he really let me stick a dildo up his ass? My thighs instinctively squeeze, and my core aches at the erotic image my mind conjures.

"You think it's hot, too, don't you? I bet your cunt is already fucking weeping for it."

Damn, he knows me well.

I bite my lip and offer a pathetic silent nod.

"Tell me, Josefine." He runs his thumb across my lips, then

settles his hand at the base of my throat. "Tell me how fucking hot you think it would be to ride my ass."

Taboo and desire ignite a flame in my core that blazes so hot I'm shaking with its intoxicating energy. *Me* riding *him?*

"Hot. As. Hell," I gasp.

He gives my throat a squeeze, then steps back and holds three fingers in the air again. "I volunteer as tribute."

Chapter 43
Josefine

"You look gorgeous, baby." Cam kisses the top of my shoulder.

I shiver in response and wring my hands in front of me. "I'm kinda nervous."

Tonight's the night I meet his parents, and I'm freaking out.

He stayed true to his word and helped me with my smutty writing exercise, but in exchange, he requested that I accompany him to a fundraising gala. At the time, I was convinced he'd gotten the short end of that stick (no pun intended), but now, as I'm bent in half, struggling to strap my stilettos, I'm not so sure.

Cam looks like a million bucks in a pair of tapered black slacks, a solid black button-down, and a gray woolen jacket with black satin lapels. His feet are still bare when he kneels and grasps my ankle, motioning for me to give him my foot. With a hand on a shelf in Millie's closet (which I have officially taken over), I balance on one leg and rest my heel in his hand.

"It's okay to be nervous, sweetheart." He buckles the strap of my nude stiletto, then sets it on the floor and taps my other ankle. "How can I make you feel better?"

I didn't have the time or the funds to purchase a new dress, but Claire offered to let me borrow one of hers. So tonight I'm decked out in a floor-length white gown covered in large red, purple, and green flowers. The front cuts in a deep V, and the straps tie in thick bows at the shoulders. It's a tight fit, but I made it work. I chose to pin my hair in a low chignon to showcase the backless design. But the best part about the gown? It has pockets.

Cam sets my foot on the floor and skates a hand up my dress until his fingers brush over my lace thong. "What would help you relax?" he asks, bunching up the front of my dress.

"Cam," I breathe, saliva already pooling in my mouth. "What are you—"

"Shh. Lean back."

Obediently, I rest against the wall of the closet.

He grasps my hand and brings the hem of my dress up, silently instructing me to hold it out of the way. Sliding my thong to the side, he teases my entrance, collecting my arousal, then rubbing my clit.

"Baby," I urge.

He looks up at me, all beautifully coiffed hair and a gorgeous smile.

"We're going to be late." Though as the words leave my lips, I greedily grind against his hand.

"Then we better get started. Be my good fucking girl," he demands, impaling me with one long finger. He drags it out like we have all the time in the world. "And scream my name when you come."

After fixing my mascara, changing my underwear, and apologizing to the driver for being late, we pile into the waiting car. Tonight's event will be held at Empire Elegance, a premier NYC venue located near Bryant Park.

Cam's parents insisted on hiring a car for us, which was generous, I suppose. Though despite how luxurious it is, discomfort swamps me. Not only am I meeting his parents, but the fundraiser we're attending is to benefit an organization spearheaded by his ex-girlfriend's father. Hayden's dad is a renowned cardiologist, and while the gala is typically held in February for American Heart Month, Dr. Draper ironically suffered a heart attack. He only recently recovered enough for such an undertaking.

I'm not sure I've ever felt so awkward, but Cam assures me that his ex-girlfriend is out of the country and will not be in attendance.

We're snapping selfies in the back seat when a text notification appears at the top of my screen.

My mother.

Frank left me.

"Dammit," I huff, dropping my chin to my chest.

"What's wrong?"

With a sigh, I switch my phone to vibrate, then slip it into the pocket of my dress. "My mom. I think her boyfriend broke up with her. I'll call her later."

I'm much too anxious about meeting Cam's parents to deal with her drama. She doesn't know about him yet, and if I call her now, I'd have to explain. I'd rather save that conversation for when he isn't within earshot.

The twenty-five-minute drive to the gala turns into nearly forty-five minutes due to traffic, and Cam tries his best to distract me with a friendly game of Never Have I Ever.

Turns out, he's never eaten asparagus or been to Hawaii. He's never owned a pet, either. The biggest revelation? He's never had sex in the back of a car.

He wears a smug smile when I admit I'd never gone skinny-dipping before the nude beach, and for a second, I think he may kick me out of the car—or bend me over—when I reveal that I have, in fact, used someone else's toothbrush without them knowing.

After showing our tickets at the door, we bypass the multi-level indoor spaces and head up to the rooftop terrace. It's gorgeous, with its sweeping panoramic views of the Hudson River, Times Square, and Midtown Manhattan.

When Cam doesn't immediately spot his parents, we make our way to the bar for cocktails. He orders two fingers of a Japanese whiskey, and I try a Cognac sparkler. The tart apple aftertaste is perfect for a warm summer evening.

I'm sipping my drink at a high-top table, eyeing the black-and-white checkered dance floor, when a middle-aged man and woman cut through the crowd and head straight for us.

"You must be Joey." The woman crowds my personal space and grasps my hands. She's petite, like Claire, and her hands are freezing. Her shoulder-length, salt-and-pepper hair is curled at the ends. Her kind eyes are more green than hazel, and her effervescent pink lipstick adds to her bubbly demeanor. She's wearing a black strapless gown that hugs her small frame and a dazzling emerald statement necklace. I immediately love her style.

"Hi, Mrs. Connelly," I reply in my best meet-the-parents voice, ignoring the buzzing sensation of my phone at my side.

Behind his wife, Cam's dad stoically pats him on the back.

"Call me Stephanie," she insists, still gripping my hands.

Only when Mr. Connelly steps up beside her does Stephanie release her hold on me.

"I'm Cliff. It's a pleasure to meet you." Though his eyes are a piercing blue, he and his son share many similar features. If this is a glimpse into the future, then holy hell, sign me up now.

"Nice to meet you too." The knots in my stomach loosen a little. His parents seem genuinely happy to meet me.

Stephanie inquires about the book I'm writing, and while I thoroughly despise that question, I grin through my response. She means well, and I appreciate her genuine interest.

Beside us, father and son have fallen into a civil conversation. After a few minutes, Cam squeezes my hand and subtly nods at the couple about his parents' age who are approaching our table.

They embrace Cliff and Stephanie before taking turns hugging Cam like he's their favorite person in the world. My insides tingle with a twinge of jealousy.

They don't even acknowledge my existence until Stephanie offers an introduction. With a sort of motherly charm, she caresses the back of my arm, just over my tattoo.

"This is Joey," she says. "Cam's..." She trails off, looking from her son to me with a hint of an uncertain frown.

"Girlfriend," Cam replies with a giant grin, pulling me into his hip.

My heart skips a beat at the word. We haven't had that conversation yet, though I suppose fucking a person's ass with a dildo should warrant "the talk."

Thankfully, the Drapers are promptly whisked away by other attendees, and Cliff and Stephanie politely excuse themselves, promising to meet up with us on the dance floor later.

"Your parents seem nice," I say, brushing a piece of Cam's hair off his forehead.

Beads of sweat have collected at his temple. The sight alone leaves me wanting to drag him into the bathroom so I can lick them away before dropping to my knees the way he did in the closet before we left.

"I'm sorry this is how you're meeting them for the first time, but I—"

"You called me your girlfriend." The words tumble out of my mouth before I have a chance to rein them in.

Cam, a man who stands tall with confidence no matter what the situation, ducks his head and rubs at the back of his neck. And if I'm not mistaken, his cheeks have gone pink. "About that..." His lips tip up in a smile.

I step closer and put a hand to his chest. Beneath my palm, his heart pounds a furious beat. I want to tell him I liked it. I can taste the words on my tongue, and the desperate look in his eye silently urges me to go for it, but before I can, I'm gently tackled from behind.

"Joey!"

I spin and come face to face with Claire. She's almost unrecognizable without a nest of hair on the top of her head and her glasses. She's stunning, dressed in a strapless, floor-length gown. The maroon bodice is fitted, and the fabric flares at the hips. Her simple black choker matches her black heels. Her dark hair falls a couple of inches below her shoulders and is set in loose curls. She looks phenomenal.

"Claire!" I gasp. I'm thrilled to have an ally here, but conflicted, because I'd finally found the courage to tell Cam that I liked being called his *girlfriend*. Though now that I've had a moment, his ex-girlfriend's dad's uppity fundraiser is probably not the right place to confess.

After hugging me, she embraces her brother, then throws her clutch on the table next to mine. The band plays the first notes of Diana Ross's "I'm Coming Out," and she yanks me by the wrist.

"Let's dance!" she crows over the trumpets.

Before I know it, I'm on the dance floor with my *maybe boyfriend's* sister.

Cam is leaning against the table, one foot crossed in front of

For the Plot

the other, the glass of whiskey in his hand resting at his belt. His face is painted with an irresistibly devastating grin, his eyes turned up at the sides as he watches me. I pull my attention back to Claire, who's motioning for me to twirl in her arms. God, we must look ridiculous, but we're having a blast all the same.

The band goes into a Michael Bublé song next—the one about being terrified to love again and promising to never run. Before I can exit the dance floor, warm breath hits the back of my neck. "My turn." Cam's voice, deep and sensual, sends a ripple of lust through me.

Claire bows out, but Mr. and Mrs. Connelly appear nearby. Stephanie's eyes sparkle as she spies us over her husband's shoulder. I smile at her but am quickly lost in the man holding me. We don't speak, but our bodies converse, nonetheless. In my stilettos, I'm at the perfect height to burrow into his neck and inhale his cologne.

My phone buzzes again in my pocket, but I ignore it. I needed this moment. Cam slides his hand a little lower, and I glance up at him. When he kisses me on the forehead, I swear he transfers images to my mind. Visions of what a life with him could be like flash by cinematically: more sleepovers, more movies in the park, more working side by side on hotel balconies, more food-induced gastric moans, more moans in general, more reading each other's favorite books and talking endlessly about them.

But I'm interrupted yet again by the buzzing in my pocket. The incessant vibrations have finally piqued my curiosity, so I fish it from my dress.

"Hold on, I'm so sorry."

An unknown California number flashes on the screen, but just as I slide my finger over the screen, the call ends. A series of missed calls and voicemail notifications pop up immediately after.

"What's going on?" he asks, his voice urgent.

"I'm not sure, actually," I admit, unlocking my phone. "Can you give me a minute?" Without waiting for a response, I stride off the dance floor.

I scroll through my missed calls as I rush to the restroom, and once I'm locked in a stall, I tap on the most recent voicemail.

"This is Santa Monica Medical Center. We're calling again regarding Elin Beckham. Please call us back at—"

My stomach drops to the floor. Worst-case scenarios flood my brain. Is she injured? Or worse?

With shaky hands, I tap the number in my list of recent calls and hold the phone to my ear. I'm transferred twice before I'm connected with a nurse who can answer my questions. He informs me that my mom fell and hit her head at a bar and assures me that her CT came back normal. She did, however, need stitches and is in no condition to return home on her own.

I can't believe this is fucking happening right now.

"She's under observation right now, but she will likely be discharged in the next couple of hours. Is there someone close by who can pick her up?" the nurse asks.

Tears well in my eyes, and I pinch the bridge of my nose. My mind is racing a million miles per minute. I wish I could teleport to California. I don't have contact information for any of my mom's friends. Brooks and Tyler are nearby. I'll try Brooks first. That way I can avoid adding awkwardness to this clusterfuck.

Only...*shit*. He's at a film festival in San Francisco this weekend.

Heels click-clack on the bathroom floor, and the stall door beside me swings shut, but I ignore the intrusion. "Yeah. I'll call them." I hang up without even saying thank you or goodbye.

For weeks after we broke up, Tyler called and left message after message, begging me to take him back. After several failed attempts to win me back, the rude texts began. Eventually he stopped contacting me altogether, so I hold my breath, worried that when he sees my number on his screen, he'll hit decline or block me.

But after the second ring, the phone connects, and I exhale.

"Joey?" He sounds dumbfounded, and rightfully so.

"Oh, thank god you answered. Tyler, it's my mom," I whisper, my voice cracking.

"What happened?"

"She's at the hospital. She fell and needed stitches. I'm in New York, and I don't know what to do. I didn't know who to call." The tears are flowing now, and my body is shaking. "Do you—do you think you can go get her?"

My chest is tight in anticipation of his reply, but he doesn't leave me waiting long. "Of course. Which hospital?"

The vise threatening to cut off my airway loosens immediately. "Santa Monica Medical Center."

"Okay, I'm on my way, Beck," he assures me. "It's okay."

"Thank you. I'll book a flight. Hopefully I can get out of here tonight."

After a hasty goodbye and a promise from Tyler that he'll contact me as soon as he gets eyes on my mom, I exit the stall. I startle when I catch sight of Stephanie at the sinks, and my face heats when I catch my own reflection in the mirror behind her. My hair is falling out of its knot, and my eyes are smudged with mascara.

She picks up a white cloth and dampens it, then guides me to a captain's chair in the lounge area of the restroom.

"Want to tell me what's going on?" she asks, handing me the cloth. The crow's feet next to her green eyes deepen when she offers a warm smile.

Trying my best to conceal my emotions, I give her a very basic rundown.

"Oh, honey." She crouches before me and rubs my arm. "Is she all right? Is she in LA?"

I nod.

"How can I help?"

Cam was right about his mom. She has a caring soul. I've only just met her, yet she's ready to jump in and help in any way she can. I'm not used to that kind of treatment.

"Umm, I don't know," I hedge, feeling uncomfortable with such concern from a virtual stranger. "I'm going to try to get on the red-eye." I hold up my phone to check the time.

"Our driver will take you to your apartment, then to the airport," she says, her eyes warm and her expression soft. "It'll be faster that way."

My lips quiver and my chest tightens. Accepting her help may make me all squirrelly inside, but she's right—the town car will be much faster.

"Thank you," I choke back tears.

I don't have time to find Cam. God, I hope he understands. I need to grab my clutch and go. I'll book a flight in the car. I stand and head for the door, ready to ask Stephanie to relay the message to him, when a husky voice in the hall mentions his name. I freeze in the doorway, and Stephanie does too.

Mr. Connelly and Dr. Draper stand a few feet away, both wearing scowls.

"I wish that son of yours would get his head on straight," Dr. Draper asserts. "What's he doing bringing that girl to my fundraiser anyway, after what he did to Hayden?"

Oh, does he not know it was his daughter who rocked the boat?

Cliff shifts his weight and crosses his arms in front of him, but he's angled away, so his facial expressions are hard to make out.

"I hear this new girl doesn't have a real job, and Cameron's still off gallivanting around the world taking pictures. Why's he throwing his life away? He really fucked up by not marrying my daughter."

I've heard enough. I'm not the traditional type and no, my career choice doesn't guarantee stability, but I do not need some rich prick talking about me behind my back.

I springboard off the doorframe, leaving Stephanie in the dust. She calls after me, but I don't turn around. I have tunnel vision. For my wallet. For the town car. To my apartment. To the airport. To my mom.

Chapter 44
Cameron

When Joey excuses herself, I consider running after her, but knowing her, she'd prefer a few moments of privacy. I finish my whiskey at the table, politely decline a few *let me set you up with my daughter* offers, and scare off a man who's trying to rub up on my sister on the dance floor before I've reached my *let Joey have some space* capacity. I figured she would be back by now, and I'm starting to get worried. When I scan the room and don't spot her, I head to the bathrooms, where I run smack into my parents and Dr. Draper, who are engaged in a whisper-screaming match.

"You don't get to talk about my son like that." My father shoves a finger into Dr. Draper's chest, the vein in his forehead bulging.

"What's going on?" I demand, stomping straight up to them.

"Oh, Cameron, there you are," my mom rushes out, tugging on my arm.

My dad is still looming over Dr. Draper, but I let her drag me a few feet away. "What's going on? Where's Joey?"

"She left, honey."

My heart drops to my stomach. "What do you mean, she left?" I bark, chest heaving. If one of these assholes was nasty to her—

"She got a call. Her mom was injured." My mother pats my back, frowning.

"What?" My mouth goes dry, and I force my mind to focus. Why didn't she come find me? Is she still here?

My mom mentions the town car and a red-eye, and that's all the information I need. I flee.

In the eight minutes I wait for an Uber outside the venue, I call Joey six times, but she doesn't answer. On the ride to my apartment, I book a one-way ticket to LA. There's a red-eye leaving both JFK and LaGuardia. I don't know which one she will be on, but I take my chances with LaGuardia because it's closer. Either way, we'll end up in the same place. My hands tremble and my heart practically beats out of my chest. I can't hold still, so I tap my feet and try her again. When she doesn't pick up, I text her: *Please call me back.*

Thankfully, Ezra is home. I call him next, and by the time I walk through our apartment door, he's already throwing my toiletries into a bag.

While I pull out a change of clothes, I tell him what little I know.

"You really like this girl, don't you?"

My chest squeezes so tight it's hard to breathe. Bending in half, I grasp my hair and tug, then straighten quickly. "God, Ezra, I feel like I'm losing my fucking mind." But I can't help myself.

"Do you love her?"

She consumes me.

"I've never felt this way about anyone before."

We haven't even known each other long, but it's been clear to me since the moment I saw her in Greece again this spring that this is exactly how my life is supposed to unfold. It's fate.

As I'm zipping my carry-on, the tattoo on my forearm catches my eye. It's inspired by the cover of my favorite book. It's a reminder that the universe will help me achieve what I want.

I check the time on my phone, then strip and toss my suit on the bed. I pull on a pair of jeans and a T-shirt, and by the time I hustle out the front doors of my building, the Uber is pulling up. Thank fuck, too, because I'm cutting it close.

But the universe has my back, I can feel it.

I'm a jittery mess as I head straight for security, scanning the people around me for my petite brunette. She must feel so alone right now. I've respected her wishes and let her keep me at a distance, but I'm done with that shit now. I want more. I deserve more. And she does too—she's just too afraid to ask for it. When we were on the dance floor, her soul and mine were speaking. I've never felt so attuned to a person as I did in that moment. Maybe I shouldn't have called her my girlfriend before speaking with her about it first, but god dammit, I want everyone to know she's mine.

Especially her.

The line at security is outrageous for how late it is. The people around me probably think I'm strung out. I can't stop twitching and bouncing around. Either that, or they suspect I have heroin shoved up my ass.

According to the airline app, the plane is already boarding. I offer to hold a baby for the couple in front of me just to move things along, and they respond to my offer with glares that promise they're about ten seconds from calling the police. That's fair.

I fly by the people flagged for pat-downs and race to the terminal. It's only when my phone vibrates in my pocket that I falter.

It's Joey.

Chapter 45
Josefine

I MAKE a mental note to thank Stephanie for letting me borrow the town car. Without Tom, I wouldn't have made the flight. The man could be a stunt driver for *Fast & Furious*.

On the ride here, my mind raced, conjuring up all kinds of scenarios of what I'll find when I touch down in LA. Will this accident be enough to convince her to go to rehab? I doubt it. She refused the last time I begged.

When I've located my row, I settle into the middle seat—my least favorite, but beggars can't be choosers. I was too panicked to bother with making a seat selection when I booked. So far, no one is sitting on either side of me, so I cross my fingers that one of them remains vacant.

I adjust the nozzle so the air is directed at me and pull on my shirt with my thumb and forefinger to cool my sweaty cleavage. Before leaving the apartment, I carefully hung Claire's dress, then threw on a pair of black leggings and a T-shirt Cam left behind.

Cam.

I feel horrible that I ran out on him, but getting to my mom

For the Plot

was my only thought. Until Dr. Draper's nasty remarks, that is. The way he spoke about Cam made me want to punch him in his smug, slimy face.

I'm anxious to get in the air, but people are still boarding, so I resign myself to being patient and pull my phone from my purse. I saw his name flash on my screen more than once, but from the looks of my notifications, he's been trying to reach me nonstop for the last ninety minutes or so.

He answers on the first ring.

"Joey!" He's out of breath and his voice is almost drowned out by background noise; he's probably still at the fundraiser. "Are you okay? How's your mom?"

My heart lurches. He's got the biggest damn heart. I squeeze my eyes shut, trying my best to prevent the tears burning behind them from breaking through. "I think she's okay," I say, my voice cracking. "And, um, someone is picking her up." I almost say that someone is my ex, but I'll explain that later.

"Where are you?"

"I'm on a plane," I reply, worrying my bottom lip. "I'm so sorry I ran off like that. Tell your parents I'm sorry too. I got the call from the hospital about my mom, and I had to move quickly if I was going to make it on the red-eye. I hope you're not mad."

"Of course I'm not mad, sweetheart." He huffs, the sound crackling down the line, then mutters a *thanks* to someone. "Are you okay?"

"I'm—I don't know." When I got the call, all I could think about was getting to my mom, but now that I have a moment to breathe, I feel so alone. In the rush of things, I haven't even called my aunt and uncle. If I told Aunt Rachel I needed her, she probably would have flown out with me.

A flight attendant comes over the loudspeaker to tell us to take our seats, and there's an echo in the phone.

"I think we're getting ready for takeoff. I'll call you when we land." With that, I hit the End button and switch my phone to airplane mode.

"Sir, please take your seat. We're readying for takeoff," a flight attendant says from a few rows in front of me.

As I'm leaning forward, blindly searching in my bag for my AirPods, a pair of shoes appears in my periphery, then a body sinks into the aisle seat on my left. *So much for having the row to myself.*

Giving up on locating my AirPods, I grab for my seat belt, ready to scoot over to the window, but a hand grasps mine, stopping the movement.

Chapter 46
Josefine

MILLIE and I have watched a lot of romance movies over the years. I feast on the suspense over the will-they-won't-they moments, like when one person races against the clock through the airport. Or when the wind sweeps away a stranger's phone number onto the street. Or a wedding is interrupted by a desperate confession.

But never in my wildest dreams did I think this could be my reality.

"Cam," I gasp, and a shiver runs through my body. "What are you doing here?"

"Flying to LA. What does it look like?" He winks. He brings my hands to his lips and presses a kiss against my skin in the shadow of the brim of his ball cap.

"No," I exhale. "I mean, that's sweet of you, but—no." He can't fly out to LA for me. That's just crazy.

Shifting in my direction, with his knees jammed into the seatback in front of him, he speaks. "I'm not trying to be sweet. I'm trying to be there for you. Don't push me away." His voice is clear and unwavering.

I regard him for a moment, taking in the seriousness in the set of his jaw and the genuine compassion behind his eyes. "My life in California is messy," I warn, "and—and it's about to get messier." He has no idea.

The plane is taxiing. There's no way out of this now. The overhead lights turn off and the strip of lights flicker above the windows, illuminating along the length of the plane.

"And you think that's going to scare me away? I can handle messy, Joey. I didn't quit my job and give up my inheritance to play it safe. I gave it up to live life on my own terms. And I want to be there for you. I want to do this. *I'm* choosing this. I'm choosing *you*. Let me choose you."

My heart cracks open and tears finally tumble down my cheeks, despite my attempt to keep them inside. "I don't deserve you."

Cam hasn't let go of my hand. In fact, he's clutching harder, and his left leg is bouncing like a jackhammer now that we're moving down the runway.

"Are you a nervous flier?"

With his eyes still shut tight, he juts his chin in confirmation. "Just during takeoff and landing," he mumbles, white-knuckling the armrest to his left.

I hold his hand in my lap and lean over him so I can rub calming circles over his chest.

"Did you ever read the book *We're Going on a Bear Hunt* as a child?"

The plane lifts off then, and he cracks one eye open skeptically at my random question.

"Remember what they did every time they reached a new hurdle? The snowstorm? The cave?"

He nods, and his grip loosens just a fraction, so I continue. "They observed the obstacle and considered their best course of action. They couldn't go under it or over it, so they went through it. Flying's a lot like that."

A smile surfaces on his smooth face, and he drops his head back against his seat and lets it loll, his eyes glowing in contemplation.

I nuzzle into his shoulder, ignoring the way the armrest stabs into my ribs.

"The same goes for you, you know," he says.

I lift my head to meet his gaze beneath the brim of his hat.

"With your mom," he clarifies. "We'll get through it."

The way he says *we* has my insides lighting up like constellations in the night sky.

Once the plane has evened out, Cam breaks away to lift the armrest between us.

"You must be exhausted." He drapes an arm over my shoulders and tugs me into his sturdy body. He kisses the top of my head and strokes my hair. I nearly purr like a kitten at his tranquil touch. He's about to find out that playing with my hair is my kryptonite.

Sometime later, I'm woken by a subtle shifting of Cam's body. I sit up straight and wipe at my chin, mortified when my hand comes away damp.

All he does is give me a soft smile. Removing his hat, he chuckles. "Sorry to wake you, but my arm's asleep."

He rubs and shakes out his arm as I stretch out my neck. The brown noise of the engines drowns out the rustling of passengers around us who are struggling for comfort with their makeshift neck pillows, and random overhead lights look like polka-dots in the otherwise dark cabin.

I unbuckle my seat belt and slide to the window seat. "Come." I pat my thigh, motioning for him to lay his head in my lap. He obeys, kissing my knee, then settling in.

Running my fingers through his hair, I rest my head against

the fuselage. And for the first time in hours, a sense of calm covers me like a blanket. Bring on the bear, because with Cam by my side, I can get through anything.

Sometime after three, we deboard at LAX. Neither of us checked bags, so we head straight outside to locate a taxi. When we exit through the automatic doors, I inhale the familiar Southern California air. Although the smell of pollution is similar to that in New York City, it's much less humid here.

While we wait, I turn my phone off airplane mode and wait while a slew of texts pops up. I immediately open the one from Tyler: *I was able to get your mom into that rehab facility in Palm Springs.*

My lungs seize. He got a facility lined up without even checking with me? I know the place he's talking about too. It's super exclusive. There's no way we can afford it. This is so like him—making decisions for me.

Cam takes my carry-on and brushes a hand down my arm like he can sense the rage bubbling up inside me. Just a simple touch from him dulls the fury. "What's wrong?"

Scattered and overwhelmed, I wave him off and furiously tap out a response on my phone.

He steps closer and lays his hand over the top of my screen. When I look up at him, his kind eyes are narrowed and his mouth is a flat line, like he means business. "I know you're used to doing everything on your own, but you don't have to anymore. And, baby?" He steadies me with his hand at the back of my neck and brushes the pad of his thumb against my cheek. "You are worthy of so much. If this is going to work, you need to talk to me, okay? I promise I'm not going anywhere."

I give him a curt nod and am rewarded when a light sparks in his eyes.

"You're right."

A taxi pulls up then, and he guides me inside. Once we're settled, he watches me, expectation clear in his expression.

So I dive in. When I tell him I called Tyler for help, he doesn't even bristle. He nods and listens as I relay how he picked my mom up from the hospital, then brought her to the rehab center without my permission.

"I'm sorry he didn't discuss it with you first." He squeezes my hand. "*And* I'm glad she's in a safe place."

He's right, but— "I can't afford this rehab center. A thirty-day stint will be tens of thousands of dollars," I squeak.

Nausea creeps up like a slow, relentless shadow, followed by a boiling, dizzying sensation—no doubt from a combination of exhaustion and stress. With a sharp breath, I push it all down and smother it with a lid.

The rehab center in Palm Springs is two hours from LAX, so Cam suggests we stop at my mom's so we can sleep for a few hours and promises we'll head east first thing in the morning.

It's nearly seven in New York, so I text Aunt Rachel in case she's still sleeping. She immediately calls me and puts me on speakerphone. I tell her and Uncle Ethan everything I know while Cam thumbs away on his phone beside me in the taxi, one hand on my lap the entire time.

I decline their offer to fly out but promise to update them as soon as I know more and if I need their help.

When we pull up to my mother's modest bungalow, the street is eerily quiet. A lone streetlamp bathes her carport in a dim glow.

I exhale a sigh of relief when her spare key is still buried in moss in a planter. When I open the front door, the faint scent of takeout greets us.

To be honest, I expected the place to be worse, but it's mostly tidy. The only thing out of sorts is an empty Styrofoam container on the counter next to her cell phone. At first glance, the main living space looks rather untouched.

"Is this where you grew up?"

"No. I never lived here. My mom moved shortly after I started college."

I left San Diego to put some space between my mom and me, but living in the house my father died in without me became too unbearable for her.

We walk down the hall. Flicking on the light, I take in the guest bedroom. I stayed here for a couple of days after my breakup, but I haven't been back since.

Cam embraces me from behind, resting his chin at the top of my head. My hair is down but kinked from the flight, with remnants of hairspray from the gala.

I turn in his arms and mumble into his chest. "Thank you for being here."

He squeezes harder when my sniffles turn to sobs, and he doesn't let go. He supports me when my legs feel like they're about to give out, and he rubs my back when the waterworks finally release.

"I've got you." He kisses me on the top of my head.

I focus on the steady rise and fall of his chest.

I love this man, and I think he might love me too.

Chapter 47
Josefine

I'M SURPRISINGLY REFRESHED after a solid four hours of sleep. Enough so, even, to conquer whatever is waiting for me in Palm Springs. I passed out while Cam showered last night, and this morning, I linger under the hot water longer than intended. I dress in a flowy white spaghetti-strap top tucked into a pair of cutoff jeans and a boho-like kimono. With my hair in a giant claw and a pair of Birkenstocks on my feet, I'm ready to head out. After filling my mom's car with gas and grabbing coffees and bagels to-go, we are finally on the highway. If traffic is light, we should arrive at the rehab center before noon.

Cam looks relaxed in chino shorts, a fitted tee, and white sneakers. Neither of us remembered to pack sunglasses in our mad rush, so we're donning cheap gas station frames. While he drives, I text Tyler: *On my way to Palm Springs. Thank you again.*

The iconic palm-lined streets aren't as glamorous when one's mother is in rehab on the other side. We pull up to the front of Desert Haven Recovery Oasis. At first glance, the vibe is far more luxury resort and spa than inpatient facility, especially when the valet greets us.

On the drive over, I researched a more affordable center closer to my mom's house, but because of poor reception, I couldn't get through to reserve a spot. Now that we're here and the service has improved, I'll try again. First, though, I need to see my mom. She may not agree to it.

We're hit with a burst of cool air as we pass through the automatic doors. Just inside, I stumble to a halt. Because my ex is sitting on a sofa in the lobby. He promptly rises when he catches motion at the door and strides my way.

"Hi." I give him a curt nod.

Cam steps closer to my side in solidarity.

"Hey, Beck." Tyler gives me a crooked smile. His button-down is buttoned a little too down, giving me a clear view of the tattoos on his chest. What was once *Josefine* is now a field of pine trees. "It's good to see you."

I'm not sure how to reply. I'm definitely not delighted to see him, but he did pick up my mom from the hospital and drive two hours to bring her here.

I don't waste time on superficial politeness, but I do offer my gratitude. "Thank you for your help last night."

Why is he still here?

His eyes linger on me a little too long, and when he finally glances at Cam, he nods in his direction and scowls. "Who's this guy?"

Looping my pinkie with Cam's, I say, "This is Cameron. My" —*oh what the hell*—"boyfriend."

He wraps my hand in his and squeezes.

It's the first time I've said the word aloud, but dang, if it doesn't feel right. Maybe introducing my new boyfriend to my ex-boyfriend isn't the best way to declare my feelings, but I refuse to tiptoe around them anymore.

Tyler crosses his arms at the same time Cam extends his for a handshake.

"I'm going to see what I can find out about my mom," I say, attempting to break the tension, but the guys don't take their eyes off each other.

Ignoring the little puffing-of-the-chests ritual, I approach the woman behind the desk and present my ID.

"Hi, my mother, Elin Beckham, was brought here last night, *er,* this morning," I correct myself. "I'd like to check her out, actually."

"Oh?" Behind her wide-frame glasses, the woman's brows raise and her eyes widen.

"Yes. If you could just bill me for one night, I can pay now." I brace myself for the cost.

The woman, Dahlia, according to her name tag, is silent as she turns to her computer. Only the soft click of her nails on the keyboard can be heard. That, and two men huffing down my neck.

"It looks like the bill has been taken care of, Ms. Beckham," Dahlia says.

"What? I haven't even seen a bill yet."

She peers up at me. "According to our records, the cost of a thirty-day stay for your mother has been paid."

Dumbfounded, all I can do is gape at her for a moment. "And my mom agreed to this?"

"Yes," she confirms. "I can have someone bring you to her now if you'd like."

I nod, then turn to the two men behind me.

"How?" I choke out, turning to Tyler, who must have covered the cost. "Did you—" I'm so shocked I can't form the words.

With a tilt of his head, he shrugs.

"I can't—I don't—" I stutter. "I can't pay you back right now, but I promise I will."

"Don't worry about it, Beck." He slides his hands into his pants pockets. "Consider this my apology."

And with a silent salute, he turns on his heel and strides for the door.

Before I have time to process what's happening, a tall, skinny man appears and offers to escort me to see my mother. They only allow one person at a time, so Cam takes a seat in the lobby, but not before kissing the side of my head.

I'm led to a living space that looks like it was ripped from the pages of *Architectural Digest*. My mother is sitting on a brown leather sofa in front of floor-to-ceiling windows that overlook a man-made lake with a fountain. She looks thinner than when I last saw her, though I can't be sure because she's wearing a flowing long-sleeve linen pants outfit.

On the drive over, I imagined I'd have to play the role of adult, per usual, but seeing her after all this time provokes the instinct to be the child. I crumple in her arms as exhaustion spills out of my pores. She doesn't let go as we settle into the sofa. When I pull away, I examine the side of her head.

"Are you okay?" I ask, eyeing the bandage at her temple.

With tears in her eyes, she nods.

I allow myself to relax against the cushion. "What happened?"

Trembling, she explains how Frank broke up with her. Something about her being too needy and nagging, and to be honest, I don't follow the whole jumbled story. After she texted me, she took some pills (she doesn't mention which) and walked to a bar a few blocks from her house. When the bartender cut her off, she hopped off the barstool, and that's when she slipped and hit her head on the bar. She doesn't remember much after that, but she was told that the bartender called an ambulance. She ducks her chin and wipes at her eyes when she admits that she doesn't remember being brought to the facility.

"But I'm going to stay." She clears her throat, and an instant later, an employee magically appears with a pitcher of water infused with cucumber and mint. "The whole thirty days. I promise."

Wiping the tears falling from my eyes, I hug her again. "Thank you, Mom."

I don't know what's to come. I don't know whether she'll stay sober and get her life back on track, but it's a step in the right direction.

Cam is on the phone when I return to the lobby but quickly pockets the device when he sees me.

"How did it go?" He studies my face, brow furrowed, and wipes at my cheek.

"Good, actually." The way the weight lifts from my shoulders when I say the words is such a relief. "She's going to go through with the program."

"That's great news."

I nod. "Let's take off. I can drive you back if you're tired, but I think I'm going to stay in LA until she's released." That would keep me here until mid-August. "I'm not sure what will happen after she finishes here."

"Actually..." He guides me through the automatic doors to wait for the valet. "Hotel Connelly has a location here. We can stay as long as we need to."

"In Palm Springs?" I whip around to face him, feeling a little dizzy at the discovery. I may need to sit down. Or throw up.

"Yes. I've already cleared it with my folks. You can write your book, and I can do some marketing work for the hotel while your mom gets better."

My heart soars at the prospect. Throwing my arms around him, I kiss his neck. Twelve hours ago, I was in panic mode. Now, though, an overwhelming sense of calm washes over me. I have a healthy new partner, and my mom is finally in rehab.

Cam insisted we bring our luggage today. Now I'm wondering if he planned this all along. Thank god the two of us are so attached to our laptops. In my haste, I may have forgotten a thing or two, but that little piece of technology goes with me everywhere. As long as we've got Wi-Fi where we're going, we'll be set for work for the next month.

We check into our hotel room—oh, excuse me; our penthouse suite—and find a late lunch waiting for us inside. A little bit of everything: hamburgers, waffles, chicken nuggets, french fries, salad, and enough fruit to feed the entire population of a small island, as well as bottles of sparkling water and iced green tea.

After stuffing our faces while watching reruns of *The Office* on the sectional sofa, Cam excuses himself to shower.

Now that my belly is full and my adrenaline is deflating, the California king in the largest bedroom (of three) is calling my name.

The door to the bathroom is cracked, and the sound of running water acts as a lullaby. Before I let it ease me into slumber, I fire off a text to my aunt and uncle, and Millie, then settle in. I remove my hair clip and set it on the table next to where Cam's phone is plugged in. The screen comes to life when a text notification pops up. While I'm not trying to be nosy, my eyes can't help themselves. I think it's human nature.

The notification banner shows a preview of a text from Ezra: *You paid for her mom's rehab? You're—*

What the hell?

I thought Tyler covered the bill.

Flying off the bed, I yank the phone from the charger and

barge into the bathroom. At the commotion, Cam wipes the fog from the shower glass and squints at me.

Holding up his phone, I take a step closer and straighten my shoulders. "What's this about?"

"I can't see anything." He turns off the water, and when he opens the shower door, I can't help but drink him in. But I shake off the hit of desire that bombards me each time I'm met with the sight of his perfectly wet body.

He reaches across me for a towel, dripping water onto the shoulder of my kimono. After wrapping the towel around his waist, he takes his phone and calmly examines the evidence. The frown deepens.

"Is it true?" I demand. "Wait, are you not mad that I snooped at your messages?"

"No. I have nothing to hide," he says, leaning his hip against the counter.

"Obviously you hid this from me!" I mirror his position so we're face to face, one hip propped against the vanity.

"If you're trying to pick a fight, it's not going to work." He sets his phone to the side and tucks a strand of hair behind my ear. "I wasn't trying to hide it from you. I was trying to do it anonymously. There's a difference."

"But you can't—" I scan his face. "How?"

"My inheritance." He lifts one shoulder.

"What do you mean your inheritance? I thought you gave it up."

He adjusts the towel around his waist, the muscles of his chest and abs rippling as he does. "I did. But my parents had a talk, and my dad reconsidered."

"When did this…" I trail off and run through the events of the last twenty-four hours.

"When you were in the shower this morning."

I grasp his hand and hold it to my chest. "I'll pay you back, I promise."

"No." He pushes off the counter, towering over me, a flash of determination crossing his face. "You won't."

"But that's a lot of money."

"A drop in the bucket." He takes half a step closer and cups my jaw.

For the millionth time today, tears obscure my vision. He opens his arms, and I dive into his chest without hesitation and drag my nose across his chest, breathing in his scent.

"Did you just sniff my armpit?" he laughs.

I don't pull away. "I'm making a memory."

It's said that a person's sense of smell has the power to trigger emotion and memories. I never want to forget how I feel right now.

It's not enough that I'm pressed against his bare skin; I want to be *in his skin*.

"Tell me, what do I smell like?" He sighs. "Please say *like peppermint and pipe tobacco*."

"You did not just reference *The Parent Trap* while I'm having a moment," I giggle.

"I did," he laughs back. "Why were you sniffing my armpit?"

"I told you. I'm making a memory." While I didn't mean to sniff his armpit specifically, I inhale again, though this time much more dramatically. He smells of the hotel's body wash: orange and bergamot.

"I can't believe you're smelling my armpit. You're so—"

"I love you."

He goes rigid for an instant, then angles back, fixing his wide-eyed expression on me. There's a fierce sort of sparkle glinting in his irises. "What?"

Draping my arms over his shoulders and threading my fingers at his nape, I pull him close, until his lips hover over mine.

"I love you, Cam," I breathe.

His full lips are warm as he devours mine. When I part my lips in invitation, he slides his tongue inside greedily, drugging me with his taste. There's a savage intensity to our kiss, a divine ecstasy.

Just as I shiver in delight, he pulls away. "I love you too," he whispers into my soul. Then he seals his vow with another kiss.

I tug on his towel, loosening its hold.

And suddenly, I'm not so sleepy.

Chapter 48
Cameron

When that asshole let Joey believe he paid for her mother's rehab, I considered punching his smug skinny face right there in the middle of the lobby. Instead, though, I let him have his moment. But the second Joey went back to see her mom, I flew out the door after him.

Mr. Fuckboy was waiting for the valet when I approached.

He turned and nodded in a pathetic greeting as I loomed over him.

"You got the balls to match that lie back there?" I asked.

He scanned the portico, probably looking for backup, but it was just the two of us. "What are you talking about?"

I crossed my arms in front of me, making sure to puff up just a little. He's toned, but I'm much bigger. "We both know you didn't pay for her mom's rehab."

I saw the moment it clicked for him.

"*You.*" He shifted on his feet, scanning our surroundings once again. "You gonna tell her?"

"Nope," I replied, getting in his face. "It was awfully nice of you to pick Elin up from the hospital and get her a spot at this fancy rehab." I offered him a smarmy smile. "But after today, you will not contact Joey again."

Without waiting for a response, I turned on my heel and strode inside.

Facilities like Desert Haven typically don't allow patients to receive visitors for the first thirty days of treatment, so it took some finagling on my end to get Joey in to see her mom—another thing I handled while she was in the bathroom getting ready this morning—but it was worth the effort. Elin agreed to complete the treatment, and getting eyes on her mom had to be a huge weight lifted for Joey.

My dad's call this morning was a surprise, to say the least. We've got a long way to go, but the transfer he made to my account this morning—one large enough to pay for Elin's rehab and then some—was a great way to begin apologizing.

While I may never have the relationship I dream of having with my dad, it's progress, and I'll take what I can get.

Even though I didn't foresee any of this happening, I know it's exactly where I'm meant to be.

And right now? My breathtakingly beautiful girl just confessed her love to me.

Finally.

Then she tugged my towel free.

My stomach clenches, and a chill courses through my veins. I want her so fucking bad.

"Baby," I whisper, sucking the side of her neck, slipping my fingers beneath her kimono and letting it drop to the floor.

She glides her hands down my damp chest, and when she teases the dark hair below my navel, my dick twitches. Dipping lower, I untuck her silky shirt and step back so I can pull it off. Once she's free, I cup her pert breasts and roll her nipples between my fingers.

She groans, arching into my touch, and I can't help but press right back, rubbing my hard cock against her belly. The fabric of her cutoffs is rough, so I make quick work of unbuttoning them and shimmying them down her hips.

She kicks them to the side, and then she's standing before me in only a gray thong. The fabric is already drenched, and her bare chest is heaving as she regards me.

I spin her around to face the mirror and cup her pussy. Capturing her gaze in the mirror, I rasp, "You're fucking soaked, Josefine. Did saying you love me cause this? Or did this happen when I said the words to you?"

"Both," she breathes.

I twist her around to face me again. Fuck, I want to tell her that she's all mine, that our pasts don't matter. That how we got here doesn't matter. Instead, I explore her body. It's different now. The fear of losing her is gone. For the first time, I'm confident that she won't hold back. This time, I feel like we have all the time in the world.

I caress her ribs, then make my way to her hips, and then her ass. I love the feel of her perfect ass in my hands.

"Arms around me, baby." She follows my instruction, and I hoist her up, her legs wrapping around my naked waist, capturing my hard length between us.

In the bedroom, I lay her on the bed. She inches back on the mattress, but I grab her ankles and yank her to the edge, relishing the way her tits jiggle when I do.

Looping my fingers under the elastic of her thong, I tug. I drag my nails along the length of her legs all the way down, watching chill bumps erupt on her smooth skin.

"Spread those legs, sweetheart. I wanna see just how wet you are for me."

The first time we had sex in that rundown B&B, it was obvious she liked my filthy mouth. With each word, her breaths would quicken and her pupils would dilate. She's reacting the same way now, playing with her nipples and squirming against the sheets. She plants her feet flat on the mattress, baring herself to me. I have the best view in the house. I rub my hand over my cock at the sight of her glistening cunt.

Shit, I want to go slow, but I also want to fucking devour her.

I want to fuck her pretty pussy with my mouth until she's begging for relief. Then I want her to gag on my cock until she's a sloppy, whimpering mess. I want to take my time, but my girl has other plans. Wearing a smirk, she dips two fingers into her entrance, then sucks them into her mouth.

Oh, fuck me now. I love this woman.

I bring her knees over my shoulders, and with a hungry groan, I lower my head and get to work. And it's the best kind of work. Her gasps and moans are like my own private instruction manual, telling me exactly what to do. Spreading her lips, I lap at her, bottom to top, before blowing against her clit.

"Again," she commands.

I gladly repeat the action. Then I trail the tip of my tongue along her nerve endings before sinking into her.

She clings to my hair as she cries out. "Yes. That feels so good, baby. Please. Don't stop."

Obediently, I impale her with my tongue. She squeezes her thighs together, trapping my head, anchoring me to her core. She's feral, and it only makes me more ravenous. I flick and suck and slide two fingers inside, curling in a way that has her back arching off the bed and thrusting her tits toward heaven.

Heaven, indeed. With my head buried between her legs and with the way she's crushing me with her thighs, that's exactly where I may end up. *Death by pussy.* I can think of worse ways to go.

When she begins bucking her hips and chanting my name, I slip a third finger inside her. She tugs at my roots in response, holding me precisely where she wants me.

"Don't stop, Cam. Please," she begs, "Keep going. I'm so close."

That's it, baby. Let go.

I work double-time, lapping against her clit and stroking her inner wall, finding that perfect spot.

And she shatters.

Her pussy clenches around my fingers, and she lets out a series of fierce groans. Her cunt pulses with pleasure, her whole body twitching with aftershocks. I slide my fingers out and gently lap at her clit as she rides out the last of her release. It's not until her legs slip off my shoulders and her body goes limp that I come up for air.

Drowsy with lust and chest heaving, she lifts onto her elbows.

I rise from the floor and crawl up her body. Still drenched with her release, I kiss her softly. "How do you feel, baby?"

"Incredible," she sighs.

"Mmm." I pull back a fraction and harden my expression. "Now use that talented mouth and suck my cock."

Chapter 49

Cameron

For a moment, Joey's expression remains tender. She brushes my hair off my brow, though it falls back down. But in the span of one heartbeat, a wicked gleam surfaces in her eyes. "Grab the headboard."

Yes fucking ma'am.

I do as I'm told, and she shimmies her way down the mattress until her mouth lines up with my dick. She nuzzles into the light smattering of hair, breathing me in. On instinct, I jut my hips forward, but she wraps her arms around my thighs, halting my movement.

When I dip my chin to get a good look at her, she releases a soft sound low in her throat. Then she kisses the tip of my cock. My dick twitches, making her giggle, and in response, she flicks my head with the tip of her tongue.

Her lips part in invitation. When I move my hips again, she doesn't stop me, but rather guides me between her lips. She gags and I pull back. Fuck, that's hot, hearing her choke around my cock.

With a whimper, she wraps one hand around my shaft. The

other holds steady to my hip. She teases my head, then sucks me all the way in. Her obscene noises make me desperate. I've never needed to fuck someone so much.

"You like that, baby? My cock shoved down your throat?"

She nods and mumbles "fuck my face" around my dick.

"Oh god." I squirm above her and lower to my forearms. I'm so fucking close already, but I'm not ready to blow. No. I'm saving that for her pussy. I want to see my cum leaking from her tight hole.

Though it's torture, I pull away. I roll to my side and guide her up the bed so she's on her side too. Fuck, those tits look extra gorgeous pressed together like this. Catching her breath, she feathers her fingers against my arm and trails them down my ribs and my hips before clasping my cock once again.

"I'm so glad you're the only one who's fucked me bare," she whispers, stroking my length, then cupping my balls.

My lungs expand to their fullest, and the caveman in me beats his chest. "Only you, baby."

"There's only you."

A gluttonous moan escapes her lips as she rubs my tip against her slit. I'm barely holding back my release, but I can't wait to feel her warm cunt pulse around my cock.

Enough of this teasing.

I grasp the base of her throat and squeeze lightly. "My cock is screaming for your pussy."

"My pussy's weeping for your cock," she sobs.

I shove her onto her back and loom over her. With one look from me, she spreads her legs, beseeching. I want her more than ever. I sit back on my heels, breathless, and take in the view. I thrust two fingers into her still soaked center. She pushes against me, riding my hand with enthusiasm. All the while, I pump my cock with my free hand, lost in her. In this moment. I can't pull my gaze away.

"Come here," she breathes.

I slide my fingers out, savoring the feel of her heat, and cage her in with my forearms.

"Kiss me," she requests, cupping my neck and pulling until my lips meet hers.

Our kiss is languid, yet full of electricity.

Without letting up, she reaches between us and notches the head of my cock at her entrance. "I'm yours," she whispers into my mouth. "Take me."

And I do. I press in, giving her a minute to adjust to my size, then out and slam into her.

I'm hers too. She can take everything.

There are no words for how good it feels to be buried in her tight warmth. The way her pussy welcomes me and sucks me all the way to the hilt. My attention locked on her face, I thrust in deep, embedding myself in her.

"God, you're pretty," I pant.

Her tits bounce with every thrust of my hips, tempting me to capture them with my mouth. I suck one perfectly peaked nipple, eliciting a groan from her, then I repeat the movement with the other.

"Ah, yes," she whines, wiggling her hips. "You feel so fucking good. Deeper." She's homed in on the place where our bodies connect in the most physical way.

"Eyes on me."

She obeys, dragging her attention to my face. Her pupils are blown wide, and her mouth is parted. She's so goddamn beautiful.

"That's my girl. You take my cock so well."

She snakes her hands down my back to grab my ass and grinds against me. I pump faster when she digs her nails into my skin and pour my desire into her mouth, needing the connection.

It's not enough that my dick is buried inside her. I want to burrow under her skin and live there.

I'm so fucking gone for this girl.

"So close," she pants. "Need. More."

Sweat beads at my temples as I pick up my pace and drag my hand down to her swollen clit.

"Yes, right there." She gasps when I rub my thumb around it in circles, and grinds against me harder, faster. "I can't—I'm gonna—"

"Take what's yours, baby. Fucking come on my cock."

And she does. Her back arches, and she unleashes a primal moan. My vision blurs at the edges, and I follow her over the edge, crying out as I unload inside her. Her tight pussy squeezes me, rhythmically draining me until there's nothing left to give.

Shivering, I collapse onto my beautiful girl. The pulse point on her neck beats rapidly against my nose as I saw sharp breaths in, then out again. We're a shaking, sweaty mess.

Groaning, I pull out from between her legs, careful not to put too much weight on her. With one leg hooked over hers, I rest my head on her breasts, ghost circles over one sensitive nipple, and plant a kiss in the middle of her chest, over her beating heart.

She runs delicate fingers through my hair, then up and down my back. "I love you."

"I love you, Joey," I breathe into her heart.

Chapter 50
Josefine

One Month Later

THEY—WHOEVER they may be—say a person should write the book they want to read.

As the daughter of someone with substance abuse, I chose to write a book that adolescents and young teens could turn to for comfort in times of confusion and isolation. Because that's how I felt growing up: confused and alone.

I didn't start out with a committed deadline or goal, really. Just a dream to write and publish a book someday.

But Cam lit a fire inside me.

With my mom tucked safely inside a bougie rehab center, surrounded by some of the best therapists in the world (I looked it up), a huge weight was lifted off my shoulders. That relief alone opened up a part of my creativity that had been sealed shut for as long as I can remember.

Cam suggested we take a couple of days to decompress before making any big decisions about how to spend the month. And by "decompress," he meant "have lots of sex."

When our decompression period was over, we devised a plan. First, I made it clear that we weren't actually living together, but rather on a "work-retreat-like vacation." Whether I was kidding myself or not with this reframe, he appeased me.

Next, I promised to try my best to communicate my needs, even if all I could think to say was "I don't know how to express my needs." Having a simple script to communicate better was liberating.

While I wrote, Cam worked for his parents. Traditional office life isn't his jam, but it was only temporary. This time, though, he didn't experience the same pressure from his father as he once did.

Brooks drove out to Palm Springs for a couple of nights and helped me clean up certain plot holes and kill off an unnecessary character—metaphorically speaking.

Though I hoped the change of scenery and finally allowing myself to open my heart to Cam would magically give me the motivation and inspiration I'd need to finish the book, writing is ultimately a slow process. No number of hyped-up texts from Millie, Brooks, and Ari can extract me from feeling like I'm suddenly stuck.

Worse yet, I'm beginning to question my ability. *Why can't I finish it? Why do my words read like they were written by a chimpanzee?*

I've been meeting with a new therapist via video weekly, and she's encouraging me to "trust the process" and practice patience and compassion for myself.

She and Cam are quick to remind me that being a Creative—with a capital C—is mentally taxing. As if I don't already know. Some days, I feel like I'm absolutely losing it. Our suite is covered in sticky notes. I'm pretty sure housekeeping thinks I'm investigating a murder with the way I've tacked them on every surface.

For the Plot

But I'm terrified of forgetting the ideas that hit me in the shower or sprout in the middle of the night.

Cam hasn't batted an eye at my creative madness. Rather, I think he understands the sense of urgency—though he's taken to wearing earplugs to bed so I'm less likely to wake him in the middle of the night while I record voice memos on my phone.

But now I'm at a standstill with my book. The words, once flowing like a waterfall, have dried up.

And tomorrow is the day my mom is released from rehab. Will she be healed? Will she fall back into her old ways? Fuck, I wish I could see into the future. Or at least have a set of super-bright headlights.

Chapter 51

Josefine

As I zip the last of my bags, a dull seasick feeling sweeps over me. I shrug it off, and when my vision blurs at the edges, I attribute it to my inconsistent use of blue-light-blocking glasses. For zero-point-two seconds, my stomach plummets and I worry I'm pregnant. But I literally finished my period three days prior, so I push that fear aside.

Carrying my bags to the door, I can no longer ignore the concerning sensations happening in my body. A large knot clings to my diaphragm like a leech, making it impossible to take in a full breath. I pour a glass of water from the sink, my hands trembling, but swallowing makes me feel like I'm drowning.

I rest my elbows on the edge of the sink, and when the tightness in my chest and tingling down my arms don't subside, I seek out Cam.

"What is it, baby?" he asks when he spots me standing outside the shower door.

I hold my right arm tight against my body like a ball of yarn. If I let go, I fear the anxiety may unravel into a full-blown panic attack.

He doesn't even bother with a towel when he steps out from the shower. He grasps my shoulders and ducks his head so I'm forced to look at him. "What's wrong?"

I try to take a deep breath, but the knot at the base of my lungs has turned into a baseball, making it next to impossible to force air past. "I think I'm about to have a panic attack," I sputter.

Without a word, he guides me to the bed. "Lay down, sweetheart."

Obediently, I crawl in. Cam follows, drawing the sheets over us and curling up behind me, drenching my sundress in the process.

"We're going to breathe together, okay?" he says, wrapping his arms tightly around my chest.

"Follow my breath, baby. Inhale. *Exhale*," he directs. "Inhale. *Exhale*."

Fighting back sobs, I coerce myself to match the rise and fall of his chest. Though it takes many tries, he remains patient, whispering "that's it" and "almost there" until my vision returns and my breaths come easier.

Rolling over, I press my face into his chest, inhaling orange and bergamot, imploring the scent to take me to the memory of the moment we confessed our love.

"Thank you," I whisper.

"Always, baby." He kisses the top of my head.

Enveloped in his arms, I share my fears about which version of my mom will greet me today and about whether I'll ever finish my book.

Cam holds not only me, but space for my worry. We lie in bed for what could be minutes or an hour until my breaths are even and full again.

When his bare ass crawls out of bed, I laugh.

"That's the only time you're allowed to laugh when I'm naked," he teases, pulling me up beside him.

I hug him, then glide my hands down his fine ass, giving his cheeks a squeeze. "I love you."

The whirlwind of unease and apprehension my anxiety caused fades as soon as I see my mom. She looks healthier than she has in a decade, and not just because of the on-site salon at Desert Haven. While false hope lurks in the shadows, the light at the end of the tunnel shimmers in the distance.

My mom is already enrolled in an outpatient program close to home and is optimistic about her recovery. She talks the entire drive to Santa Monica, and I'm turning around to look at her so much that I have to ask Cam to pull over so I can jump in the back seat to keep from getting carsick. She met Cam for the first time when we picked her up, but by the time we make it back home, she has already fallen in love with him.

We stay with her, but by the end of the week, she kicks us out, claiming I'm suffocating her.

I'm not ready to return to the other side of the country just yet, so we find a furnished apartment available for sublease a few blocks away. Like most places in Southern California, it doesn't have central air. That's the true test of any relationship. Making it through the hottest days of summer without AC and coming out on the other side.

It doesn't take Cam long to find clients in the area. After uploading more pictures from Crete and Palm Springs onto his socials, he collects quite the SoCal clientele. Seeing him do what he loves makes my heart so happy.

For a few months now, Mom and I have been going to therapy together once a week. After she apologized for not being the parent I needed her to be, I accepted that she did the best she could while struggling with extreme grief. Following my dad's death, she was paralyzed over where to go or what to do next. It was painful to share our truths—and there were a lot of tears—but I feel optimistic about her treatment plan.

While we can't change the past, and while I have more work to do on my own, we're slowly rebuilding our relationship, and I'm hopeful about where we're headed.

The most surprising part about sharing therapy with my mom is how it opened my creative floodgates and allowed me to finish my book. Spoiler alert: All the good words aren't actually taken. *I finally found them.*

In honor of this huge accomplishment, Cam took me to Catalina Island for the weekend, where we pretended to be back on Crete (complete with another round of sensory-deprivation play).

Writing this book would not have been possible without therapy and a supportive partner, and while I feel deep sorrow that my dad is not here to witness this dream come true, I know that wherever he is, he's proud.

Cam once asked me if the young woman in my book finds her way in life.

My response was "I don't know."

But now, on the day I've submitted my debut novel, *Plot Twist*, for publishing, I can finally say: *Yes, she does.*

Epilogue

Cameron

"Are you serious?"

"Positive," I reply, picking up my old-fashioned from the coffee table.

Joey and I were greeted by the yellows, oranges, and reds of fall in New York City when we returned yesterday. Thanksgiving is right around the corner, though the streets and landmarks are adorned with festive holiday decorations already. I love how the city comes alive with holiday spirit and the way the crisp fall air adds to the cozy ambiance.

After living out of suitcases for four months, Joey was ready to reunite with her wardrobe. Millie is back from another tour, so I said my goodbyes at their apartment to give the two of them time to catch up.

While I slept terribly without my girl last night, I have my own catching up to do. Starting with informing Ezra that I'm moving out.

"She's it for me, man," I admit. "We've been living together since July anyway."

To celebrate the completion of Joey's book, I swept her away to Catalina Island for a weekend. The terrain and landscape are so similar to Crete that we felt like we were back on the island that serendipitously brought us together not once, but twice.

"How do you feel, gorgeous?" I asked, running my fingers through her hair.

It was still damp from the bath we'd taken the night before.

"I feel more settled than I've ever felt before."

Her expression showed it. For months, she had been stressing about her mom and her book.

"Yeah?" I cocked a brow. "Why is that?"

She set her espresso cup on the small table between us, then climbed onto my lap. Her robe gaped open, gifting me the perfect view of her tits. She played with the hair at my nape. I'd let it grow far too long over the last few months, but Joey liked it. She said it gave her more to grab on to.

"Because of you." She kissed my jaw and nuzzled into my neck.

"I love you." I played with the belt around her robe. The feel of the terry cloth brought images of the previous night to mind. This time, her senses were the ones deprived.

I had swirled ice around her nipples and sucked them into my mouth before licking the water left behind off every part of her body. Every. Part. I'd reveled in the way she shivered and squirmed on the mattress, clawing at the sheets and letting out desperate mewls.

The way her cunt had convulsed around my tongue, then my fingers, then my cock, had nearly made me lose my mind. Her last climax dragged on forever. When I'd finally spilled inside her, I basked in the way my cum leaked out of her pussy with every electric spasm.

"I love you too." She traced the tattoos on my arm.

We made small talk for a few minutes, but when she mentioned dreading the pull-out sofa and being ready to find a place that feels like home, I took my shot. "What do you think about moving in together?"

She sat back and blinked at me. "Are you serious?"

"I've never been more serious, but if you're not ready or if—"

"Yes!"

The shock of her sudden consensus caused words to wedge in my throat. But when she broke into the brightest smile, I exhaled a long sigh of contentment. Joy bubbled in her laugh, and we drank in each other's kisses before I carried her back to bed and took my time showing her just how happy she makes me.

Ezra clinks his glass of whiskey against mine in congratulations, but that isn't even the biggest surprise I have up my sleeve.

ME

Joey doesn't suspect anything does she?

MILLIE

Dude

Cool it

I'm leaving now. She thinks I'm going to Sam's

The coast is clear. Come get your girl

Joey's book doesn't release for another few weeks, but I'm surprising her with a private book launch with her closest friends. She doesn't want to celebrate, but publishing a book is a huge accomplishment, so Millie and I got to work on a surprise.

She thinks I'm taking her to see a special showing of *Singing in the Rain* at a nearby theater tonight, but I have a stop to make first.

I meet Millie at the Black Hole to check in. I find Iris in the kitchen and thank her profusely for closing the café early tonight. In response, she hands me a sign to hang on the door that reads *Closed for a private event.*

Mark is catering, of course, and from the look of the food setup, he and his wife went overboard. Ari picked up the custom cake I ordered—a confectionary replica of Joey's book—and is setting it up as the focal point. My parents and Claire arrive as I'm headed out to get tonight's guest of honor.

Joey looks hot as fuck in black faux-leather leggings, an oversized cream-colored sweater, and spike-heeled boots.

"Ready to go?" she asks, greeting me with a kiss on my cheek.

I brush the loose curls that fall over her shoulder back and take a peek at my watch. "We have some time. I thought we could look at a few apartments I found online first."

"Um, sure," she says, tilting her head.

She pulls out her laptop and plops onto the sofa with me.

We look through one after another, but her shoulders are hunched and her lips are turned down just a fraction. Shit. Is she having second thoughts?

I close the laptop and set it on the table, then shift so I'm facing her. "Okay, what's going on?"

With her head dipped so her hair hangs around her face, she tangles her fingers in the ends. "I don't think we should look for apartments."

"What?" My body heat rises.

She grasps my hand and pulls it to her chest and finally looks up at me, her bottom lip trapped between her teeth. "What if we take a year to travel?"

"Travel?"

"Yeah. I can promote my book from anywhere in the world. And you can take on projects anywhere we go. You were so successful these last few months in California, so why not expand to other places?"

"What about all that talk about having a real bed and a place to call home?"

She straddles my lap and captures my face in her hands. "Baby," she says, "wherever you are, that's my home."

About four blocks from her apartment, Joey's cursing her heels, so I offer her a ride on my back. When I stop outside the Black Hole and set her on her feet, I convince her that we should pop in and grab a coffee on our way. Someone had the foresight to pull the window shades down, and I do my best to keep Joey turned so she can't see the closed sign.

A collective "surprise!" erupts from inside, startling her. With a jump, she spins to me, her eyes wide and her mouth agape. Grasping her shoulders, I turn her to face our friends, then step out of the way as they all rush her. Every one of them is holding an advanced copy of her book and a Sharpie.

Elin and Brooks flew in, and Talulah, looking like a proud grandmother, is here, standing next to Claire. Opposite them, Ezra's propped up against a table; he said he was bringing his new girlfriend, but there isn't a face here I don't recognize. Even Peg and Fran are here, tears welling in their eyes. Iris is behind the bar, fussing with a tray of pastries.

Joey makes her way around the room and is speechless when she sees the cake. Once everyone has hugged and smothered her with praises, she finds me at the bar.

She dives into my chest and giggles. "I can't believe you did this."

I grasp her chin and lift it. "You think anything's been added to the secret menu while we were gone?"

She narrows her eyes, but without argument, she turns and asks, "Anything new?"

"Actually," Iris says, her voice an octave too high. "We do have a new drink. We named it after a book written by a local author." With a wink, she places a plastic to-go cup on the counter in front of us. "It's called Plot Twist."

Joey gasps and her eyes go wide when she gets a good look at the cup. Specifically, the item lying on top of the lid, held secure by a straw through the middle.

A green amethyst gemstone set in yellow gold.

She covers her mouth with one hand when she looks to me, then back to the ring, then back to me again.

"You remembered," she whispers, her eyes welling with tears.

Of course I remembered. Green—the color of her dad's eyes.

I gather her hands in mine and take a deep, cleansing breath. "Truth or *dare?*"

Her lips twitch as she surveys me. "Dare."

"I dare you to marry me."

Her eyes light up, and that lip twitch morphs into a full, knowing smile. "That's quite the dare," she sings, wrapping her arms around my neck.

With shaking hands, I pull her body tight against mine and bury my lips in her hair.

She cups my cheeks and locks her eyes to mine. "Are you sure?"

Squeezing her with all I have, I choke back tears. "I've never been more sure of anything."

Bonus (Spicy) Scene

Cameron

"What about this one?"

"Are you out of your damn mind, woman? I said I'd let you stick a dildo up my ass, not the Chrysler Building!"

I never thought I'd be standing in the middle of a sex shop with the woman I had a one-night stand with in Greece, but here I am.

The adult entertainment store stands proudly on a street corner in Brooklyn and came highly recommended by Joey's friend, who works here and at FrenchSHEs.

"Oh, sugar, it's not as scary as it looks." Stevie takes the box with a picture of a purple dildo made to look like a real penis, veins and all, from Joey's hands. "But let's start you off with something less intimidating." They set the box back on the shelf and drag their long sparkly nails across the vast selection.

Some may consider it taboo, but the thought of her riding me with a strap-on is nothing but sexy in my eyes.

Of course, since I agreed, I've done a little research and *prepping* on my own, but ultimately, I trust her and am fucking chomping at the bit to do this.

"What about one of these?" Stevie asks.

"What's the difference?" Straining to get a better look at the pictures, I notice that both boxes advertise "five inches." That seems manageable. I think.

"One is strapless and one has a harness." Stevie hands us one of the boxes and grabs another off the shelf. "But you could get a boxer-brief to use instead of a harness. Whichever you prefer. Oh, and they vibrate."

I turn to Joey, but she's examining the box in her hand. If she feels uncomfortable, she sure isn't showing it.

"What's the benefit of the strapless one?" she inquires. "How does it even work?"

Stevie removes the dildo from its box and answers matter-of-factly, without a hint of judgment. "The smaller end"—they point to the more bulbous side of the dildo—"is inserted in you. And the other side goes inside him."

We both study the neon orange silicone toy.

"Some folks," Stevie says, "think it's more comfortable because there aren't any straps to deal with, and the person with a vulva can enjoy penetration at the same time. Others don't like it because you have to work a little harder to keep it in place. It's totally up to you."

When neither of us speaks, they go on. "If you want the stability of the harness, but also want the penetration, we have that option too."

Joey's eyes light up. "Yes! That's what I want." She turns to me. "If that's okay with you?"

Seeing her this excited is a huge turn-on. "Baby, I want this to be good for you too. Sounds perfect."

I accept a box containing a dildo that's black instead of jack-o-lantern orange and not at all "realistic."

"Wonderful, sugar." Stevie collects the box from Joey and

Bonus (Spicy) Scene

motions us toward the front of the store. "Need any lube?" they ask from behind the cash register.

"No, thanks." I have plenty at home.

Stevie throws in a small bottle anyway before handing us the bag with a wink.

When I exit the bathroom after my shower, I find my gorgeous girl climbing onto my bed, her perfect bum on display. She wiggles her ass and peeks over her shoulder, one brow cocked. When she flips over and props herself up on the pillows, all the air leaves my lungs.

"Holy fuck."

Joey is completely naked, save for the black thong that's harnessing the silicone dildo we picked out together.

Licking her lips, she drags her gaze up and down my body. It's filled with so much heat it's like a physical caress.

"C'mere, baby," she says, scooting to one side of the bed.

She's spread a towel over the sheet and set a box of tissues and a bottle of lube on the nightstand.

Following her instructions, I settle beside her. She plants a kiss to my forehead, then my temple and down my jaw before brushing her supple lips against the corner of my mouth. Her kisses are calm and deliberate, grateful.

I return the sentiment with my hands. I stroke the smooth skin at her collarbone, then drag my fingers between her breasts and down her soft stomach until I reach the neoprene harness.

"Is it comfortable?"

"Surprisingly, yes." It looks just like a thong, except the sides are adjustable and there's a circular cutout in the front designed to house the dildo.

"Do you already have it in?" I ask, referring to the shorter side that's meant to slide inside her.

She nods.

"*Fu-u-ck.*" My heart lurches in my chest at the same time a zap of lust shoots straight to my dick. "How do you want me, gorgeous?"

"On your back."

With a peck to her lips, I stretch out and grasp my cock. I can't help but give it a good stroke as I drink my girl in.

She situates herself between my legs and pulls her hair into a knot on the top of her head, then directs me to slide the pillow and towel under my hips.

I flinch when she presses her cold hands to my thighs to spread my legs apart.

"Sorry," she mumbles.

"It's okay. Are you nervous?"

She shakes her head. "No, I'm so turned on right now. You look so fucking hot like this."

With her hand at the base of my hard cock, she ducks down and sucks me into her mouth, making my hips jerk. She pumps my shaft while she keeps her mouth focused on the head.

When she pulls away, I silently curse her absence, but my ire is quickly forgotten when she snaps the cap off the bottle of lube.

"I'll take good care of you, baby," she promises, massaging the liquid into her fingers.

"I trust you."

When she swirls a fingertip at my entrance, I lock eyes with her. Silent commitments are exchanged.

"Okay?"

I nod and lace my fingers behind my head, giving her full access.

Gently, she slips the tip of one finger inside. We've messed around with anal play, so the sensation is one I'm familiar with, but the anticipation of what's to come has me clenching anyway.

Joey, so in tune with my body, pauses. "Relax, baby."

On my next exhale, she works her finger inside a little farther. I wrap my hand around my cock on instinct and squeeze the head as she slides that finger in and out of my tight hole. God, she's going to make me come so fucking hard.

"How does it feel?"

"Good," I grunt. "Add another. Stretch me out, baby."

Her eyes widen, and she bites on her bottom lip. My girl loves watching me bottom for her.

With her fingers deep inside me now, massaging my prostate, I can't help but stroke my cock.

"Uh-uh," she *tsks*, slapping my hand away. "Not yet. Are you ready for me to take you?"

"God, fuck, please," I beg. I'm so fucking ready for her to claim me.

When she slides her fingers from me and holds out a hand, I paw at the bottle of lube she left lying beside me, pop the cap, and squirt a dollop into her palm.

"More."

With a groan, I comply, then pour a generous amount over on my cock, being sure to let it drip between my cheeks too.

With her hand, she coats the dildo. I'm entranced, watching her, though a part of me is grateful it's not very thick.

"Ready?" She smiles. Her tender expression is in juxtaposition with all my dirty thoughts.

I nod a little forcefully because, fuck, my cock is aching to be stroked.

Joey guides the tip to my entrance, but she doesn't push in.

"What's wrong?"

With a hand behind her back, she pulls a small remote from

the elastic. With one touch, the dildo whirs to life, and she trembles in response to the vibrations inside her.

"*Ahh*," she groans.

"Feel good, gorgeous?"

She closes her eyes, leaning into the sensation, then pulls her lips between her teeth and moans. Goddamn. Watching her enjoy her pleasure feels even better than experiencing my own sometimes.

But fuck if I'm not about to burst. "Joey?"

She opens her eyes, though her lids are heavy. "Hmm?"

"Please fuck me now."

I shuffle my feet out wider and spread my cheeks to give her better access. With a small scoot forward, she runs the tip of the vibrating dildo along my shaft and over my balls, then over my hole. She glances at my face, checking in, then turns her attention back to the salacious scene. Then, slowly, gently, she slides through the tight ring of muscle.

"Oh fuck," I hiss, breathing deeply and willing myself not to tighten around the toy.

She stops there, waiting for me to adjust. "You're doing so well, baby." She rubs my thigh, urging me to relax, and when I obey, she slides even farther inside. "This still okay?"

"Yes," I breathe. "Move. I need you to move."

With one hand on my hip and the other gripped around the dildo, she rocks back and forth. My balls contract with each slide, making it nearly impossible not to touch myself.

"Baby. You look so fucking hot taking my silicone dick like a good boy," she praises.

Grasping her hips, I pull her closer to me, forcing the dildo deeper inside. Damn. I'm so fucking full. I drop my head back against the pillow, squeeze my eyes tight, and let out a moan.

The intense vibrations from the dildo cause my thighs to

Bonus (Spicy) Scene

shake. Any minute, I'm going to blow, and by the hedonistic look on Joey's face, she's right there with me.

"How is it for you?"

"So good. I need you to touch me," I beg.

Without hesitation, she grasps my cock, and at the same time, she thrusts into me.

"Oh, god," I cry out.

She stills, as if considering whether my response was one of ecstasy or pain.

"Again," I pant, driving my hips to encourage her pace. "I'm close."

She spits on her fingers, then slides them beneath the harness, giving her clit some attention. She continues pumping into me, her tits bouncing wildly above me.

Fuck, she looks powerful.

She picks up her speed, furiously working her clit, and her moans get louder.

"Cam," she groans, splaying her free hand on my chest for support.

I cover it with mine, steadying her as she falls apart above me. And that does it. The scream she lets out catapults me into my own ecstasy. Cum shoots up my abdomen, mixing with my sweat and coating our hands. Joey moans in approval, her eyes ablaze. She's never looked so stunning.

There's a slight burn when she gently removes the toy from inside me. She switches it off, then reaches for a tissue to wipe my stomach clean.

With a huff, she collapses next to me, then gets to work loosening the sides of the harness. Once she's removed her end of the dildo, she shimmies it down her legs and tosses it to the side.

Desperate to have her in my arms, I roll over and pull her close, nuzzling into her breasts.

Bonus (Spicy) Scene

"How was that, baby?" She runs her fingers through my hair, massaging my scalp.

"Mhmph, s'good," I mumble, sinking into her touch, too spent for coherent words.

"Next time, I want to take you from behind," she says.

I huff out a laugh. "Next time?"

"I can't believe you let me do that." A dreamy sigh escapes her. "Thank you."

I raise my head to kiss her lips. "Anything *for the plot*."

What I really mean is, *anything for you.*

One Last Thing

Want to know what's written inside Cam's letter to Joey? Scan the QR code to find out.

Come hang out in Katie's Chaos Crew on Facebook and interact with Katie. Early announcements, exclusive content, bonus giveaways, and so much more!
Come for the chaos. Stay for the happy ending.

Be sure to sign up for Katie's newsletter on her website so you never miss a thing about Cam, Joey, and the upcoming All for Love series.

Did you love the book? Please consider leaving a review and telling a friend. This is super helpful to indie authors.

Acknowledgments

Writing a book has been one of the wildest rides of my life! I was actually writing another story when Cam & Joey banged on my brain and refused to leave. They've been a blast to write, but would not be who they are today without some amazingly supportive people in my life.

To my earliest readers–Ali, Alisa, Bobbi, Catalina, Cayce, Jane, Jenn, Jennifer, Josefine, Lottie, Kate, Krystyn, Malia, Rachel, and Sanyae. Thank you for loving Cam and Joey and offering me the most thoughtful and tender feedback.

Immense gratitude to Lulu. You hyped me up when this book was merely a manic thought in a text. You never faltered in pumping me up when I sent screenshots of my manuscript and asked "IS THIS STUPID? YES OR NO?!" I'm so glad we bonded over smut on an island in Greece. Thank you for listening to my tangents, filling in holes when I needed them, and reminding me that everything is... "for the plot!"

And to Ghillian, who listened to the frenzied description of my book in its earliest stages in a hotel room on Crete for hours. You laughed and gasped at all the right places and told me you loved it all. I'm thrilled we met in a library all those years ago. You checked out a book I was returning—the best "meet-cute" friendship.

To my beautiful book club nerds in Virginia. Thank you for enriching my life and being my cheerleaders.

Thank you, Alyx, for supporting me during a time when I grew into my most authentic self.

Salina, my pseudo-therapist. I appreciate you always showing interest in my passion even if you don't know what the hell I'm talking about. You have helped keep me sane throughout this entire process. (Also, sorry about all the "P-words.")

And to my actual paid therapists–thank you for teaching me to have more self-compassion, let go of my perfectionistic tendencies, and live alongside my anxiety. (I'm trying!)

To my BFF, Dana. Thank you for reading my book even though you hate reading. I'm sorry for all the years in our childhood I made you play "school" and corrected your grammar and spelling. Karma's a bitch because my editor finally got me back.

Speaking of editors... Beth, you're the real star of the show. My writing improved tremendously because of you. Thanks for your patience with all the technical difficulties living on an island brought me. You were an absolute delight supporting me through this whole experience. (Note: Beth did not edit my Acknowledgments so all the grammar mistakes are on me.)

Thank you to my beta and proofreader, Kristen H.

Kristen R., thank you for your valuable beta feedback and assisting me through important stages of writing this book.

It gives me chills to think about how serendipitous it is to meet certain people at the right time; how random strangers on the internet have become some of the most important people in my life.

Adriana Locke, thank you for selflessly answering my emails flooded with All The Questions. I would be lost without your early guidance.

Auden Dar, thank you for writing my favorite book and allowing me to stitch it into my own. I will be forever grateful.

Thank you, Hannah Bonam-Young, for letting me include you in my pages too. You taught me that "an environment I can't control is a memory in the making" and shit, if that isn't the theme of writing a book!

M.A. Wardell, you're a gem for always answering my questions, being transparent, telling me you can never have enough fucks, and fact-checking and approving the bonus scene. And a big thank you to Matt's husband for asking "Do you want a good book or a *great* book?"

Rachael, thank you for bringing Cam and Joey to life, the late night/early morning (stupid time difference) chats, and sending me your unhinged live reactions. They gave me life!

Hannah, you came into my life at the right time, and are one of the most generous people I know. "Thank you" will never feel like enough. (Oh, and you are so funny!)

Jenny, who knew visiting your grandparents and playing in my pool as a kid would lead to us working together one day? Thank you for your invaluable critiques as a beta reader, as well as designing my beautiful website.

Ronnie, thank you for the unending texts, voicemails, and video chats. Your support, hype, and advice as a beta, accountability partner, and friend mean more to me than you'll ever know!

Lauren—alpha reader turned brand designer turned cover artist, and now my Book Doula ™. Thank you for being with me every step of the way and helping me birth my book baby. You're the Schmidt to my Nick and stuck with me until the end. *No takesie-backsies.*

To my in-laws and sisters, Blake, Mary, Ann Marie, and Michelle. Thank you for supporting me unconditionally. (I hope I remembered to tell you which chapters to skip!)

Thank you, Mom, for all the notebooks you ever gave me. It was money well spent because look where they brought me. Dad, I wish you were here to see my dreams come true. (Even if I'd ban you from reading the contents inside.) While you're not on this side of eternity to celebrate, I can still feel just how proud you are.

My cool and amazing kids. I hope you remember this time as lots of movies and treats and not Mom running around saying "fuck" a lot. Thank you for all the notes left on my desk filled with words of encouragement, and celebrating with me every step of the way. I appreciate your patience when I was really stressed and snappy. I hope I did a good job repairing those moments. I love you all so much!

My husband, Blake. My Favorite Person in the Whole Wide World. I couldn't have done this without you. It was hard on both of us for me to make the transition from stay-at-home-mom to work-from-home-mom, but we did it. I'm grateful for every extra meal and chore you took on so I could make my dreams come true. Thank you for knowing when to push me, and when to hug me and tell me I'm a "good girl." Oh! And thank you for helping me with the anatomy portion of this book. (You know, because you're a doctor.)

A huge thanks to my incredible Street Team. Your generosity means the world to me.

And to YOU, for reading this book. I appreciate every kind, encouraging, and unhinged message. Thank you for every like, share, and comment on social media. As a new and indie author, this is the greatest gift you can give me.

About the Author

Katie Van Brunt writes steamy rom-com stories with banter and lots of texts on page. She's a total mood reader, has a love-hate relationship with spin class, and is working on being more spontaneous.

Before writing romance, she was a dance and yoga instructor. Originally from Florida, she has also lived in California, North Carolina, and Virginia, and the island of Crete in Greece, but she currently resides in O'ahu, Hawai'i with her husband and three children—until their next adventure..

www.katievanbrunt.com

Printed in Great Britain
by Amazon